"MacLean is very good at setting up the conflict and bringing together various characters so that every angle that seems to be right turns out to be re[...]"

"MacLean wings his [...] through a thoroughly professional tale about a gang of mild-mannered terrorists who are methodically blowing up the dikes of Holland.... crisp, sure, and satisfying."

Cosmopolitan

"MacLean sticks to the tight plotting and stylistic simplicity that have been his trademarks over the years and he develops characters with a remarkable ease as every word carries the reader a step closer to the ultimate climax."

Richmond Times-Dispatch

A MAIN SELECTION OF THE LITERARY GUILD

ALISTAIR MacLEAN

FLOODGATE

FAWCETT CREST • NEW YORK

A Fawcett Crest Book
Published by Ballantine Books

Library of Congress Catalog Card Number: 83-45013

ISBN: 0-449-20343-1

This edition published by arrangement with Doubleday and Company, Inc.

Manufactured in the United States of America

First Ballantine Books Edition: May 1985

To
David & Judy

Prologue

THE TWO ODDLY similar incidents, although both happening on the night of February 3, and both involving army ammunition storage installations, had no discernible connection.

The occurrence at De Doorns in Holland was mysterious, spectacular and tragic: the one at Metnitz in Germany was a good deal less mysterious, unspectacular and faintly comic.

Three soldiers were on guard at the Dutch ammunition dump, set in a concrete bunker about a mile north of the village of De Doorns, when, about one-thirty in the morning, the only two citizens who were awake in the village reported a staccato burst of machine-pistol fire—it was later established that the guards were carrying machine pistols—followed immediately by the sound of a gigantic explosion, which was found to have blasted in the earth a crater sixty-five yards wide by thirteen deep.

Houses in the village suffered moderately severe damage but there was no loss of life.

It was presumed that the guards had fired at intruders and that a stray bullet had triggered the detonation. No traces of the guards or the supposed intruders were found afterward.

In Germany, a group calling themselves the Red Army Faction, a well-known and well-organized band of terrorists, claimed that they had easily overcome the two-man guard at the U.S. NATO arms dump near Metnitz. Both men, it had been claimed, had been drinking, and when the intruders had left both were covered with blankets—it had been a bitterly cold night. The U.S. Army denied the drinking allegation but made no mention of the blankets. The intruders claimed that they had acquired a quantity of offensive weapons, some so advanced that they were still on the secret list. The U.S. Army denied this.

The West German press heavily favored the intruders' account. When it came to penetrating army bases, the Red Army Faction had an impressive record; when it came to protecting them, the U.S. Army had an unimpressive one.

The Red Army Faction customarily list the nature of their thefts in meticulous detail. No such details of the alleged secret weapons were published. It has been assumed that, if the Faction's account was true, the U.S. Army (or the U.S. Army through the German government) had issued a stop order to the press.

1

"IT IS CLEAR that it is the work of a madman." John de Jong, tall, lean, gray, ascetic and the general manager of Schiphol Airport, looked and sounded very gloomy and, in the circumstances, he had every justification for looking and sounding that way. "Insanity. A man has to be deranged, unhinged, to perform a wanton, mindless, pointless and purposeless task like this." Like the monkish professor he so closely resembled, De Jong tended to be precise to the point of pedantry and, as now, had a weakness for pompous tautology. "A lunatic."

"One sees your point of view," Van de Graaf said. Colonel Van de Graaf, a remarkably broad man of medium height with a deeply trenched, tanned face, had about him an imperturbability and an unmistakable cast of authority that accorded well with the chief of police of a nation's capital city. "I can understand and agree with it but only to a certain extent. I appreciate how you feel, my friend. Your beloved airport, one of the best in Europe—"

"Amsterdam airport *is* the best in Europe." De Jong spoke as if by rote, his thoughts elsewhere. "Was."

"And will be again. The criminal responsible for this is, it is certain, not a man of a normal cast of mind. But that does not mean that he is instantly certifiable. Maybe he doesn't like you, has a grudge against you. Maybe he's an ex-employee fired by one of your departmental managers for what the manager regarded as a perfectly valid reason but a reason with which the disgruntled employee didn't agree. Maybe he's a citizen living close by, on the outskirts of Amsterdam, say, or between here and Aalsmeer, who finds the decibel level from the aircraft intolerably high. Maybe he's a dedicated environmentalist who objects, in what must be a very violent fashion, to jet engines polluting the atmosphere, which they undoubtedly do. Our country, as you are well aware, has more than its fair share of dedicated environmentalists. Maybe he doesn't like our government's policies." Van de Graaf ran a hand through his thick, iron-gray hair. "Maybe anything. But he could be as sane as either of us."

"Maybe you'd better have another look, Colonel," De Jong said. His hands were clenching and unclenching and he was shivering violently. Both of those were involuntary but for different reasons. The former accurately reflected an intense frustration and anger; the latter was due to the fact that, when an ice-cold wind blows east-north-east off the Ijsselmeer, and before that from Siberia, the roof of the main concourse of Schiphol Airport is no place to be. "As sane as you or I? Would you or I have been responsible for this—this atrocity? Look, Colonel, just look."

Van de Graaf looked again. Had he been the airport manager, he reflected, it would hardly have been a sight to gladden his heart. Schiphol Airport had just disappeared, its place taken by a wave-rippled lake that stretched almost as far as the eyes could see. The source of the flooding was all too easy to locate: close to the big fuel-storage tanks just outside the perimeter of the airport itself, a wide breach had appeared in the dike of the canal to the south: the debris, stones and mud that were scattered along the top of the dike on either side of the breach left no doubt that the rupture of the containing dike had not been of a natural or spontaneous origin.

The effect of the onrush of waters had been devastating. The airport buildings themselves, though flooded in the ground floors and basements, remained intact. The damage done to the sensitive electric and electronic machinery was very considerable and would almost certainly cost millions of guilders to replace, but the structural integrity of the buildings was unaffected; Schiphol Airport is very solidly built and securely anchored to its foundations.

Aircraft, unfortunately, when not operating in their natural element, are delicate artifacts and, of course, have no means at all of anchoring themselves. A momentary screwing of Van de Graaf's eyes showed that this was all too painfully evident. Small planes had drifted away to the north. Some were still floating aimlessly around. Some were known to be sunk and out of sight, and two had their tail assemblies sticking up above the water—those would have been single-engined planes, carried down head-first by the weight of the engines in their noses. Some two-engined passenger jets, 737's and DC9's, and three-engined planes, Trident 3's and 727's, had also been blown out of position and were scattered randomly over a large area of the airfield, their noses pointing in every-which direction. Two were tipped on their sides and two others were partially submerged, with only parts of their upper bodies showing; their undercarriages had collapsed. The big planes, the 747's, the Tri-Stars, the DC10's, were still in situ, held in position by their sheer massive weight—these planes, fueled, can weigh between three and four hundred tons. Two, however, had fallen over to one side, presumably because the undercarriages, distant from the onrush of water, had collapsed. One did not have to be an aeronautical engineer to realize that both planes were write-offs. The port wing of each was angled upward at an angle of about twenty degrees and only the roots of the starboard wing were visible, a position that could only have been accounted for by the fact that both wings must have broken upwards somewhere along their lengths.

Several hundred yards along a main runway an undercarriage projecting above the water showed where a Fokker Friendship, accelerating for takeoff, had tried to escape the floodwaters and failed. It was possible that the pilot had not seen the approach of the water, possible but unlikely; it was more likely that he had seen it, reckoned that he had nothing to lose either way, continued accelerating but failed to gain lift-off speed before being caught. There was no question of his plane's having been engulfed; in those initial stages, according to observers, there had been only an inch or two of water fanning out over the airfield, but that had been enough to reach the Fokker aquaplane, with disastrous results.

Airport cars and trucks had simply drowned under the water. The only remaining signs of any wheeled vehicles were the projecting three or four steps of aircraft boarding ramps and the top of a tanker; even the ends of two crocodile disembarkation tubes were dipped forlornly into the murky waters.

Van de Graaf sighed, shook his head and turned to De Jong, who was gazing almost sightlessly over his devastated airfield, as if still quite unable to comprehend the enormity of what had happened.

"You have a point, John. You and I are sane, or at least I think the world at large would think so, and it is not possible that we could have been responsible for such appalling destruction. But that doesn't mean that the criminal responsible for this wanton destruction is insane; we will doubtless find, either through our own efforts or because he chooses to inform us, that there was a very compelling reason for what he did. I shouldn't have used the word 'wanton' there, you shouldn't have used words like 'mindless' and 'pointless.' This is no random, arbitrary, spur-of-the-moment act of an escaped mental patient: this is a deliberately calculated act designed to produce a deliberately calculated effect."

Reluctantly, as if by a giant effort of will, De Jong looked away from the flooded field. "Effect? The only effect it has on me is one of sheer outrage. What other effects could there be? Do you have any suggestions?"

"None. I've had no time to think about it. Don't forget I've only just come to this. Sure, sure, we knew yesterday that this was promised, but like everyone else, I thought the idea was so preposterous as to be not worth considering. But I have two other suggestions. I suggest that we'll achieve nothing by staring out over Lake Schiphol; and I suggest we're not going to help anyone or anything by hanging around here and getting pneumonia."

De Jong's briefly pained expression showed what he thought of the term "Lake Schiphol," but he made no comment.

The staff canteen was an improvement on the rooftop inasmuch as there was no wind, but it wasn't much warmer. All electric heating had been short-circuited, and the butane heaters that had been brought in had as yet had a minimal effect on the chilled atmosphere. An abundance of hot coffee helped; something rather more sustaining, Van de Graaf reflected, would have been in order, but for those with a taste for schnapps or jonge jenever, the presence of the airport manager had a markedly inhibiting effect. As became his ascetic appearance, De Jong was a lifelong teetotaler, a difficult thing to be in Holland. He never made a point of this, he had never even been heard to mention this, but, somehow, people just didn't drink anything stronger than tea or coffee when De Jong was around.

Colonel Van de Graaf said: "Let's summarize briefly what we know. It has to be brief because we know damned little. Three identical messages received yesterday afternoon, one to a newspaper, one to the airport authorities—in effect, Mr. De Jong—and one to the Rijkswaterstaat of the Ministry of Transport and Public Works." He paused briefly and looked across at a burly, dark-bearded man who was placidly polluting the atmosphere with the smoke from what appeared to be an ancient pipe burning still more ancient tobacco. "Ah! Of course. Mr. Van der Kuur. The Rijkswaterstaat deputy Projects Engineer. How long to clear up this mess?"

Van der Kuur removed his pipe. "We have already started. We seal off the breach in the canal with metal sheeting—a temporary measure only, of course, but sufficient. After that— well, we do have the best and biggest pumps in the world. A routine job."

"How long?"

"Thirty-six hours. At the outside." There was something very reassuring about Van der Kuur's calm and matter-of-fact approach. "Provided, of course, that we get a degree of co-operation from the tugboat men, barge men and private owners whose boats are at the moment resting on the mud at the bottom of the canal. The boats that settled on an even keel are no problem; those that have fallen over on their sides could well fill up. I suppose self-interest will ensure cooperation."

Van de Graaf said: "Any loss of life in the canal? Or anybody hurt?"

"One of my inspectors reports a considerable degree of high blood pressure among the skippers and crews of the stranded craft. That apart, no one was harmed."

"Thank you. The messages came from a man or a group signing themselves F.F.F.—it was not explained what those initials were meant to stand for. The intention, it was said, was to demonstrate that they could flood any part of our country whenever and wherever they wished by blowing up a strategically placed dike and that accordingly they intended to give a small-scale demonstration that would endanger no one and cause as little inconvenience as possible."

"As little inconvenience! Small scale." De Jong was back at his fist clenching. "I wonder what the devil they would regard as a large-scale demonstration?"

Van de Graaf nodded. "Quite. They said the target was Schiphol and that the flooding would come at eleven A.M. Not one minute before eleven, not one minute after. As we know, the breach was blown at precisely eleven A.M. At police headquarters, quite frankly, this was regarded as a hoax—after all, who in his right mind would want to turn Schiphol Airport into an inland sea? Perhaps they saw some symbolic significance in their choice—remember, the Dutch navy defeated the Spanish navy at this very spot when the present Schiphol really was a sea. Hoax or not, we took no chances. The canal was the obvious choice for any saboteur, so we had both sides of the north bank of the canal closely examined. There were no signs of any kind of disturbance that could have indicated a preparation for the blowing of the dike. So we assumed it was some kind of practical joke." Van de Graaf shrugged, palms uplifted. "As we know too late, nothing was further from the mind or minds of the F.F.F. than fun and games."

He turned to the man seated on his left side. "Peter, you've had time to think. Have you any idea—sorry, gentlemen, sorry.

... Some of you may not know my colleague here. Lieutenant Peter van Effen. Lieutenant Van Effen is my senior detective lieutenant. He is also an explosives expert and, for his sins, the head of the city's bomb-disposal squad. Have you figured out yet how it was done?"

Peter van Effen was an unremarkable figure. Like his boss, he was just over medium height, uncommonly broad and looked suspiciously as if he were running to fat. He was in his late thirties, had thick dark hair, a matching dark mustache and an almost permanent expression of amiability. He didn't look like a senior detective lieutenant, in fact, he didn't even look like a policeman. Many people, including quite a number of people in Dutch prisons, tended to take Van Effen's easy-going affability at face value.

"It didn't take much figuring, sir. Anything's easy with hindsight. But even had we had foresight, there was nothing we could have done about it anyway. We'll almost certainly find two boats tied up bow-to-stern alongside the north bank. Unusual, but there's no law, say, against an engine breakdown and a sympathetic owner of a passing vessel stopping to lend a hand. I should imagine that we'll find that those boats were almost certainly stolen because there is traffic on the canal, and any habitual waterway user would have been able to identify them.

"The two boats would have been very close or even overlapping, leaving a clear, hidden area where scuba divers could work. If this took place during dusk or at nighttime, as I'm sure it did, they would have bright lights on deck, and when you have those on, anything below gunwale level is in deep shadow. They would have had a drilling machine, something like the ones you use on oil rigs, only, of course, this one would have been on a very small scale and operated horizontally, not vertically. It would have been electrically powered, either by batteries or generator, because the exhausts of a petrol or diesel plant make a great deal of noise. For an expert, and there are literally hundreds of experts operating on or around the North Sea, this would have been a childishly simple operation. They would drill through to, say, a foot of the other side of the dike—we may be sure they would have taken very careful measurements beforehand—withdraw the bit and insert a waterproof canvas tube packed with explosives, maybe just plain old-fashioned dynamite or TNT, although a real expert would have gone for amatol beehives. They would then attach an electrical timing device, nothing elaborate, an old-fashioned kitchen alarm clock will do well enough, plug the hole with mud and gravel—not that there would be a chance in a million of anyone ever looking there—and sail away."

"I could almost believe, Mr. Van Effen, that you masterminded this operation yourself," Van der Kuur said. "So that's how it was done."

"It's how I would have done it, and within the limits of a slight variation, that's how they did it. There is no other way." Van Effen looked at Van de Graaf. "We're up against a team of experts, and the person directing them is no clown. They know how to steal boats, they know how to handle them, they know where to steal drilling equipment, they know how to use equipment and they're at home with explosives. No wild-eyed, slogan-chanting cranks among this lot; they're professionals. I've asked head office to notify us immediately if they receive any complaints from factories, wholesalers or retailers of the theft of any equipment from the manufacturers or distributors of drilling equipment. Also to notify us of the theft of any vessels from that area."

"And beyond that?" Van de Graaf said.

"Nothing, we have no leads."

Van de Graaf nodded and looked down at the paper he held in his hands. "That message from the mysterious F.F.F. No indication whatsoever as to the reason behind this threatened— now actual—sabotage. Just a warning that nobody should be at ground level at eleven A.M. this morning and that all planes should be flown out yesterday afternoon or evening to adjacent airfields, as the needless destruction of property formed no part of their plans. Very considerate of them, I must say. And even more considerate, John, was the phone call you got at nine o'clock this morning urging you to evacuate all those planes immediately. But, of course, we all knew it was a hoax, so we paid no attention. Would you recognize that voice again, John?"

"Not a chance. It was a woman's voice, a young woman and speaking in English. All young women speaking English sound the same to me."

Fist clenched, De Jong gently thumped the table before him. "They don't even hint at the reason for carrying out this—this monstrous action. What have they achieved by this action? Nothing. Absolutely nothing. I repeat that any person or persons who behave in this fashion have to be mentally unbalanced."

Van Effen said: "I'm sorry, sir, I disagree. I do agree with what the colonel said on the roof—they're almost certainly as sane as anyone. No one who is mentally unbalanced could have carried out this operation. And they're not, as I said, wild-eyed terrorists throwing bombs in crowded marketplaces. In two separate warnings they did their best to ensure that neither human lives nor property would be put at risk. That was not the behavior of irresponsible people."

"And who, then, was responsible for the deaths of the three people who lost their lives when that Fokker Friendship cartwheeled and crashed on takeoff?"

"The saboteurs, indirectly. One could equally well say that you were, also indirectly. It might be argued you might at least have considered the possibility that the threat was not a hoax, taken even the most remote possibility into account and refused permission for the Fokker to take off at exactly eleven A.M. But that permission was given, personally, I understand, by you. It is as certain as certain can be that the saboteurs had carefully checked landing and takeoff schedules and made sure that there were no planes either taking off or landing at or near that time. That Fokker, as the private plane of a German industrialist, was therefore not listed on the scheduled departures. I suggest, Mr. De Jong, that it's futile and perhaps self-destructive to ascribe the blame for those three deaths to anyone. Sheer bad luck, an unfortunate coincidence in timing, an act of God, call it what you like. There was nothing planned, nothing calculated, no motive behind those deaths. It was nobody's fault."

De Jong had substituted finger drumming for table thumping. "If those evil people were as considerate as you say, why didn't they postpone the explosion when they saw people boarding the plane?"

"Because we don't know that they were in a position to see anything and, even if they were, they were almost certainly unable to do anything about it. Had the explosives been activated by a radio-controlled device, sure, they could have stopped it. But, as I told you, I'm pretty certain it was an electrical timer and to deactivate that they would have had to assemble a boat, scuba gear and diver—and all in broad daylight—in a matter of minutes. In the time available, that would have been impossible."

There was a faint but unmistakable sheen of sweat on De Jong's forehead. "They could have phoned a warning."

Van Effen looked at De Jong for a long moment, then said: "How much attention did you pay to the previous warning this morning?"

De Jong made no reply.

"And you've just said that the saboteurs have achieved nothing, absolutely nothing, by their action. I know you're upset, sir, and it seems unfair to press the point, but can you really be so naive as to believe that? They've already made a considerable achievement. They have achieved the beginnings of a climate of fear and uncertainty, a climate that can only worsen with the passing of the hours. If they've struck once, apparently without a blind bit of motivation, are the chances not high that they will strike again? If they do, when? If they do, where? And, above all, there's the why. What overpowering reason do they have to behave as they do?" He looked at Van de Graaf. "Soften up the victim but keep him in suspense as to your purpose in behaving in this fashion. It's a novel form of blackmail and I see no reason why it shouldn't work. I have the strong feeling that we are going to hear from the F.F.F. in the very near future. Not to state the reasons for acting as they do, certainly not to make any specific demands. Dear me, no. Not that. That's not the way you conduct psychological warfare. One turns the wheel that stretches the rack very, very slowly over a calculated period of time. Gives the victim time to ponder more deeply about the hopelessness of his situation while his morale sinks lower and lower. At least that's how I believe they operated in the Middle Ages—when using the actual instrument, of course."

De Jong said sourly: "You seem to know a lot about the workings of the criminal mind."

"A little." Van Effen smiled agreeably. "I wouldn't presume to tell you how to run an airport."

"And what am I to understand from that?"

"Mr. Van Effen just means that a cobbler should stick to his last." Van de Graaf made a placatory gesture with his hand. "He's the author of the now-established textbook on the psychology of the criminal mind. Never read it myself. So, Peter. You seem sure the F.F.F. will contact us very soon, but not to tell us about themselves or their objectives. Tell us what? The where and the when? Their next—ah—demonstration?"

"What else?"

A profound and rather gloomy silence was ended by the entrance of a waiter who approached De Jong. "Telephone, sir. Is there a Lieutenant Van Effen here?"

"Me." Van Effen followed the waiter from the canteen and returned within a minute and addressed himself to Van de Graaf.

"Duty sergeant. Apparently two men reported their boats missing some hours ago. One is a pleasure-boat owner. The sergeant who took their complaint didn't think it necessary to notify our department. Quite right, of course. The boats have now been recovered. One, it would seem, was taken by force. The boats are in our hands. I told them to take a couple of fingerprint men aboard, return the boats to the owners but not to allow the owners aboard. If you can spare the time, sir, we can interview the two owners after we leave here; they live less than a kilometer from here."

"A promising lead, yes?"

"No."

"I don't think so either. However, no stone unturned. We may as well go now and—"

He broke off as the same waiter reappeared and approached him. "Phone again. For you this time, Colonel."

Van de Graaf returned in a matter of seconds. "John, have you such a thing as a shorthand typist?"

"Of course. Jan?"

"Sir?" A blond youngster was on his feet.

"You heard the colonel?"

"Yes sir." He looked at Van de Graaf. "What shall I say?"

"Ask her to take that phone call and type it out for me. Peter, you have clairvoyance, the second sight."

"The F.F.F.?"

"Indeed. The press, I need hardly say. The F.F.F. have their publicity priorities right. Usual anonymous phone call. The subeditor who took the call was smart enough to tape-record it, but I'd be surprised if that is of the slightest help. A fairly lengthy statement, I understand. Shorthand is not my forte. Let us possess our souls in patience."

They had possessed their souls for not more than four minutes when a girl entered and handed a type-written sheet to Van de Graaf. He thanked her, looked briefly at the sheet and said, "Action this day would appear to be their motto. This, I understand, is their statement in full, and a fairly arrogant example of its kind it is, too. This is what the F.F.F. says:

"'Next time, perhaps, the responsible citizens in Amsterdam will listen to what we say, believe what we say and act accordingly. It is because you did not believe what we said that a misadventure occurred today. For this misadventure we hold Mr. De Jong entirely responsible. He was given due warning and chose to ignore that warning. We deplore the unnecessary deaths of the three passengers aboard the Fokker Friendship but disclaim all responsibility. It was not possible for us to arrest the explosion.'" Van de Graaf paused and looked at Van Effen. "Interesting?"

"Very. So they had an observer. We'll never find him. He could have been in the airport, but hundreds of people who don't work here visit here every day. For all we know, there could have been someone outside the airport with a pair of binoculars. But that's not what is interesting. The four first-aid men who brought in the most seriously injured passengers did not know at the time whether the three men who were later pronounced dead were, in fact, dead or alive. Two of them, I understand, died after admission, but none were officially pronounced dead until the doctor certified them as such. How did the F.F.F. know? Neither the doctor nor the first-aid men could have been responsible for leaking the news, for they would be the obvious suspects and all too easily checked on. Apart from them, the only people who knew of those deaths are in this room." Van Effen looked leisurely around the sixteen men and three women seated at the canteen tables, then turned to De Jong.

"It hardly needs spelling out, does it, sir? We have an infiltrator here, an informant. The enemy has a spy in our camp." Again he carried out the same slow survey of the room. "I do wonder who it can be."

"In this room?" De Jong looked both disbelieving and unhappy at the same time.

"I don't have to repeat the obvious, do I?"

De Jong looked down at his hands, which were now tightly clasped on the table. "No. No. Of course not. But surely, well, we can find out. *You* can find out."

"The usual rigorous inquiries, is that it? Trace the movements of every person in this room after the Fokker crashed? Find out if anyone had access to the phone or, indeed, used a phone? Sure, we can do that, pursue the rigorous inquiries. We'll find nothing."

"You'll find nothing?" De Jong looked his perplexity. "How can you be so sure, so sure in advance?"

"Because," Van de Graaf said, "the lieutenant has a policeman's mind. Not a bunch to be underestimated, are they, Peter?"

"They're clever."

De Jong looked from Van de Graaf to Van Effen, then back to Van de Graaf. "If someone would kindly explain—"

"Simple, really," Van de Graaf said. "It hasn't occurred to you that the F.F.F. didn't have to let us know that they knew of the deaths. Gratuitous information, if you like. They would know that we would know this. They would know, as the lieutenant has just pointed out, that we would know that someone had informed them and that someone would have to be one of us. They would be certain that we would check on the possibility of someone here having made a phone call, so they made certain that no one here made a phone call. He passed the word on to an accomplice who is not in this room; the accomplice made the call. I'm afraid, John, that you have another mole burrowing away inside here. Maybe even more. You are aware, of course, that every word of our conversation will be reported back to the F.F.F., whoever they may be. We will, naturally, go through the motions and make the necessary routine inquiries. As Van Effen says, we will, surely, draw a blank."

"But—but it all seems so pointless," De Jong said. "Why should they be so devious so as to achieve nothing?"

"They're not really devious and they do achieve something. A degree of demoralization, for one thing. More important, they are saying that they are a force to be reckoned with, that they can infiltrate and penetrate security when they so choose. They are giving the message that they are a highly organized group, again, one that is capable of carrying out any threats that it chooses to make and one that is to be ignored at our peril.

"Speaking of threats and perils, let's return to the F.F.F.'s latest phone call. They go on to say: 'We are sure that the Dutch people are well aware that, in the face of an attacker determined to bring it to its knees, it is the most defenseless nation in the world. The sea is not your enemy. We are, and the sea is our ally.

"'You will not need reminding that the Netherlands has about eight hundred ten miles of sea dikes. A certain Cornelius Rijpma, president of the Sea Polder board in Leeuwarden, in Friesland, is on record as saying some months ago that the dikes in his area consist of nothing more than layers of sand, and that if a big storm comes they are certain to break. By a "big storm," one would assume that it would have to be a storm of the order of the one that breached the delta defenses in 1953 and took 1,850 lives. Our information, supplied to us by the Rijkswaterstaat, is that—'"

"What! What!" Van der Kuur, red-faced and almost incoherent with anger, was on his feet. "Are those devils daring to suggest that they got information from us? Damn them! Impossible!"

"Let me finish, Mr. Van der Kuur. Can't you see that they're using the same technique again, trying to undermine confidence and demoralize? Just because we know that they have contacts with one or more of Mr. De Jong's staff is no proof that they have any with your people. Anyway, there's worse to come. They go on: 'Our information is that a storm of not more than seventy percent of the power of the 1953 one would be sufficient to breach the dikes. Mr. Rijpma was talking about vulnerable dikes. Of the Netherlands' eight hundred ten miles of dikes almost exactly one hundred eighty-six have deteriorated to a critical condition. By the best estimates, no repairs will be carried out to the threatened dikes for another twelve years, that is to say, 1995. All we propose to do is to accelerate the advent of the inevitable.'"

Van de Graaf paused and looked around. A chilled hush seemed to have fallen over the canteen. Only two people were looking at him, the others were either gazing at the floor or into the far distance; in both cases it was not difficult to guess that they didn't like what they saw.

"'The dikes cannot be repaired because there is no money to repair them. All the money available, or likely to be available in the future, is being sunk or will be sunk into the construction of the East Schelde storm-surge barrier, the last link in the so-called Delta Plan designed to keep the North Sea at bay. The costs are staggering. Due to gross original underestimates, cost overruns and inflation, the likely bill will probably be in excess of nine billion guilders—and this massive sum for a project that some engineering experts say will not work anyway. The project consists of sixty-three lock-gates fitted between enormous, eighteen-thousand-ton free-standing concrete pillars. The dissident experts fear that heavy seas could shift the pillars, jam the locks and render the barrier inoperable. A shift of one inch would be enough. Ask Mr. Van der Kuur of the Rijks-waterstaat.'"

Van de Graaf paused and looked up. Van der Kuur was on his feet again, every bit as apoplectic as before; his normal air of pipe-puffing imperturbability was a very thin veneer indeed.

"Lies!" he shouted. "Rubbish! Balderdash! This is defamation! Lies, I tell you, lies!"

"You're the engineer in charge. You should know. So really, there's no need to get so worked up about it." Van de Graaf's tone was mild, conciliatory. "The dissidents the F.F.F. speak about—they have no hydraulic engineering qualifications?"

"The dissidents! A handful. Qualifications? Of course. Paper qualifications! Not one of them has any practical experience as far as this matter is concerned."

Van Effen said: "Does anybody have on this project? Practical experience, I mean. I understood that the East Schelde involved completely untested engineering techniques and that you are, in effect, moving into the realms of the unknown." He raised a hand as Van der Kuur was about to rise again. "Sorry. This is all really irrelevant. What is relevant is that there is a mind or minds among the F.F.F. that is not only highly intelligent but has a clear understanding about the application of practical psychology. First, they introduce the elements of doubt, dismay, dissension and the erosion of confidence into Schiphol. Then they apply the same techniques to the Rijks-waterstaat. And now, this evening or tomorrow morning, through the medium of every paper in the land, and through television and radio, they will introduce those same elements into the nation at large. If you ask me, they have—or will have—achieved a very great deal in a very short space of time. A remarkable feat. They are to be respected as strategists if not as human beings. I trust that the traitor in our midst will report that back to them."

"Indeed," Van de Graaf said. "And I trust the same traitor will understand if we don't discuss the steps we plan to undertake to combat them. Well, ladies and gentlemen, to the final paragraph of their message and incidentally, no doubt, to introduce some more of what the lieutenant referred to as doubt, dismay, dissension, erosion of confidence or whatever. They go on to say: 'In order to demonstrate your helplessness and our ability to strike at will wherever and whenever we choose, we would advise you that a breach will be made in the Texel sea dike at four-thirty this afternoon.'"

"What!" The word came simultaneously from at least half a dozen people.

"Shook me a bit, too," Van de Graaf said. "That's what they say. I don't for a moment doubt them. Brinkman"—this to a uniformed young police officer—"contact the office. No urgency, probably, but check that people on the island know what's coming. Mr. Van der Kuur, I'm sure I can leave it to you to have the necessary men and equipment to stand by." He consulted the sheet again. "Not a big operation, they say. 'We are sure that damage will be minimal but it might behoove the citizens of Oosterend and De Waal to stand by their boats or take to their attics shortly after four-thirty. Very shortly.' Damned arrogance. They end up by saying: 'We know that those names will give you a fairly accurate idea as to where the charges have been placed. We defy you to find them.'"

"And that's all?" Van der Kuur said.

"That's all."

"No reasons, no explanations for those outrages? No demands? Nothing?"

"Nothing."

"I still say we're up against a bunch of raving maniacs."

"And I say that we're up against clever and calculating criminals who are more than content to let us stew in our own juice for the time being. I wouldn't worry about the demands, if I were you. These will come in due time—their time. Well, nothing more we can achieve here—not, on reflection, that we have achieved anything. I bid you good day, Mr. De Jong, and hope that you'll be back in operational services sometime tomorrow. It'll take days, I suppose, to replace the machinery ruined in your basements."

On their way out, Van Effen made a gesture to Van de Graaf to hold back. He looked casually around to make sure that no one was within earshot and said: "I'll put tails on a couple of gentlemen who were in that room."

"Well, you don't waste time, I will say. You have, of course, your reasons."

"I was watching them when you broke the news of the proposed Texel breach. It hit them. Most of them just stared away into space and those who didn't were studying the floor. All of them, I assume, were considering the awful implications. Two did neither. They just kept on looking at you. Maybe they didn't react because they are cool . . . or perhaps because it didn't come as news to them."

"Straw. You're just clutching at straws."

"No. Shadowing straws. Besides, isn't that what a drowning man is supposed to do?"

"With all the water that's around, present and promised, you might have picked a less painful metaphor. Who?"

"Alfred van Rees."

"Ah. The Rijkswaterstaat's Locks, Weirs and Sluices man. Preposterous. Friend of mine. Honest as the day's long."

"Maybe the Mr. Hyde in him doesn't come out until after sunset. And Fred Klassen."

"Klassen? He's Schiphol's security chief, as you know damned well. Preposterous."

"That's twice. Or is he a friend of yours too?"

"Impossible. Twenty years unblemished service. The *security* chief?"

"If you were a criminal and were given the choice of subverting any one man in a big organization, who would you go for?"

Van de Graaf looked at him for a long moment, then walked on in silence.

2

BAKKEREN AND DEKKER, the two boat owners who had been involuntarily deprived of their vessels the night before, were, as it turned out, brothers-in-law. Bakkeren was phlegmatic about the borrowing of his boat and not particularly concerned by the fact that he had not yet been allowed to examine his boat to see what damage, if any, had been done to it. Dekker, by contrast, and understandably, was seething with rage. He had, as he had informed Colonel Van de Graaf and Detective Van Effen within twenty seconds of their arrival at his suburban home, been rather roughly handled during the previous evening.

"Is *no* man safe in this godforsaken city?" He didn't speak the words, he shouted them, but it was reasonable to assume that this was not his normal conversational custom. "Police, you say you are, police! Ha! Police! A fine job you do of guarding the honest citizens of Amsterdam. There I was, sitting in my own boat and minding my own business when those four gangsters—"

"Moment," Van Effen said. "Were they wearing gloves?"

"Gloves!" Dekker, a small, purpling, intense man, stared at him in disbelief. "Gloves! Here am I, the victim of a savage assault, and all you can think of—"

"Gloves."

Something in Van Effen's tone had reached through the

man's anger; one could almost see his blood pressure easing a few points. "Gloves, eh? Funny, that. Yes, they were. All of them."

Van Effen turned to a uniformed sergeant. "Bernhard."

"Yes, sir. I'll tell the fingerprint men to go home."

"Sorry, Mr. Dekker. Tell it your way. If there was anything that struck you as unusual or odd, let us know."

"It was all bloody odd," Dekker said morosely. He had been, as he had said, minding his own business in his little cabin, when he had been hailed from the shore. He'd gone on deck and a tall man—it was almost dark and his features had been undistinguishable—had asked him if he could hire the boat for the night. He said he was from a film company and wanted to shoot some night scenes and offered a thousand guilders. Dekker had thought it extremely odd that an offer of that nature should have been made at such short notice and with night falling; he had refused. Next thing he knew, three other men had appeared on the scene, he'd been dragged from the boat, bundled into a car and driven to his home.

Van Effen said: "Did you direct them?"

"Are you mad?" Looking at the fiery little man, it was impossible to believe that he would volunteer information to anyone.

"So they've been watching your movements for some time. You weren't aware that you were under surveillance at any time?"

"Under what?"

"Being watched, followed, seeing the same stranger an unusual number of times?"

"Who'd watch and follow a fishmonger? Well, who would think they would? So they hauled me into the house—"

"Didn't you try to escape at any time?"

"Would you listen to the man." Dekker was justifiably bitter. "How far would you get with your wrists handcuffed behind your back?"

"Handcuffs?"

"I suppose you thought that only police used those things. So they dragged me into the bathroom, tied my feet with a clothesline and taped my mouth. Then they locked the door from the outside."

"You were helpless?"

"Completely." The little man's face darkened further at the recollection. "I managed to get to my feet and a hell of a lot of good that did me. There's no window in the bathroom. If there had been, I don't know of any way I could have broken it, and even if I had, there was no way I could shout for help, was there? Not with God knows how many strips of plaster over my mouth.

"Three or four hours later—I'm not sure how long it was— they came back and freed me. The tall man told me they'd left fifteen hundred guilders on the kitchen table—a thousand for the hire of the boat and five hundred for incidental expenses."

"What expenses?"

"How should I know?" Dekker sounded weary. "They didn't explain. They just left."

"Did you see them go? Type of car, number, anything like that?"

"I did not see them go. I did not see their car, far less its number." Dekker spoke with the air of a man exercising massive restraint. "When I say they freed me, I meant that they had unlocked and removed the handcuffs. Took me a couple of minutes to remove the strips of tape and damnably painful it was, too. Took quite a bit of skin and my mustache with it too. Then I hopped through to the kitchen and got the bread knife to cut the ropes round my ankles. The money was there, all right, and I'd be glad if you'd put it in your police fund because I won't touch their filthy money. Almost certainly stolen anyway. They and their car, of course, were to hell and gone by that time."

Van Effen was diplomatically sympathetic. "Considering what you've been through, Mr. Dekker, I think you're being very calm and restrained. Could you describe them?"

"Ordinary clothes. Raincoats. That's all."

"Their faces?"

"It was dark on the canal bank, dark in the car, and by the

time we reached here they were all wearing hoods. Well, three of them. One stayed on the boat."

"Slits in the hoods, of course." Van Effen wasn't disappointed, he'd expected nothing else.

"Round holes, more like."

"Did they talk among themselves?"

"Not a word. Only the leader spoke."

"How do you know he was the leader?"

"Leaders give orders, don't they?"

"I suppose. Would you recognize the voice again?"

Dekker hesitated. "I don't know. Well yes, I think I would."

"Ah. Something unusual about his voice?"

"Yes. Well. He talked funny Dutch."

"Funny?"

"It wasn't—what shall I say—Dutch Dutch."

"Poor Dutch, is that it?"

"No. The other way around. It was very good. Too good. Like the news-readers on TV and radio."

"Too precise, yes? Book Dutch. A foreigner, perhaps?"

"That's what I would guess."

"Would you have any idea where he might have come from?"

"There you have me, Lieutenant. I've never been out of the country. I hear often enough that many people in the city speak English or German or both. Not me. I speak neither. Foreign tourists don't come to a fishmonger's shop. I sell my fish in Dutch."

"Thanks, anyway. Could be a help. Anything else about this leader—if that's what he was?"

"He was tall, very tall." Dekker tried his first half-smile of the afternoon. "You don't have to be tall to be taller than I am, but I didn't even reach up to his shoulders. Four, maybe five inches taller than you are. And thin, extremely thin; he was wearing a long raincoat, blue it was, that came way below his knees and it fell from his shoulders like a coat hanging from a coat hanger."

"The hoods had holes, you say, not slits. You could see this tall man's eyes?"

"Not even that. This fellow was wearing dark eyeglasses."

"Sunglasses? I did ask you to tell me if there was anything odd about those people. Didn't you think it odd that a person should be wearing a pair of sunglasses?"

"Odd? Why should it be odd? Look, Lieutenant, a bachelor like me spends a lot of time watching movies and TV. The villains always wear dark glasses. That's how you can tell they're villains."

"At night? Still, you're right."

Van Effen turned to Dekker's brother-in-law. "I understand, Mr. Bakkeren, that you were lucky enough to escape the attentions of those gentlemen."

"Wife's birthday. In town for a dinner and show. Anyway, they could have stolen my boat any time and I would have known nothing about it. If they were watching Maks here, they would have been watching me and they'd know that I only go near my boat on weekends."

Van Effen turned to Van de Graaf. "Would you like to see the boats, sir?"

"Do you think we'll find anything?"

"No. Well, might find out what they've been doing. I'll bet they haven't left one clue for hardworking policemen to find."

"Might as well waste some more time."

The brothers-in-law went in their own car, the two policemen in Van Effen's, an aging and battered Peugeot with a far-from-aging engine. It bore no police distinguishing marks whatsoever, and even the radio telephone was concealed. Van de Graaf lowered himself gingerly into the creaking, virtually springless seat.

"I refrain from groaning and complaining, Peter. I know there must be a couple of hundred similar wrecks rattling about the streets of Amsterdam and I appreciate your passion for anonymity, but would it kill you to replace or reupholster the passenger seat?"

"I thought it lent a nice touch of authenticity. But it shall be done. Pick up anything back in the house there?"

"Nothing that you didn't. Interesting that the tall, thin man should be accompanied by a couple of mutes."

Van Effen nodded.

De Graaf went on. "It has occurred to you that if the leader, as Dekker calls him, is a foreigner, then his henchmen are also probably foreigners and may very well be unable to speak a word of Dutch?"

"It had occurred and it is possible. Dekker said that the leader gave orders, which would give one to understand that they spoke, or at least understood, Dutch. Doesn't necessarily follow, of course. The orders may have been meaningless and given only to convince the listener that the others were Dutch."

"Pity that Dekker has never ventured beyond the frontiers of his own homeland. He might—I say just might—have been able to identify the country of origin of the owner of that voice. I speak two or three languages, Peter, you even more. Do you think, if we'd heard this person speaking, we'd have been able to tell his country?"

"There's a chance. I wouldn't put it higher than that. You're thinking, sir, of the tape recording that this newspaper subeditor made of the phone call they received. Chances there would be much poorer—you know how a phone call can distort a voice. And they don't strike me as people who would make such a fairly obvious mistake. Besides, even if we did succeed in guessing at the country of origin, how the hell would that help us in tracking them down?"

Van de Graaf lit up a black cheroot. Van Effen wound down his window. Van de Graaf paid no attention. He said: "You're a great comforter. Give us a few more facts—or let's dig up a few more—and it might be of great help to us. Apart from the fact, not yet established, that he may be a foreigner, all we know about this lad is that he's very tall, built along the lines of an emaciated garden rake and has something wrong with his eyes."

"Wrong? The eyes, I mean, sir? All we know for certain is that he wears sunglasses at nighttime. Could mean anything or nothing. Could be a fad. Maybe he fancies himself in them. Maybe, as Dekker suggested, he thinks sunglasses are *de rigueur* for the better-class villain. Maybe, like the American President's Secret Service bodyguards, he wears them because any potential malefactor in a crowd can never know whether the agent's eyes are fixed on him or not, thereby inhibiting him from action. Or he might be suffering from nyctalopia."

"I see. Nyctalopia. Every schoolboy knows, of course."

"Funny old word to describe a funny old condition. I am told it's the only English-language word with two precisely opposite meanings. On the one hand, it means night blindness, the recurrent loss of vision after sunset, the causes of which are only vaguely understood. On the other hand, it can be taken to mean day blindness, the inability to see clearly except by night, and here the causes are equally obscure. A rare disease, whatever meaning you take, but its existence has been well attested to. The sunglasses, as we think of them, may well be fitted with special correctional lenses."

"It would appear to me that a criminal suffering from either manifestation of this disease would be laboring under a severe occupational handicap. Both a housebreaker, who operates by daylight, and a burglar, who operates by night, would be a bit restricted in their movements if they were afflicted, respectively, by day or night blindness. Just a little bit too farfetched for me, Peter. I prefer the old-fashioned reasons. Badly scarred about the eyes. Cross-eyed. Maybe he's got a squint. Maybe an eye whose iris is streaked or parti-colored. Maybe walleyed, where the iris is so light that you can hardly distinguish it from the white or where the pupils are of two different colors. Maybe a sufferer from exophthalmic goiter, which results in very pro-tuberant eyes."

"Now who's being esoteric?"

"Maybe he's only *got* one eye. In any event, I'd guess he's suffering from some physical abnormality by which he would be immediately identifiable without the help of those dark glasses."

"So all we've got to do is to ask Interpol for a list, world-wide, of all known criminals with eye defects. There must be tens of thousands. Even if there were only ten on the list, it still wouldn't help us worth a damn. Chances are good, of course, that he hasn't even got a criminal record." Van Effen pondered briefly. "Or maybe they could give us a list of all albino criminals on their books. They need glasses to hide their eyes."

"The lieutenant is pleased to be facetious," Van de Graaf said morosely. He puffed on his cheroot, then said, almost wonderingly, "By Jove, Peter. You could be right."

Ahead, Dekker had slowed to a stop, and now Van Effen did also. Two boats were moored alongside a canal bank, each about twelve or thirteen yards in length, with two cabins and an open poop deck. The two policemen joined Dekker aboard his boat; Bakkeren boarded his own, which lay immediately ahead. Dekker said: "Well, gentlemen, what do you want to check first?"

Van de Graaf said: "How long have you had this boat?"

"Six years."

"In that case, I don't think Lieutenant Van Effen or I will bother to check anything. After six years, you must know every corner, every nook and cranny on this boat. So we'd be grateful if you'd do the checking. Just tell us if there is anything here, even the tiniest thing, that shouldn't be here; or anything that's missing that should be here. You might, first, be so good as to ask your brother-in-law to do the same aboard his boat."

Some twenty minutes later the brothers-in-law were able to state definitely that nothing had been left behind and that, in both cases, only two things had been taken: beer from the fridges and diesel from the tanks. Neither Dekker nor Bakkeren could say definitely how many cans of beer had been taken, they didn't count such things, but each was adamant that his fuel tank was down by at least five gallons.

"Five gallons each?" Van Effen said. "Well, they wouldn't have used a half gallon to get from here to the airport canal bank and back. So they used the engine for some other purpose. Can you open the engine hatch and let me have a torch?"

Van Effen's check of the engine-room battery was cursory, seconds only, but sufficient. He said: "Do either of you two gentlemen ever use crocodile clips when using or charging your batteries—you know, those spring-loaded grips with the ser-rated teeth? No? Well, someone was using them last night. You can see the indentations on the terminals. They had the batteries in your two boats connected up, in parallel or series, it wouldn't have mattered, they'd have been using a transformer, and ran your engines to keep the batteries charged. Hence the missing ten gallons."

"Which was, I suppose," Dekker said, "what that gangster meant by incidental costs."

"I suppose it was."

Van de Graaf lowered himself, not protesting too much, into the springless, comfortless passenger seat of the ancient Peugeot just as the radio telephone rang. Van Effen answered, then passed the phone across to Van de Graaf, who spoke briefly and returned the phone to its concealed position.

"I feared this," Van de Graaf said. He sounded weary. "My minister wants me to fly up with him to Texel. Taking half the Cabinet with him, I understand."

"Good God! Those rubbernecking clowns. What on earth do they hope to achieve by being up there? They'll only get in everyone's way, gum up the works and achieve nothing; but then, they're very practiced in that sort of thing."

"I would remind you, Lieutenant Van Effen, that you are talking about elected ministers of the Crown." If the words were intended as a reprimand, Van de Graaf's heart wasn't in it.

"A useless and incompetent bunch. Make them look important, perhaps get their names in the papers, might even be worth a vote or two among the more backward of the electorate. Still, I'm sure you'll enjoy it, sir."

Van de Graaf glowered at him, then said hopefully: "I don't suppose you'd like to come, Peter?"

"You don't suppose quite correctly, sir. Besides, I have things to do."

"Do you think I don't?" Van de Graaf looked and sounded very gloomy.

"Ah! But I'm only a cop. You have to be a cop and a diplomat. I'll drop you off at the office."

"Join me for lunch?"

"Like to, sir, but I'm having lunch at an establishment, shall we say, where Amsterdam's chief of police wouldn't be seen dead."

"I wouldn't want to be seen dead with the ministers at Texel. Where are you eating?"

"La Caracha it's called. Your wife and daughters wouldn't approve, sir."

"Business, of course?"

"Of course. A little talk with a couple of our friends in the Krakers. You asked me a couple of months ago to keep a discreet, apart from an official, eye on them. They report occasionally, usually at La Caracha."

"Ah! The Krakers. Haven't had much time to think of them in the past few months. And how are our disenchanted youth, the anti-everything students, the flower men, the hippies, the squatters?"

"And the drug pushers and gunrunners? Keeping a suspiciously low profile, these days. I must say I feel happier, no, that's not the word, less worried when they're heaving iron bars and bricks at our uniformed police and overturning and burning the odd car, because then we know where we are; with this unusual peace and quiet and uncharacteristic inactivity, I feel there's something brewing somewhere. And it's not coffee."

"You're not looking for trouble, Peter?"

"I've got the nasty feeling I'm going to find it anyway. Looking will be quite unnecessary. Yesterday afternoon, when that call came from the F.F.F., I sent two of our best people into the area. They might come across something. An off-chance. But crime in Amsterdam is becoming more and more centralized in the Kraker area, as you know—and the F.F.F., wouldn't you say, qualify as criminals?"

"Birds of a feather? Well, maybe. But the F.F.F. seem like pretty smart boys, maybe too smart to associate with the Krakers, who could hardly be called the intellectual titans of crime."

"The F.F.F. So far we've got a pretty tall fellow, with maybe something wrong with his eyes and maybe of foreign extraction. Practically got it all wrapped up."

"Sarcasm doesn't become you. All right, all right, no stone

unturned, any action is better than nothing. What's the food like at La Caracha?"

"For that area, surprisingly good. I've had a few excellent meals—" He broke off and looked at Van de Graaf. "You are going to honor us at the table, sir?"

"Well, I thought, I mean, as chief of police—"

"Of course, of course. Delighted."

"And no one will know where I am." Van de Graaf seemed cheered at the prospect. "That damned radio phone can ring its head off for all I care. I won't be able to hear it."

"Nobody else will be able to hear it either. That damned phone, as you call it, will be switched off the moment we park. How do you think the dockland citizens are going to react when they hear a phone go off in this relic?"

They drove off. By and by Van de Graaf lit another cheroot, Van Effen lowered his window further and Van de Graaf said, "You've checked up on the proprietor of La Caracha. What's he called?"

"He prefers to be known just as George. I know him moderately well. He's held in high regard among the local people."

"A kindly man? A do-gooder? Charitable? An upstanding citizen, you would say?"

"He's reputed to be a ranking member of three, perhaps four, successful criminal organizations. Not drugs, not prostitution; he despises those and won't touch them. Robbery, it is said, is his forte, usually armed, with or without violence, according to the amount of resistance offered. He himself can be extremely violent. I can testify to that personally. The violence, of course, was not directed at me; you have to be out of your mind to attack a police lieutenant, and George is far from being out of his mind."

"You do have a genius for picking your friends, associates or whatever you call them, Peter." Van de Graaf puffed at his cheroot and if he was ruffled in any way he didn't show it. "Why isn't this menace to society behind bars?"

"You can't arrest, charge, try and convict a man on hearsay. I can't very well go up to George with a pair of handcuffs and say, 'People have been telling me stories and I have to take you in.' Besides, we're friends."

"You've said yourself that he can be excessively violent. You can pull him in on that."

"No. He's entitled to eject any person who is drunk, abusive, uses foul language or is guilty of causing an affray. That's the limit of George's violence. Ejection. Usually two at a time. The law says he can. We are the law."

"Sounds an interesting character. Unusual, one might say. Two at a time, eh?"

"Wait till you see George."

"And how do you propose to introduce me?"

"No need to emphasize the police connections. Just Colonel Van de Graaf. This is, shall we say, a semi-official visit."

"I may be recognized."

"Colonel, there isn't a self-respecting criminal in this city who wouldn't recognize you at a distance of half a mile. When their kids are misbehaving they probably whip out your picture, show it to their offspring and tell them if they don't mend their ways, the bogeyman will come and get them."

"Extremely witty. You're not exactly unknown yourself, Peter. I'd be curious to know what the—ah—criminal element hereabouts think about you."

"You don't have to be curious. They think I'm bent."

The unprepossessing entrance to La Caracha was located halfway down a lane so narrow that not even a car could enter it. The cracked plaster of the tiny entrance porch, the fading and peeling paint belied the barroom that lay beyond. This was well lit and clean, with gleaming knotty-pine walls, half a dozen tables, each with four small armchairs instead of the usual metal or plastic seats, a semicircular bar flanked by fixed stools and, beyond the bar, the barman. When one looked at him, one forgot about the rest of the room.

He was tall. Large. Huge. Very tall and very broad, he probably weighed at least two hundred and eighty pounds. He wore a splendid Mexican sombrero—one assumed there was some connection between his headgear and the vaguely Latin name of the restaurant—a white shirt, a black string tie, an

open black waistcoat and black leather trousers. The absence
of a gunbelt and a holstered Peacemaker Colt struck the only
discordant notes. The eyes were dark, the bushy eyebrows black
and the equally black mustache, equally bushy, luxuriant and
drooping down past the corners of his mouth, perfectly com-
plemented the spectacular sombrero. The craggy face appeared
to have been hacked from granite by an enthusiastic but ungifted
stonemason. He was the epitome of all those "Wanted" portraits
that used to adorn the walls of nineteenth-century western
American saloons.

"That's George?"

Van Effen didn't bother to answer the superfluous question.

"When he ejects them two at a time I assume he uses only
one hand."

George caught sight of them and hurried around the corner
of the bar, a wide, welcoming smile revealing startlingly white
teeth. The nearer he approached, the bigger he seemed to become. His outstretched hand reached them while he was still
some distance away.

"Welcome, Peter, my friend, welcome. *And* Colonel Van
de Graaf. My word, this is indeed an honor." He pumped the
colonel's hand as if he were a twin brother he hadn't seen for
twenty years.

Van de Graaf smiled. "You know me then?"

"If there is anyone in the city who doesn't recognize our
commissioner of police, he must either be blind or never read
newspapers or magazines. Peter, as of this moment, my reputation is made." He looked at Van de Graaf and dropped his
voice. "Provided, of course that this is not an official visit."

"Purely unofficial," Van de Graaf said. "Regard me as the
lieutenant's guest."

"It is my pleasure to celebrate this auspicious occasion,"
George said. "Borreltje, jonge jenever, whiskey, beer, wine—
La Caracha has an excellent cellar. No better in Amsterdam.
But I recommend my bessenjenever, gentlemen. Ice just be-
ginning to form on the top." He touched his lips. "Incompa-
rable."

So it proved, and in the quantities that George supplied, the red-currant gin was as formidable as it was incomparable. George remained with them for a few minutes, discoursing freely on a variety of subjects but mainly and inevitably about the dike breach that had brought back into existence the long-vanished Haarlem Lake.

"No need to look for the perpetrators of this crime among the professional criminals of the Netherlands." George sounded very positive. "I use the word 'professional' because one would have to exclude the pitifully amateurish types among the Krakers, hotheaded madmen capable of any atrocity, no matter how many innocents suffer, in the name of their crazy and woolly ideals, totally amoral lunatics, mindless idiots who love destruction for destruction's sake. But they are not Dutchmen, though they may have been born in this country; they're just members of a terminally sick subculture that you'll find in many other countries.

"But I don't think they're responsible for the Schiphol flooding. However much one may deplore the action of the saboteurs, one has to admire the clearheaded intelligence that lies behind it. Nobody with such intelligence would associate with the morons who make up the Krakers, though that's not to say the Krakers couldn't be employed in some subordinate capacity where they wouldn't be allowed to know enough to do any damage. But no Dutchman, however criminally minded, would or could have been responsible. Every Dutchman is born with the belief, the certain knowledge, that our dikes are inviolable: it is an act of faith. I am not—what is the word, gentlemen?— I am not xenophobic, but this is a foreign-inspired idea, being carried out by foreigners. And it's only the beginning. There will be further atrocities. Wait and see."

"We won't have to wait long," Van de Graaf said. "They've said they are going to breach the Texel sea dike at four-thirty this afternoon."

George nodded, as if the news had come as no surprise to him.

"So soon, so soon. And then the next dike, and then the next, and the next. When the blackmail demands come, as come they must, for nothing other than blackmail can lie behind this, they will be horrendous." He glanced toward his bar, where a group of men were making urgent signals that they were dying of thirst. "You will excuse me, gentlemen."

"An extraordinary fellow," Van de Graaf said. "He would have made a splendid politician—he could hardly be accused of being at a loss for words. Strange type to be a criminal alleged to be associated with violence—he's clearly a well-educated man. So, on the other hand, were a number of fa-mous—notorious, rather—and highly successful criminals in the past. But I find him especially intriguing. He seems well into the criminal mind but at the same time he thinks and speaks like a cop. And he got on to the possibility that those criminals might come from another country in a fraction of the time that it took us to arrive at the possibility—and, unlike us, he had nothing to help or guide him toward that conclusion. Maybe you and I are fractionally less clever than we like to think we are."

"Maybe you should hire George, sir, on an ad-hoc basis, substantive rank of sergeant, as a dike-breach investigator. Rather a fine title, don't you think?"

"The title is fine, the idea is not. Set a thief to catch a thief—the idea never did work. Do not jest with your superior in his hour of need. Speaking of need, when do we eat?"

"Let's ask." George had returned with fresh supplies of bessenjenever. "We'd like lunch, George."

"The colonel will eat here? La Caracha is doubly honored. This table will do?"

"I'm expecting Vasco and Annemarie."

"Of course." George picked up the drinks tray and led the way up four steps into a dining room, bright, cheerful and so small that it held only two tables. George produced a menu. "Everything is excellent. The *Rodekool met Rolpens* is superb."

"Shall we have the superb, Peter?" Van de Graaf said.

"Fine. And, George, as our chief of police is with us, I think the expense account could stand a bottle of reasonable wine."

"Reasonable? Do I believe my ears? A *superb* wine to go with a superb dish and strictly on La Caracha. A Château

Latour, perhaps? I have said that there is no better cellar than mine in the city. Equally beyond dispute is the fact that I have by far the best Bordeaux cellar." George handed them their aperitifs. "Sharpen your appetites, gentlemen. Annelise, I promise, will excel herself."

When George left, Van de Graaf said: "Who's Annelise?"

"His wife. Less than half his size. He's terrified of her. A wonderful cook."

"She is aware of his, what shall we say, extracurricular activities?"

"She knows nothing."

"You mentioned a Vasco and an Annemarie. Those, I assume, are your informants. George seems to know about them."

"He knows them pretty well. They're friends."

"Does he also know that they're working undercover for you?" Van Effen nodded and Van de Graaf frowned. "Is this wise? Is it politic? Is it, dammit, even professional?"

"I trust George."

"Maybe you do. I don't have to. To say you have the best Bordeaux cellar in Amsterdam is to make a pretty large claim. That would cost money, a great deal of money. Is he into the hijacking and smuggling rackets too, or does he earn enough from his extracurricular activities to buy honestly on the open market?"

"Look, sir, I never said George was a rogue, thief, crook, gangster or whatever. I was only quoting the neighborhood opinion of him. I wanted you to make up your own mind about him. I think you already have, only you still have reservations owing to the fact that you have a nasty, devious, suspicious mind which is why, I suppose, you're the city's chief of police. Annelise knows nothing about George's extracurricular activities, as you call them, because there are none. George has never earned an illegal guilder in his life. He's totally straight, and if every man in Amsterdam were as honest as he is, you'd join the unemployed by nightfall. I was certain you'd caught on to this when you said he thought and spoke like a cop. He is—or was—a cop, and a damned good one, a sergeant in line for his inspectorate when he decided to retire last year.

Phone the chief of police in Groningen and find out who he'd give a bag of gold for to have back on his staff."

"I am staggered," Van de Graaf said. He didn't look staggered, he just sat placidly puffing his cheroot and sipping his bessenjenever as if Van Effen had been discussing the weather or crops. "Different. Yes, different." He didn't say what was different. "Might have given me some kind of warning, though."

"Thought you'd guess, sir. He's got cop written all over him. At least he had until he grew his mustache after retirement."

"Any specialties?"

"Drugs and counterterrorism. I should have said drugs, then counterterrorism."

"Drugs? The only drug in the province of Groningen comes out of a gin bottle. Here's the place for him. Or, if I take you rightly, was. Why was he taken off? Who took him off?"

"Nobody. Nature took him off. To be a successful narcotics cop you have to be able to merge unobtrusively into your background. You've seen him. He wasn't built to merge into anything."

"What's more, they've never even *seen* a terrorist up north."

"They're not all that thick on the ground down here either, sir. Maybe that's why George resigned—no challenge, nothing left for him to do."

"A waste. An intelligence like that devoting its life to serving up superfluous calories to already overweight Amsterdamers. Could be useful. Maybe there's something to your idea of ad-hoc recruitment. In an emergency, we could always have him co-opted."

"Yes, sir. I thought that to co-opt anyone you required a committee, a quorum."

"There's only one committee and quorum in the Amsterdam police force, and I'm it. If you think he could be of help, just ask me. In fact, don't bother to ask me. All I care about at the moment is food. I'm hungry."

"Ah, yes. George normally serves up hors d'oeuvres. Maybe he thought there was no urgency." He surveyed Van de Graaf's ample frame. "Superfluous calories. However." He rose, opened a wooden cupboard door to reveal a refrigerator, opened this and said, "Half a smoked salmon. Smoked trout. Mountain ham. Gouda, Edam, and a few other odds and ends."

"There are no limits to the heights you might reach, my boy." Some time later, the first sharp edge of his appetite temporarily blunted, he said, "If you're too busy or too cowardly to accompany me to Texel, may one ask what you intend to do?"

"Depends on what I learn from Annemarie and Vasco. If anything. On balance, however, I think I'll go and do what poor George couldn't, merge unobtrusively among the Krakers in their garden suburb."

"You! You're mad. The unchallenged bête noire of Krakerdom. Two minutes after your arrival all activity and conversation will wither on the vine."

"I've been there more than once in the past and the vine has remained unaffected. I don't wear this rather nice pinstripe you see before you or my official uniform. I wear other garb. My Kraker uniform. I don't think I've ever discussed my wardrobe with you before." Van Effen sipped some more bessenjenever. "I've a sealskin jacket with lots and lots of tassels and a coonskin hat with a wolverine's tail attached to the back. Rather dashing, really." Van de Graaf closed his eyes, screwed them tightly shut and then opened them again. "The trousers are made of some other kind of skin, I don't know what it is, with lots of little leather strips down the sides. Moccasins, of course. Those were a mistake. The moccasins, I mean. They leak. Then my hair and my mustache are blond, not platinum, you understand, that would attract too much attention."

"The rest of your outfit doesn't?"

"The dye is impervious to any rainstorm. Have to use a special detergent to get it off. A painful process. Then I wear half a dozen rings, solid brass, on my right hand."

"That the hand you hit people with?"

"Among other things I'm a Green Peace, anti-nuclear, environmental pacifist. I also have a multicolored bead necklace, double chain and an earring. One earring. Two are passé."

"This, some day, I must see."

"I can get you one like it, if you want." Van de Graaf closed his eyes again and was saved further comment by the arrival of George with lunch. George served the *Rodekool met Rolpens*, opened the Château Latour with a suitably reverential air and departed. The meal was a simple one, red cabbage, rolled spiced meat and sliced apple, but, as George had promised, splendidly cooked; as was customary in Amsterdam, there was enough food for four. The wine was not simple: it was, also as promised, superb.

They had just finished when George brought coffee. "Annemarie is outside."

"Bring her in, please."

Annemarie was a young lady of striking appearance. Her turtleneck pullover of indeterminate color had once, perhaps, been white. It was about four sizes too large for her, a defect she had tried to remedy by hauling a three-inch studded belt tightly about her midriff. As she had a rather slender waist, the effect was incongruous in the extreme—she resembled nothing so much as a potato bag tied around the middle. The faded and patched blue jeans were fashionably frayed at the cuffs and she teetered, rather than walked, into the room on a pair of stained short leather boots with ludicrously pointed high heels. The condition of her streaky blond hair showed that she regarded combs as an unnecessary luxury. Jet-black mascara had been applied with a heavy hand, as had the turquoise eye shadow. The ghastly pallor of her face, which could only have been caused by an overenthusiastic application of some cheap powder, was in stunning contrast to the two circular red patches on her cheeks, which owed nothing to nature, either. The lipstick was purple and the blood-red nail varnish, which showed when she removed the cigarette holder from between her stained teeth, was chipped and flaking. The nose-wrinkling smell of her penny perfume suggested that she had been bathing in it, although the impression was overwhelming that she hadn't bathed in anything for a very long time. Brass earrings tinkled as she teetered.

Van Effen looked at Van de Graaf but Van de Graaf didn't

look at him; he was either mesmerized or petrified by the apparition before him. Van Effen cleared his throat, loudly.

"This is Annemarie, sir."

"Yes, yes, Annemarie." Van de Graaf was still staring at her, and by a visibly conscious effort of will, he turned his head to look at Van Effen. "Of course, of course. Annemarie. But there are one or two things I haven't had the opportunity yet to discuss with you and—"

"I understand, sir. Annemarie, my dear, would you mind for a few minutes—I'm sure George will give you something." She blew a long puff of smoke, smiled and tottered from the room.

"Annemarie, my dear." Van de Graaf sounded and looked appalled. "Annemarie, my dear. You in your Kraker uniform and that—that creature, what a couple you would make. Levelheaded, I'd always thought you, eminently sensible—this has to be some kind of joke. Where on earth did you pick up that hussy, that harlot, that harridan, that ghastly spectacle? God, that makeup, that bordello perfume!"

"It's not like you, sir, to go by appearances. Snap judgments—"

"Snap judgments! Those preposterous shoes. That filthy jersey that was built for—for a gorilla—"

"A very practical jersey, sir. That way no one would suspect the existence of the Beretta she carries strapped beneath her waist."

"A Beretta! That creature, that spectacle—she carries an automatic? That—that caricature of a human being with a gun? You must be mad." He drew deeply on his cheroot. "No, you're not mad. I'm not complaining, Peter, but it's been a shock to my system."

"I can see that, sir. Should have warned you, I suppose. She does have rather an effect on people who make her acquaintance for the first time. That awful harridan is in fact a lovely young woman, or would be if she soaked in a bath for about an hour. She's very nice, charming, really, intelligent, speaks four languages, is a university graduate and is also a policewoman from Rotterdam. Don't you see, sir, I'm making a point. If she can fool the chief of police, who has become chief of police by, among other things, being fooled by fewer people than anyone else around, she can fool anyone."

"How did you come by this paragon?"

"Exchange basis. Not a very fair exchange. I knew she'd spent six months underground in Rotterdam, and we had no one comparable up here. It wasn't easy, but my opposite number down there is a friend of mine."

"Why wasn't I informed of this?"

"Because you gave me a free hand, remember. I would have informed you if there had been anything to report. So far there has been nothing. Didn't want to bother you with trifles."

Van de Graaf smiled. "I doubt whether that explosion of paints and scents would care to be called a trifle. Have her in, would you?"

Van Effen did so and Van de Graaf waved her courteously to a seat. "Sorry you were kept waiting. You know who I am?"

"Of course. Colonel Van de Graaf. My boss." The slightly husky voice was low and pleasant, at complete variation with her appearance.

"Lieutenant Van Effen told you?"

"He didn't have to, sir. I work for him and I know he works for you. And I've seen your picture dozens of times."

"That outfit you're wearing, Annemarie. Don't you feel it makes you look rather . . . conspicuous?"

"Among the people I'm supposed to be investigating? Compared to some of the clothes worn there, mine are low-key, positively understated. Isn't that so, Peter?"

"Ah! Peter, is it? A lowly ranker addresses my senior lieutenant by his given name?"

"On orders, sir. We've been out a couple of times together—"

"Among your—ah—friends?"

"Yes, sir."

"I wish I had seen that."

"We do form rather a colorful couple. I told Annemarie that it would be less than desirable to call me Lieutenant in such company. I told her to call me Peter and always think of me as Peter. That way you don't make mistakes. Someone drummed this into me years ago."

"I was the drummer. I understand that you carry a gun, young lady. You can use it?"

"I was trained at the police range."

"Ever used it?"

"No. And I must admit I hope I never have to."

"Would you use it?"

"I don't know. If it was to stop someone from killing a person, well, perhaps, yes. But I couldn't kill a person. I don't like guns. I'm afraid I'm not very brave, sir."

"Nonsense. Your sentiments do you credit. Feel exactly the same way myself. And it takes a brave girl to venture into Krakerland."

She half-smiled. "That's where the turtleneck comes in so useful. They can't see the pulse in my neck."

"Rubbish. How are things among your friends? Anything untoward or exciting afoot?"

"They're not a very exciting lot, sir. Rather dull, really. Most of them are not the social rebels and anti-authority storm-troopers they would like to be thought to be. Of course, there are the drug pushers and drug users, and there is a hard core that trade in armaments, selling Russian small arms to the Irish Republican Army and other disaffected elements. But Peter has told me not to bother about the arms-running side."

"Disaffected elements? I like that. So, Peter, the young lady does not concern herself with gunrunning. Why?"

"*You* ask *me*, sir? America, Russia, Britain, France trade in arms—legally—to the tune of billions of dollars yearly. The Israelis do it, as do the Iranians, Libyans and God knows how many other countries. All with their governments' blessings. Who are we to become all God-fearing, moralistic and holier-than-thou when private enterprise moves in on a tiny scale? Anyway, I know you're not really interested in that side. The only things you really are interested in are drugs and those mysterious and increasing threats to the royal family and members of the government."

"Yes, yes, of course. Anything interesting to report on any of those fronts?"

Annemarie shook her head. "Vasco—you've heard of Vasco?"

"Yes. Never met him, though. Supposed to meet him today. In fact, I thought I was meeting him with you."

"I thought so, too. We'd arranged to meet in a café close by here almost an hour ago. No signs, which is most unlike Vasco."

"This friend of yours—he's a dyed-in-the-wool true-blue Kraker?"

"Well, he seems to be but he can't be, can he? They have some kind of leaders, nobody with any personality or charisma, a kind of loose council, and Vasco appears to be a member or close to it. But he says he's basically against them and I believe him. After all, he works for you. Sort of."

"But you're of two minds about him?"

"My intelligence, if I have any, says that—well, I'm ambivalent about him. My instincts trust him."

"Peter?"

"Her instincts are right. He's a cop. Detective sergeant."

"A policeman." Annemarie's lips were compressed, her eyes angry. "Thank you. Thank you very much."

"Don't be childish," Van Effen said. "You told him you were a policewoman?"

She didn't answer and Van de Graaf said hastily, "It's the need-to-know principle, my dear. He didn't even tell me. I take it he thinks I didn't need to know. You were about to say something about Vasco?"

"Yes. Could be important. I don't know. He told me late last night that he thought he had a lead. He said he had just been approached by one of the council, a person who knew that he, Vasco, moved quite often about the outside world—to them, everything beyond their suburban boundaries is the outside world. He said he was being taken to a meeting about midnight to meet someone important. I don't know who the person was. But I got a look at him as he left."

Van Effen said, "Who was the person who approached him? Can you describe him?"

"I can describe him, all right. Short, balding, pepper-and-salt beard and a bad squint in his right eye."

Van de Graaf looked at Van Effen. "Another eye disorder, but this one for real. This person have a name?"

"Julius."

"Julius what?"

"Just—" She hesitated. "Julius Caesar. I know it's crazy, but then they're crazy. Nobody out there ever uses his real name. Right now, as far as names are concerned, they're going through a historical phase. That's the kind of follow-my-leader sheep they are. We've got Alexander the Great, Genghis Khan, Charlemagne, Lord Nelson, Helen of Troy, Cleopatra—I could go on. They go for macho men or beautiful women, everything that they're not. Anyway, Julius Caesar."

Van Effen said: "And that's all you know? No indications as to what kind of lead it was?"

"No." She pursed her lips. "That's not to say that Vasco didn't know."

"An odd comment to make," Van de Graaf said. "What do you mean?"

"Nothing. I just don't know whether he knows or not."

"Dear me." Van de Graaf studied her quizzically. "You don't trust your fellow officer?"

"He doesn't trust me."

"Well. This does make for a happy relationship in the field."

Van Effen said: "Sergeant Westenbrink doesn't distrust her. It's just that three years working undercover tends to make you secretive, a loner."

"Westenbrink, is it. I thought I knew all my sergeants."

"He's from Utrecht, sir."

"You cast a wide net. Lieutenant Van Effen, Annemarie, works on the same principle as Vasco, whose name is not Vasco. The need to know. How can you be hurt when you see me being treated in this cavalier fashion?"

George entered, apologized, picked up a phone set from a side table and placed it in front of Annemarie. She lifted the receiver, listened to the crackling voice for all of two minutes, said, "Thank you. Five minutes," and hung up.

Van Effen said: "The Hunter's Horn, I presume. What's the message from Vasco?"

"The Hunter's Horn." Van de Graaf frowned. "I trust that's not the Hunter's Horn that—"

"There's only one—ah—establishment of that name in Amsterdam. Beggars can't be choosers. Apart from La Caracha, it's our only safe house in Amsterdam. A private connection, Colonel. The fair name of the Amsterdam police department remains unbesmirched."

"Not to know," Van de Graaf muttered. "Not to know."

"You're half right," Annemarie said, almost reluctantly. "It was the Hunter's Horn. But it wasn't Vasco."

"Never said it was. I said, 'What's the message from Vasco?' It was Henri. Henri, sir, is the owner. Vasco is under observation but whoever is tailing him didn't know, wasn't to know, that it's virtually impossible to follow Vasco without Vasco being aware of it. So he couldn't come here. The person or persons following him would have raised their eyebrows if they saw you here; they'd have gone into shock if they'd found me, which would have been a small disaster for us and the end of the usefulness of both Vasco and you, Annemarie. So the only place left for Vasco was the Hunter's Horn. Even there he couldn't use the telephone, for he would still be being watched. So he wrote a small note for Henri, who did the telephoning. You're to ask me a question and you're to give Henri my answer inside five minutes."

Annemarie sighed. "Did you have to spoil it for me?" Then she brightened. "But you didn't get it all, did you?"

"I'm brilliant at deducing the obvious, not clairvoyant. The rest, what I didn't get, can wait, including the reasons why Vasco is going to call me back."

"I didn't say that?"

"Henri did. The message."

She made a moue. "It went like this. Two tails. Understand can't ditch. Meet two—"

Van de Graaf interrupted. "What was that meant to mean?"

"Westenbrink's shorthand, I imagine," Van Effen said. "Only two ways of getting rid of his tails. He could throw them into the nearest canal, which he's perfectly capable of doing, or he could easily have lost them, which he is again perfectly capable of doing. Either course of action would have ended any connection he's succeeded in making."

Annemarie went on: "Meet two, three men four-thirty Hunter's Horn." She pushed across a piece of paper.

"Stephan Danilov," Van Effen read. "Pole. Radom. Explosives expert. Oil-well fires. Texas. Clear enough. Interesting, sir?"

"It is indeed. How do you feel about blowing up banks?"

"Should be interesting to see the law from the other side. They'll bring along a Polish speaker, of course."

Annemarie said, "You think this is a Polish criminal group."

"No. Just to check on me."

"But if they speak to you in—"

"If they speak to him in Polish, my dear," Van de Graaf said, "he'll answer in Polish, in which language he's fluent. Your friend from Utrecht, Peter, of course knew this."

Annemarie said: "But—but you'll be recognized. Everybody in that—that ghetto knows you, I mean, knows who you are."

"Ninny. Sorry, but please. If you think I'm going to present myself as Lieutenant Van Effen, you can't be feeling too well. I shall, in the best traditions as befits the circumstances, be heavily disguised. I'll put on about fifty instant pounds—I have a suit and shirt designed to add the excess avoirdupois—fatten my cheeks, tint hair and mustache, wear a sinister scar and a black leather glove. That's to disguise the fearful scars and burns I sustained when—let me see, yes, of course—when I was putting out this oil fire in Saudi Arabia or wherever. It's remarkable what a single black glove does. It becomes the focal point for identification in nearly everyone's mind, and if you're not wearing it, you're not you, if you follow me. And don't call Krakerdom a ghetto—it's an insult to decent Jews."

"I didn't mean to—"

"I know. I'm sorry. Call Henri, tell him it's O.K. and to let a few minutes pass before giving Vasco the nod."

She made the call and hung up. "Everything seems all right. A few minutes." She looked at Van Effen. "You already have all the details you want. Why have Vasco make the call?"

"Why have Vasco make the call?" Van Effen tried to look patient. "Vasco goes back every afternoon to this empty block of flats that they've taken over under so-called squatters' rights. He's been under surveillance since his meeting with the council or whatever they call themselves since last night, and it's a safe assumption that he'll remain under surveillance until the time of the meeting in the Hunter's Horn. How's he supposed to have communicated with me to arrange this meeting? Telepathy?"

Van de Graaf cleared his throat and looked at Annemarie. "You must forgive our lieutenant his Old World gallantry. Do you go back to the dreadful place now?"

"Very soon."

"And you stay there overnight?"

She gave a mock shudder. "There are limits, sir, to my loyalty to the police force. No, I don't sleep there at nights."

"No raised eyebrows among the fraternity?"

"Not at all, sir. I have a gentleman friend who comes calling for me every evening. The Krakers understand this sort of thing."

"And you go back in the morning?"

"Yes, sir." She put her hand to her mouth to cover a smile but Van de Graaf had seen it.

"You are amused, young lady." His tone had lost some warmth.

"Well, yes, I am a little, sir. Your voice and expression of disapproval and disappointment. This friend is really a very gallant gentleman. Especially as he's married."

"Naturally." Van de Graaf was not amused.

"He takes me to his cousin's house, leaves me there and comes for me in the morning. That's why he's gallant, because he's very much in love with his wife. His cousin, Colonel Van de Graaf, is a lady."

Van de Graaf said: "The chief of police is in his usual condition, namely, out of his depth." He was noticeably relieved. "You will, of course, Peter, have carried out a check on this cousin, this lady?"

"No, I have not." Van Effen spoke with some feeling. "I wouldn't dare."

Van de Graaf frowned briefly, then leaned back and laughed. "Behold our intrepid lieutenant, Annemarie. He's terrified of his young sister. So you're staying with Julie?"

"You know her then, sir?"

"My favorite lady in all Amsterdam. Except, of course, for my wife and two daughters. I'm her godfather. Well, well."

The phone rang. Van Effen picked it up and listened for perhaps half a minute, then said: "Can anyone overhear my voice if I speak?" Apparently nobody could, for Van Effen said, "Say that you'll give me half a minute to think it over." At the end of that period Van Effen spoke again. "Say to me: 'Stephan, I swear to you it's no police trap. My life on it. And if it were a police trap, what would my life be worth then? Don't be silly.'"

A few moments later Van Effen said: "That was fine. Will you be coming with them? Fine. Be sure to tell whoever comes with you—I'm sure it won't be the gentlemen who have you under surveillance at the moment—that I have a police record in Poland and have a United States extradition warrant out against me. I shall be wearing a black leather glove." He hung up.

"Nice touch about the police record and extradition warrant," Van de Graaf said. "Two statements they have no way of checking on. You will be carrying a gun, I assume?"

"Certainly. It would be expected of me and I'll have it in a shoulder holster that should make it apparent to the most myopic that I am armed."

Annemarie said doubtfully: "Perhaps they will take it off you before discussions start. Just as a precaution, I mean."

"One must take a chance about those things. I shall be brave."

"What Peter means," Van de Graaf said dryly, "is that he

always carries a second gun. It's like his single-glove theory, that people only concentrate on one thing at a time. It's in that book of his, I'm sure. If a person finds a gun on you and relieves you of it, he's relieved himself and has got to be pathologically suspicious to start looking for another."

"It's not in the book. I don't put thoughts like those in criminal minds. Curious, sir, that we'll both be engaged in something interesting at exactly four-thirty—you and the minister, schnapps in hand, peering down at the Texel sea dike from the safety of your helicopter seats while I am entering the lion's den."

"I'd switch with you any time," Van de Graaf said morosely. "I should be back from Texel by six—damn little I can do up there anyway. Let's meet at seven."

"Provided we both survive—you the schnapps, me the lions. The 444 would be in order, sir?"

Van de Graaf didn't say that the 444 would be in order: on the other hand, he didn't say it wouldn't.

3

THE CHINOOK HELICOPTER, a big, fast experimental model on demonstration loan from the U.S. Army of the Rhine, suffered from the same defect as other, smaller and less advanced models: it was extremely noisy, the rackety clamor of the engines making conversation difficult and at times impossible. This wasn't helped by the fact that it had two rotors instead of the customary one.

The passengers were a very mixed bag indeed. Apart from Van de Graaf and his Minister of Justice, Robert Kondstaal, there were four other cabinet ministers, of whom only the Minister of Defense could claim any right to be aboard. The other three, including, incredibly, the Minister of Education, were there only because of the influence they wielded and their curiosity about things that in no way concerned them. Much the same could have been said about the senior air force officer, the brigadier general and rear admiral who sat together behind Van de Graaf. Flight-evaluation purposes had been their claim. The evaluation tests had been completed a week ago; they were along purely as rubberneckers. The same could be said of the two experts from the Rijkswaterstaat and the two from the Delft Hydraulics laboratory. Superficially, it would have seemed, their presence could be more than justified, but as the pilot had firmly stated that he had no intention of setting his Chinook down in floodwaters and the experts, portly gentlemen all, had indicated that they had no intention of descending by winch or rope ladder only to be swept away, it was difficult to see how their presence could be justified. The handful of journalists and cameramen aboard could have claimed a right to be there; but even they were to admit later that their trip had hardly been worthwhile.

The Chinook, flying at no more than six hundred sixty feet and about a third of a mile out to sea, was directly opposite Oosterend when the sea dike broke. It was a singularly unspectacular explosion—a little sound, a little smoke, a little rubble, a little spray—but effective enough for all that: the Wadden Zee was already rushing through the narrow gap and into the polder beyond. Less than a third of a mile from the entrance to the gap an oceangoing tug was already headed toward the breach. As the pilot turned his Chinook westward, presumably to see what the conditions were like in the polder, Van de Graaf leaned over to one of the Rijkswaterstaat experts. He had to shout to make himself heard.

"How bad is it, Mr. Okkerse? How long do you think it will take to seal off the break?"

"Well, damn their souls, damn their souls! Villains, devils, monsters!" Okkerse clenched and unclenched his hands. "Monsters, I tell you, sir, monsters!" Okkerse's upset was understandable. Dikes, the construction, care and maintenance of, were his raison d'être.

"Yes, yes, monsters," Van de Graaf shouted. "How long to fix that?"

"Moment." Okkerse rose, lurched forward, spoke briefly to the pilot and lurched his way back to his seat. "Got to see it first. Pilot's taking us down."

The Chinook curved around, passing over the waters flooding across the first reaches of the polder and came to a hover fifty feet above the ground and some sixty-five feet distant. Okkerse pressed his nose against a window. After only a few seconds he turned away and gave the wave-off signal to the pilot. The Chinook curved away inland.

"Clever fiends," Okkerse shouted. "Very clever. It's only a small breach and they chose the perfect moment for it."

"What does the time of day matter?"

"It matters very much. Rather, the state of the tide matters. They didn't pick high tide, because that would have caused heavy flooding and great destruction."

"So they can't be all that villainous?"

Okkerse didn't seem to hear him. "And they didn't pick low tide because they knew—how, I can't even guess—that we would do what we are just about to do and that is to block the gap with the bows of a vessel. See that oceangoing tug down there? At low water the tug probably wouldn't have found enough water to get close to the dike." He shook his head. "I don't like any of this."

"You think our friends have inside information?"

"I didn't say that."

"I suggested that to your friend John de Jong. That those people have either an informant in or somebody employed in the Rijkswaterstaat."

"Ridiculous! In *our* organization? Preposterous!"

"That's more or less what John said. Nothing's impossible. What makes you think your people are immune to penetration? Look at the British Secret Service, where security is supposed to be a religion. They're penetrated at regular intervals and with painful frequency. If it can happen to them with all their resources, it's ten times more likely to happen to you. That's beside the point. How long to seal the breach?"

"The tug should block off about 80 per cent of the flow. The tide's going out. We've got everything ready to hand—concrete blocks, matting, divers, steel plates, quick-setting concrete. A few hours. Technically, a minor job. That's not what worries me."

Van de Graaf nodded, thanked him and resumed his seat beside Kondstaal. "Okkerse says it's no problem, sir. Straight-forward repair job."

"Didn't think it would be a problem. The villains said there would be minimal damage and they seem to mean what they say. That's not what worries me."

"That's what Okkerse has just said. The worry is, of course, that they can carry out their threats with impunity. We're in an impossible situation. What would you wager, sir, that we don't receive another threat this evening?"

"Nothing. There's no point in wondering what those people are up to. They'll doubtless let us know in their own good time. And there's no point, I suppose, in asking you what progress you've made so far."

Van de Graaf concentrated on lighting his cheroot and said nothing.

Sergeant Westenbrink wore an off-white coverall, unbuttoned from throat to waist to show off a garishly patterned and colored Hawaiian shirt, a Dutch bargee's cap and a circular brass earring. Compared to those among whom he lived and had his being, Vasco, Van Effen thought, looked positively underdressed but was still outlandish enough to make himself and the two men sitting opposite him across the table in the booth in the Hunter's Horn look the pillars of a respectable society. One of them, clad in an immaculately cut gray suit, was about Van Effen's age, darkly handsome, slightly swarthy, with tightly curled black hair, black eyes and, when he smiled—which was often—what appeared to be perfect teeth. Any Mediterranean country, Van Effen thought, or, at the outside, not more than two generations removed. His companion, a short, slightly balding man perhaps ten or fifteen years older than the other, wore a conservative suit and a hairline mustache, the only really and slightly unusual feature in an otherwise unremarkable face. Neither of them looked the slightest bit like a bona fide member of the criminal classes, but then, few successful criminals ever did.

The younger man—he went, it seemed, by the name of Romero Agnelli, which might even have been his own—produced an ebony cigarette holder, a Turkish cigarette and a gold-inlaid onyx lighter; any of which might have appeared affected or even effeminate on almost any man; with Agnelli, the display of all three seemed inevitable. He lit the cigarette and smiled at Van Effen.

"You will not take it amiss if I ask one or two questions."

He had a pleasant baritone voice and spoke in English. "One cannot be too careful these days."

"I cannot be too careful any day. If your question is pertinent, of course I'll answer it. If not, I won't. Am I—ah—accorded the same privilege?"

"Certainly."

"Except you can ask more what you consider pertinent questions than I can."

"I don't quite understand."

"Just that I take it that we're talking a potential employer-employee relationship. The employer is usually entitled to ask more questions."

"Now I understand. I won't take advantage of that. I must say, Mr. Danilov, that you look more like the employer class yourself." And indeed, Van Effen's overstuffed suit and padded cheeks did lend a certain air of prosperity. It also made him look almost permanently genial. "Am I mistaken in thinking that you carry a gun?"

"Unlike you, Mr. Agnelli, I'm afraid I'm not in the habit of patronizing expensive tailors."

"Guns make me nervous." The disarming smile didn't show a trace of nervousness.

"Guns make me nervous, too. That's why I carry one in case I meet a man who is carrying one. That makes me very nervous." Van Effen smiled, removed his Beretta from its shoulder holster, clicked out the magazine, handed it to Agnelli and replaced his pistol. "That do anything for your nerves?"

Agnelli smiled. "All gone."

"Then they shouldn't be." Van Effen reached below the table and came up with a tiny automatic. "A Lilliput, a toy in many ways, but lethal up to twenty feet in the hands of a man who can fire accurately." He tapped out the magazine, handed this in turn to Agnelli and replaced the Lilliput in its ankle holster. "That's all. Three guns would be just too much to carry about."

"So I should imagine." Agnelli's smile, which had momentarily vanished, was back in place. He pushed the two magazines across the table. "I don't think we'll be requiring guns this afternoon."

"Indeed. But something *would* be useful." Van Effen dropped the magazines into a side pocket. "I always find that talking—"

"Beer for me," Agnelli said. "And for Helmut, too, I know."

"Four beers," Van Effen said. "Vasco, if you would be so kind—" Vasco rose and left the booth.

Agnelli said, "Known Vasco long?"

Van Effen considered. "A proper question. Two months. Why?" Had they, Van Effen wondered, been asking the same question of Vasco?

"Idle curiosity." Agnelli, Van Effen thought, was not a man to indulge in idle curiosity. "Your name really is Stephan Danilov?"

"Certainly not. But it's the name I go by in Amsterdam."

"But you really are a Pole?" The elder man's voice, dry and precise, befitted his cast of countenance, which could have been that of a moderately successful lawyer or accountant. He spoke in Polish.

"For my sins." Van Effen raised an eyebrow. "Vasco, of course."

"Yes. Where were you born?"

"Radom."

"I know it. Not well. A rather provincial town, I thought."

"So I've heard."

"You've heard? But you lived there."

"Four years. When you're four years old, a provincial town is the center of the world. My father—a printer—moved to a better job."

"Where?"

"Warsaw."

"Aha!"

"Aha yourself." Van Effen spoke in some irritation. "You sound as if you know Warsaw and are now going to find out if I know it. Why, I can't imagine. You're not by any chance a lawyer, Mr.—I'm afraid I don't know your name."

"Paderewsky. I am a lawyer."

"Paderewsky. Given time, I would have thought you could have come up with a better one than that. And I was right, eh?

A lawyer. I wouldn't care to have you acting for my defense. You make a poor interrogator."

Agnelli was smiling but Paderewsky was not. His lips were pursed. He said brusquely: "You know the Tin-Roofed Palace, of course."

"Of course."

"Where is it?"

"Dear me. What have we here? The Inquisition? Ah. Thank you." He took a glass from a tray that a waiter, following Vasco, had just brought into the curtained booth and lifted it. "Your health, gentlemen. The place you're so curious about, Mr.—ah—Paderewsky, is close by the Wista, on the corner of the Wybrzeze Gdanskie and the Slasko-Dabrowski Bridge." He sipped some more beer. "Unless they've moved it, of course. Some years since I've been there."

Paderewsky was not amused. "The Palace of Culture and Science."

"Parade Square. It's too big."

"What do you mean?"

"Too big to have been moved, I mean. Twenty-three hundred rooms are a lot of rooms. A monstrosity. The wedding cake, they call it. But then, Stalin never did have any taste in architecture."

"Stalin?" Agnelli said.

"His personal gift to my already long-suffering countrymen." So Agnelli spoke Polish, too.

"Where's the Ethnographic Museum in Warsaw?"

"It's not in Warsaw. Mlociny, six miles to the north." Van Effen's voice was now as brusque as Paderewsky's had been. "Where's the Nike? You don't know? What's the Nike? You don't know? Any citizen of Warsaw knows it's the name given to the Heroes of Warsaw Monument. What's Zamenhofa Street famous for?" An increasingly uncomfortable Paderewsky made no reply. "The Ghetto Monument. I told you you'd make a lousy lawyer, Paderewsky. Any competent lawyer, for the defense or the prosecution, always prepares his brief. You didn't. You're a fraud. It's my belief that you've never even been in Warsaw and that you just spent an hour or so studying a gazetteer or guidebook." Van Effen placed his hands on the table as if preparatory to rising. "I don't think, gentlemen, that we need detain each other any longer. Discreet inquiries are one thing, offensive interrogation by an incompetent, another. I see no basis here for mutual trust and, quite honestly, I need neither a job nor money." He rose. "Good day, gentlemen."

Agnelli reached out a hand. He didn't touch Van Effen, it was just a restraining gesture. "Please sit down, Mr. Danilov. Perhaps Helmut *has* rather overstepped the mark, but have you ever met a lawyer who wasn't burdened with a suspicious mind? Helmut—or we—just happened to choose the wrong suspect. Helmut, in fact, has been in Warsaw, but only, as you almost guessed, briefly and as a tourist. I, personally, don't doubt you could find your way about Warsaw blindfolded." Paderewsky had the look of a man who wished he were in some other place, any place. "A blunder. We apologize."

"That's kind." Van Effen sat down and drank more beer. "Fair enough."

Agnelli smiled. Almost certainly a double-dyed villain, Van Effen thought, but a charming and persuasive one. "Now that you've established a degree of moral ascendancy over us, I'll reinforce that by admitting that we almost certainly need you more than you need us."

Not to be outdone, Van Effen smiled in turn. "You must be in a desperate way." He lifted and examined his empty glass. "If you'd just poke your head round the corner, Vasco, and make the usual SOS."

"Of course, Stephan." There was an unmistakable expression of relief in his face. He did as asked, then settled back in his seat.

"No more interrogation," Agnelli said. "I'll come straight to the point. Your friend Vasco tells me that you know a little about explosives."

"Vasco does me less than justice. I know a great deal about explosives." He looked at Vasco in reproof. "I wouldn't have thought you would discuss a friend—that's me, Vasco, in case you've forgotten—with strangers."

"I didn't. Well, I did, but I just said it was someone I knew."

"No harm. Explosives, as I say, I know. Defusing bombs I know. I'm also fairly proficient in capping wellhead oil fires, but you wouldn't be approaching me in this fashion if that was your problem. You'd be on the phone to Texas, where I learned my trade."

"No oil fires." Agnelli smiled again. "But defusing bombs— well, that's something else. Where did you learn a dangerous trade like that?"

"Army," Van Effen said briefly. He didn't specify which army.

"You've actually defused bombs?" Agnelli's respect was genuine.

"Quite a number."

"You must be good."

"Why?"

"You're here."

"I am good. I'm also lucky, because no matter how good you are, the bomb you're trying to defuse may be your last one. Peaceful retirement is not the lot of a bomb-disposal expert. But as I assume you have no more unexploded bombs than you have oil wells, then it must be explosives. Explosives experts in Holland are not in short supply. You have only to advertise. That I should be approached in a clandestine fashion can only mean that you are engaged in activities that are illegal."

"Have you never been? Engaged, I mean?"

"All depends upon who defines what is illegal and what is not and how they define it. Some people hold definitions that are different from mine and wish to discuss the matter with me. Very tiresome they can be, those alleged upholders of justice. You know what the British say—the law is an ass." Van Effen considered. "I think I put that rather well."

"You've hardly committed yourself. May one ask—delicately, of course—whether this postponed discussion, the one you are avoiding, has anything to do with your vacationing in Amsterdam?"

"You may. It has. What do you want me to blow up?"

Agnelli raised his eyebrows. "Well, well, you can be blunt. Almost as blunt as you can be, shall we say, diplomatic."

"That's an answer? An explosives expert is good for only one thing—exploding things. You wish me to explode something? Yes or no?"

"Yes."

"Two things. Banks, boats, bridges, anything of that kind I'll blow up and guarantee a satisfactory job. Anything that involves injury, far less death, to any person, I won't have any part of."

"You won't ever be called upon to do any such thing. That's also a guarantee. The second thing?"

"I don't seek to flatter you when I say that you're a smart man, Mr. Agnelli. Such people are usually first-class organizers. To seek the help of a last-minute unknown to help you execute some project that may have been in the planning stage for quite some time doesn't smack to me of preparation, organization or professionalism."

"A very valid point. In your position I would adopt the same disbelieving or questioning attitude. You have to take my word for it that I am a member of a highly organized team. But, as you must well know, the best-laid plans, et cetera. An unfortunate accident. I can explain to your satisfaction. But not just at this moment. Will you accept our offer?"

"You haven't made one yet."

"Will you accept an offer of a job in our organization, on, if you wish, a permanent basis, on what I think you'll find a very satisfactory salary plus commission basis, your special responsibility being the demolition of certain structures, those structures to be specified at a later date."

"Sounds *very* businesslike. And I like the idea of commissions, whatever they may be. I agree. When do I start and what do I start on?"

"You'll have to bear with me a little, Mr. Danilov. My brief for this afternoon is only of a limited nature—to find out if, in principle, you are prepared to work with us, which I'm glad to say you seem to be. I have to report back. You will be contacted very shortly, sometime tomorrow, I'm sure."

"You are not the leader of this organization?"

"No."

"You surprise me. A man like you acting as a lieutenant—well, this leader I must meet."

"You shall. I promise."

"How will you contact me? No phones, please."

"Certainly not. You will be our courier, Vasco?"

"My pleasure, Mr. Agnelli. You know where to reach me any time."

"Thank you." Agnelli stood up and gave his hand to Van Effen. "A pleasure, Mr. Danilov. I look forward to meeting you tomorrow." Helmut Paderewsky didn't offer to shake hands.

As the door closed behind them, Sergeant Westenbrink said, "I need another beer, Lieutenant."

"Peter. Always Peter."

"Sorry. That was pretty close. The ice was very thin at times."

"Not for a practiced liar. I rather gather that you've given them the impression that I'm a desperate and wanted criminal?"

"I did mention that there was the odd extradition warrant out for you. But I didn't forget to emphasize your generally upright and honest nature. When dealing with your fellow criminals, of course."

"Of course. Before you get the beer, I have a phone call to make. Well, get it anyway."

Van Effen went to the bar and said to the man behind it, "Henri, a private call, if I may."

Henri, the proprietor, was a tall, gaunt man, sallow of countenance and lugubrious of expression. "You in trouble again, Peter?"

"No. I hope someone else will be, soon."

Van Effen went into the office and dialed a number. "Trianon? The manager, please. I don't care if he is in conference, call him. It's Lieutenant Van Effen." He hung on for a few moments. "Charles? Do me a favor. Book me in as from a fortnight ago. Enter it in the book, will you, in the name of Stephan Danilov. And would you notify the receptionist and doorman.

Yes, I expect people to be inquiring. Just tell them. Many thanks. I'll explain when I see you."

He returned to the booth. "Just booked myself—Stephan Danilov, that is—into a hotel. Agnelli pointedly did not ask about where I might be staying, but you can be sure that he'll have one of his men on the phone for the next couple of hours, if need be, trying to locate me in every hotel or pension in the city."

"So he'll know where you are—or where you're supposed to be." Vasco sighed. "It would help if we knew where *they* were."

"Should know soon enough. There have been two separate tails on them ever since they left the Hunter's Horn."

Van Effen, appearance returned to normal, asked the girl at the *Telegraph*'s reception desk for the subeditor who had taken the F.F.F.'s first telephone message. This turned out to be a fresh-faced and eager young man.

"Mr. Morelis?" Van Effen said. "Police."

"Yes, sir. Lieutenant Van Effen, isn't it? I've been expecting you. You'll be wanting to hear the tapes? Maybe I should tell you first that we've just had another message from the F.F.F., as they call themselves."

"Have you now? I suppose I should say, 'The devil you have,' but I'm not surprised. Happy tidings, of course."

"Hardly. The first half of the message was given over to congratulating themselves on the Texel job, how it had happened precisely as they had predicted and with no loss of life; the second half said there would be scenes of considerable activity on the North Holland Canal, a mile north of Alkmaar, at nine o'clock tomorrow morning."

"That, too, was to be expected. Not the location, of course. Just the threat. You've taped that, too?"

"Yes."

"That was well done. May I hear them?"

Van Effen heard them, twice over. When they were finished he said to Morelis, "You've listened to those, of course?"

"Too often." Morelis smiled. "Fancied myself as a detective, thought maybe you would give me a job, but I've come to the conclusion that there's more to this detecting business than meets the eye."

"Nothing struck you as odd about any of the tapes?"

"They were all made by the same woman. But that's no help."

"Nothing odd about accents, tones? No nuances that struck you as unusual?"

"No, sir. But I'm no judge. I'm slightly hard of hearing, nothing serious, but enough to blunt my judgment, assuming I had any. Mean anything to you, Lieutenant?"

"The lady is a foreigner. What country I've no idea. Don't mention that around."

"No, sir. I rather like being a subeditor."

"We are not in Moscow, young man. Put those tapes in a bag for me. I'll let you have them back in a day or two."

Back in his office, Van Effen asked to see the duty sergeant. When he arrived Van Effen said, "A few hours ago I asked for a couple of men to be put on a Fred Klassen and Alfred van Rees. Did you know about this, and if you did, do you know who was given the assignment?"

"I knew, sir. Detective Voight and Detective Tindeman."

"Good. Either of them called in?"

"Both. Less than twenty minutes ago. Tindeman says Van Rees is at home and seems to have settled in for the evening. Klassen is still on duty at the airport or, at least, he's still at the airport. So, nothing yet, sir."

Van Effen looked at his watch. "I'm leaving now. If you get word from either, a positive, not negative report, call me at the Dikker en Thijs. After nine, call me at home."

Colonel Van de Graaf came from a very old, very aristocratic and very wealthy family and was a great stickler for tradition, so it came as no surprise to Van Effen when he approached their table wearing dinner jacket, black tie and red carnation. His approach bore all the elements of a royal progress; he seemed to greet everyone, stopped to speak occasionally and waved graciously at those tables not directly in his path. It was said of Van de Graaf that he knew everybody who was anybody in the city of Amsterdam; he certainly seemed to know everybody in the Dikker en Thijs. Four paces away from Van Effen's table he stopped abruptly, as if transfixed.

The girl who had risen from the table with Van Effen to greet Van de Graaf had this momentarily paralyzing effect not only on Van de Graaf but on a wide cross section of the males of Amsterdam and beyond. She was of medium height, wore a rather more than well-filled ankle-length gray silk gown and no jewelry whatsoever. Jewelry would have been superfluous, and no one would have paid any attention to it anyway; what caught and held the attention, as it had caught the riveted attention of the momentarily benumbed colonel, was the flawless classical perfection of the features, a perfection only enhanced, if this was possible, by a slightly crooked eyetooth, visible when she smiled, which seemed to be most of the time. This was no simpering and empty-headed would-be Miss Universe, churned out with repetitive monotony by a Californian-style production line. The finely chiseled features and delicately formed bone structure served to highlight character and intelligence. She had gleaming auburn hair, great hazel eyes, and a bewitching smile. It had, at any rate, bewitched the colonel. Van Effen cleared his throat.

"Colonel Van de Graaf. May I introduce Miss Meijer. Miss Anne Meijer."

"My pleasure, my pleasure." Van de Graaf grabbed her outstretched hand in both of his and shook it vigorously. "My word, my boy, you are to be congratulated. Where *did* you find this entrancing creature?"

"There's nothing to it really, sir. You just go out into the darkened streets of Amsterdam, stretch out your hands and— well, there you are."

"Yes, yes, of course. Naturally." He had no idea what he was saying. He seemed to become aware that he had been holding and shaking her hand for an unconscionably long time, for he eventually and reluctantly released it. "Remarkable. Quite remarkable." He didn't say what he found remarkable and didn't have to. "You cannot possibly live in this city. Little, my dear, escapes the notice of a chief of police, and I think it would be impossible for you to be overlooked even in a city of this size."

"Rotterdam."

"Well, that's not your fault. Peter, I have no hesitation in saying that there can be no more beautiful lady in the city of Amsterdam." He lowered his voice a few decibels. "In fact, I would come right out and say that she is the most beautiful in the city, but I have a wife and daughters, and these restaurants have ears. You must be about the same age as my daughters. May I ask how old you are?"

"You must excuse the colonel," Van Effen said. "Policemen are much given to asking questions; some chiefs of police never stop."

The girl was smiling at Van de Graaf while Van Effen was speaking and, once again, Van Effen could have been addressing a brick wall. "Twenty-seven," she said.

"Twenty-seven. Exactly the age of my elder daughter. And *Miss* Anne Meijer. Bears out my contention—the younger generation of Dutchmen are a poor, backward and unenterprising lot." He looked at Van Effen, as if he symbolized all that was wrong with the current generation, then looked again at the girl. "Odd. I know I've never seen you, but your voice is vaguely familiar." He looked at Van Effen again and frowned slightly. "I look forward immensely to having dinner with you, but I thought—well, Peter, there were one or two confidential business matters that we had to discuss."

"Indeed, sir. But when you suggested we meet at seven o'clock, you made no exclusions."

"I don't understand."

The girl said, "Colonel."

"Yes, my dear?"

"Am I really such a hussy, a harlot, harridan and ghastly spectacle? Or is it because you don't trust me that you want to speak privately with Peter?"

Van de Graaf took a pace forward, caught the girl by the

shoulders, removed one hand to stop a passing waiter and said: "A jonge jenever. Large."

"Immediately, Colonel."

Van de Graaf held her shoulders again, stared intently into her face—he was probably trying to equate or associate the vision before him with the creature he had met in La Caracha— shook his head, muttered something to or about the same nameless deity and sank into the nearest chair.

Van Effen was sympathetic. "It comes as a shock, I know, sir. A brilliant makeup artist, don't you think? If it's any consolation, sir, she also fooled me once. But no disguise this time—just a wash and brush-up." He looked at her consideringly. "But well, yes, rather good-looking."

"Good-looking. Hah!" Van de Graaf took the gin from the waiter's tray and quaffed half the contents at a gulp. "Ravishing. At my age, systems shouldn't be subjected to such shocks. Anne? Annemarie? What do I call you?"

"Whichever."

"Anne. My dear. I said such dreadful things about you. It is not possible."

"Of course it's not. I couldn't believe Peter when he said you had."

Van Effen waved a hand. "A loose translation, shall we say?"

"Very loose, I hope." Wisely, Van de Graaf did not pursue the subject. "And what, in heaven's name, is a girl like you doing in a job like this?"

"I thought it was an honorable profession?"

"Yes, yes, of course. But what I meant was—well—"

"What the colonel means," Van Effen said, "is that you should be an international stage or screen star, presiding over a Parisian salon, or married to an American oil millionaire— billionaire, if you like—or a belted English earl. Too beautiful, that's your trouble. Isn't that it, Colonel?"

"Couldn't have put it better myself."

"Dear me." Anne smiled. "Doesn't say much for your Amsterdam girls. You mean you only employ ugly girls?"

Van de Graaf smiled for the first time that evening. "I am

not to be drawn. The chief of police is famed for his powers of recovery. But you—you—among those dreadful Krakers and dressed like a—like—"

"Harlot? Hussy?"

"If you like, yes." He put his hand on hers. "This is no place for a girl like you. Must get you out of it. Police is no place for you."

"One has to earn a living, sir."

"You? You need never earn a living. That, Anne, is a compliment."

"I like what I'm doing."

Van de Graaf didn't seem to have heard her. He was gazing at some distant object out in space. Van Effen said to the girl, "Watch him. He's at his most cunning when he goes into a trance."

"I am not in a trance," Van de Graaf said coldly. "What did you say your surname was?"

"Meijer."

"You have a family?"

"Oh yes. The usual. Parents, sisters, two brothers."

"Brothers and sisters share your interest in law and order?"

"Police, you mean. No."

"Your father?"

"Again police?" She smiled as people smile when recalling someone of whom they are very fond. "I couldn't imagine it. He's in the building business."

"Does he know what kind of business you are in?"

She hesitated. "Well, no."

"What do you mean, well, no? He doesn't, does he? Why?"

"Why?" She seemed to be on the defensive. "He likes us to be independent."

"Would he approve of what you are doing? And that was no answer you gave me. Would he approve of his darling daughter mingling with the Krakers?"

"Is this what it's like to be a suspect, sir, and to be grilled? Am I supposed to have done something wrong?"

"Of course not. Would he approve?" The entranced colonel

of a few minutes previously could have belonged to another world.

"No."

"You put me in a quandary. I don't like you being in this. You, apparently, do. Your father wouldn't. To whom should I listen—you or your father?"

"The question hardly arises, sir. You don't know my father."

"Child!"

"What does that mean? I don't understand."

"I know your father. Very well. We've been friends for over thirty years."

"Impossible! You can't know him. You've only just met me and you didn't even know me." She was no actress and was visibly upset. "This is—this is a trick of some kind."

"Annemarie." Van Effen touched her arm. "If the colonel says he's a friend of your father, then he is. Come on, sir."

"I know. When next you write or phone, Anne—if you ever do—give my warmest regards to David Joseph Karlmann Meijer."

Her eyes widened. She opened her mouth as if to speak, closed it again and turned to Van Effen. "I think it's my turn for a drink."

Van de Graaf looked at Van Effen. "My old friend David— we've gone sailing, fishing, skiing, hunting over the years— we were even up exploring the Amazon before this young lady here was born—owns a huge construction company. He also owns one of the biggest cement factories in the Netherlands, oil refineries, tankers, an electronics firm and God knows what else. 'One has to earn a living, sir,'" he mimicked. "Earn a living! Cruel, cruel landlord throwing the poor orphan out into the snow. Ah!" He turned to look at the maitre d' at his elbow. "Good evening. The young people will choose for me. But first, another jonge jenever." He looked at Annemarie. "Must have something to cry into. They say gin is best."

After the orders had been taken and the maitre d' and his minions departed, Van Effen said, "You have a scenario, sir, and you don't like what you see."

"I don't like it at all. Two things. If anything happens to

this young lady—well, David Meijer's wrath is fearful to behold—and it's considerably worse to be the object of it. Secondly, disguise or no disguise, Anne's identity may be discovered. It can happen, as you know all too well, Peter: a slip of the tongue, an unguarded reference, some careless action; there are too many possibilities. What a windfall for a penniless Kraker or, even worse, a professional kidnapper. Her father would pay five, ten million guilders to get her back. Do you like it, Peter?"

Van Effen made to speak, then glanced at the waiter who stood by his side.

"Lieutenant Van Effen. Phone."

Van Effen excused himself. Van de Graaf said, "Well, do *you* like it?"

"Not the way you put it but—I don't want to seem impertinent, sir, to disagree with my boss, but I think you put it too strongly. I've been doing this kind of work for some months in Rotterdam and nothing has ever happened to me. And while there may be no Krakers down there, the criminal elements are a great deal tougher than they are here. I'm sorry, Colonel, but I think you exaggerate the dangers. I'm rather good at disguises—you as much as said so yourself. I have a gun. Best, of course, is that no one in Amsterdam knows me."

"I know you."

"That's different. Peter says that you know everyone—and you must admit that it was a very remote chance that you knew my father."

"I could have found out easily enough. Peter knows?"

"Only my name. Not who I am, not until you spoke about it just now. I must say he didn't seem particularly surprised." She smiled. "He could, of course, have been unconcerned or uninterested."

"You're fishing for compliments, my dear." She made to protest, but he held up his hand. "In your case, indifference is impossible. The lieutenant cares very much for people. That doesn't mean he goes around showing it all the time. It's a learned habit. I know he didn't know. I'm equally sure Julie does."

"Ah. Julie. Your favorite lady in all Amsterdam?"

"I now have two favorite ladies in all Amsterdam. With the usual provisos, of course."

"Your wife and daughters, of course."

"Of course. Don't stall. You're very good at stalling, you know, Anne, at diverting me from the topic at hand, which is you, and don't give those big innocent eyes."

"Julie knows," she said. "How did you know that, sir?"

"Because I know Julie. Because she's clever. Because she's a woman. Living so close to you, she's bound to notice things that others wouldn't. Clothes, jewelry, personal possessions— things the average working girl wouldn't have. Even the way you speak. Fine by me if Julie knows, she'd never tell anyone. I'll bet she's never even told her brother. You like living there?"

"Very much. And Julie, also very much. I think she likes me, too. I have the honor to sleep in the bedroom that used to be Peter's. I believe he left about six years ago." She frowned. "I asked her why he'd left, it couldn't have been an argument, they're obviously terribly fond of each other, but she wouldn't tell me, just said I'd have to ask Peter."

"Did you ask him?"

"No." She shook her head very firmly. "One doesn't ask the lieutenant personal questions."

"I agree that he does rather give that impression. He's quite approachable really. No secret about his departure—he left to get married. Marianne. A very lovely girl, even although I do say it about my own niece."

"She's your niece?"

"Was." Van de Graaf's voice was somber. "Even in those days Peter was the best, most able cop in the city; far better than I am, but for God's sake don't tell him so. He broke up a particularly vicious gang of people who specialized in a nice mixture of blackmail and torture. Four brothers, they were, the Annecys, God knows where they got their name from. Peter put two of them away for fifteen years. The other two just vanished. Shortly after the conviction of the two brothers, someone, almost certainly one or both of the two brothers who had not been brought to justice, placed in Peter's weekend canal boat a huge bomb wired up to the ignition switch—same technique as was used by the murderers who assassinated Lord Mountbatten. As it happened, Peter wasn't aboard his boat that weekend. But Marianne and their two children were."

"Dear God!" The girl's hands were clenched. "How awful. How—how dreadful!"

"And every three months or so since that time, he receives a postcard from one of the two surviving Annecy brothers. Never any message. Just a drawing of a noose and a coffin, a reminder that he's living on borrowed time. Charming?"

"Horrible! Just horrible! He must be worried to death. I know I would. Wondering every night when I go to sleep—if I could sleep—whether I would wake up in the morning."

"I don't think he worries much—if he did he'd never show it—and I know he sleeps well. But that's the reason—although he never mentions it—why he doesn't return to live with Julie. He doesn't want her to be around when the bomb comes through his window."

"What a way to live! Why doesn't he emigrate somewhere, live under an assumed name?"

"If you ever get to know Peter van Effen—really know him, I mean—you'll wonder why you ever asked that question. Anne, you have an enchanting smile. Let me see it again."

She gave a puzzled half-smile. "I don't understand."

"He's coming back. Let me see how good an actress you are."

And, indeed, when Van Effen returned to the table she was smiling, a person at ease with the world. When she looked up and saw the expression—more accurately, the total lack of expression—on his face, she stopped smiling.

"About to ruin our dinner, are you, Peter?" Van de Graaf shook his head. "And such a splendid meal we've ordered."

"Not quite." Van Effen smiled faintly. "Might put us off our third bottle of Bordeaux or Burgundy or whatever. Perhaps even the second bottle. First, let me put you briefly in the picture as to what happened earlier today. Yes, sir, I'll have some wine, I feel I could do with a mild restorative. I've been offered a job—at, I'm sure, a far higher salary than I'm ever likely to get in this police force—to blow something up. What, I don't know. Could be the Amsterdam-Rotterdam bank, for all I know. Maybe a boat, bridge, barge, barracks, maybe anything. Haven't been told yet.

"As you know, Vasco brought those two characters to the Hunter's Horn this afternoon. Prosperous and respectable citizens, but then, no successful criminal ever looks like one. We were all very cagey and crafty, toing-and-froing, sparring and giving nothing away for most of the time. Then they made me this definite offer of a job and I accepted. They said they would have to report back to their superiors but would definitely contact me tomorrow and give me details of the job to be done and what my rewards would be for this. Vasco was to be the courier. So we shook hands like gentlemen and parted with expressions of goodwill and mutual trust.

"I had two sets of tails waiting at a discreet distance from the Hunter's Horn. I've had a report—"

"Goodwill and mutual trust?" Annemarie said.

Van de Graaf waved a hand. "Figurative. Proceed, Peter."

"I've had news of both sets of tails. The first say that they lost Agnelli and Paderewsky—that's what they called themselves—"

"Good God!" Van de Graaf said. "Agnelli and Paderewsky. A famous industrialist and a famous pianist. Aren't they original?"

"That's what I thought. Lost them in a traffic jam, they say. Claimed that they hadn't been spotted. Pure accident. The report about the other two makes me wonder, to say the least."

"'About' the other two?" Van de Graaf said. "Not 'from'?"

"About. They were found in an alley. Barely able to call for help, barely conscious. Unable to move and both in agony. Each man had both kneecaps smashed. A sign used in Sicily and certain American cities that some people don't like being followed and that those who were doing the following won't be doing it again for some time to come. They weren't knee-capped—no guns. Iron bars. They're under surgery. Neither man will be able to walk for months, neither will ever be able to walk properly again. Nice, isn't it, sir. And a new development in our fair city. Another instance, one supposes, of the steady advance of American culture."

"Crippled?" Annemarie's voice was low, barely above a whisper. "Crippled for life. How can you—how can you joke about such things?"

"I'm sorry." Van Effen looked at her, saw that some color had gone from her face, and pushed her glass closer to her. "Take some. I'll join you. Joking? I never felt less funny in my life. And it's not just an American practice, sir; it's become a very popular pastime in Northern Ireland in recent years."

"So your other tails were given the slip and nothing accidental about it." Van de Graaf sampled his Bordeaux. He smacked his lips appreciatively. "Excellent. Our friends seem to have a considerable expertise in both evasive and direct action. Professionals. And gone to ground. Ah. All is not lost. The chateaubriand. You said you would share this with me, my dear."

She appeared to give a tiny shudder. "I know it's trite, silly, but I don't think I could eat a thing."

"Maybe the moles will come out of their burrows tomorrow," Van Effen said. "I'm still hoping that they will keep their promise and make contact with me."

Annemarie stared at him, almost blankly. "You must be mad," she said in a low voice. She seemed genuinely puzzled. "Either they'll come and give you the same treatment, perhaps worse, perhaps dispose of you permanently, or they won't come at all. After they carried out that savage attack on those poor men they could have examined them and found out that they *were* policemen. They must have been carrying something that would identify them as policemen, even guns. Were they carrying guns?" Van Effen nodded. "Then they'll know you are a policeman because they'll know you must have had them followed since they left the Hunter's Horn. You like the idea of suicide?" She reached out and touched Van de Graaf's wrist. "You mustn't let him do it, sir. He'll be killed."

"Your concern does you credit." It was Van Effen who answered, and he seemed quite unmoved by her plea. "But quite uncalled for. The villains don't necessarily know that I set the tails on their tracks. They might not even have noticed them until long after they left the Hunter's Horn and would have no reason to connect me with them. That's one thing. The other thing is the fact that though the colonel is your father's friend, that doesn't give the father's daughter the right to advise the colonel. A fledgling policewoman. A chief of police. It would be laughable if it weren't so presumptuous."

She looked at him, her eyes hurt as if she had been struck, then lowered her gaze to the tablecloth. Van de Graaf looked at Van Effen, shook his head slightly, and took the girl's hand.

"Your concern *does* do you credit. It does. But it doesn't give me much credit in your eyes. None. Look at me." She looked at him, the hazel eyes at once solemn and apprehensive. "Van Effen is right. The foxes have to be flushed from their covers, and this, at the moment, seems the only way to do it. So Peter will go—I would never order him to go—and with my consent. Good heavens, girl, do you think I would use him as live bait, a lamb to the slaughter, a Daniel in the lion's den, a tethered goat for the tiger? My word, I do have a way with metaphors. I guarantee, my girl, that, when and if the meeting does take place, both the Hunter's Horn and the surrounding area will be alive with invisible armed men. Invisible to the ungodly. Peter will be as safe as a man in a church."

"I know. I'm silly. I'm sorry."

"Pay no attention to the colonel's comforting words," Van Effen said. "I'll probably be riddled with bullets. Police bullets. Unless somebody remembers to point out to them that I'm in disguise. Ironic if they shot the wrong man. Same outfit as before. Just let them concentrate on the black glove. That's me."

A waiter approached their table. "Sorry, Lieutenant. Another call for you."

Van Effen was back inside two minutes. "Well, no surprise, surprise. The F.F.F., again, mysterious message, no doubt stepping up their demoralizing campaign. They say there *could* be some havoc wreaked along the North Holland Canal tomorrow at Alkmaar at nine A.M., but they have made no guarantee that there will be. All they have promised is that there will be some quite considerable activity."

Van de Graaf said: "That was all?"

"All. Seems utterly pointless and meaningless. What the devil do you think they're up to now?"

"It's not pointless. That's just the point—to make us wonder and worry about just what the devil they *are* up to now. They want to create uncertainty, confusion and demoralization, and it would seem to me that they're going the right way about it. Speaking of the F.F.F., sir, how was your pleasure trip to Texel this afternoon?"

"Complete waste of time. I was accompanied, as you more or less predicted, by a bunch of old women."

"You don't intend to be at Alkmaar at nine A.M. tomorrow?"

"I intend to be in Amsterdam at nine A.M. tomorrow. What am I supposed to do? Lurk around and nab anyone who looks as if he is acting suspiciously, such as gloating over the scene of the crime?"

"An unpromising course of action. You've got friends in the university, sir. Specifically, in the linguistics department?"

Van de Graaf said to Annemarie, "I'm supposed to look startled at this sudden switch and ask, 'Why on earth do you ask that?'" He looked at Van Effen. "Well, why on earth *do* you ask that?"

"I listened to the F.F.F.'s tapes in the *Telegraph*'s office earlier on this evening. A woman's voice. A young woman, I would say. And not Dutch, I'm sure."

"Interesting. Very. Back to our mysterious foreigners again. Any educated guesses as to the country of origin of the caller?"

"That's the trouble, sir. I speak the odd language, sure, but I'm not what you might call an educated linguist. Regional accents, nuances, pronunciation—that is quite definitely not my field."

"And you think the university could help?"

"It's a chance, sir. As you say, no stone unturned. Or tape. The tapes are in my office."

"I'll do what I can. You may as well get to your feet, Peter. A purposeful waiter comes your way."

Van Effen rose, met the waiter, spoke briefly and moved on. When he took his seat again, he said: "The opposition is stirring. Whatever opposition that might be. That was my hotel, the Trianon. Message relayed through the office, of course."

Van de Graaf said patiently: "And how long have you been staying in the Trianon, Lieutenant? You have been evicted from your own apartment?"

"The register book says that I have been there for two weeks. I arranged that about five o'clock this afternoon."

"Dear, dear. Falsifying register books is a civil offense."

"I've no time to be arrested at the moment. Romero Agnelli or one of his men must have been very busy phoning around and have at last located me as staying at the Trianon. They have posted a watcher in the shadows—in a little old Fiat, actually. I have arranged for another watcher to watch the original. Well, can't disappoint them. I shall turn up there later on tonight."

"You lead an active life," Van de Graaf said. "I assume that you do not intend to spend the night there?"

"You assume correctly, sir. I shall park my car at the back of the hotel, where I'll be picked up by a police taxi and deposited at the front door. Then I pass through the hotel, exit by the rear entrance and drive home. It's a nuisance, no more."

"And here, again," Van de Graaf said, "comes your own private and personal nuisance. My word, you *are* popular tonight."

Van Effen looked, sighed, rose, spoke briefly to the waiter again and disappeared toward the telephone booths.

"Ah, a brandy," he said on his return. "Thank you, sir. That was Sergeant Westenbrink—Vasco. Message again via the office, of course. Agnelli has been in touch with him. They would, they say, very much like to meet me at eleven A.M., tomorrow morning. Same place. This can mean one of two things."

"I know what it means," Van de Graaf said. "Either they're on to us or they're not on to us. It is quite possible that they had no idea that they were being shadowed ever since leaving the Hunter's Horn this afternoon. On the other hand, it's perfectly possible that they did know. If they did, they can have only one purpose in wanting to meet you again: to see how much you know, what danger your knowledge offers, and how best they can eliminate this danger. It should, I imagine, all be very discreet. And, if they suspect you and suspect that you in turn suspect them, they're being clever; in that case one would have expected them to opt for a neutral rendezvous, for if they suspect you're an undercover policeman or working as an agent for the police, then they must automatically suspect that the Hunter's Horn is a police hangout. But, of course, to go elsewhere would be to tip their hand that they know." Van de Graaf sighed. "All very devious. Designed to spread confusion and doubt on all hands. Maybe they've been taking lessons from the F.F.F. Or vice versa. Another brandy, Peter? No? In that case I suggest we be on our way. I expect we'll be having a rather long day tomorrow. Do you have any particular plan for this young lady?"

"I shall think up some onerous task by and by. As yet, no."

"Um." Van de Graaf pondered. "You, Anne, are, of course, seen quite often in the company of Sergeant Westenbrink."

She smiled. "I find it difficult to think of him other than as Vasco. Yes, of course. We have to talk and it seems the best— and also the easiest—thing to do it openly."

"Quite. Do you come and go as you like there?"

"Of course. That's the whole point of being us. No hours, no rules, no regulations. You do as you like, you're as free as the air."

"It would cause no undue comment if you were not to turn up for a day, even two days?"

"No." She hesitated. "Am I supposed to be intelligent and know what you're getting at, sir?"

"You're intelligent enough. It's just that you lack the training and experience to have a nasty, suspicious mind, such as is possessed by Lieutenant Van Effen, and I hope you always will."

Annemarie shook her head, almost imperceptibly, then looked questioningly at Van Effen, who said, "The colonel is right, you know."

"I don't know. That is, I'm sure he's right, but I don't know what he's right about. If you're having fun with me, I don't think it's very fair."

"We aren't having fun with you, Annemarie. Teasing or diminishing people is not our idea of having a good time. Look. All this is a matter of connections. It's possible—I'd say at least a fifty-fifty chance—that Agnelli and company are on to us. In that case, Vasco is also under suspicion because he introduced them to me. And because you are known to associate with Vasco, you, in turn, come under suspicion. What the colonel's suggesting is that you lie low for a day, maybe two. Depends on how things develop. I have the feeling, irrational, perhaps, that the development is going to be rapid. It's not a pleasant thought for the colonel or myself that you should fall into those people's hands. Think of those two detectives, the tails who ran out of luck. We already know that those people are ruthless, that the inflicting of pain is a matter of indifference to them. It may even be a pleasure. How would you care to be taken by them and tortured? I am not trying to scare you, Annemarie. I'm talking about something that's halfway between a possibility and a probability."

"I think I've already told you." Her voice was very quiet. "I'm not particularly brave."

"And then they'd know who it was they had on their hands. They'd be over the moon. Another lovely blackmailing trump in their hands, in addition to their still undisclosed trumps. Apart from your own health, you'd be putting us in an impossibly difficult situation."

"Couldn't have put it better myself," Van de Graaf said.

She smiled faintly. "I'm a coward. I'll do what I'm told."

"Not told, my dear, not told," Van de Graaf said. "Just a suggestion."

Again the faint smile. "It sounds like a good suggestion to me. Where shall I stay?"

"With Julie, of course," Van Effen said. "An unobtrusive armed guard will be lurking in the vicinity. But before you go into purdah, as it were, there's one thing I want you to do for me."

"Of course."

"I want you to go to Vasco in the morning. Tell him what we've told you and tell him to disappear. I know where he'll disappear to and I'll contact him there when it's safe."

"I'll do that." She was silent for a moment. "When you asked me to do something for you and I said 'Of course,'— well, I wish now I hadn't. You see what you've done to me, Peter. I'm a quivering wreck."

"You're not quivering, and for a wreck you look in pretty good shape to me. You may be jumped on there and then your gallant fellow Krakers would look the other way?"

"Yes."

"We are accustomed to those injustices, are we not, Colonel? Nothing will happen to you. You'll be under constant surveillance, and by constant I mean sixty seconds every minute. The trusty Lieutenant Van Effen, suitably disguised—not the Hunter's Horn disguise, of course—and lumbered with his usual arsenal—there's a thought for you, Colonel. I think I'll carry a third gun tomorrow when I meet Agnelli and his friend or friends. They already know that—"

"That you carry two guns," Van de Graaf said, "and so their minds will, of course, be preconditioned against the idea of you carrying a third."

"That's the idea. So, no problem, Annemarie. I won't be further away than fifteen feet at any time."

"That's nice. But you've put all sorts of unpleasant thoughts in my head. I could be jumped on, in your words, anywhere and any time between here and Julie's house."

"More injustice. No worry. I will transport you there in the safety and comfort of my own limousine."

"Limousine!" Van de Graaf said. "Comfort! My God!" He bent a solicitous eye on the girl. "You have, I trust, not forgotten your air cushion?"

"I don't understand, sir."

"You will."

They left the restaurant and walked along the street until they came to the colonel's car, parked, as usual, in a "No Parking" area. Van de Graaf kissed the girl in what he probably regarded as an avuncular fashion, said good night and climbed into his gleaming Mercedes. The back seat of his Mercedes. Colonel Van de Graaf had a chauffeur.

Annemarie said, "I understand now what the colonel meant about an air cushion."

"A trifling inconvenience," Van Effen said. "I'm having the seat fixed. Orders. The colonel complains."

"The colonel does like his comforts, doesn't he?"

"It may not have escaped your attention that he was built for comfort."

"He's very kind, isn't he? Kind and courteous and considerate."

"It's no hardship to be all those things when the object of them is as beautiful as you."

"You do have a nice turn of speech, Lieutenant."

"Yes, I do."

She was quiet for a moment, then said, "But he is rather a snob, isn't he? A fearful snob."

"In the interests of discipline, I must speak severely. You can't expect me to condone, far less agree with, denigrating remarks about our chief."

"That wasn't meant to be denigrating. It was just an observation. I refuse to get to the stage where I must watch every word I say. This is still an open society. Or is it?"

"Well, well."

"Go on. Say it. 'Spoken with spirit' or something like that."

"I don't think I will. But you're about as wrong with your snobbism as you were about your warm-hearted Arthur bit."

"Arthur?"

"Our chief's first name. Never uses it. I've never figured out why. Regal connotations. Sure he's kind and thoughtful. He's also tough, shrewd and ruthless, which is why he is what he is. And he's no snob. Snobs pretend to be what they are not. His is a very ancient, aristocratic and wealthy lineage, which is why you'll never find me contesting a restaurant bill with him. He was *born* with the knowledge that he is different, the one percent of the one percent. Never occurs to him to question it. He's convinced that he radiates the spirit of democracy."

"Tough or not, snob or not, I like him." She spoke as if that settled the matter, without specifying what the matter was.

"Arthur, as you may have observed, has a way with the ladies. Especially when he's off duty, which is what he considered himself to be tonight."

"Are you never off duty? Am I always a policewoman?"

"Never thought about it that way. But I will. Think about it, I mean."

"You're too kind." She lapsed into silence and remained that way for the rest of the drive. Only Van Effen spoke. He called his office and requested an armed guard for his sister's flat.

It was not difficult to understand why Van de Graaf had said that Julie van Effen was his favorite lady in all Amsterdam. With hair black and shining as a raven's wing, a delicately molded face and high, Slavonic cheekbones, she was far more than just merely good-looking. But her attraction for Van de Graaf, as for a great many others, almost certainly lay in her laughing eyes and laughing mouth. She was almost permanently good-humored—except when she encountered injustice, cruelty, meanness, selfishness and quite a few other things of which she disapproved, when she could become very stormy— and seemed to love the whole world with the exception of those who encountered her formidable disapproval. She was one of those rare people who radiate happiness, a quality in her that more than tended to conceal the fact that below it all lay a fine mind. Cabinet ministers do not habitually employ dim-witted secretaries, and Julie was a cabinet minister's secretary, private, personal, confidential and discreet.

She was also very hospitable and wanted to cook them a meal as soon as they had entered. It was not easy to believe that this happy beauty was also a cordon bleu chef, which she was. Next, she offered sandwiches and desisted only when she learned that they had already eaten.

"The Dikker en Thijs, was it? Well, the police always did

know how to look after themselves. For a working girl, it's new herring, red cabbage and sausage."

"For this particular working girl," Van Effen said, "it's the ministerial canteen. A gourmet's paradise, so I'm told—we cops aren't allowed near the place. Julie, alas, has no will-power—well, you've only to look." Julie had as nearly perfect a figure as it was possible to imagine. She treated this badinage with lofty contempt, ruffled his hair in passing and went to the kitchen to prepare some coffee and a café schnapps.

Annemarie looked after her departing form, turned to Van Effen and smiled. "She can wrap you round her little finger any time, can't she?"

"Any time and any day," Van Effen said cheerfully. "And, alas, she knows it. 'Minx' is the word for her. Something I have to show you, in case you're in the house alone." He led her to a picture on the wall and pushed it to one side to reveal a red button set flush with the wallpaper. "What's known to the trade as a personal-attack button. If you think you're in danger, suspect it or even sense it, you press this button. A patrol car will be here within five minutes."

She tried to make light of it. "Every housewife in Amsterdam should have one of those."

"As there are a hundred thousand housewives in Amsterdam—maybe two for all I know—it would come a mite expensive."

"Of course." She looked at him and didn't or couldn't smile any more. "I've been with the two of you a few times now and one would have to be blind and deaf not to realize that you're just potty about your kid sister."

"Tut, tut. I can but sigh. Of course."

"I hadn't finished. You didn't have that button installed just because you love her. She's in danger, isn't she?"

"Danger?" He caught her by the shoulders, so tightly that she winced. "Sorry." He eased his grip but left his hands where they were. "How do you know?"

"Well, she is, isn't she? In danger, I mean?"

"Who told you? Julie?"

"No."

"The colonel?"

"Yes. This evening." She looked at him, her gaze moving from one eye to the other. "You're not angry?"

"No. No, my dear, I'm not angry. Just worried. I'm not a healthy person to know."

"Julie knows about the danger?"

"Yes."

"Does she know about the postcards?" He looked at her thoughtfully and didn't change his expression as she put her hands on his shoulders and made as if to shake him in exasperation; which was a silly thing to do, as Van Effen was built along very solid lines. "Well, does she?"

"Yes. It would be difficult for her not to. The postcards come to this address. One of the Annecy brothers' ways of getting to me."

"Dear God. This—this is dreadful. How—how can she be so—so happy?" She put her head against his shoulder, as if she were suddenly tired. "How can she?"

"The old saying, I suppose. Better to laugh than to cry. You're not about to cry, are you?"

"No."

"Anyhow, the old saying doesn't quite apply here. She always was a happy child. Only, now she has to work at it."

Julie came in with coffee, stopped abruptly and cleared her throat. "Isn't it a little early in the evening—" She laid the tray down. "I hope the deafness is a temporary affliction. I said—" She stopped again, the expression on her face showing her concern, moved swiftly to where they stood, put an arm round Annemarie and gently turned her head until she could see her face. "Tears. Full of tears." She pulled a lace handkerchief from her sleeve cuff. "What's this ruffian up to?"

"This ruffian hasn't been up to anything," Van Effen said mildly. "Annemarie knows everything, Julie. Marianne, the kids, you, me, the Annecys."

"The colonel, I'll be bound."

"You'll be bound right."

Julie said, "I know, Annemarie. It's a shock. To come all

at once, it's a shock. At least it came to me bit by bit. Come. I have the sovereign remedy. A double schnapps in your coffee."

"You're very kind. If I could be excused—" She turned and walked quickly from the room.

"Well." There was a demanding note in Julie's voice. "Don't you see what you've done?"

"Me?" Van Effen was genuinely perplexed. "What am I supposed to have done now? It was the colonel—"

"It's not what you have done. It's what you haven't done." She put her hands on his shoulders and her voice went soft. "It's what you haven't seen."

"I see. I mean, I don't see." Van Effen was cautious. "What haven't I seen?"

"You clown." Julie shook her head. "Annemarie. Her heart is in her face, in her eyes. That girl's in love with you."

"What! You're not well, that's what it is."

"My beloved, brilliant dolt of a brother. But don't believe me. Ask her to marry you. A special license—which you can obtain at the drop of a hat—and you'd be married by midnight."

Van Effen looked slightly dazed. "Pretty sure, aren't you?"

"No. Absolutely certain."

"But she hardly knows me."

"I'm aware of that. After all, you've only met her, what— twenty, thirty, forty times?" She shook her head. "The feared interrogator, the writer of books on psychology, the man who can lay bare the innermost secrets of any mind with one piercing glance—well, 100 percent for theory, zero for practice."

"You're a fine one to talk. Specialist in marriage counseling—or should I say matchmaking? Ha! Six marriage proposals for certain—could have been twenty, for all I know—and you turned them all down. There speaks the voice of experience."

"Don't try to change the subject." She smiled sweetly. "Yes, indeed, there speaks the voice of experience. I didn't love any of them. *She* is deeply in love with you. I don't quite understand why."

"I need a schnapps." Van Effen opened a nearby cupboard.

"I've just brought you a café schnapps."

"First of all, I need a schnapps. Then I need one with coffee."

"Not a psychiatrist? Why do you think she's so upset?"

"She's soft-hearted, that's why."

"You should make a splendid match. Soft heart. Soft head." She took his head between her hands and studied his eyes carefully. "The hawk-eyed detective lieutenant. What you need is a pair of glasses. And you've missed your cue, haven't you? Half a dozen times, at least."

"What cue?"

"Oh dear. That wary hunted look makes you more criminal than cop. What cue? 'I wouldn't marry her if she were the last girl in the world' should have been your answer to the cue. Standard reaction, I believe." She smiled again. "But, of course, you're not standard."

"Oh, shut up."

"A well-reasoned answer." She sat and took up her coffee. "Mental myopia. I believe it's incurable."

"Oh, I don't know. I'm sure you'll find an answer." Van Effen was his old self, calm, assured, relaxed, back on balance. "I don't particularly care for cool, clinical, slightly superior, slightly amused doctors, but I have to admit you've effectively worked a cure in my case. You've cured me of any interest I might ever have had in that young lady. Or maybe that was what you wanted. I don't know." She was looking at him with parted lips and uncomprehending eyes. "I don't need—I don't want, I should say—help, advice or sympathy from you, and not just because they're uncalled-for, unhelpful, unwanted or unsolicited but because I'm perfectly capable of managing my own life without the assistance of a meddlesome young sister. I'll go check if the guard is here."

He went out, leaving Julie to stare numbly at the door he'd closed behind him, disconsolate and disbelieving, and she was still in the same position, gazing sightlessly at the door, the same expression of hurt and bafflement on her face when Annemarie came into the room. Annemarie stopped, looked in puzzlement at the unhappy face, hurried across the room to

Julie's chair, dropped to her knees and said, "What's wrong, Julie? What's wrong?"

Julie looked away from the door and slowly turned her head. "Nothing. Nothing's wrong."

"Nothing's wrong? Oh God! Nothing. First me, then you. Tears. And you look—you look so woebegone." Annemarie hugged her. "Nothing wrong! Julie! Don't treat me like an idiot."

"I'm the idiot. I've just made a mistake."

"You? I don't believe it. Mistake. What mistake?"

"The mistake of forgetting that Peter is not only my brother, he's a policeman and heir apparent to the colonel. You didn't know that, did you?" Julie sniffled. "Common knowledge. Van de Graaf is due to retire this year, but he's in no hurry to retire as long as Peter is already doing most of his job for him."

"Never mind the colonel. Where's that ruffian?"

Julie tried to smile. "Second time tonight he's been called a ruffian by two different girls. I'll bet it's never happened before. He's left."

"Gone? Gone for the night?"

"No. Just to check on the guard." Julie smiled again, a more successful effort this time. "He may be gifted at reducing people to tears, but I'm sure he cares for us."

"He's got a funny way of showing it. What did he *do* to you, Julie? What did he say?"

"Do? Nothing, of course. Say? I stepped out of line, I guess, and he brought me back into line. That's all."

"You expect me to be satisfied with that?"

"No, I don't, my dear. But can we leave it just for the moment? Please?"

They had finished their coffee by the time Van Effen returned. He appeared to find nothing amiss or, if he did, chose not to comment on it.

"Guard's here," he said. "Armed to the teeth. And I have to go now."

"But your coffee—"

"Another time. I am, as they say, summoned forth. Julie, there's something you must do for me. Could you—"

"Must?" She smiled. "An order or request?"

"What does that matter?" Rarely for him, Van Effen was irritated. "Do what I ask—please, note the please—or I'll take Annemarie away with me."

"My word! Such threats. And if she chooses to remain here or I ask her to stay?"

"Rotterdam. Tomorrow morning. Ex-policewoman. You don't disobey orders in the police and remain on the force. Sorry, Annemarie, that was not directed at you. Julie's not being very bright tonight. Don't look shocked, little sister, if you can't see I'm serious, then you've become uncommonly stupid. Develop diplomatic flu for the next day or so. Annemarie is in as much danger as you are, and I want the two of you here together. Annemarie, nine-fifteen."

He went to the door and opened it, looked at the two solemn faces and shook his head.

"Exit the gallant lieutenant into the dark and dreadful night."

He closed the door quietly behind him.

4

THE TALL, THIN young man in the dark and dripping raincoat would rarely have called for more than a passing glance or a comment or the fact that he did look rather unprepossessing, an impression increased by the hair plastered to his head by the heavy rain and the ill-trimmed black mustache he sported. The mustache, in fact, had not been trimmed at all; he had been in an unusual hurry that morning and had pasted it on ever so slightly askew.

He was standing almost in the middle of the square when he saw her, angling across and coming almost directly toward him. Annemarie, her war paint back in position again, looked as miserable and bedraggled as the young man, who now stepped out into her path.

"Annemarie is it?"

Her eyes widened and she looked quickly around. Despite the near torrential rain there were a fair number of people around and a flower and vegetable open-air market only steps away. She looked again at the young man, who was smiling, a pleasant smile despite his over-all appearance.

"Please don't worry, miss. Hardly the place where anyone would think to carry out a kidnapping. You must be Annemarie—there couldn't be two people answering the description I was given. I'm Detective Rudolph Engel." He brought a badge from his pocket and showed it to her. "I could, of course, have stolen this. Lieutenant Van Effen wants to see you. He's in his car."

"Why should I believe you? Why did he send you? He knew where I was. He could have come to see me. What car does he have?"

"A black Peugeot."

"You would know that, wouldn't you?"

"Yes." The young man was patient. "When you've worked under someone for five years, you do know something about him. The lieutenant said to me, 'Miss Meijer is very suspicious. Mention the Amazon, her father, the colonel and someone's "lack of courage." ' I have no idea what he meant."

"I do." She took his arm. "I'm sorry."

Van Effen, relaxed behind the wheel of his car, was this morning sporting a homburg hat and a big square beard of the type favored by Sephardic Jews. He looked round as Annemarie opened the passenger door and looked in.

"Good morning, my dear."

"Good morning, he says. What are you doing here, Peter?"

"Sheltering from the rain. It's coming down in buckets. You must have noticed. Come in, come in."

She sat down and looked at him accusingly. "Fifteen feet, you said. Never more than fifteen feet away. Sixty seconds in every minute. That's what you said. Where were you? Your promise to look after me! Fine promise."

"Man proposes, God disposes." If Van Effen was remorse-stricken, he concealed it well. "Besides, you were being looked after. By proxy. Don't tell me you didn't see a rather elderly gentleman hanging around, slightly stooped, gray beard, gray coat and a white stick. He was looking after you."

"I saw him. That creature! He couldn't have looked after a kitten."

"Whatever that means. That creature is young, fit, a judo expert and a very accurate shot."

"Beards," she almost muttered. "Beards, mustaches, that's all they can think of. Disguises! Well, thank you, someone was there, but you broke your promise."

"It was politic to do so. I was close behind and you were less than a hundred yards from your rendezvous when I caught sight of no other than Mr. Paderewsky following you even more closely than I was. Mr. Paderewsky is shrewd, observant and doesn't like me, which is a nasty combination. He might just have recognized me, especially when I was in close attendance on you. I had taken the precaution of taking two of my detectives with me—think nothing of the fact that we obviously care so much about you—and I decided discretion was the better part of foolhardiness. Hence the switch."

Engel said through Van Effen's open window, "Anything further, sir?"

"No. Not here. Don't lose sight of our friend when he shows."

"Well, I've seen him, sir. There can't be one other bald, pepper-and-salt beard with a squint around."

"Julius Caesar?" Annemarie said.

"None other. I didn't tell Rudolph here what his name was. He wouldn't have believed it. A close but not too close eye on our Julius. And make sure there are always a few people around. I'd rather lose him than lose you. Don't forget what happened to your two colleagues yesterday."

"I won't forget, sir." The expression on his face was testimony enough to that. He turned and walked away into the rain.

"Mollified?" Van Effen started the engine and drove off.

"A bit." She smiled a little. "Did you have to tell him I was a coward?"

"I did not. Someone was, I said."

"It doesn't matter, because I am. I don't like riding around in this car, for instance."

"It takes time to get seats fixed. And what's that got to do—"

"Please. I mean that this car is known. To criminals."

"Pfui. There are a couple of hundred like this in the city."

She said sweetly, "A couple of hundred with the same license plates?"

"What's that got to do with anything? *You* know the license number of this car?"

"More or less. Rotterdam. Three nines. We are trained to be observant, remember?"

"But not observant enough to notice that these are clip-on plates, not screwed. Today, this car is registered in Paris with a big 'F' at the side to prove it. I have access to an unlimited number of plates." She made a face but said nothing. "You should be interested in more important things. Such as the latest antics of the F.F.F."

"Yes?"

"There were no antics. They didn't blow the dike of the North Holland Canal. They called in to both the papers and the police less than ten minutes ago. Positively hugging themselves, they are. Said they never promised they would blow the canal—which is quite true—only that there would be considerable activity in that area at nine o'clock this morning. There was, they reported, very considerable activity, which is again quite true. All rescue and repair teams were there, waiting, as were considerable numbers of police and army, not to mention air force helicopters. They claimed to have taken a good number of aerial photographs of the scenes, just for keepsakes."

"You believe that, too?"

"Certainly. I have no reason to disbelieve it."

"But aerial photographs? How could that be possible?"

"It would be all too simple, I'm afraid. There would be any amount of helicopters buzzing about there this morning. An extra one wouldn't be noticed especially, as is highly likely if it was carrying some official markings."

"What was behind this pointless exercise?"

"It was very much to the point. Just in case we missed the point, they spelled it out. They said that in the space of twenty-four hours they had reduced the country, most especially the authorities, to a state of frustrated helplessness. The so-called authorities—they had a number of cynical and very unpleasant remarks to make about the government, the police, the army and those whose duties it was to look after the safety and welfare of dikes, locks, weirs, sluices, dams and I forget what else—were totally powerless to do anything to stop them. All they had to do, they said, was to stay at home, stick a pin into a map, phone the papers, sit back and never go within a hundred miles but still guarantee that the law, the army, the repair and rescue teams would be out in full force. It was, they said, both an entertaining and gratifying situation."

"And not a word about their purposes, no hint?"

"No hint, but a suggestion that we might soon know what their demands are going to be. They didn't use the word 'demands,' but they can have meant nothing else. Tomorrow, they said, they were going to flood a really large area of the country and after that they would probably have talks with the government. Can you imagine? The sheer cold arrogance of it all. They speak as if they are an independent sovereign state. Next, one supposes, they'll be calling for an open debate in the UN." He glanced at his watch. "Plenty of time. Two minutes to remove this outfit—no washing or soaking required—and five minutes to put on my Hunter's Horn uniform. I suggest coffee."

She put a hand on his arm. "You really are going there, aren't you, Peter."

"Of course. I've said so. Somebody has to, and as I am the only person who's been in contact with them, it has to be me. How else do you think the law would ever get anywhere unless it's prepared, just once in a while, to take the initiative?"

"I wish you weren't going. I feel certain something is going to happen. Something awful. You could be hurt, even killed, or, maybe even worse, crippled for life. You know what they did to those two men. Oh Peter!" She was silent for a moment, then said, "If I were your wife, I'd stop you."

"How?"

"I don't know," she said miserably. "Appeal to your better nature, love for me, something like 'For my sake, if you care about me, please don't go.' Something clever like that," she said bitterly.

"Well, you're not my wife, and even if you were, I'd still go. I'm sorry that sounds hard and selfish and cruel, but it's my job and I have to go." He put his hand on her arm. "You're a very kind girl and I do appreciate your concern."

"Kind?" She caught his wrist and gently removed his hand from her arm. "Concern!"

"Annemarie!" Van Effen's surprise was genuine. "What on earth's wrong?"

"Nothing. Just nothing."

Van Effen gazed ahead for some moments, sighed and said, "I don't think I'll ever understand women."

"I don't think so either." She seemed to hesitate, then said, "I don't want to go to a coffee shop."

"If you wish we won't. Why not?"

"I don't much care for wearing this face in public. Where there are decent people around. It doesn't matter back there. And I don't think you are particularly keen on being seen among the same public with a freak."

"I know what's behind the war paint, so it doesn't matter to me." He paused. "Maybe I don't know anything about women, but I always know when they're telling fibs."

"I'm telling fibs?"

"Of course."

"Well yes, I am. Can't we have coffee at Julie's place? It's only another five minutes."

"Sure. Time I have. I know you're very fond of Julie. But are you also worried about her?"

"I think she's worried about me. Even though she knew you would be there, she didn't like the idea of my going back to that place."

"You didn't answer my question. You're not, perhaps— well, just a little bit worried about her?"

She remained silent.

"The Annecy brothers. Would you believe, I've never even seen either of them? I regard them as a fairly distant menace."

"The menace I'm thinking of is a great deal nearer to home. Well, not menace. Problem, rather."

"This is something new on me. A bagatelle, whatever it is. Give me the name of this person or problem and I'll attend to it."

"Indeed, Lieutenant." Something in the tone of her voice caught Van Effen's attention and he gave her a long, speculative look. "And how do you attend to this bagatelle, when the bagatelle in question is yourself?"

"Ah. Me again. I don't suppose there's any point in repeating the old complaining question?"

"Which is?"

"What the hell am I supposed to have done this time?"

"By your standards, I suppose, absolutely nothing."

"I detect a certain sarcasm? Or is it irony? I've noticed an increasing use of it. Not becoming, Annemarie. You should do something about it. Well, what *have* I done?"

"Reduced a lovely girl to tears. Not once, but three times. And when I say lovely, I don't just mean beautiful. I mean the nicest, kindest, warmest person I've ever met."

"Julie?"

"Julie! Who else would I mean? Or do you have a whole collection of ladies that you go around reducing to tears?"

"What's she crying about?"

"What's she—I don't know what to say. I can't believe you're cruel, indifferent. But don't you care that she's upset?"

"Of course I care. I'd care more if I knew why she was upset."

"I wonder. You'll think it funny. For one thing, you left last night without a good-night hug and kiss. You've never done that before, she says."

"Funny? It's ludicrous. My men getting hospitalized, a gang of lunatics threatening to inundate our country, another gang of lunatics wanting to hire me to blow up the palace or whatever, nations toppling, and I'm supposed to be worried about smooches? Soon fix that."

"Of course you will. A double ration of affectionate farewells. Georgie, Porgy, pudding and pie, kissed the girls and made them cry."

"Shakespeare?"

"English nursery rhyme." Her voice was curt. "Perhaps a bagatelle. What does matter is that she says she hurt two people she loves because she was meddlesome. I suppose she means you and me. Said she thought she was helping but that she was too clever or too stupid for her own good."

"That's her problem. A little bit of self-analysis never did anyone any harm."

"Self-analysis! *You* told her she was interfering and too smart for her own good. Anybody's good."

"Julie told you that?"

"Of course she didn't. She's too loyal—misplaced loyalty, perhaps. Julie would never have said that—she's too unselfish to think about herself. But it sounds exactly like you."

"I'll say I'm sorry. Very, very sorry."

"And, of course, you'll tell her that I told you to."

"No. I must say it's a sad thing to be held in such low esteem by two ladies you love."

"The lieutenant is pleased to be flippant," she said coldly.

"Flippancy? Never. You don't believe me?"

"No, I don't believe you."

"I care very much about you. But as a matter of principle and in the interests of discipline, a barrier must remain between the officer class and rankers."

"Oh, shut up!" The tone was one of pure exasperation.

"The principle doesn't seem to be standing up very well," Van Effen said gloomily. "And the barrier's flat. So much for discipline."

Annemarie gave no indication that she had heard a word he'd said.

Julie, polite but reserved, had gone to make coffee, Annemarie had headed for the bath and Van Effen spoke to the guard, a man called Thyssen, who assured him that all was quiet and that the man he had relieved had had a similarly uneventful night. Julie entered the living room just as he did; she was still quiet and unsmiling.

"Julie?"

"Yes?"

"I'm sorry."

"For what?"

"I've hurt you."

"You? Hurt? How?"

"That's right. Make it easy for me. I know you've been upset, most likely still are. Annemarie told me."

"Did she tell you why?"

"No. But it didn't take my analytical mind, the one you're always denigrating, very long to figure it out. In retrospect, I could have been more tactful. But I've things on my mind, lots of things. Apart from those things, you're upset, Annemarie is upset because you're upset, and I'm upset because the two of you are upset. I've got to go out and see some ugly customers, and I can't afford to be upset. I have to be careful, crafty, cunning, calculating, watchful and ruthless, and I can't be any of those things if I'm upset. And I'll only be upset if you insist on remaining upset, so you'll have me on your conscience for the rest of your life if something happens to me, such as being shot in the head, thrown off a high building or drowned in a canal. Are you still upset?"

She came close to him, linked her hands behind his neck and put her head on his shoulder. "Of course I am. Not because of last night, but because of what you've just said. You're the only brother I have, and I suppose I have to love someone." She tightened her grip. "One of those days the gallant lieutenant is going to go out into what he calls the dreadful night and the gallant lieutenant is not going to come back."

"This is the morning, Julie."

"Please. You know what I mean. I feel fey, Peter. I feel something dreadful is going to happen today." She tightened her grip even more. "I do so wish you weren't going out. I'd do anything in the world to stop you. You know that this is not the first time—that I've felt this way, I mean—it's been three or four times, and I've been right every time. Change your appointment, Peter, please, darling. I know, I just know I won't feel this way tomorrow."

"I'll come back, Julie. I love you, you love me, I know you'd be terribly sad if I didn't come back. So I'll have to come back, right?"

"Please, Peter. Please!"

"Julie, Julie." He smoothed her hair. "You lot certainly do wonders for my morale."

"What do you mean, 'you lot'?"

"Annemarie's been at it too. Feeling fey, I mean. Prophesying death, doom and disaster. You can imagine how this cheers me up no end. Tell you what. A compromise. I promise you I won't be lured astray by any bad men or go anywhere with them from the Hunter's Horn. I'll listen to what they say. Basically, I think that I'll arrange to meet them again at a time and place of my own choosing, this being after I've learned what their plans are for me. So, a deal. If you promise me one of your cordon bleu lunches—finest French wine, of course— for one o'clock, I'll promise I'll be here at one."

Still with her hands linked behind his neck, she leaned back and looked at him. "You will?"

"Just said so. Your eyes are funny. About to weep salt tears for the gallant lieutenant?"

"I was thinking about it." She smiled. "I've changed my mind. I'll think about the lunch menu instead."

Annemarie came in. She was wearing a bathrobe that was much too large for her and a towel wound around her still-wet hair. She smiled and said, "It's difficult to move around this house without interrupting private conversations. Sorry I look such a fright."

"You can frighten me at any time," Van Effen said cheerfully. "She really isn't too bad-looking, is she, Julie?"

"She's the most beautiful girl *you've* ever seen."

"In my profession you don't get to see many girls, beautiful or otherwise." He looked at Julie. "You're not too bad yourself. But, then, I'm used to your face. It's a toss-up. And who am I to quibble in—or at—such company?"

"Ah, it pleases the lieutenant to be carefree and lighthearted, Julie," Annemarie said. "He was anything but this morning. What have you done?"

"We've been conducting a mutual admiration party," Van Effen said.

"No, we haven't. And I haven't been appealing to his better nature either—I wouldn't know where to look for it. I think maybe we're slightly unfair to the poor man. Both you and I, it seems, have been full of bad omens and predicting all sorts of awful things that are going to happen to him. He was just suffering from gloom and despondency, that's all."

"He wasn't the only one," Annemarie said. "Your cloud seems to have lifted a bit, too."

"You're choking me," Van Effen said.

"Ah!" She unclasped her hands. "Peter says he isn't going to do anything brave today. Just going to the Hunter's Horn, meeting whoever is there, making arrangements for another meeting and then leaving. Going to find out what their plans for him are. Thing is, he's going directly there—where he'll be guarded by heaven knows how many armed detectives—and coming directly back again."

Annemarie smiled, her relief as obvious as Julie's. "That *is* good." The smile slowly vanished. "How do you know he'll keep his word?"

"An officer's word—" Van Effen began.

"Because he's coming back at one o'clock. For lunch. Extra special. French wine. He knows what I'm like if anyone is late for my meals, far less misses them. Besides, I'd never cook for him again."

"Banned for life? No, not that. I'll be back. Guaranteed."

Annemarie said, "Is he coming for us or for the lunch?"

"The lunch, of course. Us he can see any time."

"Not *or*—*and*," Van Effen said. "A peaceful hour. I may well be called upon to attend to something about two o'clock. The F.F.F., I mean."

"I thought," Annemarie said, "that they weren't going to do anything until some undisclosed time tomorrow."

"I was about to tell you but I was interrupted."

Julie said, "Somebody interrupted *you*?"

"What?" Annemarie said.

"The F.F.F. promise to entertain us at two o'clock this afternoon. Same place on the North Holland Canal north of Alkmaar as promised this morning—they say the mines have been planted since yesterday, that they elected not to fire them and defy us to find them—and also the Hagestein sluice."

"The what?" Julie said.

"A sluice. Technically, I believe, an adjustable weir. Concrete structure to control the flow of water. South of Utrecht, on the lower Rhine. They may attack one or the other, they say, or both, or neither. The old uncertainty principle. Well, time to dress for my appointment."

He squeezed his sister's shoulders, kissed her, did the same to an astonished Annemarie, said, "Someone has to uphold the law," and left.

Julie looked at the closed door and shook her head. "There are times, I feel, when someone should pass a law against him."

Van Effen, dressed as he had been the previous afternoon, parked his car—not the Peugeot—in a side street three blocks away from the Hunter's Horn and made his way to the back entrance of the restaurant. This door was kept permanently locked. Van Effen had the key. He entered, passed into the semi-darkness of the passageway beyond and had just relocked the door when something hard jabbed with painful force into the small of his back.

"Don't move."

Van Effen didn't move. He said, "Who is it?"

"Police."

"You have a name?"

"Raise your hands." A torch flicked on behind him. "Jan, see if he has a gun."

Hands fumbled at his jacket and he felt his shoulder-holstered gun being removed. Van Effen said: "So. My hands are up. My gun is gone. May I turn around?"

"Very well." Van Effen turned. "Is that the way, Sergeant Koenis, to teach your men to search for weapons?" He lowered his hands and hitched up his trousers. There was an ankle holster, each with its Lilliput, attached to each leg. "Put on the overhead light."

The light came on. The man with the gun said: "Good God. Lieutenant Van Effen. Sorry about that, sir."

"Just as long as you didn't shoot me full of holes, Sergeant.

Nothing to be sorry for. Semi-dark, and, with my back to you, my trademarks, scar and black glove, weren't visible. And, of course, you weren't expecting me to enter this way. I'm just glad to see that you and your men are so on the alert."

"I didn't even recognize your voice."

"Cheek padding. It does alter the voice somewhat. How many men do you have here, Sergeant?"

"Five, sir. Two with machine pistols."

"And in the street outside?"

"Another five. Behind first-floor windows. Another two machine pistols."

"Very gratifying to see that the colonel places so high a value on his lieutenant." He turned to the young policeman who held the gun in his hand. "Do you think I could have my property back?"

"Yes, sir. Sorry, sir. Of course." The policeman was highly embarrassed. "I won't make *that* mistake again."

"I know you won't. Go and ask Henri if he'll come here—Henri's the sad-looking man behind the bar."

When Henri appeared, lugubrious as ever, he said, "I hear you've been held at gunpoint, Peter. Must have been a rather unusual experience for you. My fault. I forgot to tell the sergeant that you had your own key. Never expected you to come that way."

"No harm. Customers. How many?"

"Three only. And yes, they're regulars. Any more come in when you and your visitors are talking and I'll keep them well away. No one will be able to hear a word you say."

"Except you, of course."

Henri almost smiled. "Except me. The gentleman who was here said they wouldn't find the microphone even if they looked for it. He asked me if I could find it and I couldn't. Not in my own bar. He said he thought it was highly unlikely that they would look anyway."

"I think so too. Switch on the recorder in the office as soon as they come through the door. I shall be off now and make a respectable entrance through the front door. They've probably got someone watching."

* * *

Van Effen was sitting in the booth nearest the door when the three men entered, Agnelli in the lead. Van Effen stood and shook hands with Agnelli, who seemed no less genial than he had on the previous occasion.

"Very pleased to meet you again, Mr. Danilov," Agnelli said. "Helmut, of course, you know." Paderewsky didn't offer to shake hands. "And this is my brother, Leonardo."

Leonardo Agnelli did shake hands. He bore no resemblance to his brother. He was short, squat and had black beetling brows. The brows in themselves meant nothing, he'd just been born that way; in his own ugly way he seemed just as harmless as his brother, which again, of course, meant nothing. Introductions over, Van Effen sat down. Agnelli and the other two men remained standing.

Agnelli said: "This is your favorite booth, Mr. Danilov?"

Van Effen looked slightly puzzled. "I don't have a favorite booth. This is—well, it's just the one furthest away from the rest of the customers. I thought you might appreciate the privacy."

"We do, we do. But would you mind if we went to another?"

Van Effen gave them more of the same puzzled frown. "Not at all. But I think I'm entitled to . . . Stop! I have it. The concealed microphone. A splendid basis for mutual trust." He appeared to think briefly. "Might have done the same myself."

"You're an explosives expert." Agnelli sounded apologetic. "Such people usually—always, I believe—have a considerable knowledge of electronics."

Van Effen smiled, stood, moved out into the aisle and waved a hand toward the empty booth. "A thousand guilders to the first man to find the concealed microphone that I've just spent hours installing under the fascinated gaze of the proprietor and his customers. A thousand guilders for a few seconds' work. I have a generous nature."

Agnelli laughed. "In that case, I don't think we need bother to move." He sat and gestured that the other two should do the same. "Not joining us, Mr. Danilov?"

"Of course. I think we all should have beer."

Van Effen ordered, sat and said, "Well, gentlemen, to the point."

"Certainly." Agnelli smiled. "That's the way I prefer it. We have reported to our leader and he seems to approve our choice."

"I had hoped to see him here this morning."

"You'll see him later. At the Dam Square. The royal palace, to be precise, part of which, with your expert assistance, we intend to blow up tonight."

Van Effen spilled some of the beer that he had just picked up. "You did say the royal palace?"

"I did."

"You're quite mad." Van Effen spoke with simple conviction.

"We don't think so. Nor are we joking. Will you do it?"

"I'll be damned if I will."

Agnelli smiled his easy smile. "What is this? You have been overcome by righteousness? You're suddenly a law-abiding upholder of justice and the straight and narrow path?"

"None of those things. But you must understand that although I operate mainly outside the law and have a past that wouldn't bear rigorous examination, in fact, any kind of examination, I'm in most ways a pretty normal citizen. I've come to like the Dutch, and, although I don't know them from Adam, I respect, even admire, their royal family."

"Your sentiments do you credit, Mr. Danilov. Believe me, I even share them. But I hardly think those are your real reasons for refusing. You said yesterday afternoon that you would not become involved in any operation where there might arise the danger of risk to limb, far less to life. Is that not so?" Van Effen nodded. "I assure you no such risk will arise tonight."

"Then you just want to cause a harmless explosion inside the palace?"

"Precisely."

"And why in heaven's name should you want to cause a harmless explosion inside the palace?"

"You are not to concern yourself with that. It is, as you may well guess, a purely psychological gesture."

"How am I to know it will be harmless?"

"You'll be able to satisfy yourself on this score when you get there. The explosion will take place inside an empty cellar. There are empty cellars on either side of it. All four doors are lockable and we will remove the keys after they have been locked. There are also empty cellars above. There is absolutely no danger to anyone involved."

"There's danger to us. The palace is heavily guarded. Word has it that the guards are likely to ask questions of an intruder after they've shot him dead. My aversion to people getting killed includes myself."

"*Please*, Mr. Danilov. We are not simple-minded. Do I look like a person who would embark upon an operation like this without every detail having been meticulously planned beforehand?"

"I'll grant that. You don't."

"Then you may rest easy. We will encounter no trouble. As an additional assurance, both our leader and I will be there with you. We have no more ambition to end up there than you have."

"What's this bomb like?"

"I'm not sure." Agnelli smiled. Van Effen had practically committed himself. "I'm not an explosives man. Such talents as I have lie elsewhere, more in the organizing field, shall we say. I understand that it weighs six or eight pounds and is made of some material called amatol."

"What are the cellars made of?"

"Made of? You mean the walls?"

"What else could I mean?"

"I really couldn't tell you."

"I don't suppose it matters. I was just trying to figure the blast effect. If the cellars are deep and have—"

"Those cellars are very deep."

"So. And with the palace on top they'll have to support a very considerable weight. I don't know how old this particular part of the palace may be, I know nothing about the palace, but the walls would have to be pretty stoutly built. Reinforced concrete is unlikely. Dressed stone, I should guess, and thick. Your little firework is hardly likely to dent them. All the people in the palace will be aware of is a slight shake, if that, a tremor that wouldn't raise any eyebrows at the nearest seismographic station, wherever that may be. As for the sound factor, it would be negligible."

"Are you sure?" Agnelli's tone was unaccustomedly sharp.

"If my assumptions are correct, and I see no reason why they shouldn't be, then I'm sure."

"No loud bang?"

"They wouldn't hear it in the palace drawing rooms, far less out in the Dam Square."

"How could one ensure that it is heard?"

"Bring along enough spare amatol, let me have a look at the walls and I'll tell you. Tell me, is it your intention just to leave the explosives there, lock the doors, throw away the keys—it will have occurred to you, of course, that there will be duplicates?"

"Those we have."

"And arrange for the bang after you're clear of the palace?" Agnelli nodded. "Then why on earth do you want me for a simple job like this? I've little enough in the way of conscience, but I'd feel downright guilty taking money. A young teenager in his first year in a physics or chemistry lab could do this. All you require is a battery, any old alarm clock, an electric cord, a fulminate-of-mercury detonator, a primer and you're off. Even simpler, all you require is a length of slow-burning RDX fuse. What you don't want is an expensive explosives expert— me. It's a matter, Mr. Agnelli, of professional pride."

"This *is* a job for a professional. It's to be set off by remote radio control."

"A teenager in his *second* year in a physics or chemistry lab. Can't you do it yourselves?"

"For good reasons we want an expert. The reasons are not for you."

"You have the technical data for this radio-controlled device?"

"A professional needs an instruction book?"

"Only an amateur would ask a professional such a stupid question. Of course I need an instruction book, as you call it, but it's not instructions I require but data. These systems are not difficult if you know how they work. Problem is, there are quite a number of different systems. As far as the device and the control are concerned, I need to know such things as voltage, wattage, wavelength, radio range, type of detonator, the nature of the triggering mechanism, the type of shielding and a few other odds and ends. You have this? The data, I mean?"

"We have. I shall bring it along tonight."

"You will not. No offense, Mr. Agnelli, but only an amateur would suggest that I start to learn about this device on the spot. I want to be so thoroughly familiarized with the data that I can leave them all behind before I go near the place. I need those data at least an hour in advance."

"Or no deal?"

"I wouldn't insult you by threats or blackmail. I assume that a reasonable man recognizes a reasonable request?"

"He does. We'll send it around at, say, six-thirty this evening?"

"Fine." Van Effen paused briefly. "Well, well. We have been making diligent inquiries, haven't we?"

"It really wasn't very difficult. We come now to the delicate question of remuneration—although I did promise it would be on a generous scale."

"You did mention the possibility of permanent employment?"

"I did."

"Then let's regard this as a test demonstration. You know— efficiency, reliability, professionalism. If I measure up, let's then discuss payment for future jobs."

"Fair and generous. So fair, in fact, that I feel almost diffident about raising the next delicate point."

"I hate for you to embarrass yourself. Let me raise it for you."

"This is more than generous."

"My nature. You have given me highly secret and very valuable information for which the police would doubtless reward me handsomely." Van Effen knew from Agnelli's brief frown, then renewed smile that he had guessed correctly. "I shall not be giving this information to the police. Reasons? One, I am not a double-crosser. Two, I don't like the police and they don't like me—I don't want to be within a long distance of any policemen. Three. Purely selfish and financial—I am certain I can make a great deal more money from working for you on several occasions than I can from betraying you once. Four, I do not wish to spend the rest of my life with a hit man or hit men only one step behind." Agnelli was smiling very broadly now. "The fifth is the most compelling reason. From what you have just told me you obviously have informers, contacts inside the palace, who would immediately alert you to the presence of the police. As there could and would be only one person who could have betrayed you, I could, possibly, be summarily disposed of, although I think you would find it much more elegant to turn me over to the police and suggest that they have a look at extradition requests from Poland and the United States. I think I would prefer the States—I might at least get a semblance of a fair trial there. I am not wanted, of course, under the name of Danilov: but the description of villains is usually pretty thorough and there can't be many wanted men going round with a facial scar and a ruined left hand like mine. You can understand, Mr. Agnelli, why I give the police a very wide berth."

"I must say that you and the law don't appear to have a great deal in common. Thank you, Mr. Danilov, for having done my delicate task for me. That was exactly what I did have in mind. I am sure that you are going to be a very valuable member of our team."

"I can be trusted, you think?"

"Unquestionably."

"Then I am doubly honored." Agnelli raised an eyebrow. "I didn't have to remove the magazines from my guns today."

Agnelli smiled, stood, shook hands and left with his two companions. Van Effen went to the office, listened to the playback of the recording, expressed his satisfaction and thanks to Henri, pocketed the tape and left.

* * *

As had now become his custom, Van Effen parked his car at the rear of the Trianon but entered by the front door. A nondescript little man, seemingly engrossed in a newspaper, was seated close by the desk. Van Effen spoke to the man behind it.

"I'd like a menu, please." He paid no attention to the seated man. "Thank you." He ticked off some items on the menu. "I'll have that, that and that. And a bottle of Burgundy. In my room at twelve-thirty, please. After that I don't want to be disturbed—so no phone calls, please. I'd be glad if you would give me a wake-up call at four o'clock."

Van Effen took the lift to the first floor, walked down the stairs and peered cautiously around the corner. The little man had gone. He went across to the desk.

"I see you've lost a valued customer, Charles."

"Hardly valued, Lieutenant. He drinks one tiny gin every hour or so. That's his third time here since last night. He is rather obvious, isn't he?"

"He doesn't seem to think so. Will you cancel my lunch, Charles?"

Charles smiled. "Already canceled."

Van Effen left the Trianon a few minutes later, his appearance returned to normal.

"Well," Van Effen said, "were you worried stiff about me?"

"Of course not," Julie said. "You told us there was nothing to worry about."

"Liar. You, too."

"Me?" Annemarie said. "I haven't said a word yet."

"You were about to. Your concern is perfectly understandable. A jonge jenever, large. The very jaws of death, I tell you."

"Tell us about brave Daniel," Julie said.

"In a moment. First of all, I must phone the colonel. He will be consumed with anxiety about his trusty lieutenant."

"It's twelve-thirty," Julie said. "If I know the colonel, his only concern now is what aperitif he's going to have before lunch."

"You do him an injustice. And, incidentally, me." He took the drink from his sister. "May I use your bedroom?"

"Of course."

Annemarie said, "I thought—"

"There's a phone there."

"Ah. State secrets."

"Not at all. Come along. Both of you. It'll save me from having to repeat myself."

He sat down on Julie's bed, opened a bedside cupboard and extracted a phone. Annemarie said, "That's a curious-looking instrument."

"Scrambler phone. Any eavesdropper who is locked into your telephone hears only garbled nonsense. A device at the recipient's end works in reverse and makes the jumble intelligible again. Much used by secret services and the better class of spy. Very popular with criminals, too. The original connection was to my apartment, but I can also call Van de Graaf on it."

He got through immediately. "Good morning, Colonel. . . . No, I have not been attacked, kidnapped, tortured, assassinated or otherwise set upon. . . . Quite the contrary. Positively cordial. . . . No, there was a newcomer. Romero Agnelli's brother. Genial Mafia type, quite friendly, really, rejoicing in the name of Leonardo Agnelli. . . . Yes, it is rather splendid, isn't it, and yes, we've made some arrangements. I am engaged to blow up the royal palace at eight P.M. . . . No, sir, I do not jest." He covered the mouthpiece and looked at the two startled, wide-eyed girls. "I think the colonel's drink has gone down the wrong way. Yes, sir, amatol. Triggered by a remote-controlled radio device, details of which I shall be receiving this evening. . . . Certainly I intend to do it. They're depending on me. . . . No, it's deep in the cellars. There will be no loss of life. . . . Very well."

He covered the mouthpiece with one hand and gave his empty glass to Julie with the other. "I'm to keep a respectful silence while he communes with himself before telling me what to do. I don't need telling, and I almost certainly won't agree with what he suggests."

"Blowing up the royal palace." Annemarie looked at Julie, who had just brought in the jenever bottle. "The palace. Blowing it up. He's mad. You—you're a policeman!"

"A policeman's lot is a hard one. All things to all men. Yes, I'm listening." There was a long pause. Julie and Annemarie studied his face covertly but closely. He gave no indication as to what he was thinking, although he did permit himself the occasional thoughtful expression as he sipped some more jenever.

"Yes, I understand. Alternatives. First, you can pull me off altogether and, of course, I would have to accept that decision. But there's a difference between pulling me off a job and putting me back onto it again. Should this prove to be the first in a series of bomb outrages—and you know better than anyone that those things almost invariably happen in cycles—then I should have to refuse to be assigned to the investigation on the grounds that I was fortunate enough to be given the opportunity to investigate this group's activities and you denied me the opportunity. . . . Certainly, sir, you could ask for my resignation on the grounds of refusing to obey orders. I would refuse to resign. You'd have to fire me. And then, of course, you would have to explain to your minister that you fired me because you had made a mistake, because you had refused to listen to me, because you wouldn't give me the chance to stop what may be a new crime wave before it started, because you had backed your own judgment against mine and you were wrong. Throw as many chestnuts as you like into the fire, Colonel. I refuse to pull them out. And I refuse to resign. Excuse me, sir."

Julie had sat down beside him on the bedside and she put both hands on his telephone arm as if trying to pull it away.

"Stop it, Peter, stop it." Despite the fact that Van Effen had prudently covered the mouthpiece, her voice was low, tense, urgent. "You can't talk to the colonel like that. Can't you see that you're putting the poor man in an impossible situation?"

Van Effen looked at Annemarie. From her compressed lips and slowly shaking head it was evident that she was of the same opinion as Julie. Van Effen looked back at his sister and she visibly recoiled from the expression on his face.

"Why don't you hear me out instead of indulging in a repetition of last night's interference and blundering into things you know nothing about? You think *he's* in an impossible situation? Listen to what I say and judge what kind of position I'm in." She slowly removed her hands and just looked at him, her expression uncomprehending. Van Effen raised the phone again.

"Forgive the interruption, Colonel. Julie says that I have no right to talk to you in this fashion and that I'm putting you in an impossible situation. Julie, alas, doesn't know what she's talking about. Annemarie, who is also here, agrees with her but she wouldn't know what she's talking about either. In fairness to them I must say that, judging by the way they are looking at each other, they don't think I know what I'm talking about either. You people are only on the periphery; I'm the man in the middle. An impossible situation, she says. Consider your alternatives.

"I go ahead as planned with Agnelli and company. You, you say, will ensure my safety. In the first place you are duty-bound—you claim—to notify the royal household, using as justification the many threats that have been made against the royal family in recent months. You will have the Dam Square invisibly cordoned off by snipers. You will have anti-terrorist police squads inside the palace itself. It has apparently never occurred to you that those criminals have their moles and informants pretty thick on the ground and that the presence of even one extra policeman will be immediately reported. I have been warned that if any such thing happened they would know that there could have been only one source, one person, through whom this information reached the police. And I don't think— I *know*—that the palace security is pitiful and that those spies move freely within the gates. Lift that telephone to the palace, to your anti-terrorist squads, to any other policeman, and you might as well reach out for pen and paper and write and sign my death warrant." That was, Van Effen was aware, pitching it rather strongly.

"Ensure my safety? You'll ensure my death, Van Effen in a better world by midnight. What's one detective lieutenant less just so long as your pettifogging rules and hidebound regulations are concerned? Maybe—no, I'm sure—that Julie and Annemarie don't like me very much at the moment, but I think they'll have the grace to testify at the inquest that I did do my best to save my own miserable skin.

"That, of course, is the absolute worst scenario, and I've no intention of being any part of it. I've been thinking during our conversation, and I've changed my mind about one thing. You've offered me two alternatives. One leads to being fired, the other to the old pine box. I'm not quite in my dotage yet, and I think it would behoove me to find some form of work where I'll be faced with threats of neither dismissal nor extinction. If you send one of your boys round to Julie's place, I'll let him have my written resignation. At the same time I'll give him the tape recording I made in the Hunter's Horn this morning. I hope that you and your university friends will be able to make something of it and of the other tape-recorded telephone messages. Sorry about this, Colonel, but you leave me with no option; I seem to have run out of alternatives." He replaced the telephone in the bedside cupboard and left the room.

When Julie and Annemarie rejoined him he was sitting relaxed in an armchair, legs crossed and jenever in hand. For a man who had just made such a momentous decision he seemed relaxed.

Julie said, "May I say something?"

"Certainly. Compared to what the colonel said and what he is no doubt thinking at this moment, your slings and arrows are as nothing."

She smiled faintly. "I haven't lost my senses or memory. I have no intention of being—how did you put it so charmingly last night—cool, clinical, superior or handing out unwanted and unsolicited advice. I am sorry for what I said in the bedroom. I didn't know you were in so impossible a situation. But if I go on to say that I also think you've put the colonel in a fearful fix, you'll probably say that you appreciate that a lieutenant's life is as nothing compared to the colonel's finer feelings. Well, I still say I'm sorry, but—"

Annemarie interrupted. "Julie?"

"Yes?"

"I wouldn't bother saying sorry to him again. I don't for a moment believe he's in an impossible situation. Look at him. He's getting high blood pressure trying not to laugh out loud." She gave him a considered glance. "You're not very active, I see. I thought you came in here to write out your resignation."

He frowned, looked off into the middle distance, then said, "I've no recollection of saying that."

"That's because you never had any intention of writing one."

"Well, well. We'll make a lady detective of you yet. You're right, my dear, I did not. How could I? How could I leave Uncle Arthur alone to cope with the rising wave of crime in Amsterdam? He needs me."

Annemarie said to Julie, "If I were to say to him that he is as Machiavellian as he is big-headed, do you think he would fire me?"

Van Effen sipped. "Fortunately, I am above such things. And you must never confuse Machiavellianism with diplomacy, or big-headedness with intelligence."

"You're right, Annemarie. I'm sorry I said 'sorry,'" Julie looked at Van Effen with something less than affection. "And what are you going to do now?"

"Wait."

"Wait for what?"

"The phone. The colonel."

"The colonel!" Julie said. "After what you said to him?"

"After what he said to me, you mean."

"You're going to have a long wait." Annemarie spoke with conviction.

"My dear children—you sadly underestimate the colonel. He is infinitely shrewder than either of you. He knows very well what the score is. He's taking some time to make this call because he's figuring out a way to beat a strategic retreat without loss of dignity, peace with honor, if you will. Now there, if you like, does go a man with a Machiavellian mind—after forty years battling with the underworld one does develop a certain cast of mind. I told the colonel that he had left me with no place to go. Van de Graaf, being Van de Graaf, realized at once what I meant—that *he* had no place to go."

Julie said, "Seeing you're so clever, would you mind—"

"No need to be unpleasant. Look—am I treating you with unfailing courtesy?"

"I suppose. What's the colonel going to say?"

"That on consideration—or on re-consideration—he's going to give me carte blanche. The eight P.M. assignation is on."

"It would be nice to see you wrong for once," Julie said. "No, I didn't really mean that. I only hope you are wrong."

For a time no one spoke. The girls kept looking at each other, at the ceiling, at the floor, at the telephone on the coffee table by Van Effen's side. Van Effen wasn't looking at anything in particular. The phone rang.

Van Effen picked it up. "Ah! Yes . . . I accept that. Maybe I did step out of line. But I was provoked." He winced and held the telephone some distance away from his ear. "Yes, sir, you were provoked too. . . . Yes, I thoroughly agree. A wise decision, if I may say so. . . . Of course, you will be kept in the picture, sir. . . . No, they don't trust me. . . . Yes, sir, here. Good-bye."

He hung up and looked at Julie. "Why aren't you in the kitchen, my girl? I distinctly smell burning. I was asked for lunch—"

"Oh, do be quiet. What did he say?"

"Carte blanche. Eight P.M."

Julie looked at him, her face still, for what seemed a long time but could only have been a few seconds, then turned and went to the kitchen. Annemarie made a couple of steps toward him, stopped and said, "Peter."

"Don't say it. I've already got out of one difficult situation. Don't you and Julie put me in an impossible one."

"We won't. I promise. You know that we can't help what we feel, and you can't blame us for that. But you could blame us if we did start talking about it, so we won't. That's sure." She smiled. "Now, isn't that considerate."

"Very. Do you know, Annemarie, I do believe I'm beginning to like you."

"Like me?" She gave him a quizzical look. "So you didn't even like me when you kissed me this morning? Absentmindedness, I suppose. Or do you just go around kissing policewomen as a matter of routine? Something to do with morale, no doubt."

"You're the first."

"And, no doubt, the last. We all make mistakes, whatever I mean by that cryptic remark. *Who* doesn't trust you?"

"Who doesn't—what?"

"Something you said to the colonel."

"Ah. My criminal associates. We parted at the Hunter's Horn professing mutual trust and faith. Didn't stop them from staking a man out at the Trianon. An irritation. No problem."

"And after lunch?"

"Stay here a bit. The colonel is going to call me. That will be after we hear what, if anything, the F.F.F. have been up to at two o'clock. The colonel is convinced that they will not blow up the Hagestein. Frogmen have found no traces of any underwater charges in position."

Van Effen called his office and asked for the desk sergeant. "The men on Fred Klassen and Alfred van Rees. They called in at noon?" He listened briefly. "So Van Rees has lost our man. Chance or on purpose, it doesn't matter. I assume you have the license number. All officers on patrol. Not to approach. Just locate. Note this number and call me here."

Lunch was a beautifully prepared but hardly festive meal. Julie and Annemarie were determinedly over-bright and over-cheerful, and the harsh edges of strain occasionally showed through. If Van Effen noticed anything, he made no comment; still, her brother, Julie knew, rarely missed anything.

They had coffee in the living room. Shortly after two o'clock a young motorcycle policeman came to collect the Hunter's Horn tape.

Julie said, "I hear that you are awaiting a call from the colonel. After that?"

"Your bed, my dear, if I may. I don't know when I can expect to sleep tonight or even if I will sleep, so I think an hour or two might be of some value. That hour or two, of course, would be helped along by the brandy you have—unaccountably—so far failed to offer me."

The colonel's call came when Van Effen was halfway through his brandy. It was a brief call and one-sided. Van Effen said "yes" several times, "I see" a couple of times, then told the colonel good-bye and hung up.

"The F.F.F. blew up the North Holland dike at exactly two P.M. Extensive flooding, but shallow and no lives lost. Not according to first reports. The Hagestein weir was not touched. As the colonel says, he expected this. The frogmen had located no charges and he is convinced that the F.F.F. were unable either to approach the weir or conceal charges. He's further convinced that their blasting techniques are primitive and limited only to simple operations like blowing up dikes and canal banks."

"But you're not convinced of this, are you?" Julie said.

"I'm neither convinced nor unconvinced. I know no more about it than you do. Maybe the colonel finds it preferable, more comforting to think along those lines, maybe the F.F.F. want the colonel—us, the country—to think along those lines. They have all the hallmarks of being a devious and highly organized bunch. That impression, too, may be deceptive. Are they a simple-minded group trying to make us think they are devious, or a devious-minded group trying to make us think they are simple? Figure it out for yourselves. I can't. I'm going to rest lightly. Turn on the radio, would you? The F.F.F. have, it seems, got into the habit of making a public announcement after what they no doubt regard as being one of their master strokes. Don't bother to wake me to convey their next dire threat. In fact, don't bother me for anything."

He had barely dropped off when Julie came in and shook him awake. He opened his eyes and, as was his custom, was almost instantly awake. He said, "This is the way you don't disturb me? The heavens have fallen?"

"I'm sorry. A letter came for you."

"A letter? An exhausted man is torn from his slumbers—"

"It came by special delivery," she said patiently. "It has *Urgent* stamped all over it."

"Let me see." He took the envelope from her, glanced briefly at the address and postmark, opened the envelope, half extracted the contents, pushed them back inside again and slid the envelope under the pillow. "And I'm disturbed by this. One of my fellow officers trying to be witty. Next time, be sure the heavens have fallen in."

"Let me see what was inside that letter," Julie said sharply. She sat on the bed, laid her hand on his arm and said in a gentle voice, "Please, Peter?"

Van Effen made to speak, said nothing, reached under his pillow, retrieved the envelope and gave the contents to Julie. It was not a letter, just a plain postcard, blank on one side. On the other side was a crude drawing of a coffin and a hangman's noose.

Julie tried to smile. "Well, it has been three months since the last one, hasn't it?"

"So?" Van Effen sounded indifferent. "It's been, as you say, three months. And what's happened in that three months? Nothing. And no reason on earth why anything should happen in the next three months."

"If it's so unimportant, why did you hide it?"

"I didn't hide it. I put it away in the full view of my little sister whom I didn't want to upset."

"May I see that envelope, please?" She took it, looked at it and handed it back. "All the others had come from other countries. This one is postmarked Amsterdam. That was the first thing you saw and that's why you put it away. The Annecy brothers are in Amsterdam."

"Maybe. Maybe not. This postcard could have come from any country to a friend or accomplice in Amsterdam who sent it on to this address."

"I don't believe that. Kid sister or not, I'm all grown up and a big girl now. I can think for myself, I can feel for myself. I *know* they're in Amsterdam. And so, I'm sure, do you. Oh Peter. It's all too much. One set of madmen threatening to flood our country, another set going to blow up the palace, and now this." She shook her head. "Everything at once. Why?"

"It is an unusual set of circumstances."

"It is a—oh, do be quiet. Do you have *no* idea what is going on?"

"I've no more idea than you have."

"Maybe. Maybe not. I'm not sure I believe you. What are we going to do? What are *you* going to do?"

"What do you expect me to do? Patrol the streets of Amsterdam until I find some character carrying a coffin over his shoulder and a noose in his hand." He put his hand on her arm. "Please excuse momentary irritation. There's nothing I can do. Second thoughts, yes. I can go back to sleep. Next time, hold the heavens up!"

"You're hopeless." She half smiled, rose, shook her head again when she saw that his eyes were already closed, and left the room.

He had barely dropped off for the second time when Julie returned. "Sorry again, Peter. The colonel. I told him you were asleep, but he said it didn't matter if you were dead, I was to bring you back to life again and get you to the phone."

Van Effen touched the bedside cupboard. "He could have used the scrambler."

"Probably using a public phone."

Van Effen went through to the living room, took the call, listened briefly, said, "I'm leaving now," and hung up.

Julie said: "Where?"

"To meet a person the colonel says may be a friend. I don't know his name." Van Effen put on shoulder holster, tie and jacket. "Things, as you said, Julie, tend not to occur singly. First, the dike nut cases. Then the palace nut cases. Then the Annecy nut cases. Now this."

"Whatever 'this' may be. Where's your friend?"

"Wouldn't you know. He's in the mortuary."

5

THE OLD TOWN of Amsterdam may well be unique in the attraction of its tree-lined winding canals, its medieval charm, its romance, its almost palpable sense of history, its nostalgic beauty. The city mortuary wasn't like that at all. It didn't possess a single attractive feature, it had no charm, medieval or modern, was totally and irredeemably ugly. It was clinical, functional, inhuman and wholly repellent. Only the dead, one would have thought, could have tolerated such a place; but the white-coated attendants, while not much given to whistling at their work, seemed no different from your average office worker, factory mechanic or farm laborer: this was their job and they did it in the best way they could.

Van Effen arrived to find Van de Graaf and a serious young man, who was introduced as Dr. Prins, waiting for him. Dr. Prins was attired in the regulation uniform of white coat and stethoscope. It was difficult to imagine what function a stethoscope played in a mortuary: possibly to check that incoming admissions were, in fact, dead on arrival; more probably, it was just part of the uniform. Van de Graaf was in a somber mood, but this was not due to his surroundings, for over the long years, Van de Graaf had become more than accustomed to mortuaries; what he was not accustomed to was having to leave his fish course and a bottle of perfect Chablis almost untouched on a restaurant table.

Dr. Prins led them to a long, cavernous, tomblike chamber, the furnishings of which—exclusively in concrete, white tiles, marble and metal—accorded well with the chilled atmosphere. An attendant, seeing Prins approach, opened a metal door and pulled out a wheeled rack that ran smoothly on steel runners. A shrouded form lay on this. Dr. Prins took the top corner of the sheet.

"I have to warn you, gentlemen, that this is not a sight for weak stomachs."

"My stomach couldn't possibly be in worse condition than it is," Van de Graaf said. Prins looked at him curiously and pulled back the sheet. What lay revealed was indeed, as the doctor had said, not a sight for the queasy. Dr. Prins looked at the faces of the two policemen and felt vaguely disappointed; not by a flicker of expression did they display whatever emotions they might have felt.

"Cause of death, Doctor?" Van de Graaf said.

"Multiple, massive injuries, of course. Cause? An autopsy will reveal—"

"Autopsy!" Van Effen's voice was as cold as the mortuary itself. "I do not wish to be personal, Doctor, but how long have you held this post?"

"My first week." The slight pallor in his face suggested that Dr. Prins was himself having some problems with his internal economy.

"So you won't have seen many cases like this. If any. This man has been murdered. He hasn't fallen off the top of a high building or been run over by a heavy truck. In that case the skull or chest wall or pelvis or the femoral bones or tibia would have been crushed or broken. They haven't. He's been battered to death by iron bars. His face is unrecognizable, kneecaps smashed and forearms broken—no doubt when he was trying to defend himself against the iron bars."

Van de Graaf said to the doctor, "He was, of course, wearing clothes when he was brought in. Anyone been through them?"

"Identification, you mean, Colonel?"

"Of course."

"Nothing that I know of."

"It doesn't matter," Van Effen said. "I know who it is. I recognize that scar on the shoulder. Detective Rudolph Engel. He was shadowing a man known as Julius Caesar—you may remember Annemarie mentioning this character in La Caracha."

"How do you know this?"

"Because I was the person who told Engel to do the shadowing. I also warned him that there was more than a degree of danger attached and that he was on no account to be in a position where he would find himself without people around. I reminded him what had happened to the two detectives who had trailed Agnelli. He forgot or disobeyed or was carried away by curiosity or enthusiasm. Whatever it was, it cost him his life."

"But to murder him in this savage fashion?" Van de Graaf shook his head. "Even to kill him at all. Well, it does seem an unbelievable instance of overreacting."

"We'll probably never know the truth, sir. But if we do we'll probably find out that he wasn't disposed of just for shadowing but because he'd found out something they couldn't let him live to report. High stakes, Colonel."

"High indeed. It might help to have a word with this—ah—Julius Caesar."

"Probably couldn't find him in the first place. He'll have gone to ground, left Amsterdam or, most likely, shaved off his pepper-and-salt beard and got himself a wig for his bald pate and a pair of glasses to conceal his squint. Besides, even if we did pull him in, what have we got to charge him with?"

They thanked Dr. Prins and left. As they were passing through the entrance hall, a man at the desk called the colonel and handed him a phone. The colonel spoke briefly, handed back the phone and rejoined Van Effen.

"Not destined to be our afternoon, I'm afraid. Office. Just heard from the hospital. One of our men there. Just been fished out of a canal, it seems."

"What's he doing in hospital? You mean he's not drowned?"

"No. Touch and go, it seems. We'd better have a look."

"Identity?"

"Not established. Still unconscious. No papers, no badge.

But carrying a gun and a pair of handcuffs. So they guessed it was a cop."

In the hospital, they were led to a private room on the first floor from which a gray-haired doctor was just emerging. He saw Van de Graaf and smiled.

"My old friend! You don't waste time, I must say. One of your men has just had a rather unpleasant experience. A very close thing, very close, but he'll be all right. In fact, he can leave in an hour or two."

"So he's conscious?"

"Conscious and in a very bad temper. Name of Voight."

"Mas Voight?" Van Effen said.

"That's him. Little boy saw him floating face-down in the water. Luckily there were a couple of dockworkers close by. They fished him out and brought him here. Couldn't have been in the water more than a minute or so."

Voight was sitting up in bed and looking disgruntled. After the briefest of courteous inquiries as to his health, Van de Graaf said, "How on earth did you come to fall into that canal?"

"*Fall* into the canal!" Voight was outraged. "Fall into—"

"Shh!" said the doctor. "You'll just do yourself an injury." He gently turned Voight's head; the blue and purple bruise behind the right ear promised to develop into something spectacular.

"Must have run out of crowbars," Van Effen said.

Van de Graaf frowned. "And what is that meant to mean?"

"Our friends are being active again. Detective Voight was keeping an eye on Alfred van Rees and—"

"Alfred van Rees!"

"You know. The Rijkswaterstaat man. Locks, weirs, sluices and what have you. Unfortunately it would seem that Detective Voight couldn't watch Van Rees and his own back at the same time. Last report, Voight, was that you had lost Van Rees."

"A patrolman found him again. Gave me the address. I drove down and parked by the canal, got out—"

"What canal?" Van Effen said.

"The Croquis Kade."

"The Croquis Kade! And Van Rees. You astonish me. Hardly the most salubrious part of our fair city."

Voight rubbed his neck. "I didn't find it very salubrious either. I saw Van Rees and another man coming out of this doorway and then they went back in again. Why, I don't know. I wasn't in a police car, and as far as I know they've never seen me, never suspected I was following them. And then—well, the next thing I knew I was in this bed. Never even heard a footstep behind me."

"Did you get the house number?"

"Yes. Thirty-eight."

Van Effen picked up the bedside phone, told the switchboard it was police and urgent, gave them his office number and said to Van de Graaf, "I don't suppose that anyone will still be at Number thirty-eight. But we may find something there—if, that is, they didn't see Detective Voight being fished out of the canal. If they did, it'll be clean as a whistle. Question of search warrant, sir?"

"Damn the search warrant." Van de Graaf was obviously rather shaken that his old friend Van Rees could be involved in illegal activities. "Effect an entry by any means."

Van Effen was through to his office almost immediately, asked for a certain Sergeant Oudshoorn, got him in turn just as quickly, gave him the address and instructions and listened for a brief period.

"No, Sergeant. Take four men. One at the front door, one at the back. . . . No warrant. The colonel says so. Yes. Take the damned door off its hinges if you have to. Or shoot the lock away. Detain anyone you find inside. Don't leave there. Radio report to station and await instructions." He hung up. "Sergeant Oudshoorn seems to relish the prospect."

They told Voight to call home, have dry clothes brought, go home and rest, and said good-bye. In the passageway Van de Graaf said, "It can't be. Impossible. Man's a pillar of society. Good heavens, I even put him up for my club."

"Could be a perfectly innocent explanation, sir. The state of Voight's neck and his immersion in the canal seem to suggest otherwise. Remember, I suggested in Schiphol that perhaps he was a Jekyll by day and a Hyde by night. Maybe I got it wrong. Maybe he's a daylight Hyde." As they approached the hospital entrance, Van Effen stopped abruptly. Van de Graaf stopped also and looked at him curiously.

"One rarely sees an expression of concern on your face, Peter. Something amiss?"

"I hope not, sir. Something's been nagging away at the back of my mind but I haven't had time to think about it. Not until now. This call you got while you were lunching—at least, when you were about to have lunch—did it come from the station?"

"Of course. Sergeant Bresser."

"Where did he get his information from?"

"The hospital, I presume. Bresser said he'd tried to find first you, then Lieutenant Valken, and failing to find either, he contacted me. Does it matter?"

"This matters. Young Dr. Prins at the mortuary is neither experienced nor very bright. For all he knew or suspected to the contrary, Engel might have fallen off the top of the Havengebouw, or been the victim of a street or industrial accident. The mortuary does *not* call in senior police officers unless they know or suspect that the victim did not meet a natural end. So the chances are that the call did not come from the hospital. Bresser's a stolid, unimaginative man. Thinking is not his forte. Was it your idea to call me up at Julie's and ask me to come along?"

"You're beginning to get me worried now, too, Peter, although I don't know why. Your name had been mentioned in the call but whether it was Bresser's suggestion you come along or mine, I'm not clear. Damn these lunches."

"Moment, sir." Van Effen went to the nearest telephone and dialed a number. He let it ring for perhaps fifteen seconds, then dialed again while Van de Graaf watched him at first in perplexity, then in apprehension, then with the sick dawning of understanding. He was at the front door and holding it open when Van Effen replaced the phone and came running toward him.

* * *

Van Effen didn't even bother to knock on Julie's door, which he unlocked with the key he'd fished out coming up in the lift. The living room appeared to be in perfectly normal condition, which meant nothing. Julie's bedroom was also as it should have been, but her bathroom told a different story. Thyssen, the guard, was lying on the floor, perfectly conscious and in apparent danger of suffering an apoplectic stroke, whether from rage or an effort to free himself from the ropes that bound wrists and ankles it was difficult to say. Perhaps he had been having difficulty in breathing through his gag. They freed him and helped him to his feet, for he was unable to stand; if the blued hands were anything to go by, the circulation of his feet must have been almost completely blocked off too. Whoever had tied him had worked with a will.

They helped him through to the living room and into an armchair. Van Effen massaged circulation back into hand and feet—not a pleasant process if one were to judge by Thyssen's repeated winces and screwing shut of the eyes, while Van de Graaf brought him a glass of brandy. He had to hold it to the man's lips, as Thyssen had yet to recover the use of his hands.

"Van der Hum," Van de Graaf said, referring to the brandy. "A universal specific and, in the circumstances, despite regulations—"

"The man who makes the regulations can break the regulations."

They had barely sipped from their glasses when Thyssen recovered enough strength to seize his, lift his trembling hand to his mouth, and drink half the contents in one gulp; he coughed, spluttered, then spoke for the first time.

"God, I'm sorry, Lieutenant! Most damnably sorry! Your sister—and that other nice lady." He drained his glass. "I should be taken out and shot."

"I don't think it will come to that, Jan," Van Effen said mildly. "Whatever happened is no fault of yours. What did happen?"

Thyssen was so overcome with anger, bitterness and self-reproach that his account was so disjointed and repetitive as to be at times incoherent. It appeared that he had been approached by a Dutch army major—who would ever have harbored suspicions about an army major?—who had produced a pistol fitted with a silencer, forced Thyssen to produce his key and open the door, pushed him inside, followed and advised the women not to move. He had been followed into the room almost immediately by three furniture-removal men; at least, they were dressed in heavy leather aprons of that type. What was atypical about them was that they wore hoods and gloves. Beyond that, Thyssen could tell nothing; he had been taken into the bathroom and tied, gagged and left lying on the floor.

Van Effen went into Annemarie's bedroom—the one that had formerly been his—took one quick look around and returned.

"There's a pile of Annemarie's clothes lying on the bed and a wardrobe missing. They were tied, gagged and carried out in it—to anyone watching, legitimate furniture removing. They must have been keeping tabs on me, sir, about the time you made the call to me from the restaurant. They would have had a furniture van parked nearby and would have moved in as soon as they saw me leave. Very neat. Ironic, isn't it, sir; both of them this morning were full of gloom and foreboding—and prophecies of disaster. Feeling fey, they called it. They were both convinced that the something terrible was going to happen to me; unfortunately, they picked the wrong subject for concern."

Van de Graaf, a second glass of Van der Hum in his hands, paced up and down. Even forty years in the police had left him without Van Effen's ability to mask his emotions; anger and worry fought for dominance in his face.

"What are those devils up to? What did they want—and *who* did they want? Anne? Julie? Or both?"

"Julie." Van Effen handed him the postcard he and Julie had looked at earlier in the afternoon. Van de Graaf took it, examined both card and envelope and said, "When did this arrive?"

"Just after lunch. Julie was very upset, but I pooh-poohed it, laughed the matter off. Clever Van Effen. Brilliant Van Effen."

"So your friends have returned, the Annecys back in Amsterdam. Lost no time in making their presence known and got at you in the very best way possible. God, I'm sorry, Peter."

"Feel sorry for the girls. Especially for Annemarie. It was just her fiendishly bad luck to be here when they came for Julie. It was that towering genius, Van Effen, of course, who had insisted that she remain here for her own safety. The demands should be arriving quite soon. You will not have forgotten, sir, that the Annecys were—and doubtless still are—specialists in blackmail." Van de Graaf shook his head and remained silent. "It's kind of you not to say so, Colonel. But you will also not have forgotten that they are specialists in torture, which was the real reason I hunted them down."

"We haven't been very clever so far," Van de Graaf said.

"Kind of you to say 'we,' sir. You mean me." Van Effen refilled Thyssen's glass, did the same for his own and sank into an armchair.

After perhaps two minutes, Van de Graaf looked at him and said: "Well, surely there's something we should be doing? Shall we start by making inquiries among the flat neighbors, the people living opposite?"

"To check on the modus operandi of the kidnappers? A waste of time, Colonel. We wouldn't find out any more than we already know. We're dealing with professionals. Although even professionals can make mistakes."

"I haven't seen any so far." The colonel was gloomy.

"Nor have I. I'm assuming that Julie was the target." Van Effen reached for the telephone. "With your permission, sir, I'll find out. Vasco. Sergeant Westenbrink. Aside from her 'gentleman friend' he was the only one who knew where Annemarie lived. They—whoever 'they' are—may have tried to find out by methods I don't care to think about."

"You think it likely? Or possible?"

Van Effen dialed a number. "Possible, yes. Likely, no. I don't think there's anyone in Amsterdam who could follow Vasco without his being aware of it; by the same token I don't think that there is anyone in the city who could be followed by Vasco and be aware of it. . . . Vasco? Peter here. Anyone been taking an interest in you since you left this morning? . . . Talked to nobody? Annemarie and my sister Julie have been taken away. . . . Within the past hour and, no, we have no idea. Put on your best civilian suit and come around, will you?" Van Effen hung up and said to Van de Graaf: "Julie it was. Nobody's been banging Vasco with crowbars."

"And you've asked him to join you?"

"Us, sir. He's far too valuable a man to be lying low and doing nothing. And, with your permission, sir, I'd like to try to recruit George."

"Your La Caracha friend? You said yourself he wasn't very good at merging into backgrounds."

"That's for Vasco. George, on the mental side, as you saw for yourself, is very acute and knows the criminal mind probably better than anyone I know; on the physical side he's a splendid insurance policy. So, progress. Damned little, but progress nonetheless."

"What kind?"

"I think it's now fairly safe to say that the Annecy brothers and the would-be blowers-up of the royal palace are working in cahoots. How else would the Annecys know that Rudolph Engel, who had been following one of the palace gang's intermediaries, had been done in and delivered to the morgue?"

"The palace gang, as you call them, could have done the kidnapping. The Annecys could have told them."

"Two things, sir. What possible motive could Agnelli and his friends have in abducting Lieutenant Van Effen's sister? None. The Annecys have a very powerful motive. The second thing is that it doesn't matter a damn whether the Annecys gave Agnelli this address or not; the point is that they sure as hell know each other."

"And how does this knowledge help us, Peter?"

"At the moment, it doesn't. And it may even actually put us at a disadvantage. They're not clowns and may well have figured out that we have figured out and exercise extra precautions because of that. Precautions against what, I can't imagine."

"Neither can I. We're doing nothing. There's nothing, as far as I can see, that we can do."

"One or two small things, perhaps. Alfred van Rees, to start with."

"What's Van Rees got to do with Agnelli and the Annecys?"

"Nothing. As far as we know. But we would at least be doing something about something. I suggest two tails on Van Rees. One to keep an eye on Van Rees, the other to keep an eye on the first tail. Just consider how lucky Mas Voight is to be still alive. Then I suggest we investigate Van Rees's bank statements."

"Whatever for?"

"This pillar of the Rijkswaterstaat may be giving the dike-blowers information that they couldn't get elsewhere. Selling, not giving. Could be, of course, that *if* he's picking up some money that he shouldn't, he might have it stashed away in another account under another name. But criminals—especially people who are not habitual criminals, and I assume Van Rees is not—often overlook the basics."

"Can't be done. Illegal. Man hasn't even been charged, far less convicted of anything."

"They've got Julie and Annemarie."

"So. What connection do they have with Van Rees?"

"None. Again, as far as we know. Although I was just thinking of one of the last things Julie said to me, that how extraordinarily odd it was that the dike-breakers, the palace bombers and the Annecy brothers should all happen along at the same time. Could be a coincidence. Could be too much of a coincidence. Or nothing. Maybe I just hate the whole wide criminal world. Forget it, sir. Just a suggestion."

The phone rang. Van Effen picked it up, listened, said thank you and hung up. "This should cheer us all up. There's going to be a radio broadcast of the F.F.F.'s latest communiqué in about ten minutes."

"Inevitable, I suppose. Your suggestion, Peter. Normally, I should dismiss it out of hand. But your suggestions have an extraordinary habit of turning up something." He smiled without humor. "Maybe you share—what's the word?—this precognition with your sister. We'll put those two tails on Van Rees—my God, the very idea of putting tails on Van Rees—*and* have his liquid assets discreetly investigated. I shall probably be arraigned before Parliament for this. Drag you down with me, of course." He reached for the phone. "Let me handle this."

After he had arranged matters in his customary imperious fashion and put the phone down, Van Effen said, "Thank you. Tell me, sir, do your linguistic friends at the university have all the tapes? Including the one I brought from the Hunter's Horn?" Van de Graaf nodded. "When do you expect them to be ready?"

"When they're ready, one supposes. Things move leisurely in the groves of academe."

"Think you could hurry them up, sir? National emergency, something like that."

"I can try." Van de Graaf called a number, spoke to someone he called Hector, then, still holding the phone, turned to Van Effen. "Six o'clock?"

"Five forty-five, if possible."

Van de Graaf spoke briefly, hung up and said, "Very precise about our timing, aren't we?"

"Person coming round at six-thirty to the Trianon to give me the radio data for detonating this bomb in the palace cellars."

"First I heard of it. One finds it uncommonly difficult to keep up. Rather droll, if I may say so, to find a police officer paying the courtesy of punctuality to a criminal."

"Yes, sir. Do you know—personally, I mean—any plastic surgeons?"

"Plastic surgeons! What on earth do you want with—well, I should know better, you'll have your reasons. But plastic surgeons? Do you think I know *everyone* in this city?"

"To my knowledge, sir, yes. Or nearly everyone."

"I could talk to the police surgeon."

"De Wit is *not* a plastic surgeon, sir."

"Ah! I have it. My old friend Hugh. Outstanding. Professor Hugh Johnson."

"Doesn't sound like a Dutch surgeon to me. I mean, he's not Dutch, is he?"

"English. Trained at East Grinstead. I'm told that's the best plastic surgery unit in Europe, if not the world. Man's a genius." Van de Graaf smiled. "Not as smart as the Dutch, though. Not specifically, as clever as one Dutch lady, a native of Amsterdam, whom he met here on an exchange visit. Six months after they got married he found himself domiciled in this country. Still doesn't know how it happened to him. The very man." Van de Graaf cleared his throat in a delicate fashion. "If you could give me some *slight* indication as to what you want—"

"Certainly. In the guise in which I meet Agnelli I have scars on my face and hands—remind me to tell you what I'll look like tonight when we meet at the university, otherwise you won't recognize me. I want those scars to look even more realistic and, more important, to be of such a nature that they can't easily be pulled off, washed off or scrubbed off."

"Ah. I see. I mean, I don't see." Van de Graaf pondered briefly. "Don't like this at all. You are referring, of course, to Agnelli and his friends and any suspicions they may harbor. I thought you were of the opinion that your bona fide status as an internationally wanted criminal was fairly secure."

"I believe so. But they don't sound like a lot with whom you take chances. Might even find a reason tonight to prove—without seeming to, of course—the genuineness and permanence of those scars."

Van de Graaf sighed. "We live in a devious world, a very devious world. Without wishing to give offense, Peter, I must say you seem perfectly at home in it. See what I can do. Damned phone again."

Van Effen picked it up, listened and said, "Send a man around with them, will you? Wait a minute." He turned to Van de Graaf. "Sergeant Oudshoorn. Says Number thirty-eight is deserted. Neighbors say nobody has lived there for years. Most of the furniture is gone, too. Oudshoorn—he's young, enthusiastic, I told you he'd relish this assignment, and we did give him a sort of carte blanche—has been investigating some locked cupboards and desk drawers."

"With the aid of crowbars and chisels, I suppose."

"I imagine so. I also imagine that it's extremely doubtful that we'll ever have any complaints on that score. Thing is, he says he's come across some odd-looking maps, charts and plans that he can't make head or tail of. Probably of no importance whatsoever. But we're in no position to overlook one chance in a thousand. I've asked Oudshoorn to have them sent round. Do you think that, en route, this messenger might pick up some knowledgeable lad from the City Surveyor's office who might just be able to enlighten us about those maps?"

"Chance in a thousand, as you say. Suppose you want me to do the dirty work?"

"Yes, sir." He spoke into the phone. "Tell whoever it is that's bringing the papers round to stop by the City Surveyor's office and pick up someone who will accompany him here. The colonel is arranging it."

While Van de Graaf was issuing his instructions over the phone—he never made requests—Van Effen turned on the radio and kept the volume low. When the colonel hung up the phone he still kept the volume low—the cacophonous racket of the latest music was not to Van Effen's taste—but turned it up when the noise stopped. The modulated voice of an announcer took over.

"We interrupt this program with a special news bulletin. The F.F.F. have issued another statement. It reads as follows:

"'We promised to breach the North Holland Canal or the Hagestein weir. Or both. We chose to breach the canal. The reason we did not damage the Hagestein weir is that we have never been within fifty miles of it. In spite of this we have to admit that the turnout of army, police, air force helicopters and the experts from the Rijkswaterstaat was most impressive.

"'It should now not be in doubt that we can cause flooding, of a degree according to our choosing, wherever and whenever we wish and that we can do this with impunity: the possibility of detection does not exist. The country's authorities, as we have pointed out before and have demonstrated again, are powerless.

"'We are sure that the people of the Netherlands do not

wish this state of affairs to continue. Neither, quite frankly, do we. We have certain terms that we wish to be met and would like to discuss those with a responsible member of the government. An arrangement for such a meeting, time this evening, location immaterial, should be broadcast over TV and radio at six P.M. this evening. No negotiator below the level of cabinet minister will be considered.

"'Our negotiator should not be apprehended, held as hostage or subjected to any degree of restraint. Should any of the authorities be so misguided as to do this, we would warn them that mines are already in position to the north and south of Lelystad. The mines, in this instance, are very much larger than on previous occasions and the repair of the breaches will be a matter of weeks. If our negotiator does not return to us by a certain hour to be agreed, then large portions of Oostlijk-Flevoland will be inundated. No warning will be given as to the time of those breaches; they will be sometime during the night.

"'We think it almost superfluous to point out that the responsibility for the safety of the Oostlijk-Flevoland and its inhabitants lies exclusively with the government. We do not ask for a great deal—just to speak with a government representative.

"'Should the government ignore our small request and refuse to appoint a negotiator, we shall go ahead and flood the polder. After that, when next we make a request, the government may deem it more prudent to be cooperative. We are sure that the citizens of the Netherlands would agree that for the government, motivated solely by affronted pride and stiff-necked outrage, to put this large area and those who live there at such risk, would be intolerable and unforgivable.

"'The time to cooperate is now, not when incalculable and avoidable damage has been done.

"'The mines are in position.'"

"That is the message in its entirety. The government have requested us—not ordered, requested—not to pass comment on or discuss this outrageous demand until they have decided what course of action to adopt. It wishes to reassure the people of this country that the government is confident that it has the resources at its command to meet this or any other threat."

Van Effen switched off the set. "God save us from politicians. The government is talking through a hole in its collective hat. It's been caught off-balance, hasn't had time to think—one charitably assumes it can think—and can do no better than trot out meaningless platitudes. Confident, they say. Confident of what? God's sake, they can't possibly be confident of anything, far less of themselves. Trust us, they say. I'd sooner trust the inmates of an asylum."

"Treasonable talk, Lieutenant Van Effen, treasonable. I could have you incarcerated for this." Van de Graaf sighed. "Trouble is, I'd have to incarcerate myself along with you, as I agree with every word. If the government honestly believes that the people will take their assertions at face value, then they're in even worse case than I thought. Which, I may add, I didn't think was possible. They are in an impossible situation. Do you think it even remotely possible that they don't recognize this?"

"They'll recognize it all right. Just as soon as they begin to think in terms of political survival. If they bury their heads in the sand, they'll be turned out of power within a week. An acute concern about preserving the status quo—their status quo—can work wonders. They have already blundered by having the commentator say that they have been requested—not ordered—not to discuss the affair. They have been ordered, not requested, otherwise the commentator, the news-reader, would not have used the term 'outrageous demand.' There's nothing outrageous in their demand. It's the demands that will be made when the meeting takes place—as, of course, it will do—that will be outrageous."

"Any discussion can only be speculative," the colonel said heavily. "So it's not worth the speculation. We have more urgent matters to attend to."

"There's a matter I should be attending to at this moment," Van Effen said. "I have an appointment at the Trianon. Well, a kind of appointment. There's a fellow there who will be expecting me but doesn't know that I'm expecting him. One of Agnelli's stake-outs. He's expecting to see me in my full criminal regalia—he's under the impression that I've been asleep all afternoon, and I mustn't disappoint him."

The phone rang. Van de Graaf answered it and handed it to Van Effen.

"Yes. Yes, Lieutenant Van Effen. . . . I'll wait. . . . Why should I?" He held the phone some inches from his ear. "Some clown advising me to avoid damage to my eardrums and to—" He broke off as a high-pitched scream, a feminine scream, not of fear but of agony, came from the earpiece. Van Effen jammed the phone against his ear, listened for a few seconds, then hung up.

Van de Graaf said, "What in God's name was that?"

"Julie. At least that's what the man said. Well, his words were: 'Your sister is slow in cooperating. We'll call again when she does.'"

"Torture," the colonel said. His voice was steady but his eyes were mad. "Torturing my Julie."

Van Effen smiled faintly. "Mine, too, remember? Possibly. The Annecy brothers' specialty. But it was just a shade too crude, too pat, too theatrical."

"God, Peter, she's your sister!"

"Yes, sir. I'll remind the brothers of that when I meet them."

"Trace the call, man! Trace the call!"

"No point, sir. I have good ears. I could just detect the faint overlay hiss of a recorder. That could have come from anywhere. And it's what makes me think it's a phony."

"Then why the devil was the call made?"

"Two reasons, perhaps, although I can only guess at them. I don't think they thought that I would even suspect that the call was not what it purported to be, that I would be so upset over my sister's kidnapping that I would take anything in its connection at face value. Second thing, of course, is that they're not after Julie, they're after me. This—at least to their highly suspect way of psychological reasoning—is part of the softening-up process."

Van de Graaf sat in silence, rose, poured himself another Van der Hum, returned to his seat, and said, "I hardly like to bring up this point, Lieutenant, but has it occurred to you that next time, or maybe the time after next, the Annecys may decide to abandon the psychological approach? And say something like, 'Surrender to us, Lieutenant Van Effen, or your sister will die, and we'll see to it that she dies very, very slowly. Would you do it?"

"Do what?"

"Give yourself up to them?"

"Of course. My appointment at the Trianon is overdue, sir. If there is any message for me, would you call me there? Stephan Danilov, if you remember. How long do you intend to remain here, sir?"

"Until I see those maps or charts or whatever that Sergeant Oudshoorn found, and until I can get Lieutenant Valken here to take over. I'll put him in the picture as far as I can."

"You have all the facts, sir."

"One would hope so," Van de Graaf said rather enigmatically.

When Van Effen had gone, Thyssen said curiously, "I know it's not my place to speak, sir, but would the lieutenant really do that?"

"Do what?"

"Give himself up?"

"You heard the lieutenant."

"But—but that would be suicide, sir." Thyssen seemed almost agitated. "That would be the end of him."

"It would be the end of someone, and that's a fact."

Van Effen returned, via the rear entrance, to his room in the Trianon, called the desk and asked for Charles.

"Charles? Van Effen. Has our friend returned? . . . Good. He will, I know, be in a position to hear every word you say. Kindly say the following into the phone: 'Certainly, Mr. Danilov. Coffee immediately and not to be disturbed afterward. Expecting a visitor at six-thirty.' Let me know when he's gone."

Some thirty seconds later Charles called to inform him that the lobby was empty.

Van Effen had just completed his metamorphosis into Stephan

Danilov when the phone rang. It was Van de Graaf, who was still at Julie's flat. He said he had something of interest to show Van Effen and could he, Van Effen, step round. Ten minutes, Van Effen said.

When Van Effen returned to the flat he found Thyssen gone and his place taken by Lieutenant Valken. Valken was a short, stout, rubicund character, easygoing except at the table: like the big boss, he was a trencherman of some note. Although several years older than Van Effen, he was his junior in the service, a fact that worried Valken not at all. They were good friends. Valken was, at that moment, surveying the alarmingly garbed Van Effen and speaking to the colonel.

"A reversal to type, wouldn't you say, sir? Cross between a con man and a white slaver, with just a touch of Mississippi riverboat gambler thrown in. Definitely criminal, anyway."

Van de Graaf looked at Van Effen's costume and winced. "Wouldn't trust him within a mile of either of my daughters. I don't even trust the sound of his voice." He indicated the pile of papers on the table before him. "Like to sift through all those, Peter? Or shall I just call attention to the ones that interest me?"

"Just the ones that interest you, sir."

"God, that voice. Fine. Top five."

Van Effen examined each in turn. They showed plans of what were clearly different levels of the same building; the number of compartments in each plan left no doubt that it was a very large building. Van Effen looked up and said, "And where's Van Rees?"

"Well, damn your eyes!" Van de Graaf was aggrieved. "How the hell did you know those were the plans of the palace?"

"Didn't you?"

"No, I didn't." Van de Graaf scowled, which he did rarely and with difficulty. "Not until that young architect or whatever from the City Surveyor's office told me. You do rob a man of his pleasures, Peter." Van de Graaf regarded himself as merely approaching the prime of his life.

"I didn't know. Just guessed. As I shall be inside that building within three hours, you can understand that my thoughts turn to it from time to time. Van Rees?"

"My old and trusted friend." Van de Graaf, understandably, sounded very bitter indeed. "Put him up for my *club*, by God! Should have listened to you earlier, my boy, much earlier. And we should have expedited the examination of his bank account."

"No bank account?"

"Gone. Gone."

"And so, one supposes, has Van Rees."

"Four million guilders," Van de Graaf said. "Bank manager thought it a highly unusual step to take, but—well—"

"One does not question the motives and the integrity of a pillar of the community?"

"Blackballed," Van de Graaf said gloomily.

"There are other clubs, sir. Schiphol, I assume, is still not open for operations?"

"You assume wrongly." The gloom remained in Van de Graaf's face. "Heard ten, fifteen minutes ago. First plane out, a KLM for Paris, took off about twenty minutes ago."

"Van Rees, clutching his millions, relaxing in the first class?"

"Yes."

"And no grounds for extradition. No charges against him yet. In fact, no hard evidence against him. That we'll get the evidence, I don't doubt. Then I'll go and get him. When all this is over, I mean."

"Your penchant for the illegal is well known, Lieutenant."

"Yes, sir. Meantime, I suggest that my penchants, your blackballing problem, and the fact that Van Rees is at the present moment entering French air space are not quite of primary importance. What does matter is that Van Rees—who has by this time passed over to the dike-breakers all they'll ever want to know about sluices, weirs and locks, so that they won't even miss him now—was also tied in with the would-be palace bombers. And we are as convinced as can be that the Annecy brothers are somehow in league with the bombers. It was Julie who first expressed the possibility of this idea, how too much of a coincidence can be too much of a coincidence, although I must say—with all due modesty and not with hindsight—that this possibility had occurred to me before."

"Your modesty does you credit, Lieutenant."

"Thank you, sir. It's well placed, given my appalling lack of progress. However, what we're faced with now is the probability—I would put it as high as certainty—that we are faced not with three different organizations but only with one. That should make things much simpler for us and easier to cope with."

"Oh. Of course, of course." Van de Graaf gave Van Effen the kind of look that stops well short of being admiring. "How?"

"How?" Van Effen pondered. "I don't know."

"Heaven help Amsterdam," Van de Graaf muttered.

"Sir?"

Van de Graaf was saved from enlarging on his brief statement by a knock on the door. Valken opened it to admit a lean gentleman with graying hair, rimless glasses and a faintly aristocratic air. Van de Graaf rose to his feet and greeted him warmly.

"Hugh, my friend. So kind of you to come and to come so quickly. At great inconvenience to yourself, I have no doubt."

"Not at all, my dear Chief, not at all. The patients of a plastic surgeon do not expire upon the spot if not attended to immediately. With a six-month waiting list, one can squeeze in the odd special patient here and there." He looked at the made-up Van Effen. "And if this is the patient, he's certainly odd . . . and special."

Van de Graaf made the introductions. "Professor Johnson. Lieutenant Van Effen. Lieutenant Valken."

"Ah. Lieutenant Van Effen. The colonel has explained your requirements to me. Rather unusual requirements, I may say, even in our at times somewhat bizarre profession—we tend to be called upon to remove scars, not inflict them. However."

He looked at the scar on Van Effen's face, produced a magnifying glass and peered more closely. "Not bad, not bad at all. You have quite an artistic bent, my dear fellow. Wouldn't deceive me—not when you've spent all your life studying thousands of different scars of every conceivable variety. But a layman is not a plastic surgeon, and I doubt very much whether any layman would question the authenticity of that scar. Let me see the dreadful wound concealed by that glove on your left hand." He did some peering. "By Jove, even better. You are to be congratulated. Very convenient to have it on your left hand, isn't it? But a trifle suspicious to the nasty-minded, perhaps? You are, of course, right-handed."

Van Effen smiled. "You can tell just by looking at me?"

"I can tell that left-handed persons don't carry barely concealed pistols under their left armpit."

"Too late for a transfer now, sir. I'm already identified as being a left-hand glove wearer."

"Yes. Well. I see. Your scars more than pass muster. The trouble, I suppose, is that you suspect that those scars might be subjected to some kind of test, such as with a scrubbing brush or even a hot soapy sponge?"

"A hot soapy sponge is all that is needed."

"Normally, you understand, the perfect nonremovable scar would take some weeks to achieve. I gather, however, that time is not on your side. Ah, Colonel. Is that Van der Hum I see?"

"It is indeed." The colonel poured a glass.

"Thank you. We don't generally advertise the fact, but members of our profession—well, before an operation, you understand?"

"*Before* an operation?" said Van Effen.

"A trifle," Johnson said soothingly. He took some brandy, then opened a small metal case to reveal a gleaming ladder of surgical instruments, most of them of a very delicate nature. "A series of subcutaneous injections with a variety of inert dyes. There will be no weals, no puffiness, I promise you. There will also be no local anesthetic. Takes better that way." He looked very closely at the facial scar. "Must have the position, size and color as before, you understand. Your left hand is unimportant. Nobody, I assume, has seen that scar. I can give you a much more satisfyingly horrific scar than you have now. Now, if I could have some hot water, sponge, soap."

Twenty-five minutes later and Johnson was through. "Not

my proudest achievement, but it will serve. At least, no one can pull or scrub those scars off. Have a look, Lieutenant."

Van Effen went to a mirror, looked, nodded and came back.

"First class, sir. A dead ringer for the one I had painted on." He surveyed his apparently horribly mangled left hand with melancholy admiration. "I've really been through it. After such a marvelous job, sir, it seems ungrateful to ask—but how permanent are those scars likely to be?"

"Not permanent at all. Those dyes are of a completely different chemical composition from tattoo pigments. Absorption times varies—two to three weeks. I shouldn't worry, Lieutenant—they're really quite becoming. Make you look like a man in a dangerous line of work."

Van de Graaf and Van Effen met Professor Hector van Dam, Professor Bernard Span and Professor Thomas Spanraft in the living room of Van Dam's house. They didn't look at all like professors or, more accurately, what stereotypical professors are supposed to look like. They looked more like a combination of prosperous businessmen and solid Dutch burghers, all curiously alike, all overweight, all cheerful and all with slightly flushed cheeks, which might have come from the overheated room or the large bottle of wine that circulated freely among them.

Professor Van Dam spoke. "Well, gentlemen, we think we have the answers you seek. Not too difficult, really. We have in this country linguistic specialists, both occidental and oriental—especially oriental, we have had vast experience of dealing with Asiatic languages over the centuries—as good as you will find anywhere in Europe. Professor Spanraft has come up specially from Rotterdam. No oriental knowledge in this case. I may start, perhaps, with my own small contribution."

He looked at Van Effen. "This gentleman you met in some café with the unusual name of Helmut Paderewsky. He is not Dutch and he is most certainly not Polish. He is, specifically and unquestionably, southern Irish."

"*Irish*?" said Van de Graaf.

"Even more specifically, he is a Dubliner. My qualifications for making so confident an assertion? A year as visiting scholar and lecturer at Trinity, Dublin. Bernard?"

Professor Span made an apologetic gesture with his hands. "My contribution, even smaller than Hector's, was pathetically easy. I am told that the other two gentlemen the lieutenant met in the same café with the splendid, if slightly unlikely names of Romero and Leonardo Agnelli, are dark-haired, dark-eyed and of a Mediterranean cast of countenance. Gentlemen of such appearance are not exclusively confined to an area south of the Alps. They are even to be found, as you must know, in our own predominantly fair-haired and fair-complexioned society. The Agnellis are two such."

"You are quite certain of that, sir?" Van Effen said. "I know Italy well and—"

"Lieutenant Van Effen!" Professor Van Dam was shocked. "If my colleague—"

Professor Span held up a placatory hand. "No, no, Hector, the lieutenant's query is a legitimate one. I gather that the inquiries in which he and the colonel are engaged are of a most serious nature." He smiled a deprecatory smile. "As a mere academic, of course—anyway, Lieutenant, rest assured that those gentlemen are as Dutch as you or I. My life on it. And at a guess—but an educated guess, mark you—from Utrecht. You are amazed, perhaps, by my certainty? Please do not be. My qualifications? Impeccable. I'm a Dutchman. From Utrecht. Your turn, Thomas."

Spanraft smiled. "*My* qualifications are similar to Hector's. This lady who makes all those mysterious phone calls. Young, beyond a doubt. Educated. Perhaps even highly so. Northern Ireland, specifically Belfast. My qualifications for this little analysis? Again, luck of the draw. I, too, have been a visiting scholar and lecturer. Queen's, Belfast." He smiled, then thought better of it. "Good heavens, I may even have taught the young lady."

"If you did," Van de Graaf said heavily, "you didn't teach her the right things."

* * *

Van de Graaf turned to Van Effen, who was driving a Volkswagen that evening. As it was not impossible that he might be called upon to drive one or more of Agnelli's group, it had been deemed more prudent not to use the Peugeot, where the presence of a police radio might have been inadvertently discovered. The VW's papers and insurance were, of course, made out in the name of Stephan Danilov.

"What do you make of the Irish connection, Peter?"

"I have no idea, sir. We know, of course, that petty criminals have in the past sold Russian and other Eastern bloc weapons to the Irish Republican Army; but these, as I say, were minor criminals operating on a relatively small scale. This, I feel, is bigger. The IRA never had any organization worth speaking of in this country. The F.F.F. definitely have. Where can I contact you later on this evening, sir?"

"I wish you hadn't mentioned that," Van de Graaf said. "Earlier, I had hoped to spend it in the bosom of my family. But now? If the government does decide to send an emissary to parley with the F.F.F.—good heavens, Peter, we completely forgot to listen in to the six o'clock news—the broadcast, rather, that was to state when and where the government would hold this parley."

"We've only to lift a phone. It's of no significance."

"True. This emissary I mentioned. Who, do you think, is the logical choice?"

"The Minister of Justice?"

"No other. My lord and master, whom you have frequently, actionably and accurately described as an old woman. Old women like to have their hands held. Who do you think would best play the part of nursemaid?"

"You'd make an admirable choice. In fact, I'm happy to say that you would be the best as well as the inevitable choice. Don't forget to take an umbrella big enough for both of you." Rain had begun to fall and fall so heavily that the Volkswagen's wipers failed adequately to cope with it. "You should consider yourself privileged, sir, to have a ringside seat at what may be, at least, a modest turning point in history."

"I'd rather have my own armchair by my own fireside."

Van de Graaf reduced visibility even more by drawing heavily on his cheroot. "But whatever seat I'm in tonight, it'll be a damned sight safer and more comfortable than the one you'll be in. Not that I would suppose for a moment that they have armchairs in the palace cellars." Van de Graaf, apparently concentrating on increasing the blue fug inside the car, lapsed briefly into silence; minutes later he said, "I don't like it, Peter. I don't like it at all. Too many ifs, buts and question marks."

"I have to admit that I'm not all that madly keen on it myself. But we've agreed—it's our only way in. And there's another thing I don't like too much and makes me more than glad that your friend gave those scars a degree of permanence. I mean, they may have reservations about me that I didn't suspect before."

"What makes you think that now?"

"A rather disquieting remark that one of those gentlemen let drop a few minutes ago—Professor Span, it was. He said he came from Utrecht. He is firmly of the opinion that the Agnelli brothers come from the same place."

"So?"

"It may have escaped your memory, sir, but Vasco—Sergeant Westenbrink—also comes from Utrecht."

"Damn it!" Van de Graaf said softly. The implications had struck him immediately. "Oh, damn it all!"

"Indeed. Cops and criminals generally have a working knowledge of each other. Two things may help, though. Vasco spent much of his time in Utrecht working under cover, and he's been in disguise—sort of—since he took up residence in Krakerdom. Imponderables, sir, imponderables."

"Your continued existence would seem to me to be another imponderable," Van de Graaf said heavily. "There is no call—"

"Yes, sir. I know, over and above the call of duty. Let's just say, as the British do, in for a penny, in for a pound, or, if you like, a calculated risk. By my calculations, the odds are on me." He pulled up outside Van de Graaf's house.

"I am glad that I'm not a betting man." He peered at his watch. "Six-seventeen. If I want to reach you in the next hour or so you will, of course, be in your room in the Trianon."

"Briefly only, sir. For about forty minutes, from, say, six forty-five onward, I'll be in La Caracha."

"The devil you will! La Caracha. I thought someone was delivering some data or whatever it is in the Trianon at six-thirty and that you were going to study that?"

"I don't have to look at it. I know how to operate radio-controlled detonations. When I explained to them at length the difficulties involved in radio detonation, that was for their benefit—and mine. Their benefit, to convince them that I really was what I purported to be, a whiz kid in explosives, who checks out every detail; my benefit, to find out how much they really knew about the subject, which appears to be little. Work that one out, sir—why so highly organized a group is anything but organized in what would appear to be a very—if not most—vital department. That's one of the reasons why I said that by my calculations the odds are on me—I think they may really *need* me and are leaning over slightly backwards to give me the benefit of the doubt.

"But the real reason for whatever optimism I have lies in La Caracha. You remember I asked Vasco to meet me in Julie's flat. I changed my mind about that; I think that the farther he and I—in my capacity of Danilov—keep away from the flat, the better. So I've arranged to meet him in La Caracha. I also took the liberty of phoning George and asking him if he would be interested in giving me a little assistance. He said he would be more than pleased. I did not—I repeat *not*, sir—co-opt him in your name. I thought there were some things you'd rather not know about—officially, that is."

"I see. You have a point. I sometimes wonder, Peter, how many things I don't know about, officially *and* unofficially, but now is not the time for brooding. I mean, you haven't the time. And how do you propose to have those two help guarantee your continued existence?"

"They will, I hope, be keeping an eye on me. A close eye.

Vasco, as I think I've mentioned, has no equal as a shadower. And George—well, he has other virtues."

"So I've noticed. May heaven help us all."

Agnelli's messenger arrived punctually at six-thirty, less than two minutes after Van Effen had arrived back in his room at the Trianon. A man, Van Effen reflected, ideally suited for his task—a small, drab, unremarkable nonentity of a man who could have been first cousin of the other nonentity who consumed so remarkably few drinks in the close vicinity of the reception desk in the lobby. He handed over a yellow envelope, said that someone would be around to pick Danilov up at seven forty-five and left, less than twenty seconds after his arrival.

"No," Sergeant Westenbrink said. He was seated with Van Effen and George in a small private room in La Caracha. "I don't know the Annecys—the two that you didn't put in prison, that is."

"Do they know you?"

"I'm sure they don't. I never came into contact with them. They left for Amsterdam about three years ago."

"Ah, I'd forgotten. Either of you hear this broadcast that was supposed to be made to the F.F.F.?"

"It was made," George said. "Minister of Justice's house. Eight P.M. Guarantees of immunity—I assume the government believes in the threat to turn the Oostlijk-Flevoland into a new sea."

"Well, doesn't concern us at the moment. You are sure you want to come in on this, George?"

George seemed to reflect. "Could be difficult. Dangerous. Might even be violence." He frowned, then brightened. "But one does get so tired of serving *Rodekool met Rolpens*."

"So. If you'll be kind enough to have your car outside the Trianon—or, shall I say, in the discreet vicinity—by seven-forty. Might leave in my Volkswagen, might be in the car of whoever comes to pick me up. I don't for a moment think you'll lose us but, in any case, you know we'll be heading in the general direction of the royal palace."

George said, "Does our chief of police know about us—our plans?"

"He knows about you two and that you'll be keeping a careful watch—I hope—over me. The rest, no. It would never do for us to go around breaking the law."

"Of course not," George said.

At precisely seven forty-five, Romero Agnelli himself came to collect Van Effen from the Trianon.

6

AS FAR AS one could tell, Romero Agnelli was in high good humor; but then, as far as one could tell, Agnelli was always in high good humor. Even the torrential rainfall drumming on the roof of the car had no effect on his spirits. The car was Agnelli's, a large and, Van Effen had been glad to note, fairly conspicuous green Volvo.

"Dreadful night," Agnelli said. "And worse still to come, I'm sure. Bad time of the year, this. Always a bad time. Gales, spring tides, north wind—must listen in to the eight o'clock forecast." Agnelli, Van Effen thought, was uncommonly interested in the weather conditions. "Busy day, Mr. Danilov?"

"If you call sleeping being busy, yes. Late in bed last night—late this morning, actually—and I didn't know what hour you'd keep me up tonight. You have not, Mr. Agnelli, been too free with information about your plans."

"Would you be in my situation? Don't worry, we won't keep you late. That information I sent round—it proved useful?"

"Everything I required." Van Effen pulled out the yellow envelope from under his coat. "Returned with thanks. I don't want to be found with that in my possession. Where's the radio?"

"In the trunk. In perfect condition, I assure you."

"I don't doubt it. Nevertheless, I shall want to see it. I trust the amatol, primers and rest are *not* in the trunk?"

146

Agnelli looked at him in amusement. "They're not. Why?"

"I'm thinking of the detonator. Usually made of some ful-minating powder, commonly a mercury derivative. Delicate. Doesn't like being jounced around. And I don't like being around when it's being jounced around."

"They're in a room we've hired off the Kalvetstraat."

"Would it be presumptuous of me to ask why the radio isn't with the explosives?"

"Not at all. I want to trigger the device in the palace from the Dam Square itself. Perhaps you wonder why?"

"Wonder or not, I'm not going to ask. The less I know, the better all around. I'm a great believer in the need-to-know principle."

"So, normally, am I." He switched on the car radio. "Eight o'clock. Forecast." The forecast, which came through almost immediately, was not encouraging. Wind, force seven, north, veering north-north-east, increasing, heavy rains, temperature dropping. Then followed some technical jargon about stationary depressions and a confident if depressing assertion that the weather would continue to deteriorate for the next forty-eight hours.

"Sounds bad," Agnelli said. His expression did not appear to reflect inner concern. "Lots of people, especially the middle-aged and older with longer memories, won't be feeling any too happy, especially with the recent comments about the decayed state of the dikes. Same conditions as caused those dreadful floods back in the fifties—and the dikes are in no better con-dition now than they were then."

"Putting it a bit strongly, isn't it, Mr. Agnelli? Think of the huge storm-surge barriers they've built in the delta area in the southwest."

"And what guarantee have we that the North Sea is going to be considerate enough to launch its attack against the delta area? Little point in locking your front door if the back door is falling off its hinges."

Agnelli parked his car in the Voorburgwal, reached into the back seat and produced two large umbrellas.

"Not that these are going to be much help in this downpour. Just wait a few seconds until I get the radio from the back."

Just over a minute later they were standing outside a door to which Agnelli had his own key. Beyond lay an ill-lit and dingy passageway, its floor covered with cracked linoleum. Agnelli furled his umbrella and gave a coded knock on the first door to the right—three taps, then one, then three. The door was opened by the man calling himself Helmut Paderewsky, who made an unsuccessful effort to restrain a scowl when he recognized the person accompanying Agnelli, who appeared not to notice it.

"Helmut you have met," Agnelli said and led the way into the room. Unlike the corridor, it was brightly lit and was large and furnished in surprising comfort. Leonardo Agnelli gave Van Effen a nod and a smile. Leonardo apart, there were four other people in the room, all young, all pleasant-looking and very respectable: two men and two girls, all looking like refugees from some university honors graduate course, the type that would have more than passed muster in any Parisian salon. They were also, Van Effen saw, of the type that, in the past decade, had not only been members of, but had organized and controlled so many politically motivated criminal groups in Germany and Italy. They were considerably more formidable than your common or garden-variety criminal who was concerned primarily with the accumulation of as much wealth as possible in the shortest time possible, but who would rapidly abandon all thought of ill-gotten gains if personal danger threatened; instead, they were fanatically dedicated people who would stop at nothing to achieve their own cherished utopias, no matter how bizarre, sick and undesirable those utopias might appear to the majority of their fellow men and women. They could, of course, have been genuine salon intellectuals who sought no more of life than the opportunity to discuss Proust and Stendhal, Hegelian and Kantian philosophies. But seekers after the higher truths did not commonly assemble in such secluded, clandestine fashion, especially not in the close vicinity of thirty-five pound blocks of amatol explosive, which Van Effen had observed neatly staked in a corner.

Agnelli indicated the two young men. "Joop and Joachim. They have other names, of course, but are not using them at the moment. Joop and Joachim, oddly alike in that both were thick-set, slightly stooped and wore horn-rimmed glasses, bowed slightly, smiled but refrained from reciprocal comment when Van Effen said he was pleased to meet them. Agnelli turned to a sweet-smiling brunette. "And this is Maria, who has also for the moment forgotten her surname."

"My, my," Van Effen said. "Imagine forgetting a name like Agnelli."

Agnelli smiled. "I didn't think you would be the man to miss much, Mr. Danilov. Yes, my sister. And this is Kathleen." Kathleen, petite and slender, had blue eyes, red-brown hair and a slightly humorous, slightly wry expression that in no way detracted from the fact that she was very pretty indeed.

"Kathleen?" Van Effen said. "But that's an Irish name. And, if I don't give offense, you're every man's concept of what an Irish colleen should look like. You know, the one in the song, 'I'll take you home again, Kathleen'?"

She made a mock curtsy. "You choose to flatter me. No offense. My mother is Irish. I'm quite proud of it, in my own Celtic way."

Professor Spanraft's putative ex-student, Van Effen knew. And the girl who had spoken over the telephone to the subeditor Morelis and others.

"It was promised that I would meet your leader tonight," Van Effen said. "He is not here."

"He asked me to convey his apologies," Agnelli said. "An urgent appointment that he couldn't break."

If one was courteous, Van Effen reflected, one did not break an appointment with the Minister of Justice.

"Those are all your group?"

"No." Agnelli waved a hand. "Those are all that are with us tonight."

"Pity I won't be able to further my acquaintance with them," Van Effen said. "They may be with us, but I won't be with them." He turned toward the door. "I trust they enjoy their trip to the cellars. Sorry, Mr. Agnelli. Good night."

"Wait a minute, wait a minute!" Agnelli, no longer smiling, was totally taken aback, his face registering his lack of comprehension and the sharp flush of anger.

"A minute? Not a second. Not in this company." Van Effen looked around the other equally startled and puzzled occupants of the room, his eyes and mouth dismissive and more than slightly contemptuous. "If you imagined that I was going to move into hostile territory—and no matter how good your inside information may be, the possibility of danger is always there—carrying explosives and with this bunch of amateur rubberneckers traipsing at my heels, you have to be out of your mind." He reached for the door handle. "Get yourself another demolitions man. Preferably from a madhouse."

"Is that what it is?" Agnelli smiled. "My dear fellow, those people are not coming with us. Do you think *I* am from a madhouse? Only you, Leonardo, and myself."

"Then what are all those people doing here? And don't tell me it's none of my business. I value my freedom above all things, and my freedom is endangered when unnecessary risks are taken. Don't you know that danger lies in numbers? Don't you think it's stupid to have your people holed up so near a place where you intend to carry out an illegal act? Don't you ever operate on the need-to-know principle?"

"This is *not* our base, Mr. Danilov. This is for one night only." Agnelli was slightly on the defensive, slightly uncomfortable. "Those people are here as observers."

"Observing what?"

"The effects of the explosion."

"Effects? The walls of Jericho come tumbling down? There'll be nothing to observe."

"Psychological effects. Reactions. Guide to our future plans."

"Effects on whom? The crowds thronging the Dam Square?" Van Effen looked at him incredulously. "That rain's torrential. There won't be a single living soul in the square tonight." He looked slowly round the unsmiling faces. "Sunday-school kids on a Sunday-school picnic. Cheap thrills? Or the feeling that they're not making a contribution, not really participating unless they're on the spot? God help us. Let's see all the gear you have." Enough moral ascendancy, Van Effen thought, was enough.

"Certainly." Agnelli tried not to hide the relief in his face. "Joop?"

"Yes, Mr. Agnelli." Joop opened a cupboard and brought out some boxes, which he set on the carpet and proceeded to open. "Primer. Detonators. Battery. The trigger mechanism. The setting on this—here—is activated by—"

"Joop."

"Yes?"

"Are you detonating this device?"

"No. Of course not."

"Why not?"

"Because I'm not an expert. Oh, I see. Sorry." Discomfited, Joop withdrew. Van Effen looked at Agnelli.

"You have the key for the radio box?"

"Yes, of course." He handed it over. "Please excuse Leonardo and me for a moment." Both men left by a side door. Van Effen unlocked the metal lid of the radio container and studied the controls on top of the radio. He turned the power on, touched a knob here, pulled a switch there, calibrated the gauges on a couple of dials and adjusted two wavelength bands. No one watching—and everyone was watching—could doubt the presence of an expert. He then studied the timing dial on the triggering mechanism, produced pad and pencil, made a few rapid calculations, then straightened, obviously satisfied.

"Nothing to it, really, is there?" Kathleen was smiling.

"Agreed. Can't imagine why I'm here." He stooped, locked the lid of the radio container and thrust the key into an inside pocket.

"You do trust people, don't you?" Kathleen said.

"No. Especially kids. But if you remove temptation from the reach of kids, then they can't possibly fall into it, can they? I have no wish to be blown up in the cellars of the palace."

He turned as Agnelli and his brother reentered the room. Both were dressed as policemen, Romero Agnelli as an officer, his brother as a sergeant. Van Effen surveyed them.

"You make an excellent inspector, Mr. Agnelli. Really most

becoming. Your brother looks the part, too, except for one thing: he's really at least five inches too short for the force."

"Short legs only," Agnelli said comfortably. "He's as tall as anyone when he's seated behind the wheel of a police car."

"You surprise me. About the police car, I mean. You have—ah—come into possession of one?"

"Not exactly. We have, shall we say, a car that looks exactly like a police car. Not too difficult." He looked at his watch. "A police car is expected at the palace in about twenty minutes."

"Expected?"

"But of course. We have friends and we have made arrangements. Joop, be so kind as to pack the equipment, will you?" He indicated two gray metallic cases that stood nearby.

"So you just drive up and walk inside?" Van Effen said.

"We believe in keeping things simple."

"Of course. No reason required, naturally. You just walk in."

"Yes." He indicated the two metal cases Joop was loading with equipment. "With those."

"Again, of course. You declare the contents?"

"Electronic detecting equipment. For locating hidden explosives."

"I didn't know there was any such thing."

"I don't believe there is. However, in this silicon-chipped, computerized and electroned age, people believe anything. The explosives we're looking for have—we believe—been secreted in the basements, somewhere. Underworld tip. So we go to the basements to look."

"Nervy," Van Effen said.

"Not really. Calculated risk, and we calculate that the risk is not very high. People don't normally publicize in advance the fact that they intend to do something which is the precise opposite of what they intend to do. And with those uniforms, the police car and the impressive set of credentials we have, we don't expect to experience too much trouble. We've even got a set of papers for you."

"Papers don't matter a damn to me. Nor does the fact that you haven't gone to the trouble to find me a uniform. What—"

"No uniform. You're a civilian expert. The papers say so."

"Let me finish. You two may—and very probably will—get off with your minimal disguises. But how am I going to disguise my scarred face and the fact that I have a crippled hand? My description will be in every paper in the country tomorrow."

Agnelli looked closely at the scar on Van Effen's face. "If you'll pardon the cruel remark, that really is a beauty. Joachim?" This to one of the two young men. "What do you think? Joachim, Mr. Danilov, is an art school student. He is also a makeup designer for theatrical groups. He requires quite a large case to carry all his stock-in-trade. As you can imagine, in an organization such as ours, we find our friend's specialized gifts invaluable."

"Do you have anything against beards, Mr. Danilov?" Joachim said.

"Not as long as they don't make me look worse than I already am."

"I have several in a suitably auburn shade. In your case, I'm afraid, it would have to be a beard of rather a luxuriant style. I know the one. I'll apply some paste."

"Just so long as I can get it off again."

"Forty-eight hours and it will fall off." Joachim left the room.

"About that black glove, Mr. Danilov," Agnelli said.

"I'm afraid there is nothing they can do with that."

"How can you be sure?"

"How can I be sure? If you'd a hand like mine. . . . Don't you think I'd have tried anything—everything—to camouflage it?" Van Effen let just the right note of bitterness creep into his voice.

"Nevertheless, perhaps I might see it?" Agnelli's voice was gently insistent. "I promise you I won't say 'Good God above' or swoon or anything of the kind."

Van Effen, being ostentatious without appearing to be, turned his back on the rest of the company and peeled off the black glove. He held his hand up to within a foot of Agnelli's face.

Agnelli's normally mobile face became still. He said: "I

promised you I wouldn't say 'Good God' or—but, well, I've never seen anything like it before. How in heaven's name did this happen?"

Van Effen smiled. "Legitimately, believe it or not. Someone made a mistake when we were trying to cap an oil fire in Saudi Arabia."

"One trusts he paid for the mistake?"

"There and then. He was incinerated."

"I see. In which case one might almost imagine you've been lucky." Agnelli took Van Effen's wrist and touched the scars with his fingernails. "That must hurt."

"Not the slightest. Skin's paralyzed. Stick a row of needles into it or slice it with a scalpel. Wouldn't feel a thing." It would be unfortunate, Van Effen thought, if Agnelli took him at his word. "It's unimportant. All that matters is that I can still oppose finger and thumb."

Joachim came back and Agnelli said, "Do you mind if Joachim looks at this?"

"If he's the sensitive artistic type, I should imagine he'd be better off looking elsewhere."

Joachim looked and failed to hide the revulsion in his face. "That's—that's *awful*! I couldn't—I mean—how can you bear to go about like that?"

"I don't have much option. It's the only left hand I've got."

Joachim said, "You'd better put your glove back on. There's nothing I—nothing anyone can do about that."

"Time to go," Agnelli said. "Helmut, we'll meet you and the others down in the Dam in about half an hour, perhaps forty minutes. Don't forget the radio."

"The radio?" Van Effen said. "You're going to operate the radio in this monsoon?"

"We have a minibus. Where's the key to the radio?"

"In my pocket," Van Effen said. "I thought it might be safer there."

"I'm sure you're right."

They left, taking the metal cases with them. Agnelli stopped at a door close to the entrance, opened it, went inside. He reappeared, leading a Doberman pinscher which had about it the homicidal appearance shared by many members of its breed; it was, reassuringly, muzzled.

"Is that animal as unloving as it looks?" Van Effen asked.

"I've had the good fortune never to find out. However, he's not here for the purposes of either defense or attack. Doberman pinschers can be trained to smell out explosives. Use them at airports. Fact."

"I know it's a fact. Has this dog been so trained?"

"Quite frankly, I have no idea. For all I know, his olfactory nerves may be paralyzed."

"I'm beginning to believe that you might even get off with this," Van Effen said.

They made the best time they could through the drenching rain and were back at the spot where they had parked the Volvo in the Voorburgwal. Van Effen had his hand on the door when he realized that it was not, in fact, the car in which they had arrived.

Van Effen got into the back seat beside Agnelli and said, "You leave your own car here and come back and find a police car. You know, I do believe that you are going to get away with it after all. You do have your organization."

"Organization is all," Agnelli said.

Everything went off as Agnelli had confidently expected. They were expected at the palace and their credentials received only the most cursory inspection; they and the car were so patently official that a more detailed examination could only have seemed superfluous. Besides, it was still raining heavily and it was cold, and the guards were anxious to get back into the shelter as soon as they could.

Agnelli led them to a doorway that was so completely shrouded in darkness that he had to use a pencil torch to locate the keyhole of a door, a keyhole for which, as he had promised, he had the key. He also had a succession of keys which he used two flights of stairs down to open a succession of cellars. He knew the location of every door, every light switch.

"You lived here?" Van Effen asked.

"I've been here a couple of times. One has to be fairly

meticulous about these things." He led the way through a completely empty cellar into another equally bare cellar and said, "This is the place. Not too difficult, was it?"

"I find it hard to believe," Van Effen said. "They do have security systems here?"

"Excellent ones, I'm told. But security is a relative term. There is no security net that can't be breached. Look at Buckingham Palace, for instance. One of the tightest security shields in the world, but, as has been proved several times in the past year or so, any semi-intelligent person—and, indeed, those of a considerably lower IQ—can go in and out whenever they feel so inclined. Well, Mr. Danilov, it's yours."

"Minutes only. Open this far door for me—if you have the key."

Agnelli had the key. Van Effen produced a tape and proceeded to measure the thickness of the walls. He said, "How come all these cellars are so empty?"

"They weren't a few days ago. They were pretty well filled with old furniture, archives, things that you expect to collect in a royal palace over the years. Not that we were concerned with the well-being of those antiquities, most of which were just ancient rubbish anyway. But it was no part of our plan to burn the palace down."

Van Effen nodded, said nothing, went out—accompanied by Agnelli—and climbed a flight of steps to work out the thickness of the ceiling. He returned to the cellar, made a few calculations on a piece of paper, then said, "We'll use the lot. Those walls are stouter than I expected. But the resulting bang should still be satisfactory."

"Always a pleasure to watch a pro at work," Agnelli said.

"No more than it is to watch a journeyman bricklayer. He does his five years' apprenticeship. I've done mine."

"There's a difference, I suggest, between dropping a brick and dropping a detonator."

"A skilled tradesman never drops anything." Van Effen busied himself for two minutes, then said, "Did you say that you have the duplicate keys for the cellars we've just passed through?"

"I did and I have."

"So no one else can get near this place?" Agnelli shook his head. "So. Finished."

Their departure was no more eventful than their arrival had been. Less than ten minutes after Van Effen had inserted the detonator into the primer they parked their car behind a dimly lit minibus.

As they stepped out, a figure emerged from the shadows. He came up to Agnelli. "All well, sir?"

"No problem, John."

"Good night, sir." The man got into the police car and drove off.

"More organization," Van Effen said. "Formidable."

The five people they had left in the room close by the Voorburgwal were all seated in the minibus, which, being a fourteen-seater, was considerably larger than its name suggested. Van Effen and Agnelli sat in the wide seat in the back.

Van Effen said, "May one ask how long you expect to wait here?"

"Of course." Agnelli had become more than his usual smiling self in the past few minutes; he was now positively jovial. He had shown no signs of strain inside the palace, but strain there must have been. "Not quite sure myself, to be honest. A few minutes, perhaps. Certainly no more than twenty. But first, one must beware of lurking and suspicious policemen. Leonardo? Catch."

He threw something to his brother, stood up, and shrugged his way into a long gray raincoat. Then he sat, reached below the seat, pulled out a machine that looked like and was a radio transceiver, flicked a switch that made a red light glow, and brought up a headband with one earphone, which he draped over his knee. He reached down again and brought up a microphone the lead of which was, presumably, attached to the transceiver.

"Sorry I have to keep you waiting," he said, almost apologetically. "But I, in turn, have to await a call."

"More organization," Van Effen said. "Admirable. But there is one area in which your organization falls down."

"Inescapably." Agnelli smiled. "In what respect?"

"No heat in this vehicle."

"An oversight. Maria?"

"It's by the radio."

Agnelli reached under the seat and, with some effort, started to bring up something heavy. Van Effen tensed. Shortly, Agnelli produced a large wicker basket, which he placed on the seat between Van Effen and himself. He opened the lid to reveal a splendidly appointed interior.

"What did you expect, Mr. Danilov? A picnic basket for the Sunday-school picnickers. If we cannot have external warmth, at least we can provide some of the internal variety." The contents of the basket bore out his claim. Apart from two rows of gleaming glasses and packets of sandwiches neatly wrapped in cellophane, it held a very promising variety of bottles. "We thought we might have something to celebrate this evening," he said, again almost apologetically, "and I do think we have. A schnapps, perhaps, Mr. Danilov?"

Van Effen said, "I withdraw my remarks about your organization."

Agnelli hadn't even had time to begin to pour the schnapps when the transceiver buzzer rang. He clamped on the headpiece and acknowledged the call, then listened in silence for almost a minute. He said, "Yes, they are foolish. They have no place to go. So a little persuasion to tip the balance? Call me back in one minute." He took off the headpiece. "Well, who's the volunteer to press the button?"

There were no volunteers.

"Well, then, I suggest you, Mr. Danilov. You're the man who prepared the charges, so, of course, we'll all blame you if the explosion turns out to be a damp squib or, alternatively, the palace falls down. So perhaps it's only fitting that you press the button also. That way the rest of us will all feel blameless while you—"

He wasn't given time to complete his sentence. Van Effen stabbed the button, and less than two seconds later, deep and muffled like a distant underwater explosion but very unmistakable for all that—to anyone with normal hearing, the sound must have been audible over half a mile away—the reverberation from the detonating amatol rolled across the square. Van Effen took the bottle from Agnelli's unresisting hand—Agnelli, not smiling, and with lips parted, seemed to be seeing something very far away—and poured himself a schnapps.

"Seems I'll just have to congratulate myself. A nice loud bang but the royal walls still stand. As guaranteed. My health."

"That was splendid," Agnelli said warmly. He was back on his own usual smiling balance again. "Perfectly splendid, Mr. Danilov. And no damage after all that noise. Unbelievable."

"Perhaps a little royal wine spilled on the royal tablecloth." Van Effen made a dismissive gesture. "I don't want to seem unduly modest—not in my nature, really—but that was next to nothing. Next time—if there is a next time—something a little more demanding perhaps."

"There'll be a next time. That I promise. *And* a little more exacting. That I also promise." He paused to sip some schnapps as the others, excited and elated, turned to congratulate Van Effen, then held up a hand for silence as the buzzer rang again.

"Ah! You heard it also, did you? Very, very satisfactory. Mr. Danilov is a man of his word." He was silent for almost a minute, then said, "Yes, I agree. I'd been thinking along those lines myself. Most fortuitous, most . . . Thank you. Ten o'clock, then."

He replaced headpiece and microphone, then leaned back in his seat. "Well now, time to relax."

"You relax," Van Effen said. "Not me. If you're not moving on, I am." He made to get up and a puzzled Agnelli caught his arm.

"What is wrong?"

"There's nothing wrong with me. It's just, as I've told you, that I've got a very acute sense of self-preservation. As soon as the police come to their senses—if they ever lost them, they're a pretty efficient bunch hereabouts—they're going to start questioning everyone within eyesight of the palace. I should imagine—no, I'm certain—that a minibus with eight odd characters such as us parked in a rainstorm in the Dam would be of interest. A prime target for questioning." He shrugged off Agnelli's hand and rose. "I've an acute aversion to being questioned by police. A criminal—and we are criminals—has to be some kind of undernourished lunatic to remain in the vicinity of his crime."

"Sit down. You're right, of course. Foolish of me—one should never let one's guard down. Helmut?"

Paderewsky drove off at once.

Back in the room they had so recently vacated Agnelli sank into an armchair. "Thank you, ladies, thank you. Schnapps would be fine. Now, perhaps, Mr. Danilov, we can relax."

"Safer than where we were. But relax? For me, no. Still too close. Instinct? Plain cowardice? I just don't know. Anyway, I have an appointment tonight. Nine-thirty."

Agnelli smiled. "You were pretty sure that you were going to keep that appointment?"

"Never had any reason to doubt it. No, that's not quite accurate. I never had reason to doubt that the arranging of the explosion was simple. I had ample reason to question your ability to get us in and out undetected. But then, I had no reason beforehand to be aware of your rather remarkable organizational ability. I'll have no doubts about you again."

"Nor we of you—not after tonight's performance. I had mentioned the possibility of finding a permanent niche with us. That's no longer a possibility, it's a guarantee—if you're still of the same mind."

"Of course I'm of the same mind. Tonight, you had a free demonstration. Now, I would appreciate some steady employment."

"The point I was about to raise. I think you are now entitled to be taken into our confidence."

Van Effen looked at him in silence, took a thoughtful sip of his schnapps and smiled. "Not your full confidence. You're not about to tell me your ultimate aims. You are not going to tell me how you came together. You're not going to tell me how you are financed or by whom. You are not going to tell me where you stay—although, if we're to work together in however limited a capacity, you'll have to give me some intermediate contact phone number. You're not even going to tell me why, in what would appear to be an otherwise highly organized setup, you require my services at such a late date."

Agnelli was thoughtful. "That's a lot of things you seem to be certain that we're not going to tell you. How come?"

Van Effen let a little impatience show. "Because that is the way I would behave myself. The need-to-know principle. I'm sure I don't have to remind you of that again. What I do believe is that you are about to let me into your very limited confidence about your immediate operational plans. No abnormal prescience on my part. You have to. If, that is to say, I'm to be of any use to you."

"Correct on all counts. Tell me, Mr. Danilov, are you in a position to acquire as well as set off explosives?"

"Good God!"

"Is that so extraordinary a question to ask?"

"My astonishment was not that you asked. I'm just surprised that—well, that such an organized group should embark upon what I take to be an ambitious project without the essentials to hand."

"We have some of what you call the essentials. We may not have enough. Are you in a position to help?"

"Directly, no."

"Indirectly?"

"Perhaps. I would have to make inquiries."

"Discreet, of course."

Van Effen sighed. "Please. If it were possible to obtain explosives without official permission in the Netherlands, you would already have done so."

"Sorry. Silly remark. But we have to protect ourselves. Your contact would not, of course, obtain supplies—if he could—in a legitimate fashion?"

"I'm not being indiscreet in saying that, to the best of my knowledge, my contact has never been involved in any legitimate dealings in his life. He would regard it as an affront to his professional code. He is also, incidentally, the only man in the country who knows more than I do about explosives."

"Sounds like a person whose acquaintance it might be useful to make." Agnelli studied his glass and looked up at Van Effen. "Not by any chance your friend Vasco? The person who introduced us at the Hunter's Horn?"

"Good Lord, no." Van Effen creased his brow and compressed his lips. "Vasco is hardly what you might call my friend, Mr. Agnelli. I got him out of bad trouble once, and have employed him occasionally on some none-too-demanding errands. But we are not soul-mates. I'm quite certain that Vasco knows nothing about explosives, has no access to them and would find it difficult to obtain a child's cap pistol in a toy shop."

Agnelli turned to his brother and shrugged. "Had we known that, Leonardo, you wouldn't have spent so much time looking for him this afternoon."

"Vasco frequently disappears," Van Effen said. "Has a girl friend in Utrecht, I believe. You are seriously trying to tell me that you were, also seriously, thinking of engaging Vasco's services?"

"Not exactly, but—"

"He comes in the front door and I go out the back and that's that," Van Effen said. "He's unstable, unpredictable and dangerous, whether he means to be or not."

"I don't quite understand what you mean by that."

"And I don't quite understand you. You mean you've never even bothered to check on him, his background?"

"We didn't check yours."

"You didn't have to," Van Effen said bleakly. "Not with all those extradition warrants hanging around."

Agnelli smiled. "That was this morning, and this morning has been forgotten. You know something about Vasco that we don't."

"Obviously. He's bad. Poison. The classic example of gamekeeper turned poacher. He's treacherous and a man full of hate. He hates the law and the society that law protects— or is supposed to protect. He's that most dangerous of criminals, an ex-cop gone wrong."

"A policeman?" Agnelli's surprise, Van Effen thought, was nicely done. "Police!"

"Ex. No public accusation of wrongdoing, far less a trial. Dismissed without explanation—although doubtless there would have been an explanation made to Vasco. Just try making some discreet inquiries at the Utrecht police station about a certain ex-Sergeant Westenbrink and see what kind of dusty answers you get. My friend George is a different kettle of fish entirely. A firm believer in honor among thieves. An honest criminal, if we understand such a contradiction in terms."

"This George is your explosives friend?" Van Effen nodded. "He has a second name?"

"No."

"Do you think he'd work for me?"

"George never works for anyone. He might be prepared to work *with* someone. Another thing. George never works *through* anyone. Not even through me. He's a very careful man. His police record is clean and he wants to keep it that way. He talks to principals only and then it must be face to face."

"That's the way I like it. Do you think you could get him to talk to me?"

"Who knows? I could ask. Not here, though."

"Why not?"

"Because I'd advise him against it. He knows I wouldn't do that without reason. Where can I contact you?"

"I'll contact you. At the Trianon."

"I won't make any comments about how touching your trust in me is. Tomorrow morning."

"Tonight. Ten o'clock."

"You *are* in a hurry. No point, I suppose, in asking you the compelling nature of this deadline you have to meet. Besides, I told you, I have a nine-thirty appointment."

"Ten o'clock." Agnelli rose. "You will of course try to see your friend immediately. I'll put a car at your disposal."

7

"**T**HAT'S AN ISFAHAN you're standing on," Colonel Van de Graaf said. "Very rare, very expensive."

"I've got to drip onto something," Van Effen said reasonably, "rare rug or not." He was standing before the fire in the colonel's luxuriously furnished library, steam gently rising from his saturated clothing. "Not for me a door-to-door, chauffeur-driven limousine. *I* have to cope with taxis that go home to roost with the first drop of rain and with people who seemed anxious to know where I was going. It would not have been good form to let them know that I was going to the house of the chief of police."

"Your friend Agnelli doesn't trust you?"

"Difficult to say. Oh sure, it was Agnelli who had me followed—couldn't have been anyone else. But I'm not sure that he's suspicious of me—I think, on principle—or, in his case, lack of principle—he just doesn't trust anyone. Difficult character to read. You'd probably like him. Seems friendly and likable enough—you really have to make an effort to associate him with anything like blackmail and torture—and even then you find it difficult to convince yourself. Which means nothing. I assume you had a comfortable evening, sir—that you didn't have to cope with the elements or the thought that you might be shot in the back at any moment."

Van de Graaf made a dismissive gesture that could have

meant either that such considerations were irrelevant trifles or that they could not possibly apply to him in the first place. "An interesting meeting, but only to a limited extent. I'm afraid Robert wasn't in a particularly receptive or cooperative frame of mind."

"Robert Kondstaal, our Minister of Justice, is a dithering old woman, scared to accept responsibility, unwilling to commit himself and looking to pass the buck elsewhere."

"Exactly. I couldn't have put—I've told you before, Peter, that's no way to talk about cabinet ministers. There were two of them. Names Riordan and Samuelson. One—the person calling himself Riordan—could have been in disguise. The other had made no attempt at any such thing, which can only mean that he's pretty confident about something or other. Riordan had long black hair—shoulder-length, in fact, I thought that ludicrous style had gone out of fashion ten years ago—was deeply tanned, wore a Dutch bargee cap and sunglasses. Tall."

"Anything so glaring has to be a disguise." Van Effen thought for a moment. "He wasn't by any chance *very* tall and preternaturally thin?"

Van de Graaf nodded. "I thought that would occur to you. Yes, Alpine. The fellow who commandeered that canal boat from—who was it?"

"At Schiphol? Dekker."

"Dekker. This must be the man Dekker described. And damned if I don't agree with your bizarre suggestion that this fellow—Riordan or whatever—is an albino. The dark glasses. Heavy tan to hide an alabaster complexion. Black hair to hide white. Other fellow—Samuelson—had white hair, thick and very wavy, white mustache, and white goatee beard. No albino, though—blue eyes. All that white hair would normally bespeak advanced years, but his face was almost completely unlined. But then, he was very plump, which may account for the youthful skin. Looked like a cross between a U.S. senator and some bloated plutocrat, oil billionaire or something like that."

"Maybe he's got a better makeup man than Riordan."

"Possible. Both men spoke in English, from which I assumed that Samuelson couldn't speak Dutch. Both made a point of stating that they were Irish-Americans and I have no doubt they were. I don't have to be Hector or one of his professorial friends to know that—the New York accent was very strong. Samuelson didn't say much. Riordan did nearly all the talking.

"He asked—no, he demanded—that we contact the British Government. More exactly, he demanded we act as intermediaries between the F.F.F. and Whitehall."

"Whitehall? Why, in God's name?"

"On the basis that Whitehall would be much more likely to negotiate with another government than with an unknown group such as they are. When Robert asked what on earth they could possibly want to discuss with Whitehall, they said they wanted to have a dialogue about Northern Ireland. But they refused to elaborate further until the Dutch Government agreed to cooperate."

Van de Graaf sighed. "Whereupon, alas, our Minister of Justice, seething and fulminating, while at the same time knowing damn well that they had him over a barrel, climbed onto his high horse and said it was inconceivable, unthinkable, that a sovereign nation should negotiate on behalf of a band of terrorists. He carried on for about five minutes in this vein, but I'll spare you all the parliamentary rhetoric. He ended up by saying that he, personally, would die first.

"Riordan said that he very much doubted that Kondstaal would go to such extraordinary lengths and further said that he was convinced that fourteen million Dutchmen would take a diametrically opposite point of view. Then he became rather unpleasantly personal and threatening. He said it didn't make the slightest damn difference to anything if Kondstaal committed suicide on the spot. The Oostlijk-Flevoland dike in the vicinity of Helystad would go at midnight if the government didn't agree to talk terms by ten o'clock tonight. He then produced a paper with a list of other places which, he said, were in immediate danger of going at any moment. He didn't say whether or not mines had already been placed in those areas—the usual uncertainty technique.

"Among the places he listed—there were so many that I

forget half of them—were Leeuwarden, the Noordoostpolder in the vicinity of Urk, the Amstelmeer, the Wieringermeer, Putten, the polder south of Petten, Schouwen, Duiveland and Walcheren—did we remember what happened to Walcheren during the war? Both the eastern and western Schelde estuaries were on their list, he said—did we remember what happened there in February 1953?—while Noord and Sud Holland offered a positive embarrassment of riches. That's only a representative sample. Riordan then started to make sinister remarks about the weather. Had we noticed how high the level of the North Sea had risen, how the strengthening wind had gone to the north and that the spring tides were at hand, while the levels of the Rhine, Waal, Maas and Schelde were near an all-time low? So reminiscent of February 1953, didn't Kondstaal think?

"He then demanded that they talk to a minister or ministers with the power and courage to make decisions and not a sniveling time-server bent only on preserving his own miserable political career, which was, I thought, a bit hard on Robert.

"Riordan then said that, to display their displeasure at this wholly unnecessary hiatus in negotiations, they would detonate one of several devices they had placed in public buildings in the capital. Here the two of them had a whispered conference and then Riordan announced that they had chosen the royal palace and defied anyone to find the explosives before they went off. No lives, he said, were at risk in this explosion, which would occur within five minutes of their departure. He added, almost as an afterthought, that any attempt to restrain them, hinder their departure or have them followed would inevitably mean that the Oostlijk-Flevoland dike would go not at midnight but at nine o'clock this evening. On this happy note, they left. The palace explosion, as you may know, duly occurred."

"So I believe." It seemed the wrong moment to tell Van de Graaf that it was he, Van Effen, who had pressed the button. He shivered and moved to a less damp patch on the Isfahan. "I think I'm getting pneumonia."

"There's brandy." Van de Graaf waved a hand at once indicative of preoccupation and irritation: one should be unaware of the universal specifics against pneumococci. "Schnapps, scotch—" He broke off as a knock came on the library door and a uniformed policeman admitted George and Vasco, who were, if anything, even more saturated than Van Effen had been. "Two more advanced cases, I suppose."

George said, "Beg your pardon, Colonel?"

"Pneumonia. Help yourselves. I must say I wasn't expecting you gentlemen."

"The lieutenant said—"

"I know. It just slipped his memory."

"I have a lot on my mind," Van Effen said. "Well?"

"We had a good look at them when they left the house to go to that small bus. Also had a good look at them in the Dam Square. Recognize them anywhere." George paused reflectively. "Seemed a harmless-looking bunch to me."

"Ever seen—or seen pictures of—the young assassins who made up the Baader-Meinhof gang? All they lacked were harps and halos. When I said 'Well,' that wasn't what I meant."

"Ah! That. Yes. Well." George seemed slightly embarrassed. "When you left the house—we saw you go but didn't approach you as you'd asked us not to in case you were being followed—you know you *were* followed?"

"Yes."

"We waited across the street for ten minutes, then crossed to the lighted window. The rain! Talk about standing under Niagara Falls." He waited for sympathetic comment and when none came went on, "Waited another ten minutes. We could hear music and conversation."

"I'll bet you could. So then, overcome by the rain, impatience or suspicion, you moved in. Light still on. Long-playing cassette on a recorder. Birds flown by the back door."

Both men looked sheepish.

"Hardly original. So we still don't know where they're holed up. O.K., not your fault—Agnelli's obsessed by security."

"Still could have done better," Vasco said. "Next time—"

The phone bell shrilled and Van de Graaf picked it up, listened for some time, said, "Wait a minute, sir," and cupped the mouthpiece. "Kondstaal. Seems the Cabinet is a bit shaken about the palace explosion and is convinced that the Oostlijk-Flevoland dike will go up at midnight. So they're going to parley. They want me along and suggested eleven P.M. I'd like you to be there. Eleven P.M.?"

"Eleven-thirty possible, sir? I have a couple of appointments."

Van de Graaf spoke into the phone, then hung up. "You seem to have a very crowded appointment book, Lieutenant. I can't recall your mentioning any of this to me."

"Haven't had a chance to. I have to be at the Trianon at ten o'clock to take a call from Agnelli. He's a bit short of explosives and I've promised to supply him with some."

"Explosives. Of course." Van de Graaf hardly spilled a drop as he poured himself a brandy. "Having already blown up the palace"—it was an exaggeration but a pardonable one in the circumstances—"one would expect us to supply them with more powder. And where do you intend to find these explosives? I'm sure you won't be wanting more than a few hundred tons of TNT or whatever it is."

"Me? Haven't the time. Haven't the authority, either. But I thought, perhaps, sir, if you would care to use your influence—"

"Me? The chief of police? To supply illegally come-by explosives to a group of terrorists?" Van de Graaf considered. "And I suppose you expect me to deliver it personally?"

"Good heavens, no. That's where George comes in. Sorry, George, haven't had the chance to explain this or anything. Had a long talk this evening with Agnelli about you and Vasco. I'm afraid, Vasco, that I've blackened your character beyond all hopes of redemption. You're a crooked cop, bent as a horseshoe, untrustworthy, unpredictable and only a couple of steps removed from a psychiatric ward. Agnelli was just that little bit too casual when asking questions about you. I'm certain he knows you are or were a cop. He comes from Utrecht, too. Not that that should be any bar to his employing you—after we've made certain delicate alterations to your appearance and history—in the not-too-distant future.

"George, you're an arms dealer. Heaven knows there are

enough of those around, but you're something special. The kingpin. Mr. Big. A Leopard tank? A SAM missile? Even a motor torpedo boat? George is your man. And being Mr. Big means you're important. You talk only to principals. No intermediaries, not even me. Face to face or no deal."

"I talk to this Agnelli?" George smiled widely. "You want me on the inside?"

"I have a feeling that I could do with a little help, sooner rather than later. I've no right to ask you, of course. There's Annelise and your kids. Things might get a little difficult—"

"A little difficult!" Van de Graaf could put a nicely sarcastic edge to his voice when he had a mind to. "Difficult. I don't say it's crazy because nothing's crazy if there's a chance, but I don't like it at all. It's based on the assumption that they're not on to you and that's unjustifiable. Sure, they've gone along with you so far and you with them, but that's only because, so far, it's suited you both. But if they are on to you and they decide a time has come when you're of no further use to them, then when the time comes to discard you it will be permanently. Have you the right to ask that of George?"

"I've just done that."

The phone rang again and Van de Graaf said, "Ah. Lieutenant Valken . . . Yes, yes." Van de Graaf's face became still as he listened. "Never mind if you've never heard it before. Wait till I get a piece of paper and pen." Van de Graaf wrote down a few words, told Valken good-bye and hung up. He reached for his glass.

Van Effen said: "Julie, Annemarie?"

"Yes. How do you know?"

"Valken, your face, brandy. Bad?"

"Bad enough. Phone call from the brothers. They say the girls are as well as can be expected, which can mean anything or nothing. They also say they've sent a telegram of condolences to Rotterdam." He picked up the piece of paper he'd scribbled on. "To David Joseph Karlmann Meijer."

Van Effen sipped his brandy and said nothing. George and Vasco exchanged glances of incomprehension. At length George said, "Who's he?"

"I forgot," Van de Graaf said. "You don't know, of course. Anne's—Annemarie's—father."

"Yes," George said. "I mean no. I don't understand, Colonel. What about Annemarie?"

Van de Graaf stared incredulously at Van Effen. "You mean you haven't told them?"

"I don't believe I have."

"Good God!" Van de Graaf shook his head. "More of the need-to-know principle, I suppose. One of those days, Peter, you're going to forget to remind yourself of something and that will be the end of you." Van de Graaf looked from George to Vasco. "Annemarie and Julie—Lieutenant Van Effen's sister—have been kidnapped. The Annecy brothers."

"The Annecy brothers." George was silent for a moment. "Those murderous—You put two of them away for fifteen years."

"Correction. Lieutenant Van Effen put them away, and the two that escaped have been threatening to get him ever since. They've gone one better. They've got Julie."

"And what's the significance of this message to Annemarie's father?"

"The significance lies in her father. You will find it hard to believe, George, but the father of that fearful frump who used to frequent La Caracha is one of the wealthiest men in the Netherlands. Maybe the wealthiest. And a very powerful man. He has the ear of the government. He's in a position rather similar to Dassault, the plane maker, in France. There are some areas in which they don't move without consulting him at first or, at least, listening to what he says. He has power and wealth and a daughter and now they have the daughter and may well turn his power and wealth to their own advantage. Anne Meijer is any criminal's dream hostage come true."

Van Effen put down his glass and looked at his watch. "It's time, George."

"God in heaven! I don't believe it. You look at your damned watch and say it's time to go. Doesn't it occur to you to wonder how in the hell they got that information about David Meijer?"

"Some sort of persuasion, I suppose."

"Persuasion! Torture. They tortured the poor girl!"

"What poor girl?"

"Annemarie, of course!"

The shake of Van Effen's head was emphatic. "No. Not Annemarie. The Annecy brothers—or at least the two we put away—never tortured without a reason, however twisted that reason might be. The reason was either revenge or to get information. Why should they revenge themselves on Annemarie—what has she ever done to anyone? And information— what information could they possibly get from her? They don't know who she is, who her father is. Didn't, rather. As far as they are concerned, she's only a friend of Julie's and they took her along for no reason other than the fact that she happened to be there. If they tortured anybody—and I suspect it was only a threat of torture, to get information about me—it would have been Julie. My guess is that Annemarie volunteered that information about herself as a sop to the Annecys, to turn their minds to the thought of unlimited ransom money—maybe she even mentioned her father's influence with the government, although people like the Annecys would almost certainly have been aware of that anyway—anything to distract attention from Julie. Annemarie's no fool—if she were, I wouldn't have brought her up from Rotterdam. She knows that the Annecys of this world are above all pragmatists, and that anything that would further their plans would be of a great deal more interest to them than hurting me by proxy."

"Cold-blooded fish," Van de Graaf muttered.

"Pardon, sir?"

"You could be right or you could be wrong. Damage both ways. If you're right, the Annecys' hands have been greatly strengthened and David Meijer's pocket almost certainly lightened, or will be in the very near future. If you're wrong, you're putting your head in that charming headman's noose that the Annecy brothers put on their postcards. If you're wrong, she'd have talked of many things, principally that Stephan Danilov is Lieutenant Peter van Effen. I can't take the chance that you're not wrong. My orders are that you all are not to go through with this."

George said, "Normally, Colonel, I wouldn't dream of not complying with your wishes. But these aren't normal circumstances. By refusing your request, I'm not stepping outside the law, nor am I making the point that I'm no longer a policeman. I'm just going my own way."

Van de Graaf nodded. "I can't stop *you*. But I can—" And he turned to Van Effen.

"You can force him to go his own way, too," George said. "By resigning. You'd never forgive yourself, Colonel."

Van de Graaf scowled, refilled his glass, sank into an armchair and gazed into the fire. Van Effen nodded to Vasco and the three men left the room.

Van Effen and George returned to the Trianon to find that the regular watchdog was not in his usual place. But there was another and, if possible, even more insignificant character seated some distance from the desk, sipping beer. Van Effen had no doubt that this was a replacement from the same stable. The manager called to them as they passed the desk.

"This message has just come for you, Mr. Danilov." He handed Van Effen a slip of paper that read: "May I see you in your room? Two minutes."

"Yes, of course. Thank you." Van Effen folded the paper into his pocket and led George to the lift. The promised two minutes later the manager arrived in Van Effen's room. He closed the door behind him, looked doubtfully at George and seemed to hesitate.

"No problem," Van Effen said. "My friend here is on the side of the angels. George, Charles. The manager. Charles, George. George is police."

"Ah. A word of warning, Lieutenant. I wouldn't use the back entrance tonight—somebody, a stranger to anyone around here—has taken up residence by the back door. He's in an old DAF. And you will have noticed that your old looker-after in the lobby has been replaced. There's another man, who has just started a meal in the dining room. He's seated conveniently by the door so that he can see anyone who crosses the lobby. He knows the new shadow. No words exchanged, just a brief look and an even briefer nod. No risk in that, they must have thought—they have no reason to suspect my interest in them. That's why I waited two minutes, to see if either of them made a move. No disappointment—our dining-room friend was at the public phone almost before the lift doors closed behind you. I waited until he finished his call to whatever person he was reporting your arrival. I was watching them from the mirror as the diner left the booth. Brief nod again, no words."

"When you go bankrupt, Charles, apply to me any time. I'll watch the bogeymen." The manager left.

"So," George said. "We can expect that phone call any minute now. The man in the restaurant has reported to Agnelli that Stephan Danilov has returned accompanied by George, explosives expert and illegal arms supplier. One wonders what nest of cobras they've chosen for the rendezvous."

"I don't wonder. There are no cobras here in Room 203. Charles tells us that Agnelli—it can only be Agnelli—has two other faithful but not very bright henchmen lurking around the place. Why? Surely it only required one stake-out, the one in the lobby, to advise him of our arrival. The other two are guards, part of his insurance policy—don't forget Agnelli has no reason to think that we know of their presence. There may even be others that Charles knows nothing about. This is the last place that we would think that would be chosen as a meeting point— or so Agnelli must imagine—and so we wouldn't think of arranging a reception committee here. And when he does call, you can be sure that he will announce that he will be here in a matter of minutes, so that we can't have the time to arrange one."

Thirty seconds later, Agnelli called to say that they would meet at the Trianon. He and his friends would be there in under five minutes.

"He's bringing friends, plural," Van Effen said after he had hung up. "I don't think Romero Agnelli trusts anyone. Well, can you blame him?"

From the cordial, guileless expression Agnelli wore on arrival, one could see that Van Effen was wrong. Here, patently, was a trusting man one could trust anywhere. Agnelli had brought three men along with him. His brother Leonardo, looking, if that was possible, an even more genial member of the Mafia than the last time, and two others whom Van Effen had never seen before. One of them, a burly, slightly florid, pleasant-featured character of indeterminate age—somewhere between forty and fifty, Van Effen would have guessed, but it was difficult to be sure—was introduced as Liam O'Brien; from his accent, no less than from his name, he had to be Irish. The other, a handsome young man, slightly swarthy, was introduced as Heinrich Daniken: he could have been, apart from the name, of any nationality. Agnelli did not see fit to disclose what the function of either man was.

Introductions over, refreshments proffered and accepted, Agnelli said, "Do I call you George, or do you have another name?"

"Just George." He smiled. "I'm an anonymous person."

Agnelli surveyed the vast bulk before him. "You, George, are the least anonymous-looking person I've ever seen. Don't you find it rather a drawback in your profession? Whatever that may be, of course."

"Drawback? It's a positive advantage. I'm a peace-loving man who abhors violence. When you're as big as I am, no one ever offers it to you." George, Van Effen thought admiringly, was as consummate and convincing a liar as he'd ever known. "And, of course, everybody, or nearly everybody—I think particularly of those who are sworn to uphold the law—think that everyone who is as big, fat, cheerful and harmless as I am must be able to get by very well without being able to think. It's a kind of law of nature. Well, I'm no Einstein, but I'm not yet ready to be locked away in an institution. But we haven't met to discuss personalities, Mr. Agnelli, have we? Five questions. What do you want? How much or how many? When? Where? Price?"

The slipping of Agnelli's good-humored smile was so momentary that only the most alert or observant would have noticed it, and even then it could have been as much imagined as seen. "You do get to the point quickly, don't you, George?

No time for the little business niceties, I see. Well, that's the way I prefer it myself. Like you, I have no time for beating about the bush; like you, I regard myself as a businessman." He produced a paper from an inside pocket. "Here's my shopping list. Fairly comprehensive, is it not?"

George studied it briefly. "Fairly. Well within my limited capacities, I should think. Most of the items are straightforward, especially the explosives. The ground-to-ground wire-guided missiles—these will be anti-tank missiles, although you don't say so—and the SAM ground-to-air are also easily come by, as are the plastic mines, grenades and smoke bombs." He paused, sipped brandy and frowned. "Something here I don't quite understand, don't even like. I'm not talking about the fact that you seem to be preparing to wage a limited war, even if only a defensive one—that's none of my business." He handed the list over to Van Effen. "Comment?"

Van Effen studied it for no longer a time than it had taken George, then returned the list. "Specifications."

"Exactly." George, not smiling, looked at the four men in turn, concentrating his gaze at the end on Agnelli. "This is a lethal-enough list as it is. But it could be suicidal if it got into the hands of whoever prepared this list."

Agnelli wasn't smiling either. He looked uncomfortable. "I'm afraid I don't understand."

"Then I'd better enlighten you. Specifications, as my friend Stephan has said. Explosives—no specifications. Missiles, ditto—and that applies to both types. What kind of primers? What kind of detonators? Fuses—you don't even say whether wire or chemical, how slow-burning or fast-acting. No explosives expert ever composed this list. Some bungling incompetent did. Who?"

Agnelli studied his glass for some time and said finally, "I'm the incompetent. But I did get some bungling help from my three associates here."

"God help us all," Van Effen said. "You're not fit to be let loose with a box of kiddies' fireworks. I have to ask you, not for the first time: where the hell *are* your experts?"

Agnelli smiled ruefully and spread his hands. "I'll be perfectly frank with you." Romero Agnelli, Van Effen realized, was about to lie through his teeth. "We are temporarily embarrassed. The two men on whom we rely have been called away for other duties and won't be back for a couple of days. But we thought— well, you gentlemen are both experts and—"

"That's no problem," George said. "We know what to get and can give you simple instructions on how to use them without blowing your silly heads off. Missiles are a different matter. Only a trained man can fire one of those."

"How long does that take?"

"A week. Ten days." George was exaggerating, Van Effen knew, but the other men's patent ignorance of all things military was so extensive that it was very likely a safe exaggeration. "And don't ask us, we're no military men, we're no better trained than you are."

Agnelli was silent for some time, until he said abruptly, "Do you know of anyone who is? Skilled in such matters, I mean?"

"Do you mean what I think you mean?"

"Yes."

"I do." The way George said "I do," in a tone just one degree short of impatience, made it clear that George should know.

"Who?"

George gave him a withering look. "He hasn't got a name."

"You must call him something."

"The lieutenant."

"Why?"

"Because he is a lieutenant."

"Cashiered, of course."

"Certainly not. A cashiered lieutenant is no good to me. I thought you would appreciate that a person like myself can only operate at second or third hand. A middleman, if you like. Or two."

"Ah! I see. Your supplier?"

"Mr. Agnelli. Don't expect me to answer such questions. I'll see what can be done. Where do you want this stuff delivered?"

"That depends on how soon you can deliver it."

"By noon tomorrow."

Agnelli looked incredulous, then smiled. "It looks as if I've come to the right shop. How will it be delivered?"

"By army truck, of course."

"Of course." Agnelli looked slightly but happily dazed. "This makes things a bit difficult. I thought it would be at least the day after tomorrow. Could I call up tomorrow to finalize time and place? And could you hold up delivery for at least a few hours?"

"That can be arranged." George looked at Van Effen. "Mr. Agnelli can call here? Ten A.M., say?" Van Effen nodded and George grinned at Agnelli. "We're missing one little detail."

"Oh," Agnelli said. "Yes. Of course. The price. What is this to cost us?"

"Can't say yet, but somewhere between ten and twelve thousand dollars. We offer the best discount rates in Europe. Dollars, guilders or deutsche marks. More, of course, if our— ah—services are required."

Agnelli stood up, his old relaxed and genial self again. "Of course. The price, I must say, doesn't seem exorbitant."

"One thing," Van Effen said pleasantly. "You are aware, aren't you, Mr. Agnelli, that if I were to, say, move to another hotel and register there under another name, that the chances of your ever finding either of us again would be remote?"

"Remote? They wouldn't exist." Agnelli was frowning. "Why ever should you mention such a thing?"

"Well, a state of mutual trust does exist between us, doesn't it?"

"Naturally." The puzzlement still there.

"Well, if it does, call off the watchdogs in the lobby, in the dining room and outside."

"My watchdogs?" From the expression on Agnelli's face one could see that, far from being baffled, he was stalling for time.

"If you don't, we'll throw them into the canal—suitably trussed, of course—and then move on."

Agnelli looked at him, his face for once expressionless.

"Ah, yes. You do play for keeps, don't you? I really believe you would." He smiled and put out his hand. "Very well, watchdogs retired. Shame. But they really weren't up to it."

When they had gone, Van Effen said to George, "You really should have taken up a life of crime. Too late now. Anyway, you'd have given Colonel Van de Graaf apoplexy years ago. I'll bet Annelise has no idea quite how gifted a liar you are. You have Agnelli hooked, outfoxed, outgunned and demoralized, not to say dependent; at least, let's hope so. Will you talk to Vasco later this evening and tell him that you've got an offer of employment for him in the capacity of an army lieutenant—after, of course, he's made suitable alterations to his appearance? Major alterations. We mustn't forget that Agnelli has had the opportunity of studying Vasco at close range."

"There'll be no problem." George handed over Agnelli's shopping list. He chuckled, a low roar like thunder. "I'd give a great deal to watch the colonel's face when he sees what he's got to go shopping for in the morning. You'll be seeing him, I take it, in an hour or so. Has it occurred to you that Agnelli might very well be there? Along with Riordan and this fellow Samuelson?"

"An intriguing thought. And yes, it has occurred."

"Well?"

"Well what?"

"Well what, he asks. We *know* that Agnelli is Annecy."

"We're 99 per cent certain. Don't forget that I never saw either of the two Annecy brothers that we didn't manage to catch and put away."

"The fact that you don't know him doesn't mean he doesn't know you. Of course he does—he must have seen your picture in the papers many times during the period of the arrest and trial. How do you think he's going to react when he sees before him not only the dreaded Lieutenant Van Effen but the dreaded lieutenant whose sister he's got tucked away in some dungeon—the sister who, for all you know, he spends his spare time with, testing out the latest model thumbscrews?"

"Should be interesting."

"Colonel Van de Graaf was right," George muttered. "You belong a hundred fathoms down. Just a cold-blooded fish."

"'Your ten cents will help to kill a British soldier. It's a bargain at the price—the best bargain you'll ever get.' That's what the collectors say when they go around rattling their damn tin cans in the Irish bars in the United States. Especially in the Irish bars in the Northeast. Especially in New York. Most especially of all in the borough of Queens, where the Irish are thickest on the ground. Ten cents. That's all they ask, just ten cents. And, of course, they rattle their cans whenever they hold Irish nights, Irish dances, Irish raffles, Irish whatever-you-like.

"If you've never heard that there are charitable organizations—*charitable* they call themselves—which collect for arms, then you live in another century or with your head in the sand. They claim the millions of dollars they've collected over the years have gone to support the widows and orphans of the IRA members foully slain by the murderous British. Support widows and orphans! The founder of one such charitable organization once made the mistake of telling the truth when he said, 'The more British soldiers that are sent back from Ulster in their coffins, the better.' Jack Lynch, a former Irish premier, has gone on record as saying that the money is intended for one purpose only—to *make* widows and orphans. British widows and orphans."

Riordan, abnormally tall, abnormally thin, black-haired, and dressed in a near-ankle-length black raincoat that served only to heighten his looming angularity, was shaking with rage as he stood facing his audience, his fists ivory-knuckled on the table before him. His sincerity and outrage were unquestionable, his intensity almost terrifying.

"God *knows* it's bad enough that the contributions to these infamous organizations should come from honest, God-fearing, intensely religious Catholics who are duped into thinking they are contributing to a worthy cause instead of to some damnable crew who make Murder Incorporated look like innocent children playing in a kindergarten. The money goes directly to dedicated IRA operatives. Some of it is used to buy guns at black-market sales in New York itself, auctions usually held in razed areas or empty parking lots, always by night, nearly always in the Bronx, Queens or Brooklyn. Guns, gentlemen, are rather easily come by in the fair city of New York."

In the depth of his bitterness, Riordan almost spat the words out. "The rest of the money is used by other operatives who openly travel to the southern and midwestern states where gun permits do not exist. Wherever the guns come from, they all end up in the New York area, from where they are shipped out, almost always from New Jersey or Brooklyn, with the warm encouragement and complicity of the stevedore unions and the upright U.S. customs, many of whom are first- or second-generation Irish and feel blood brothers to the murderous IRA. As the Customs Service is controlled by the U.S. Treasury Department, it is logical to suppose that those dealing in death operate with the cognizance if not the connivance of the U.S. Government. The Irish influence in Congress is as well known, as it is remarkably powerful."

"A moment, Mr. Riordan, if you would."

The interruption came from Aaron Wieringa, the Minister of Defense, a big, florid, blue-eyed and calm man, a man immensely respected throughout the country and one who would have become Premier years before if he had not been cursed with the unfortunate and crippling handicap, for a politician, of incorruptibility. "One appreciates—one can hardly fail to appreciate—that you are an angry man. We are not, I assure you, nineteenth-century ostriches, and I think it would be true to say that there is not a man in this room who does not understand that your fury is justifiable. I would not go so far as to concur in your condemnation of Washington and Congress, but that, in the current and particular circumstances, is by the by. Your opinion, as distinct from your recital of verifiable facts, is not of immediate concern.

"What *is* of immediate concern is why your wrath has seen fit to focus itself on our unfortunate country in general and the city of Amsterdam in particular. I cannot, at the moment, even begin to fathom the reason for it, although I am certain we will not be left in ignorance for long. But nothing you have said so far begins to justify your attempt to blackmail us into acting as intermediary between you and the British Government. I appreciate that you may have, and very probably do have, powerful reasons for wanting all British troops to withdraw from Northern Ireland. But how you can possibly imagine that we have the ability to persuade Britain to accede to your preposterous demands quite passes my understanding. No conceivable reason exists why they should so accede."

"A wholly conceivable reason exists, Minister. Humanitarian motives. Humanitarian motives on your part and on theirs."

"Our respective governments would be reluctant, true, to see the Netherlands flooded and countless thousands—maybe hundreds of thousands—drowned in those floods. Before even considering such awful matters, an answer to my question, please. Why us? Is it that we, because of our particular geographical situation, are peculiarly susceptible to threats of genocide?"

"Don't be naive. You have been chosen because Amsterdam is the linchpin in the whole lethal weapons operation. It is the gun-running center of northern Europe and has been for years, just as it has been the heroin center of northern Europe. This knowledge is in the public domain, and the continued existence of those two evil practices can only bespeak a deep level of corruption in both government and law enforcement." An indignant-looking Wieringa made to interrupt, but Riordan imperiously gestured him to silence. "There are, to be sure, other towns engaged in gunrunning, notably Antwerp. But, compared to Amsterdam, Antwerp is an ant on the hide of an elephant."

This time Mr. Wieringa, speaking in almost a shout, which was unknown for him, would not be gainsaid. "You mean you would find it *impossible* to flood Belgium?"

Riordan carried on as if he had heard nothing. "Not all the guns passing through Amsterdam go to Eire, of course. Some go to the RAF. Others go to—"

"The RAF!" It was Robert Kondstaal, the Justice Minister. "You suggest that the British Air Force is supplied—"

"Be quiet, idiot." Riordan, it seemed, could descend below the rhetorical level he usually set for himself. "I refer to the

Red Army Faction, the inheritors of the bloody mantle of the Baader-Meinhof gangsters of the early seventies. Some go to the Sicilian-controlled Mafia-type criminal organizations that are springing up all over West Germany. But the bulk goes to Eire.

"Do you know what it's *like* in Northern Ireland, Mr. Minister?" Nobody bothered to follow his line of eyesight to know that he was addressing the Minister of Defense. "Can you imagine the hellish conditions that exist there, the hideous tortures practiced by both the IRA and UVF, the homicidal insanity that has ruled there for fourteen years? A country ruled by fear that is tearing it to pieces. Northern Ireland will never be governed by representatives of the two communities, Protestant and Catholic, working together because they are far too bitterly divided by religion and, to a lesser extent, race. There are one and a half million people living together in a small area, but in spite of their divisions, 99.9 percent on either side have never harmed anyone or ever wished to. That 99.9 percent on either side are united in only one thing—in abhorring terrorism and in their desire to live only in peace. It is a desire that, as matters stand, can never be realized. Conventional politicians, with all the faults and frailties of their kind, are still those who observe the conventions. In Ulster, conventional politicians are an extinct breed. Moderation has ceased to exist. Demagogues and gunmen rule. The country is ruled by a handful of crazed murderers."

Riordan paused for the first time, probably as much for breath as anything else, but no one seemed inclined to take advantage of the hiatus.

"But murderers, even the crazed, must have their weapons, must they not?" Riordan said. "And so the murder weapons are shipped from Amsterdam—usually, but not always, inside furniture. The weapons are sealed in containers, of course, and if the Amsterdam customs are unaware of this they must be the worst, the blindest or the most corrupt and avaricious in Europe. Nine times out of ten, the ships unload in Dublin. How they—the containers, I mean—get past the Dublin customs I don't profess to know, but I don't think there's any question of collusion—if there were, the customs wouldn't have turned up a million dollars' worth of illegally imported arms destined for the IRA four years ago. But most of the guns do get through. From Dublin the arms containers, variously labeled but popularly as household goods, are trucked to a warehouse in County Monaghan and from there to a horticultural nursery in County Louth. Don't ask me how I know, but it would be rather difficult not to know: the people thereabouts know but don't talk. From there the weapons are taken to Northern Ireland, not smuggled over the border in the middle of the night by daredevil IRA members, but brought in during daylight hours in cars driven by women, mostly young, surrounded by laughing kids. All very innocuous.

"It's a long, long way from where a machine pistol is purchased in a midwestern state until it's in the hands of some killer crouched in the shadows of a back street in Belfast or Londonderry. A long way. But in all that long way the vital stage, the focal point, the nodal point, the venturi in the funnel is your city. And so we have come to Amsterdam." Riordan sat down.

The breaking of the ensuing silence was far from immediate. There were, altogether, eight men in Kondstaal's luxurious lounge. Three men had accompanied Riordan to the Minister of Justice's house—Samuelson, whom Van de Graaf had described to Van Effen; O'Brien, who had come to the Trianon; and Agnelli, the man George had forecast would be there. Samuelson and O'Brien thought there was nothing they could add to what Riordan had said, and Agnelli had yet to recover his full powers of speech. When he had entered the room and seen Van Effen, appearance returned to normal, sitting there, his eyes had momentarily widened, his lips momentarily parted, and a slight but noticeable amount of color had left his cheeks, and not momentarily either. Almost certainly Van Effen was the only person who had noticed the fleeting sea change that had overcome Agnelli, but, then, Van Effen was the only person who had been looking for it.

There were also four men on the other side of the negotiating table. The two ministers, plus Van de Graaf and Van Effen, and they had nothing immediately to say either, and this for excellent reasons: there was nothing they could immediately say that would be in any way helpful, and each had to admit to himself that Riordan had expressed his viewpoint with a certain degree of logical persuasion, however passionate and unreasonable, threatening and preposterous his accompanying demands might have been. It was Aaron Wieringa, glancing in turn at each of his three companions, who broke the silence.

"Before I speak, gentlemen, have any of you any comment to make?"

Van Effen said, "I have."

"Lieutenant?"

"Mr. Riordan has been surprisingly reticent about one thing. He hasn't said *why* he wants all British influence removed from Northern Ireland. If we are to negotiate on his behalf, I think we should have the right to know something of his motivation, his intentions. It may be that his intentions are so awful, so appalling, that we would risk any disaster to our country sooner than comply with his wishes. We have, of course, no reason to believe that Mr. Riordan will tell us the truth."

"The point is well taken," Wieringa said. "Well, Mr. Riordan?"

"There's no reason to swear that I'll tell the truth, because any liar would say the same." Riordan had again risen to his menacing height; he seemed to find talking easier that way. "I have talked about the 99.9 percent of good and decent people in that war-torn country who are utterly dominated by the 0.1 percent of those maniacal killers. Our sole objective is to eliminate this 0.1 percent—and enable the people of Ulster to resolve their own future in an atmosphere of peace and quiet and hope."

"Elimination?" Wieringa said cautiously. "What precisely do you mean by that?"

"We will exterminate the evil bastards on both sides. We will excise the cancer. Is that blunt enough for you?" Riordan sat down.

"It sounds like a high purpose," Van Effen said. He made no attempt to disguise the contemptuous disbelief in his voice.

"Noble and humane. Let them resolve their own future. Hardly ties in, does it, with your earlier statement that Northern Ireland will never be governed by representatives of the two communities. Has it not occurred to you that if the most rabid IRA leader were sitting in that chair, he would talk exactly as you are talking now, in order to achieve the same end—to get the British out of Northern Ireland at all costs? What assurance do we have that you are not, in fact, that rabid IRA leader?"

"You have none." This time Riordan had not risen from his chair and his voice was remarkably calm. "I can do no more. If you cannot see that I detest the IRA and all its manifestations, you must be blind. I am so appalled at the suggestion that I cannot easily find words to counter it."

There was another and even longer silence. Then Wieringa said, "I believe one calls this an impasse."

"Impasse, as you say," Riordan said. He was still seated, the time for rhetoric had apparently passed. "But surely there are certain salient factors that should help to resolve the impasse. Oostlijk-Flevoland, for instance. Leeuwarden. The Noordoostpolder. Wieringermeer, Putten, Petten, Schouwen, Walcheren and others. And I did mention that we have the royal palace mined?"

"The palace?" Wieringa said.

"Tonight's little demonstration was just that. A little demonstration. Just to prove how pathetically easy it is to circumvent your alleged security precautions."

"Save your breath, Riordan." Wieringa's voice was curt. No "Mr." this time. "The time for threats is past. Only moral considerations remain."

"Fifty-fifty," Van Effen said.

Wieringa looked at him for some moments, then nodded.

"My way of thinking, too. Thank you, Lieutenant. It is difficult to decide to drown one's country on the basis of a gamble." He looked at Riordan. "I am empowered to make decisions. I will call the British ambassador. He will call the Foreign Office in London. We shall make a radio announcement—worded in a suitably cautious fashion, you understand. Those three things I can promise. The outcome of the negotiations, of course, are not for me to predict or influence. That is understood?"

"That is understood. Thank you, Minister." There was no hint of triumph, not even satisfaction, in Riordan's voice. He stood. "Your integrity is a byword throughout Europe. I am content. Good night, gentlemen."

No one wished him good night in return.

After the departure of Riordan and his associates there was silence in the room until Wieringa had put through his telephone call. When he had replaced the receiver, he sipped delicately from his brandy glass, and said, "Comment, gentlemen?" He was remarkably cool.

"It's outrageous, disgraceful and dastardly," Kondstaal said loudly. Now that the need for action and decision-making was over, he was all fire and fury. "The good name, the honor of the Netherlands lies in the dust."

"Better, perhaps, than that its citizens should lie under flood-waters," Wieringa said. "Colonel?"

"You had to consider the balance of probabilities," Van de Graaf said. "Your decision, sir, was not only the correct one; it was the inevitable one."

"Thank you, Colonel. Lieutenant?"

"What can I usefully add, sir?"

"Quite frankly, I don't know. But, according to the colonel—and it is, I must say, a most handsome admission on his part—you are closer to those villains than anyone else in Amsterdam." He smiled. "I do not, of course, use the word 'closer' in a pejorative sense."

"Thank you, sir. I'd hope not."

"You're not really very forthcoming, are you, Lieutenant?"

"A certain uncharacteristic diffidence, sir. I may be the senior detective lieutenant in the city, but I'm pretty junior in this company. What do you want me to be forthcoming about, sir?"

Wieringa regarded the roof and said, almost inconsequentially, "I had to make a pretty important decision there." He dropped his gaze and looked at Van Effen. "Did you believe Riordan?"

Van Effen picked up his glass and considered it without drinking from it. He was obviously marshaling his thoughts. Then he said, "Four points, Minister. There are two things I believe about Riordan, one point I'm not sure whether to believe or disbelieve and a fourth where I definitely disbelieve."

"Ah! This is more—hence your cryptic remark 'fifty-fifty'?"

"I suppose. First, I believe he is definitely not IRA."

"You do, Lieutenant? In that case, why did you push him?"

"Confirmation. But I was sure before. That speech of his— that impassioned and violent denunciation of the IRA and all its methods. You'd have to be an exceptional actor to get that amount of hatred into your voice; but you'd have to be an impossibly good one to have a pulse beat like a trip-hammer in your throat."

"I missed that," Wieringa said. He looked at Van de Graaf and Kondstaal. "Either of you gentlemen—" He broke off at their mute headshakes.

"Nothing remarkable. A friend of mine, and a police officer of ours, suffers from the same sign of concern. Secondly, I believe that Riordan is not the leader, the driving force, the man in charge. Why? I can't give a shred of evidence, of proof. But he's too fiery, too unbalanced, too unpredictable to be a general."

"You wouldn't fight under him, Van Effen?" Wieringa was half smiling, half curious.

"No, sir. There's someone else. I'm certain it's not Agnelli. I would take long odds it's not O'Brien—he's got sergeant-major written all over him. I'm not saying it's Samuelson. He's an enigma, a mystery. But his presence is totally unexplained, and when any presence is as inexplicable as that, then a very big explanation is called for.

"Where I'm uncertain, whether to believe or not, is about Northern Ireland. Riordan said his only aim was to eliminate the monsters. His voice did carry what might have been re-garded as the authentic ring of sincerity and, as I've said, I don't believe he's all that good an actor." Van Effen sighed briefly, shook his head and tasted his brandy. "I know this is all rather confusing, gentlemen. Let me put it this way. I believe that he believes what he says, but I don't believe that what he believes is necessarily true. It's one of the reasons why I'm convinced he's not the kingpin. Two things. He was caught outright in a flat contradiction, yet appeared to be unaware that any such contradiction existed. Then he seems to be unaware that there could be three sets of fanatics around—the extremist Protestants, the extremist Catholics and the mediators. That's them. The mediators could be the most irresponsibly dangerous of all. To achieve the final solution, the mediators are prepared to drown a million. One could imagine what the final solution would be like in Ulster. No. Let me rephrase that. I can't imagine that."

"The same thought was in *my* mind." Wieringa spoke very slowly. "The very same. Although not so clearly formulated. In *my* mind, I mean." He smiled. "Well, that should be enough for a day—but you did mention that there was something you didn't believe."

"Yes, sir. I don't believe his threats. His immediate threats, that is. His long-range threats are a different matter. But the ones he mentioned here tonight—and the ones outlined to Colonel Van de Graaf earlier this evening—I do not believe, with the exception of the threat to Helystad in Oostlijk-Flevoland. The rest I believe to be bluff. Especially the threat to destroy the palace."

"If you say that, Lieutenant," Wieringa said, "I'm damned if I don't believe you. Why do you say so?"

"Because I don't believe they have any mines laid inside the palace. They were concerned that the explosion inside the palace tonight would be heard over a considerable area to convince you that they had, indeed, the ability to carry out their promise."

Wieringa regarded him with a puzzled expression. "You sound fairly sure about this, Lieutenant."

"No, sir. I'm certain."

"How can you be so sure?"

"I have inside information."

Wieringa looked at him in a speculative fashion but said nothing. Not so Kondstaal. He had been totally out of his depth all evening, but now he thought he was on secure and known footing and that it was time to assert himself.

"What were the sources of your information, Lieutenant?"

"That's confidential."

"Confidential!" Whether the source of Kondstaal's immediate anger was due to the reply or the fact that Van Effen had omitted the mandatory "Minister" or "sir" was difficult to say; he probably didn't know himself. "Confidential!"

"I'm trying to be discreet, sir, that's all. I don't want to divulge my sources because it may cause acute and unnecessary embarrassment. Surely you can understand that—it's so commonplace in the police world that it's hardly worth mentioning. Why don't you just take my word for it?"

"Understand it! Commonplace! Take your word!" Kondstaal's mottled complexion was rapidly assuming the hue of a turkey wattle. "You arrogant—you arrogant—you—" He made a visible effort to ward off the onset of apoplexy. "I would remind you, Lieutenant"—he put a heavy accent on the word "Lieutenant"—"that I am the Minister of Justice"—he put a very heavy accent on that, too—"whereas you are only a junior officer in the force which I personally—"

"That's unfair, sir." Van de Graaf's voice was impersonal. "Next to me, Van Effen is the senior police officer in the city of—"

"Keep out of this, Van de Graaf." Kondstaal tried to let ice creep into his voice, but his temperature control had slipped. "Van Effen! You heard me."

"I heard you," Van Effen said, then added "sir" almost as an afterthought. "I know what I'm talking about because I'm the person who placed that charge in the cellars of the royal palace."

"What! *What!*" Kondstaal's complexion would now have made any turkey-cock look to his laurels. "Good God! I can't believe it." He was halfway out of his chair. "My ears deceive me!"

"They don't. Sir. I was also the person who pressed the button that detonated the explosives."

Kondstaal said nothing, not immediately. The shocked horror of this threat to the safety of the royal family, this dreadful lèse majesté, held him in thrall. Van Effen returned to his brandy and made no attempt to keep his opinion of the Minister of Justice out of his face.

"Arrest this man, Van de Graaf," Kondstaal shouted. "This moment!"

"On what charges, sir?"

"On what charges! Have you gone mad as well as—as well as—Treason, man, treason!"

"Yes, sir. This raises problems."

"Problems? Your duty, man, your duty!"

"Problems, sir. I'm the city's chief of police. All other policemen in Amsterdam are junior to me." Every century of Van de Graaf's aristocratic lineage was showing. "Nobody in Amsterdam has the authority to arrest me."

Kondstaal stared at him, his anger gradually changing to bewilderment. He shook his head and said nothing.

"What I mean is, sir, that if Lieutenant Van Effen is to be locked up on a treason charge, then you'd have to lock me up, too, because I'm as much a traitor as he is." Van de Graaf considered. "More, I would say. I am, after all, his superior; moreover, I personally authorized and approved every action the lieutenant has undertaken." Inconsequentially, it seemed, but probably to give Kondstaal time to readjust, Van de Graaf turned to Van Effen and said, "You forgot to tell me that you personally had detonated those explosives."

Van Effen shrugged apologetic shoulders. "You know how it is, sir."

"I know," Van de Graaf said heavily. "You have so much on your mind. You mentioned that before."

"Why have you stepped outside the law, Colonel?" There was no reproof in Wieringa's voice, only a question. Wieringa had remained remarkably unperturbed.

"We did not step outside the law, sir. We are doing and have done everything in our power to uphold the law. We—Lieutenant Van Effen—have gained the entrée—and a highly dangerous entrée it is—into the ranks of the F.F.F. I think it is more than dangerous, it's close to suicidal. But Lieutenant Van Effen has persuaded me—and I most reluctantly agree with him—that it's our last best hope. Our only hope."

Kondstaal looked at the two policemen dazedly but his mind was beginning to function again, at least after a fashion. "How is this possible? Van Effen's face must be known to every criminal in Amsterdam." He had forgotten how junior Van Effen had been only moments ago.

"It is. But not the Van Effen you see before you. His appearance, voice and personality have changed to such a remarkable extent that I'd wager my pension that neither of you would recognize Stephan Danilov, which is the pseudonym he has temporarily adopted." He might have wagered something else, Van Effen reflected; Van de Graaf was so wealthy that his pension was a matter of indifference to him. "Whether the F.F.F. have uncritically accepted Stephan Danilov at his face value, we have no means of knowing. It seems incredible to me that, so far, they appear to have done so. If they have not done so or will not do so any longer, the city of Amsterdam will be requiring a new senior detective lieutenant. They will also be requiring a new police chief, which the lieutenant will probably regard as a trifling matter, because I shall have to resign. The Netherlands, of course, will be looking for a new Minister of Justice, because you, Mr. Kondstaal, are also a party to this. Only Mr. Wieringa can look forward to a safe tenure."

Kondstaal looked stricken. "I haven't said that I'm a party to anything."

Wieringa took him gently by the arm. "Robert, if you would, a word in your ear." They walked away to a distant corner of the lounge, which was fortunately as large as it was luxurious, and began to converse in low terms. Wieringa appeared to be doing most of the conversing.

Van Effen said, "What weighty matters do you think our revered ministers are discussing?"

Van de Graaf forgot to reproach Van Effen for his unseemly

and unconstitutional levity. "No prizes for guessing that. Mr. Wieringa is explaining to Mr. Kondstaal the principle of Hobson's choice. If Kondstaal doesn't go along, the Netherlands is still going to be looking for a new Minister of Justice. If Kondstaal hadn't forced you to divulge your confidential information, he wouldn't have found himself in the impossible situation he does now. Hoisted, to coin a phrase, on his own petard—or petty stupidity." Van de Graaf seemed to find it a moderately entertaining thought. He settled himself comfortably in his chair, sighed and reached out for the bottle. "Well, thank heaven everything's over for the day."

Van Effen considerately let Van de Graaf pour the brandy and sip it before producing Agnelli's shopping list. "Not quite complete, I'm afraid, sir. There's this little item."

Van de Graaf read through the list, his face ashen, then read through it again. His lips were moving, but at first no sound came. He had just got around to muttering, "This little item, that little item," when Wieringa and Kondstaal returned. Wieringa looked his normal imperturbable self, Kondstaal like a Christian to whom the Romans had just given his first preview of the lions.

Wieringa said, "What little item, Colonel?"

"This." Van de Graaf handed him the paper, put his elbow on the arm of his chair and his hand to his forehead, as if to hide his eyes from some unspeakable sight.

"High explosives," Wieringa read out. "Primers. Detonators. Grenades. Ground-to-ground missiles. Ground-to-air missiles." He looked at Van Effen but with no signs of consternation on his face. "What is this?"

"A so-called shopping list. I was going to ask the colonel to get them for me." Kondstaal, who had adopted the same attitude as Van de Graaf, made a moaning sound. "As you are the Minister of Defense, the colonel would have had to approach you anyway. I'd also like to borrow an army truck, if I may. With a little luck I may even be able to return it."

Wieringa looked at him, looked at the paper in his hand, then back at Van Effen again. "Balanced against this shopping list, as you call it, the loan of the odd army vehicle seems an eminently reasonable request. All this I can obtain without any great difficulty. I have heard a considerable amount about you, Van Effen, and I have learned a great deal more tonight. I would hesitate to question your judgment." He thought for a moment. "I think I would question my own first, so I don't question yours. No doubt it's just idle curiosity on my part, but it would be nice to know *why* you require those items."

"The F.F.F. is short of explosives and offensive weapons, so I have promised to supply them with some."

"Of course," Wieringa said. "Of course." The Defense Minister appeared to be virtually unshockable; certainly nothing showed in his eyes. Nothing was to be seen in the eyes of Van de Graaf or Kondstaal either, but that didn't mean that they were shock-proof; their shading hands still cut their eyes off from the dreadful realities of the harsh world outside.

"They also seem to be short of explosive experts, so I volunteered my services."

"You know something about explosives?"

Van de Graaf reluctantly uncovered his eyes. "He knows a great deal about them. He's also a bomb-disposal expert. I wish," he said bitterly, "that this was something simple, like defusing a ticking thousand-pound bomb."

"Yes, sir." Van Effen was addressing Van de Graaf now. "I've also recruited George and Vasco, George as another person versed in the way of explosives and Vasco as a trained missile launcher. You will understand that I did not have time to consult you on these matters."

"You can't think of everything," Van de Graaf said dully. He discovered, to his apparent astonishment, that his brandy glass was empty and set about solving this disappearance.

"Nothing illegal about recruiting those two men, Mr. Wieringa. They're police sergeants. And they weren't recruited—they volunteered. They know the dangers. There's nothing to be done about the explosives, sir, but if you could have an armorer deactivate the missiles, I'd be very grateful."

Van de Graaf lowered his glass. "So would I. So would I." Not much in the way of life had come back into his voice.

Wieringa said, "I suppose I'm just being idly curious again, but why are you and your two friends taking those appalling risks?"

"Calculated risks, sir. I hope. The reason is simple. The colonel has said that we have gained an entrée into the F.F.F. That's not quite accurate. We have been accepted—or appear to have been accepted—on the fringes. We're just on the outer strand of the spider's web. We don't know where the spider is. But if we deliver the requested items, we'll find out. They're not likely to leave missiles and missile launchers in a safe-deposit box in the Central Station."

"Impeccable logic, Van Effen. Except, of course, for one tiny flaw."

"Sir?"

"The spider may gobble you up. The scheme is quite mad—which is the only reason it might just succeed. I'd be intrigued to know where and when you arranged this."

"About an hour and a half ago. Over a drink with Agnelli." For the first time, Wieringa's monolithic calm cracked.

"Over a drink with Agnelli? Agnelli? *Agnelli!* One of those men who have just left?"

"I was Stephan Danilov then. Well, can't think of anything else, so, with your permission, I'll be on my way. The weather forecast should be interesting tonight—latest reports say flood-level danger inside the next forty-eight hours might even exceed that of February 1953. That will be the time for our friends—and it doesn't leave a great deal of time for negotiations with the British. You will remember that I said I didn't believe in Riordan's short-range threats; I'm convinced that the long-range threat, the massive flooding of the country, has been arranged and is real. One small point, Colonel. Riordan's allegations against the integrity of our customs. They're ludicrous. I know that. You know that. The world doesn't. I'm convinced that the transfers are taking place in the Ijsselmeer, Wadden Zee or the open sea. It's a navy job. God knows we've got a bad-enough name already as a gunrunning entrepôt, I wonder what it will be like when all this is over." Van Effen smiled. "Still, it's not a job that can be handled by a junior police officer;

only the ministries of Defense and Justice can cope. Good night, gentlemen."

"Moment, Peter, moment." It was Van de Graaf, and his distress was apparent. "Surely there's *something* we can do to help?"

"Yes, sir. There is. Do nothing. Absolutely nothing. *Any* attempt to help us will probably help us into our graves. Those are clever and increasingly desperate people, so please, please, don't try anything clever and desperate yourselves. Don't have the truck followed, not in any way, no matter how clever you think you are, nothing. No helicopters, no blind barrel-organist, nothing. And nothing so futile and puerile as fitting a concealed location transmitter bug to the truck—it's the first thing they'd look for. Do *nothing*."

"We take your point," Wieringa said dryly. "Nothing." His tone changed. "From what you've just said, Lloyd's of London wouldn't insure you for a 99 percent premium. But you go. For the last time—why?"

"You heard what Mr. Kondstaal said—the good name and honor of the Netherlands in the dust, and you with its citizens full fathom five. We can't have that, can we?"

"Your sister."

"What about my sister?"

"The colonel told me tonight. God only knows how you carry on as you do. I couldn't. Kidnapped."

"She's part of it."

"I would not care to be the unfortunate man who abducted her when you meet up with him."

"I've already met up with him."

"What!" For the second time Wieringa's self-control deserted him, but he recovered quickly. "When?"

"Tonight."

"Where?"

"Here. Agnelli."

"Agnelli!"

"I should have shot him full of holes. But—there's a law against it. I'm a policeman. I'm supposed to uphold the law. Sworn to it, in fact."

He left. Wieringa said, "I begin to believe some of the stories about Van Effen. The not-so-nice ones. God, Arthur, that's his *sister*. No blood in his veins. None. Ice."

"Yes, sir. Let's hope Agnelli has not hurt Julie—or the woman of ours she's with."

"What do you mean?"

"Then he's a dead man. Sure, sure, Van Effen's sworn to uphold the law—but only in front of witnesses."

Wieringa stared at him, then nodded slowly and reached for his glass.

8

AT NOON ON that February day the streets of Amsterdam were dark as dusk. At noon on that same day the streets were as deserted as those of any long-dead city. The cloud cover driven by that icy northern wind must have been black and heavy and thousands of feet in depth but it could not be seen: the torrential slanting rain that bounced knee-high off those same deserted streets limited visibility in any direction, including vertically, to only a few yards. It was not a noontide for the well-advised to venture out of doors.

Van Effen, George and Vasco were among the very few who seemed to be singularly ill-advised. They stood in the porchway of the Trianon Hotel, sheltering from the monsoon-like rain behind the side glass panels. Van Effen was subjecting Vasco to a critical examination.

"Not bad, Vasco, not at all bad. Even if I hadn't known it was you, I don't think I would have recognized you. I'm quite certain I would have brushed by you in the street and not given you a second look. But don't forget that Romero Agnelli had the opportunity of studying you very closely over the table at the Hunter's Horn. On the other hand, the clothes you wore on that occasion were so outlandish that he probably didn't spend much time examining your face. It will serve."

Vasco had indeed undergone a considerable metamorphosis. The long blond locks that had straggled haphazardly over his shoulders had been neatly, severely trimmed and parted with millimetric precision just to the center left. His hair was also black, as were his eyebrows and newly acquired and immaculately shaped mustache, all of which went very well with his shadowed, thinned-down cheeks. All dyes guaranteed waterproof. He was the maiden's conceptualized dream of what every young army officer should look like. Shirt, tie, suit and belted trench coat were correspondingly immaculate.

"They could use him in those army advertisements," George said. "You know, your country needs you." George, himself, was still George. For him, disguise was impossible.

"And the voice," Van Effen said. "I'm not worried about Agnelli, he's hardly heard you say more than a few words. It's Annemarie. I don't know whether she's a good actress, with her emotions under control or not, but I rather suspect not. It would spoil things if she flung her arms round your neck and cried, 'My savior!'"

"I have a very bad cold," Vasco said hoarsely. "My throat is like sandpaper." His voice reverted to normal and he said morosely, "Whose throat wouldn't be, in this damned weather? Anyway, I'll be the strong, silent type; I'll speak as little as possible."

"And I," George said, "shall lurk discreetly in the background until one of you has advised the ladies—if the ladies are indeed there—of my presence. But make it fast."

"We'll make it as fast as we can, George," Van Effen said. "We appreciate it's difficult for you to lurk anywhere for any length of time. And I have no doubt whatsoever the ladies will be there." He tapped the newspaper under his arm. "What's the point in holding a couple of trumps if you don't have them in your hand?"

The F.F.F.'s latest announcement had been very simple, direct and to the point. They had now with them, they said —crude words like "abducted" and "kidnapped" had been studiously avoided—two young ladies, one of them the daughter of the nation's leading industrialist, the other the sister of a senior police officer in Amsterdam. They had then proceeded to name names. Condolences, the F.F.F. had said, had been sent to both parents and brother, together with assurances that they were being well cared for and expressing the pious hope that they would continue to remain in good health.

"I do look forward to meeting those card players," George said wistfully. "I wonder what American university—or it could be Irish—offers a combined course in terrorism and psychology?"

"They're not exactly stupid," Van Effen said. "But then, we never thought they were. Another push up the back for the arm of the government—and another push into an even more impossible situation. Just ending their message with those prayerful good wishes. No threats, no hints of reprisals or what might happen to the girls, no spoken possibility of torture or even death. Nothing. The old uncertainty principle in full operation again. What, we wonder, do they have in mind? That's left to us—and, of course, it's only human nature to come up with the worst possible scenario. Bad enough to have the country threatened with inundation, but for the tenderhearted and romantic—and even among the so-called stolid Dutch there are an uncommon number of those around—the thought of what dreadful terrors may lie in store for two beautiful and innocent young women could be a great deal worse."

"Well, there's one consolation," Vasco said. He was practicing his *in extremis* voice again. "I'm sure that's the last threat about your sister's well-being that you'll be getting, Lieutenant."

"Stephan," Van Effen said.

"Stephan. I know. But I won't apologize this time." Vasco's voice was back to normal. "Once I clap eyes on that lot, there's not the slightest chance I'll forget."

"My mistake," Van Effen said. "I'm the person who's doing the forgetting—about your undercover years. I agree with you— there'll be no more threats to Julie. By the same token, I don't even think they'll bother to try to extract any money from David Meijer. Apart from the fact that they appear to have unlimited funds of their own, David Meijer is much more important to them as David Meijer—the man who, however unofficially, has very much the ear of the government and is in a position to influence them, to swing whatever decision may be under consideration. Not that I think the government has any decision under consideration. I think that matter has been effectively taken out of their hands now. The ball is now very much in the British court."

"I wouldn't very much like to be in the position of the British either," George said. "They face a position that, if it's possible, is even worse than the one our government had to face. Are they going to be dictated to, even by proxy, by a bunch of what are essentially no more than terrorists, no matter what lofty motives they may ascribe to themselves? What would happen in Northern Ireland if they did pull out—would there be strife, and murder, even massacre that might cost more than any lives that could or would be lost in the Netherlands—and, of course, we can have no idea of how many lives that might be—hundreds or hundreds of thousands? Or do they just dig in, refuse to move and sit back and let the Hollanders drown, making themselves the lepers of the world, ostracized, perhaps for generations to come, by all nations? And although this is a wicked old world, there must be still quite a few left who still subscribe to some ideals of decency and humanity."

"I do wish you'd shut up, George." Rarely for him, Van Effen sounded almost irritable. "You put the damn thing all too clearly. In a nutshell, it's a toss-up between what value is put on the lives of x number of citizens in Ulster against y number of citizens in the Netherlands." Van Effen bared his teeth without smiling. "It's difficult to solve an equation when you don't even have a clue as to what the factors are. Imponderables, imponderables. The physicists who ramble on about the indeterminates and uncertainties in quantum mechanics should have this one dumped on their laps. Me, I'd rather spin a coin."

"Heads or tails," George said. "What way do you think the coin would land?"

"I have no idea. But there's one factor that is at least faintly determinate, even although that is wildly uncertain, and that is human nature. So at a wild guess, just as wild as guessing at the toss, I would say that the British would give in."

George was silent for a few moments, one massive hand caressing his chin, then said, "The British haven't got much of a reputation for giving in. Feed any of them enough beer or scotch or whatever, and like as not someone will end up telling you that no unspeakable foreigner has ever set foot on their sacred soil for a thousand years. Which is true—and it's the only country in the world that can claim that."

"True, true. But not applicable—or at least of importance—here. This is not a case of Churchill declaiming that we will fight in the streets, hills, beaches or wherever, and that we will never surrender. That's for martial warfare, and in martial warfare the parameters and issues are clear-cut. This is psychological warfare, where the distinctions are blurred out of sight. Are the British any good at psychological warfare? I'm not sure they are. Come to that, I'm not sure that any country is—too many indefinables.

"I don't think, anyway, that it's a factor of either martial or psychological warfare. If there's any factor that's going to count, it's the factor of human nature. This is how it might just possibly happen. The British will bluff and bluster, rant and rave—you have to admit that they yield first place to none when it comes to that—throw their arms in the general direction of a mindless heaven, appeal for common justice and claim they're as pure and white and innocent as the driven snow, which, at this moment in time and conveniently forgetting their not-so-distant bloody history, they have some justification in claiming to be. What, they will ask, have we done to precipitate this intolerable situation, and why should they, luckless lambs being led to the slaughter, et cetera, be forced to find an impossible solution to an impossible problem that is none of their making? All quite true, of course. Why, they will cry, is no one in the world lifting a finger to help us, specifically those idle, spineless, cowardly, incompetent, et cetera, Dutch who can't bear to separate themselves from their cheese and tulips and gin even for the few moments it would take to eradicate this monster in their midst?

"Nobody, of course, is going to pay a blind bit of attention to what they are saying. And when I say 'they,' I don't mean the British people as a whole, I mean Whitehall, their government. And here's where the first real bit of human nature comes in. The British have always prided themselves on their compassion, fair-mindedness, tolerance and undying sympathy for the underdog—never mind what a few hundred million ex-subjects of the British Empire would have to say on that subject—and their kindness to dogs, cats and whatever else takes their passing fancy. That they may be happily existing in a world of sheer illusion is irrelevant; what is relevant for them is that what other people may regard as sheer hypocrisy is, for them, received truth. It is an immutable fact of life—British life, that is—so that if we poor Dutch even as much as got our feet wet, their moral outrage would be fearful to behold. Their indignation would be unbounded, ditto their consternation, the principles of all they think they hold dear destroyed, their finer sensibilities trampled in the mud. *The Times* letter department would be swamped in an unprecedented deluge of mail, all of it demanding that the criminals responsible for this atrocity should be held to account. X number of heads on X number of charges. John the Baptist raised to the nth.

"And now the second real bit of human nature. Whitehall is acutely aware who the John the Baptists would be. The government—any government, come to that, may regard themselves as statesmen or cabinet ministers, but deep down in their cowering hearts they know full well that they are only jumped-up politicians strutting their brief hour upon the stage. Politicians they are and politicians in those fearful hearts they will always remain. And in their little egoistic political minds they are concerned, with rare exceptions—our Minister of Defense is one—only with security of tenure, the trappings of office and the exercise of power. Their egos are their existence, and if you destroy their egos you destroy their existence or at least consign them to the political wilderness for many years to come.

"There would be a landslide defeat for them at the next election or, much more likely, they would be turned out of office very promptly. For your average cabinet minister, such a possibility is too appalling for contemplation. So we won't get our feet wet. Motivated not by their own miserable fear, cowardice, greed and love of power but by the overriding dictates of common humanity, Whitehall will gallantly bow its head to the terrorists."

There was a considerable silence, interrupted only by the hissing and drumming of rain on the windowpanes and streets and the constant rumbling of distant thunder. Then George said, "Never did have a very high opinion of politicians, did you, Peter?"

"I'm in the sort of job where I come into contact with far too many of them."

George shook his head. "That's as may be. But that's a very, very cynical outlook to adopt, Peter."

"We live in a very, very cynical world, George."

"Indeed." There was a pause, and this time George nodded his head. "But sadly I have to agree with you. On both counts. About the world. And about the politicians."

Nobody had anything more to say until a van drew up before the hotel entrance—it was, in fact, the minibus that had been used in the Dam Square the previous evening. Romero Agnelli, who was driving, wound down the window and slid back the door behind him.

"Jump in. You can tell me where to go."

"Jump out," Van Effen said. "We want to talk to you."

"You want to—what's wrong, for God's sake?"

"We just want to talk."

"You can talk inside the bus."

"We may not be going anywhere in that bus."

"You haven't got the—"

"We've got everything. Are we going to stand here all day shouting at each other in the rain?"

Agnelli slid the door forward, opened his own and got out, followed by Leonardo, Daniken and O'Brien. They hastily mounted the steps into the shelter of the porch.

"What the hell do you think you're doing?" Agnelli said. The suave veneer had cracked a little. "And what the hell—"

"And who the hell do you think you're talking to?" Van

Effen said. "We're not your employees. We're your partners—or we thought we were."

"You think you—" Agnelli cut himself off, frowned, smiled and hauled his urbanity back into place. "If we must talk—and it seems we must—wouldn't it be a trifle more pleasant inside?"

"Certainly. This, by the way, is the lieutenant." Van Effen made the introductions, which Vasco hoarsely acknowledged, apologizing for the state of his throat. Agnelli, it was clear, had no idea who he was, even going as far as to say that Vasco couldn't possibly be anything else than an army officer.

Inside, seated in a remote corner of the lounge, Van Effen unfolded his newspaper and laid it on the table before Agnelli. "I suppose you can see those headlines?"

"Um, well, yes, as a matter of fact, I can." He could hardly have failed to, for the banner headline was the biggest the newspaper could produce. It read, quite simply: F.F.F. BLACK-MAILS TWO NATIONS, which was followed by a number of only slightly smaller headlines that were concerned primarily with the perfidy of the F.F.F., the heroic resolution of the Dutch Government, the dauntless defiance of the British Government, and one or two other lies.

"Yes, well, we thought you might have read something like this," Agnelli said. "And we did think you might have been a little troubled. But only a little. I mean, I personally can see no reason for concern, or that anything has radically altered. You knew what the reasons for your employment—sorry, engagement—were and you knew what we were doing. So what has changed so much overnight?"

"This much has changed," George said. "The scope of the thing. The escalation of the plan. The sheer enormity of the matter. I'm a Dutchman, Mr. Agnelli. The lieutenant is a Dutchman. Stephan Danilov may not be Dutch-born, but he's a damn sight more Dutch than he is anything else, and we're not going to stand by and see our country drowned. And *country*, Mr. Agnelli, means people. It is certain that none of us three operates inside the law; it is equally certain that none of us would ever again operate outside the law if we thought that our actions would bring harm to any person alive.

"Quite apart from that, we're out of our depth. We are not small-time criminals but we do not act at an international level. What do you people want with Northern Ireland? Why do you want the British out? Why do you blackmail our government—or the British? Why do you threaten to drown thousands of us? Why threaten to blow up the royal palace? Or haven't you read the papers? Are you all mad?"

"We are not mad." Agnelli sounded almost weary. "It's you who are mad—if you believe all that you read in the papers. The papers have just printed—in this instance—what your government has told them to say. In a state of national emergency, and the government do regard this as such, they have the power to do so. And the government told them what *we* told them to say. They have followed our instructions precisely. We have no intention of hurting a single living soul."

"Northern Ireland is still a far cry from blackmailing the Dutch Government for a little ready cash," Van Effen said. "This, we thought, had been your original intention and one with which we'd have gone along. Quite willingly. We have no reason to love the government." He stared off into the far distance. "I have no reason to like quite a number of governments."

"On the basis of what you have told me," Agnelli said, "I can quite understand that." He smiled, produced his ebony cigarette holder, fitted a Turkish cigarette and lit it with his gold-inlaid onyx lighter, all of which demonstrated that he was at ease, in charge and back on balance again—assuming, that is, that he had ever been off it in the first place. "Cash is the basis, gentlemen, and only cash. Precisely how it is the basis I am not yet permitted to divulge, but you have my assurance that it is the sole and only motivation. And you also have my assurance—which you can take or leave as you choose—that we have no intention of bringing harm to anyone. And, quite honestly, in saying so we are not as moved, perhaps, by humanitarian considerations as you are. Organized crime on a large scale is big business and we run our affairs on a businesslike basis. Emotion is nothing, calculation all. Killing not only pays few dividends, it is usually counterproductive. A robber is pursued by the law, but only within reasonable limits; but he who kills in the process of robbery is relentlessly pursued. No, no, gentlemen, we are in the business of conducting purely psychological warfare."

George reached across the table and touched another headline. "Kidnapping young women is another form of psychological warfare?"

"But of course. One of the most effective of all psychological forms of blackmail. It touches the strings of one's heart, you understand."

"You are," George said genially, "one cold-blooded bastard." When George was at his most genial he was at his most menacing, and the slight compression of Agnelli's lips showed that he realized that he was in the presence of menace. "I wonder how you would like it if your wife, sister or daughter were held with a gun at her head or a knife at her throat? And don't throw up your hands in horror. Blackmailers never hold hostages without accompanying threats of what will happen if their blackmailing ends are not achieved. As often as not, such threats are carried out. What would it be in this case? Turning them over to some of the less uninhibited among your employees for a few hours' innocent pleasure? Torture? Or the ultimate? We are, as we have repeatedly told you, not men of violence. But if any harm were to come in any way to those women, totally harmless and innocent as we believe them to be, we would be capable of actions that you would regard as being acts of unimaginable violence. I do wish you would believe me, Mr. Agnelli."

Agnelli believed him all right. The atmosphere in the Trianon's lounge was acceptably cool, but a sheen of sweat had suddenly appeared on Agnelli's forehead.

George said, "Why, for instance, did you kidnap this Anne Meijer? Is it because her father runs a minor kingdom of his own and may be presumed to have a powerful voice with the government?" Agnelli nodded silently. "And this"—he twisted the paper to have a glance at it—"this Julie van Effen. She's only a policeman's sister. There are thousands of policemen in the Netherlands."

"There's only one Van Effen." Agnelli spoke with a considerable depth of feeling. "We know there's a nationwide hunt up for us, but we also know who's leading it. Van Effen. If we have his sister, and we do, we may clip his wings a bit."

"You don't sound as if you care for the man very much."

Agnelli said nothing; the look in his eyes said it for him.

"And you still ask me to believe that you wouldn't subject those girls to some violent forms of persuasion to achieve your ends?"

"I don't really care whether you believe me or not." Once again Agnelli was beginning to sound more than a little tired. "I believe you are quite capable of doing what you say you would do if you found out we are deceiving you. I have no doubt that you are heavily armed. I suggest you come along and see and believe for yourselves. Take a look at our hostages this afternoon. If you don't like what you see you can leave or use any other measures you think appropriate. There's nothing else I can say, and I can't speak fairer than that."

George said, "Stephan?"

"We'll go along. Mr. Agnelli's explanations may be a bit thin, but if we are to believe in the essence of what he says— and I have no reason to think that we shouldn't—then I think we all may have a great deal to lose if we are raising objections to situations that do not exist. It wouldn't be very bright of us to cut off our own noses. As Mr. Agnelli says, let's go and see for ourselves."

"Thank you, gentlemen." Agnelli didn't mop his brow, perhaps because he wasn't the brow-mopping kind, but almost certainly because he would not have regarded it as a politic thing to do. "I was by no means convinced that you would come to see it my way—you are exceptionally difficult negotiators, if I may say so—but I am glad you have done so." Moderation, reasonableness, courtesy—Agnelli could generously afford all of those now that he had had, as he thought, his own way. "Now, where's the truck?"

"Nearby garage."

"Garage? Is it safe—"

"I *own* it," George said. "For God's sake, do you think this is the first time?"

"Of course. Silly question."

"We have one or two questions," Van Effen said. "We're committed now and we've no more wish to take unnecessary chances than you have. I don't for a moment suppose we'll know where this place is until we get there. Have you a place of concealment for this truck?"

"Yes."

"How many people are going out there?"

"Apart from yourselves? The three of us, Mr. Riordan, whom you haven't met but have read about, Joop and Joachim. Why?"

"Please. My turn for questions. You travel in the minibus?"

"Well, no. We'd hoped there would be plenty of room in the truck."

No, indeed, Van Effen thought. They wanted to keep the closest possible eye on the three of them and the precious contents of the truck. "How many cars?"

"Cars?" Agnelli looked faintly surprised. "No cars. Why?"

"Why?" Van Effen looked at the ceiling, then at George, then back at Agnelli. "Why? Tell me, Mr. Agnelli, have you ever transported stolen government property before?"

"This will be a new experience for me."

"I want two cars. One to follow the truck at two or three hundred yards, the other to follow the first car at a similar distance."

"Ah! Well now, I appreciate this. You do not wish to be followed."

"I have a deeply rooted objection to being followed. It's one chance in a million. We do not take that chance."

"Good, good. Joop and Joachim. I'll phone now."

"Last question. We forgot to discuss this. Do we return to the city tonight?"

"No."

"You should have told us. We do require a toothbrush or

two. However, we guessed right and packed some gear. Three minutes in the lobby."

Back in his room Van Effen said, "George, I've said it before and say it again. Your career has been a wasted one, ruined and misplaced. That was splendid, splendid theater."

George made a mock-modest gesture of deprecation. "It was nothing."

"How to establish a moral ascendancy in one easy lesson. They're going to go out of their way not to step on our toes. And did you gather the impression, George, that they need us more than we need them? Or, at least, that *they* think so?"

"Yes. Intriguing."

"Very. Second, they know that they're not going to be followed. It was our suggestion, so that makes us trustworthy."

"Anyone can see that. It will also, we trust, make them relax their vigilance."

"We trust. Third, again thanks to you, it is certain that Agnelli has no idea whatsoever who I am. Agnelli is sadly in need of a course of instruction from you. He's a poor dissembler and overreacts too easily. It is not possible that, knowing who I was, he could have sat at the same table without giving himself away. Lastly, it seems fairly certain that we'll be safe until or unless they find out who we are or until we are no longer of any use to them—when they have achieved whatever it is they want to achieve, that is. But I think the latter unlikely. I could understand them wanting to dispose of us if we were to betray their identity, but their identity is already well known—the names of those in Kondstaal's house last night will be in every major newspaper in Europe this morning. Or by nightfall. And the TV and radio. I asked Mr. Wieringa to make specially sure about that. And didn't you love all this talk about limiting themselves solely to pure psychology and being interested only in cash returns? You believed him, of course?"

"Sure. You can always trust a man of character, like Signor Agnelli."

* * *

Agnelli, O'Brien and Daniken were waiting in the lounge when the two men descended. Van Effen said, "Fixed?"

"Yes. But one thing we overlooked—or I overlooked. I said I'd call them back. I didn't know whether to ask them to come here or not."

"We'll let them know when we move out in the truck."

"Why not call them from here?"

Van Effen looked at him as if in faint surprise. "Do *you* ever make two consecutive calls from the same phone?"

"Do I—" Agnelli shook his head. "And to think that I thought *I* was the most suspicious, most security-conscious person around. Do we move now?"

"The heating in Dutch army trucks is rather substandard. I suggest a schnapps. We have time?"

"We have. Very well. Until the lieutenant comes, I assume."

"He doesn't join us. We join him. That's why I suggested a schnapps. Takes him a little time."

"I see. Rather, I don't. He's not going to join—"

"He's leaving by the fire escape. The lieutenant has a penchant for unorthodox exits. Also, he's bashful about calling attention to himself."

"Unorthodox. Bashful. I understand now." Standing by what appeared to be a freshly painted army truck in an otherwise empty, brightly lit small garage, Agnelli surveyed the impressive figure of Vasco, who was now attired in a brand-new Dutch army captain's uniform. "Yes, I understand. The desk staff in the Trianon would have found the change intriguing. But I thought—um—the lieutenant was a lieutenant?"

"Old habits die hard. You don't change a man's name just because he changes his suit. Promoted last month. Services to queen and country."

"Services to—ah, I see." Agnelli, it was clear, didn't see at all. "And what's this bright-orange dagger flash on the radiator?"

"'Maneuvers. Do not approach.'"

"You don't miss much and that's a fact," Agnelli said. "May I look inside?"

"Naturally. I wouldn't like you to think that you'd bought a pig in a poke."

"This, Mr. Danilov, is the most unlikely-looking poke that I've ever seen." Agnelli had inspected the neatly stacked and, in the case of the missiles and launchers, highly gleaming contents of the truck and was now actually rubbing his hands together. "Magnificent, quite magnificent. By heavens, Mr. Danilov, when George here is given a shopping list, I must say that he delivers. I wouldn't have believed it."

George made a dismissive gesture. "A little assistance from the lieutenant here. Next time, something more difficult."

"Splendid, splendid." Agnelli looked toward the front of the truck and at the heavily side-curtained bench seat behind the front seats. "That, too? I see, Mr. Danilov, that you share my passion for privacy."

"Not I. Senior Dutch army officers on maneuvers."

"No matter. Mr. Riordan, I am sure, will be delighted. When you meet him you will understand why. He is a man of a singular appearance and rather difficult to conceal, which is a pity, as he does like his privacy, too." Agnelli was silent for a moment, then cleared his throat and said, "In view of all this and the very, very stringent security precautions you have taken, Mr. Danilov, I do feel a bit—in fact, very—diffident about asking—but, well, do you mind if Mr. O'Brien here carried out a closer inspection?"

Van Effen smiled. "I've often wondered what Mr. O'Brien's function might be. But this? Well, I'm slightly puzzled. If Mr. O'Brien knows more about explosives and arms than we three do, then he must be Europe's leading expert and our services would seem to be superfluous."

"Explosives, Mr. Danilov?" O'Brien was an easy smiler and, as it turned out, had a pleasant light baritone voice, a natural for the rendering of "When Irish eyes." "Explosives terrify me. I'm an 'electronics man.'"

"Mr. O'Brien is being modest," Agnelli said. "He's an electronics genius, one of the very best in the business. Security. Alarms. Installation—or deactivating."

"Ah. Burglar alarms. Photoelectric rays, pressure pads, things like that. Always wanted to meet one of those. It'll be a pleasure to watch one at work. Little enough scope, I would have thought, for an electronics man around an army truck. Wait a minute." Van Effen paused briefly, then smiled. "By all means go ahead, Mr. O'Brien. I'll take long odds against you finding one, though."

"Finding what, Mr. Danilov?"

"One of those dinky little location transmitters."

Agnelli and O'Brien exchanged glances. Agnelli said, "Dinky little—I mean, how on earth—"

"Because I removed one this morning. Rather, the lieutenant did it for me."

Agnelli, as Van Effen had said, would never stand in line for an Oscar. He was perplexed, apprehensive and suspicious, all at the same time. "But why should one—I mean, how did you suspect—"

"Don't distress yourself." Van Effen smiled. "Perfectly simple explanation. You see—"

"But this is an army truck!"

"Precisely. Far from uncommon on army trucks. Use them on their silly war games, especially at night, when there are no lights permitted and strict radio silence. Only way they can locate each other. The lieutenant knew where they were usually concealed and found and detached this one."

Vasco opened a map compartment by the driver's seat, removed a tiny metallic object, and handed it to Van Effen, who passed it over to O'Brien.

"That's it, all right," O'Brien said. He looked doubtfully at Agnelli. "In that case, Romero—"

"No, no," Van Effen said. "Go ahead and search. Be happier if you do. Damn truck could be littered with them, for all I know. Speaking personally, I wouldn't know where to start looking."

Agnelli, trying with his usual lack of success to conceal his relief, nodded to O'Brien. Van Effen and George left the truck and wandered idly around, talking in a desultory fashion. Agnelli, they could see, was displaying a keen interest in O'Brien at work, but none in them. In a far corner Van Effen said,

"Must be an interesting profession, being a professional dismantler of alarm systems."

"Very. Useful, too. If you want to get at the private art collection of some billionaire or other. Or into a secret army base. Or bank vaults."

"It's also useful if you want to blow up a dike or a canal bank?"

"No."

"I didn't think so."

Although it was only just after 1 P.M. when they left the garage, it could well have been nighttime for the amount of light left in the sky. And although it seemed impossible that the amount of rain could have increased, it had. The truck was equipped with two-speed wipers but might as well have been equipped with none at all. And the wind blew even more strongly from the north. Apart from the occasional triple tram, the streets were deserted. One might almost have thought that the efforts and intention of the F.F.F. were wasted: Holland, it appeared, was about to drown under the weight of its own rainfall.

Agnelli had made his phone call from the garage. Shortly after leaving it, at a word from Agnelli, Vasco, who was driving, pulled up outside an undistinguished café off the Utrechtse Straat. Two cars were parked there, both small, both Renaults. Agnelli got out and spoke hurriedly to the invisible drivers of the cars; he had need to hurry, he had no umbrella and his gabardine coat offered no protection at all against the pitiless rain.

"Joachim and Joop," he said on his return. "They are following us to a restaurant just this side of Amstelveen. Even the F.F.F. must eat." Agnelli was back to smiling again, but it was impossible to confirm this. The inside of the truck was totally black.

"If they can follow us," Van Effen said. "In this weather, I can see that my precautions were superfluous. I thought we were to meet your brother and Mr. Riordan. I'll be interested to meet your Mr. Riordan. If the newspaper accounts are anything to go by, he must be a most extraordinary character." He ignored George's heavy nudge in the ribs.

"He's all that. They've elected to remain in the cars—I don't suppose they fancied getting wet. We'll meet up in De Groene Lanterne."

Riordan was indeed extraordinary. For some reason known only to himself, he had elected to dress in a sweeping, neck-buttoned, black-and-white shepherd's tartan cloak with matching deerstalker, of the type favored by Highland lairds and Sherlock Holmes. As the cloak ended six inches above his knees and hence made him look even more incongruously tall and skeletal than ever, he couldn't possibly have been trying to make himself inconspicuous. He had greeted everyone civilly enough—when he wasn't declaiming against the IRA he was, it seemed, a normally grave and courteous man—raised his eyebrows at the sight of Vasco's uniform, readily accepted the explanation and thereafter remained silent, not from any wish to disassociate himself from those at the table but because he was carrying a large, intricate and expensive radio, with a pair of earphones clamped to his head. He was listening, Agnelli explained, to weather forecasts and Dutch and international news broadcasts. Agnelli didn't have to explain why.

Lunch over, Riordan elected to continue the journey in the truck, earphones still in place. He ensconced himself in the right-hand corner of the rear bench seat and seemed to approve of the heavy side curtain, which he pushed as far forward as possible. Vasco drove south during the dark afternoon, making the best speed possible, which, because of the near-zero visibility, was no speed at all. Van Effen was particularly impressed by the carefully polite attention Vasco paid to Agnelli's would-be meticulous instructions as how to drive through Utrecht. As Vasco had been born, bred, lived all his life and been a police driver in Utrecht, it said much for Vasco's heroic patience and histrionics that he three times followed directions that he must have known to be wrong.

About mid-afternoon, Riordan unhooked his earphones. "Progress, gentlemen, progress. The Dutch Foreign Minister and Defense Minister—that's that excellent Mr. Wieringa of theirs—arrived in London this afternoon and are meeting with their counterparts. A communiqué is expected. We are being taken seriously."

Van Effen said, "After those scare headlines, those banner headlines in the papers today, and all the emergency news flashes on TV and radio, did you expect *not* to be taken seriously?"

"No. But gratifying, nonetheless gratifying." Riordan reaffixed his earphones and leaned back into his corner. The expression on his face was an odd mixture of the expectant and the beatific. A man with a mission, Riordan wasn't going to miss out on anything.

Some twenty minutes later the truck pulled off to the right onto a B road and, a couple of miles farther on, turned left onto a still more minor road. It stopped at a building that appeared to be fronted by a brightly lit porch.

"Journey's end," Agnelli said. "Our headquarters—well, one of them—and our overnight stop. I think you'll be comfortable here."

"A windmill," Van Effen said.

"You seem surprised," Agnelli said. "Hardly uncommon in these parts. Disused but still functional, which is also not unusual. Large extensions and quite modernized. It has the additional attraction of being a long way from anywhere. If you look to this side you'll see the place of concealment I promised for the truck. A barn."

"And that other barnlike structure beside it?"

"State secret."

"Helicopter."

Agnelli laughed in the darkness. "End of state secret. Obvious, I suppose, since we told people that we had taken aerial photographs of those rather stirring scenes north of Alkmaar on the North Holland Canal."

"So you're now the happy owner of both army and air force property?"

"No. Not air force. Indistinguishable, though. A lick of paint here, a lick of paint there, some carefully selected registration numbers—but it's unimportant. Let's go inside and see what we can find in the way of old Dutch cheer and hospitality." Now that he had, he thought, completed his mission with a 100 percent degree of success, he was positively radiating a genial cordiality. It could well, Van Effen thought, represent his nature: he was not equipped for all the cut and thrust, riposte and parry that he had been through that afternoon.

"Not for me," George said. "I'm a businessman, and a businessman always likes to—"

"If you're referring to payment, George, I assure you—"

"Payment? I'm not referring to payment." George sounded pained. "I'm referring to standard business practices. Lieutenant, is there an overhead light? Thank you." George produced a sheaf of papers from an inside pocket and handed them to Agnelli. "Inventory of goods. You have to sign the receipt but not until I have checked the conditions of all the items—you will understand that I had no time to do so this morning—and see how they survived the transport. Ordinary business ethics." No one seemed to find it peculiar that George should use the word "ethics" in connection with stolen goods. "But some of that hospitality wouldn't come amiss as we go. Beer for me."

"Of course," Agnelli said, then added delicately, "Would you be requiring any help?"

"Not really. But it is customary for the purchaser or purchaser's agent to be present. I would suggest Mr. O'Brien. Electronics experts are accustomed to small fiddly things, and detonators are small and fiddly. A carelessly dropped detonator, Mr. Agnelli, and there wouldn't be a great deal left of your windmill. Wouldn't be a great deal left of the people once inside, either."

Agnelli nodded his satisfaction and led the way to the porch that had been added to the windmill. A tall, shock-haired and unshaven youth whose most notable facial characteristic was the negligible clearance between eyebrows and hairline moved to bar their entrance. A machine pistol was held loosely in his right hand.

"One side, Willi." Agnelli's voice was sharp. "It's me."

"I can see that." Willi scowled—it was the kind of face

that wasn't built for much else—and stared truculently at Van Effen. "Who's he?"

"Hospitable," Van Effen said. "Our genial host, no doubt. God help us. This the kind of hired help you have around here?"

Willi took a threatening step forward, lifting his gun as he did so, then subsided gently to the ground, bent over and clutching his midriff as he did so: the blow he had received there had been no friendly tap. Van Effen took the gun, removed the magazine and dropped the gun on top of the wheezing Willi. Van Effen stared at Agnelli, his expression once more a nice mix of consternation and disbelief.

"Frankly, I'm appalled. I don't like this. Is this—I mean, is he typical? You have other cretins like this on your team? People who are going to hold—no, people who are holding nations for ransom having—having—words fail me. Have you never heard of the weakest link in the chain?"

"My own sentiments exactly," Riordan said gravely. "You will remember, Romero, that I expressed my reservations about this fellow. Even as a guard, the only possible function he could serve, his limitations have been cruelly exposed."

"I agree, Riordan, I agree." Agnelli's ebullience was in temporary abeyance. "Willi is a disappointment. He'll have to go."

Willi had now slipped over onto his side. He was conscious enough, propped on one shaky elbow and grimacing with pain. Van Effen looked over his all-but-prone form to the opened doorway beyond. His sister was there, Annemarie by her side, Samuelson just behind them. The expression on both girls' faces was the same—wide-eyed, shocked, uncomprehending. Van Effen let his eyes rest on them for a brief moment, then looked indifferently away.

"Have to go, Agnelli? Have to go? If he goes, I go. Can't you see that you're stuck with him, want it or not? Stuck with him either above ground or below. Let him go and the first thing he'll do is talk his head off to the first cop he meets. No drastic methods, preferably, but his silence must be assured. I hope the rest of your Praetorian guard is a cut above this character."

"The rest are many cuts above this unfortunate." Samuelson, rubicund, smiling and looking even more prosperous than the previous evening, had gently pushed the girls apart and stepped out onto the stoop. He smelled of after-shave lotion. Rubbing his chin with an immaculately manicured hand, he peered down at Willi, then looked up at Van Effen. "You do have a direct way with you, my friend. At the same time one must admit that you come to some remarkably quick conclusions in a commendably short time. I must confess that I have occasionally felt tempted to do just what you have done, but well, explosive violence is not my forte. Ah yes, I saw it all. Very economical, very." He extended a hand. "Samuelson."

"Danilov." Judging from both the man's bearing and his speech, Van Effen knew that he was in the presence of the man who mattered. His speech. Samuelson had said so few words the previous evening that his country of origin had remained uncertain. Van de Graaf had thought him Irish-American. Van de Graaf, Van Effen thought, had been wrong. This man was English-American. Perhaps even an Englishman who had spent just long enough in the United States to pick up a slight American overtone. Van Effen gestured to the fallen man. "Sorry about this, Samuelson. One does not usually treat a host's staff in so summary a fashion. On the other hand you must admit that it's not the average guest who finds himself dealing with a subhuman with a submachine gun, poked in his face."

"A well-taken point, Mr. Danilov." Like Agnelli, Samuelson seemed given to smiles. "A breach of hospitality. It will be the last—as you yourself have personally assured. All is well, Romero?"

"Perfect, Mr. Samuelson. Everything there, everything in order. Exactly as Mr. Danilov guaranteed."

"Splendid. Mr. Danilov does have a certain aura of competence about him. Come in, come in. Wretched evening. Absolutely wretched." That, thought Van Effen, made him

English for sure. "And good evening to you, Captain. I understood you were a lieutenant."

"A very recent captain," Vasco said hoarsely. "Sorry about this throat."

"Dear me, dear me." Samuelson sounded genuinely concerned. "A hot toddy, and at once." Samuelson did not seem to find it at all amiss that a regular army captain should be in their company; but a man with so smooth, unlined a face could take many things in his stride without registering reactions of any kind. "Oh, let me introduce our two charming guests. Miss Meijer, Miss Van Effen."

Van Effen bowed briefly. "Those are the two who figured so prominently in the headlines this morning? Their photographs didn't do them justice."

Agnelli said, "Mr. Danilov and his friends were concerned about their well-being, Mr. Samuelson."

"Ah yes. Compatriots, of course. No need, no need. As you can see, both are in excellent health."

There were five other people in the room, all men. Two were earnest-looking, intellectual-looking youths cast in the mold of Joachim and Joop. The other three were older, bigger and a great deal tougher-looking, although that didn't mean that they were in any way more dangerous. They looked uncommonly like the Secret Service men who guard an American president. Samuelson didn't see fit to introduce them; as a result, indeed, of some signal that Van Effen had not seen they all quietly left the room.

"Well, now." Van Effen looked at Samuelson, Agnelli and Riordan in turn. "I don't know which of you I should address. It doesn't matter. We have delivered the material. One of our number is at present checking the explosives and armaments to see that they are in the best possible working order. We understood that some call might be made on our services— our expertise, if you want to put it that way. If you don't require us, there's no point in our remaining. We have no wish to impose ourselves on anybody."

Samuelson smiled. "You would rather go?"

Van Effen smiled in turn. "I think you are perfectly well

aware that we would rather stay. I'm as curious as the next man. Besides, it would be most interesting to know what is going to happen without having to wait to read about it in the newspapers."

"Stay you shall," Samuelson said. "We will probably have need of your expertise. We do, in fact, have plans for you. But first, perhaps, a soupçon of Borreltje. Five P.M., and five P.M., I understand, is the prescribed hour. Leonardo"—this to Agnelli's brother, who had just entered with Daniken—"be so kind as to have some hot water brought from the kitchen." Van Effen was certain that Samuelson was the man who called the tune. "And some honey. We must do something about this fearful cold the captain has. Come. Join me."

A log fire burned in an open hearth built into the windowless back wall. Adjoining this was a circular oaken bar, small but splendidly stocked. Samuelson moved behind this as Riordan said, "You will excuse me."

"Of course, James, of course," Samuelson said. Van Effen was faintly surprised. Riordan didn't look like a man who had a first name. Riordan nodded to the company and mounted a circular stairway.

Van Effen said: "Riordan doesn't approve of our heathenish practice of having a Borreltje at this hour?"

"Mr. Riordan doesn't disapprove. He doesn't drink himself, nor does he smoke, but he doesn't disapprove. I may as well tell you—for you will find out anyway and I don't wish to cause anybody any embarrassment—that Mr. Riordan regularly goes upstairs at this hour for prayer and meditation. He does this several times a day and one cannot but respect a man with such deeply held beliefs. He is very devout—and is, in fact, an ordained minister of the church."

"You all surprise me," Van Effen said. He thought briefly. "No, on second thought you don't. Seems very much in character. For such a devout character, I must say, the Reverend has certainly let loose a storm of cats in the dovecotes of Europe today."

"You must not think ill of Riordan, nor underestimate him." Samuelson spoke seriously. "He is an evangelist, a missionary fired by a burning zeal. He is genuinely appalled by what is happening in Northern Ireland and believes that if blood must be spilled to bring peace to that troubled land, then that's how it will be. In his own words, he's prepared to use the devil's tools to fight the devil."

"And you support him in all this?"

"Naturally. Why else should I be here?"

It would have been interesting, Van Effen thought, to know just why else he should be there, but it seemed hardly the time and place to raise the question. He hoisted himself on a bar stool and looked around.

The two women were in whispered consultation. Agnelli and Daniken had already occupied the stools at the farther end of the bar. Vasco, who had been wandering around looking at the paintings and brass and copper work on the walls, made his unconcerned way over to the bar and sat down beside Daniken, whom he began to engage in hoarse conversation.

"Mr. Samuelson." It was Julie. "I think I'll go to my room. I have a bit of a headache."

Van Effen remained casual, drumming his fingers idly on the bartop, a man perfectly at ease with himself. In fact, the last thing that he wanted was that either girl should go to her room. Samuelson, who had been stooping down behind the bar, came to his unwitting rescue.

"My dear Julie!" If he weren't certain that he knew what Samuelson would say next, Van Effen could have hit him. "Not to be thought of. Here we have a fine Tio Pepe. Guaranteed cure for any headache. Would you deprive me of your company?"

The girls would obviously have gladly done just that, but just as obviously they deemed it prudent to do as he said— prisoners tend to do what their jailers tell them—and came and perched reluctantly by the bar, Julie close to her brother. She glanced at him briefly, a glance that told him quite clearly what she thought of violent characters who discuss offhandedly sticking undesirable characters under the ground, then looked away. Almost at once she looked back again, fortunately not too quickly: something had just touched her right thigh. She looked at him, frowning slightly, then glanced downward. Almost at once she turned away and made a quiet remark to Annemarie, just as Samuelson's head cleared the bar again. Magnificent, Van Effen thought, she was magnificent, the best in Amsterdam wouldn't be good enough for his sister after this. She accepted her sherry from Samuelson with a correctly pleasant if somewhat forced smile, delicately sipped her drink, placed it on the bartop, opened her handbag on her lap and brought out cigarettes and lighter. She *was* splendid, Van Effen thought. She lit the cigarette, returned the case but not the lighter to her bag and, while still talking quietly to Annemarie while watching, without seeming to, the men at the bar, dropped her hand till it touched Van Effen's. A moment later, the lighter and the folded note, the top of which had been protruding between the fore and middle fingers of Van Effen's, was safely inside her closed bag. He could have hugged and kissed her and made a mental note to do so at the first available opportunity. In the meantime, he did the next best thing. He downed his Borreltje in one gulp. He had never much cared for it, but this one tasted as nectar must have done to the gods. Samuelson, ever the attentive host, hurried across to replenish his glass and Van Effen thanked him courteously. The second drink went the same way as the first.

Julie locked the bedroom door behind her, opened her bag and brought out the note, which she began to unfold. Annemarie looked at her curiously.

"What have you got there? Julie, your hands are shaking!"

"A billet-doux that I just got from a love-lorn suitor in the bar. Wouldn't your hands shake if you'd just got a love note?" She smoothed out the note so that they could read it together. It had been meticulously typed; plainly, not a scribbled note put together at the last moment.

"Sorry about the appearance and the thick accent," it said, "but you will understand that I can't very well go around in my ordinary clothes and using my ordinary voice.

"The dashing young army captain is Vasco. You will understand why he has developed this sore throat. Annemarie *might* just have been a little startled to hear his normal voice. Agnelli would have been very startled.

"George is with us. Couldn't bring him in at first because George can't be disguised. Also, couldn't have you hugging him with feminine shrieks of delight.

"You don't know us and you don't want to know us. Stay away from us but don't make it too obvious. Distant, remote and extending to us as much courtesy as you would to any other common criminals.

"Don't try to do anything clever. Don't try to do anything. The men, probably, are not dangerous but watch the women. They're shrewd and have nasty devious feminine minds.

"Destroy this note immediately. I love you both."

"And signed," Julie said, "with his own unmistakable signature." Her hands still weren't too steady.

"You said he would come," Annemarie said. Her voice was like Julie's hands.

"Yes, I did, didn't I? Didn't expect him quite so soon, though. What are we going to do—cry with relief?"

"Certainly not." Annemarie sniffed. "He might have spared us the bits about feminine shrieks of delight and shrewd and nasty devious feminine minds." She watched as Julie ignited the note over a washbasin and flushed the ashes away. "So what do we do now?"

"Celebrate."

"In the bar?"

"Where else?"

"And ignore them."

"Totally."

9

THE BARN THAT served as a garage was cold and drafty and leaking and couldn't have served as a barn for many years; the air was heavy with the unsavory smell of musty hay, although there was no trace of hay to be seen. But it was clean and well-lit enough to show that the army truck's freshly painted bodywork had vanished under a thick encrustation of mud.

George and O'Brien were bent over what appeared to be a checklist when Van Effen entered. George looked over O'Brien's shoulder and lifted an interrogative eyebrow. Van Effen gave a brief nod in return, then said, "About through?"

"Finished," George said. "All present and correct, I think."

"*Think*," O'Brien said. "Check, re-check and cross-check. Never saw a man so meticulous about anything. But I did learn a little about explosives. And a lot about drinking beer."

They switched off the lights, padlocked the doors—George pointedly pocketing the key while making some remark to the effect that signed receipts came first—and entered the mill. Julie and Annemarie were seated at a table by the fire, each with a small glass before her, a sure indication, Van Effen knew, that they had read the note. He noted, approvingly, that both girls regarded their entry with open curiosity; it would have been an odd person indeed who would have registered indifference when encountering George's vast bulk for the first time. Across the fireplace, and seated at another table, Samuelson was just replacing the handset of a state-of-the-art radio transceiver; when obtaining new equipment the F.F.F. didn't go to secondhand markets.

"All well?" Samuelson said.

"All well," O'Brien said. "Just about managed to stop George testing the detonators with his teeth. That's quite an arsenal you have there, Mr. Samuelson."

"Sign here, please." George laid three copies of the inventory on the table before Samuelson, who signed them; thus finally confirming that he was the man in charge. He smiled and handed them back to George, who solemnly handed over the garage padlock key.

"A pleasure to do business with you, George. How would you like the fee to be paid?"

"Not time for the fee yet," George said. "The inventory is only a promise. Wait for the guarantee—let's see if the damn things work."

Samuelson smiled again. "I thought businessmen always demanded cash on delivery."

"Not this businessman. If, of course, you decide not to use them, then I'll present the bill—you understand that I can't very well return them to the ordnance store. Or if you decide to dispense with our services."

"Still a pleasure, George. I'm quite certain we'll be requiring both your goods *and* your services. Well, gentlemen, we'll be hearing a rather—" He broke off, looked at Van Effen, patted the radio and said, "You know what this is, don't you?"

"A transceiver. RCA. The best, I believe. If you'd a mind to, you could reach the moon with that."

"It can reach Amsterdam, which is all I want. Helmut. Helmut Paderewsky, whom you have met, I believe."

"Yes. I rather wondered where Helmut was."

"Our voice in the capital. He has just arranged for our latest message to be made known." He glanced at the wall clock. "Exactly eight minutes. TV and radio. We've decided not to bother about newspapers any more. I am not being smug when I say that we can now get instant coverage whenever we wish it. I think you'll all find it a rather interesting message—

messages rather. Don't you think we should give them—ah—
advance notice, Romero? Mr. Danilov here has said that he
likes to know what's going on before he reads or hears about
it."

"If it is your wish, of course," Agnelli said. "But I would
rather they saw it on TV. I think it would be interesting to see
what the reaction of the average Dutch citizen would be."

"We'll wait. It's unimportant. Although I'd hardly call those
three average Dutch citizens. Ah! Our provision party has returned."

The two girls Van Effen had met the previous evening in
the room off the Voorburgwal entered, each carrying a shopping
basket. They were followed by a young man who was having
some difficulty in coping with a huge hamper.

"Welcome back," Samuelson said benignly. "A successful
expedition, I see. Ah! Introductions. Mr. Danilov, of course,
you've met. This is George, this is the captain, who for some
obscure reason is called the lieutenant. Maria. Kathleen. You
look puzzled, Mr. Danilov."

"That's a lot of food."

"True, true. But a lot of mouths to feed."

"It's a fair way to Utrecht."

"Utrecht? My dear fellow, we shop at the local village store.
Delighted to have our trade. Ah, the factor of anonymity." He
laughed. "Romero. If you would be so kind."

Romero led Van Effen to the front door, opened it and
gestured. At the foot of the steps stood a blue van. Emblazoned
on its side, in golden lettering, was the legend GOLDEN GATE
FILM PRODUCTIONS.

"Ingenious," Van Effen said.

"It is, rather. Not a famous-enough name to attract national
attention, but we're certainly well enough known locally. Been
here for almost a month now. We have a camera crew almost
continually on the move around the area. An isolated spot, this,
and it brings a touch of color into their otherwise drab lives.
No trouble at all in recruiting house and kitchen staff; we are
generous employers and very well thought of locally."

"You'd be even better thought of if they knew that this is

probably the only area in the Netherlands that's immune from flooding."

"There's that, there's that." Agnelli seemed quite pleased with the idea. "War film, I need hardly say. Hence the helicopter. Had to get official permission, of course, but that was a mere formality."

"I'd wondered how you'd managed that. You do have your nerve, that I must say."

"Just had a thought. This newly acquired truck. Change of paint and it can move around in complete freedom. War film—army truck. Follows, no?"

"Yes. This is your brainchild, of course?"

"Yes. But why 'of course'?"

"You have a certain talent for devious organization."

The TV announcer, soberly suited and tied and ominously grave in expression, looked as if he were about to pronounce a funeral oration.

"We have just received what is called an interim communiqué from London. It says that the talks about the Dutch crisis are continuing and that a further communiqué can be expected within the hour.

"It was expected that some further statements would be received from this terrorist organization calling itself the F.F.F. Those have arrived some fifteen minutes ago. They are not so much statements as threats of the very gravest nature.

"The first of those states that they, the F.F.F., expect to hear by midnight that a definite and affirmative answer—that is an answer agreeing to the F.F.F.'s demands—will be announced before eight A.M. tomorrow. If they do not hear such confirmation by midnight, the Oostlijk-Flevoland dike will be blown at five minutes past midnight. The citizens of Lelystad are advised to begin to take precautionary measures now. If they fail to do this, the F.F.F. now disclaim all responsibility for their fate.

"The second statement makes the announcement that the F.F.F. have in their possession a number of nuclear explosive devices which they will not hesitate to use, if the need arises, to achieve their ends. The F.F.F. hasten to assure the people of the Netherlands that those nuclear devices are not of the caliber of major hydrogen or atomic warheads. They are tactical battlefield devices intended for delivery by plane, rocket or shellfire. All are of American manufacture, some still on the secret list. All have been obtained from NATO bases in Germany. They have the serial numbers of those devices—they are clearly stamped on each one—and U.S. forces in Germany can confirm that those devices are, in fact, missing. If, that is, they are prepared to give this confirmation."

There was a pause while the newscaster broke off to accept and glance at a sheet of paper that had just been handed him by a studio colleague; judging from the stricken expression on the colleague's face, he had already read the message.

Van Effen looked around the room. No newscaster, he felt certain, had ever had so rapt an audience. The faces of George and the lieutenant were expressionless, but that was only because, in certain circumstances such as those, they hadn't much use for expressions; but their eyes were very still. Julie and Annemarie looked shocked. Kathleen and Maria were smiling, but their smiles were half-hearted and more than tinged by apprehension. No question they had known what was coming, but they still didn't like hearing it. Agnelli, O'Brien and Daniken looked thoughtful but not particularly gratified. But the normally genial Samuelson was reveling in every moment of it. True, he was still smiling, but there was no warmth now in his smile; there never can be in the smile of a hungry crocodile that has just spotted his lunch.

"We have here," the announcer said, "a further message from the F.F.F. They say they are prepared to release those numbers at any time, but they feel a practical demonstration to prove their possession of those nuclear devices would be much more convincing. Accordingly, they intend to explode one of those devices in the Ijsselmeer in the early afternoon of tomorrow. The power of the charge will be in the range of one kiloton—that is to say, the equivalent of one thousand tons of TNT. This is expected to cause a certain disturbance of the water, but the probable height of the accompanying tidal wave— *tsunami* is the term for it—is not precisely known. It is hoped that the inhabitants of the coastal settlements of the Ijsselmeer will not be too inconvenienced. Inconvenienced!" The newscaster almost spluttered the word, which was obviously not in the script—or the repetition of it. "Inconvenienced, they say!" He recovered himself. "The demonstration has been delayed until the afternoon in order to allow British cabinet ministers plenty of time to fly across and join their Dutch colleagues in watching this demonstration. The time and place will be announced later. The device, they add, is already in position.

"Finally, they demand some money. This money, they say, will be returned. It is not blackmail money, or ransom money, merely a temporary loan to cover operating expenses. Details of the methods of payment will be announced later this evening—this is to give the parties concerned time to arrange for the transfer. The demand is for one hundred million guilders from the government, twenty million from Mr. David Joseph Karlmann Meijer, the Rotterdam industrialist." The newscaster laid down his paper. "Viewers will not need reminding that Mr. Meijer's daughter, Anne, is being held hostage by the terrorists." Samuelson touched a switch before him and the screen went blank.

"I wish," Samuelson said in a complaining voice, "that he wouldn't call us 'terrorists,' when 'philanthropists' is more the word. I rather liked that touch about operating expenses. Anne, my dear, do sit down. You're overexcited."

Annemarie was on her feet, face pale, lips compressed, her hands unclenching and clenching into ivory-knuckled fists.

"You monster," she whispered. "You utterly evil monster."

"You think so, my dear?" He looked around the room, smiling. Van Effen was one of those who smiled back at him; there were witnesses. "Not at all. The equitable redistribution of excess wealth. Besides, it's not even that. As you heard, merely a temporary loan. Don't tell me that the wealthiest man in the Netherlands can't afford that money. I know all about your father."

"Murderer," she said softly. Her hands were hanging straight by her sides now, and they were still. The tears were rolling down her cheeks and Julie was on her feet, her arm around the girl's shoulders. "You know all about my father. You know then that he has had two heart attacks this year. You know that he came out of hospital only four days ago after his last attack." Her voice, like her shoulders, was shaking. "You've killed him."

Samuelson had stopped smiling. He frowned and said, "I did not know this. Before God, I didn't." Without apparently even pausing to think, he reached out for the handset of his RCA and pressed a button. He must have received an acknowledgment almost immediately, for he started talking into the mouthpiece rapidly and urgently, issuing instructions in a language that no one there knew but which George, from a few odd words, recognized as being Yiddish. He replaced the handset, rose, walked around behind the bar, poured himself a large brandy, and drank the contents in two or three gulps.

Van Effen rose in turn, walked round to the bar in turn and poured brandy in turn—two brandies. He carried those round to Anne and Julie, waited until they had both sipped from them and resumed his seat.

"Fine lot you are when it comes to damsels in distress." He looked at Agnelli. "That was a nice new line in threats."

"You think they were meaningless threats, Mr. Danilov? A 'line?'" Agnelli didn't seem at all reluctant to speak; like others in the room, he probably found it embarrassing not to look at Samuelson, who was on his second brandy and paying attention to nobody. "I assure you they were all genuinely intended. And will be carried out."

"So much for your word, Agnelli."

"I don't understand."

"You'd have to have a damned short memory not to. Only a few hours ago you promised us that no harm would come to any Dutch people. You warn all the Helystad people to take the necessary precautions against the breaching of the dikes. Good God, man, it's pitch-black outside and coming down in torrents. They won't be able to *see* to take precautions."

"They don't have to see. Flood level won't be more than half a yard. We've checked and checked the area. Plenty of second-floor rooms and attics—although they could remain on the ground floor if they didn't mind getting their feet wet. And plenty of boats. We've checked that also. The message was primarily for intimidation. Surely you can see that?"

"That's as may be. Where's old elastic conscience?"

"Elastic what?"

"Elastic who. Riordan. The praying priest. The God-fearing Reverend. Why wasn't he here watching?"

Agnelli smiled faintly. "He regards TV as the work of Satan. Could be right, for all I know. As you saw, he's practically married to his earphones. There was a simultaneous radio broadcast."

"You have those nuclear devices? I find it frankly incredible."

"I can show them to you."

"Well, that answers that. So our man of peace and goodwill plays around with mega explosives."

"You heard what Mr. Samuelson said to you a short time ago." Agnelli looked quickly at the bar. Samuelson, still looking at nothing and nobody but with something peculiarly tense in his stance, appeared to consider yet another brandy. "Mr. Riordan's prepared to use the devil's tools to fight the devil."

"Too late in the day to talk about pious hypocritical platitudes, I suppose. How did you get them—those nuclear devices?"

"You heard. NATO. West Germany. Specifically, U.S. bases."

"I heard that. I didn't ask where. I asked *how*." Van Effen looked away for a moment, then back at Agnelli. "I know. The RAF. The Red Army Faction."

"Yes. I would have told you, but since you've guessed it—yes."

"Jesus! The holy father upstairs must really have the original, twisted, double-dyed, infinite stretch elastic conscience. The RAF! And only last night, according to the papers—correct me if I'm wrong—he was telling Wieringa, the Defense Minister, that the RAF were the inheritors of the bloody mantle of the Baader-Meinhof gangsters of the early seventies. The fact that his own hands are stained bright red doesn't appear to worry the Reverend at all. God, I should have thought of this right away. It's only a couple of weeks since there was this successful break-in at a U.S. army ammunition depot outside Hanover. The RAF claimed responsibility and their claim was generally accepted; the RAF is rather good at this and the Americans rather poor at guarding their installations. No mention of nuclear devices. It would have been in character for the RAF to have made specific mention of this; one supposes that they did but that the U.S. Army, or the Army through the government, put a stop order on this. Anti-nuclear sentiment is high enough already in Germany without the added knowledge that a bunch of woolly-headed, harebrained young terrorists are on the loose with nuclear weapons in their suitcases."

"No prizes for that guess, Mr. Danilov. Had to be that way. And it was."

"Your information, of course, comes from the same source as the nuclear devices."

"Where else?"

"Joachim and Joop. And the two other baby-faced choirboys who were here when we arrived this afternoon."

"Who else?"

"The leisure-time terrorists, as the West Germans call them—nights and weekends only. Since the egregious Christian Klar was captured—along with two lady friends, Moonhaupt and Schultz, I think they were called—and charged with the murders of diverse politicians, prosecutors, bankers and industrialists, the RAF have pulled in their horns and are reported to have moved into neighboring countries. I suppose Holland was the natural first choice. Should be like a second home." Van Effen thought briefly, then smiled. "On the one hand the RAF, on the other your blackmailing demands on the Dutch Government. Don't you find it an inane thought, Mr. Agnelli, that the Dutch Government are going to pay the RAF for nuclear devices to be used against the Dutch people?"

Agnelli didn't have the opportunity to say, for the buzzer on the RCA rang at that moment. He lifted the handset, spoke an acknowledgment, then said, "Mr. Samuelson, for you."

Samuelson came and took the handset, listened, said, "Thank

you, Helmut, thank you very much." He hung up and looked at his watch. "Four minutes. I'm going to my room, Romero, but will be down for dinner. So will Mr. Riordan. There'll be a news flash on TV in four minutes. Please don't miss it." On his way to the stairs, he stopped by Annemarie's table. "I am sorry, Miss Meijer." No "my dear," no "Anne." "I did not know."

When the news flash came, interrupting some appropriately lugubrious offering from Handel by the Concertgebouw, it was very much what Van Effen expected. "The now notorious terrorist group, the F.F.F.," the newscaster read, "have announced that, for reasons they do not wish to discuss, the demand for twenty million guilders from Mr. David Meijer has been withdrawn, effective as from now. Miss Anne Meijer will be released and returned to her father as soon as is conveniently possible. The sum now asked from the government has been correspondingly increased to a hundred and twenty million guilders."

Apart from a slow shake of the head, which could have meant anything but probably indicated a total lack of understanding, Annemarie did not react at all. Julie smiled in delight and hugged her. George clapped a hand on Van Effen's knee and said, "Well now, my friend, what do you think of that?"

"Wonderful," Van Effen said. "Unfair to policemen's sisters, though. They should have let her go as well."

"I must admit," Van Effen said, "that it does make it more difficult to kill him, should that need arise. If, of course, our friend Samuelson was moved solely by humanitarian principles. One must not misjudge the man. Perhaps he recalled the days when he used to say his prayers at his mother's knees and his heart was touched. Equally well, he may be even more calculating than we've given him credit for."

"I can't see how you can possibly say that," Vasco said. They were pacing to and fro on the front porch. It was bitterly cold now, and the wind of gale force dimensions. They had a certain degree of privacy out there—it had been impossible to conduct a private conversation inside—but only a certain degree. There was a loft over the garage, approached, as was the custom in that area, by an external stairway. Earlier on they had seen one man go up those stairs and another come down: a change of watchman, who would have taken position behind the loft window. There were probably others similarly stationed in the other barn and in the windmill itself. Whether the purpose was to keep insiders from going out or outsiders from coming in, it was impossible to say. All that could be said was that it was done with discretion. Civilian staff were employed in the windmill, and even the hint of the maintenance of a guard—almost certainly an armed guard—would have done much to destroy the credibility of the Golden Gate Film Productions.

"I not only suggest that he may be an exceedingly cunning operator," Van Effen said. "I believe it. Sure it was moving, touching, heartrending, even, a fundamentally decent man overwhelmed by his own decency. You noticed the terms of the communiqué. Miss Anne Meijer will be released as soon as conveniently possible. For 'conveniently possible' read 'inconveniently impossible.' People will know that the poor man is trying desperately to return Annemarie to the bosom of her family but finds it impossible to do so without jeopardizing his own plans and safety. But he has made the offer. Mr. David Meijer, who has not, I assume, accumulated his millions or billions or whatever without having some faint glimmer of intelligence somewhere, will know exactly what the score is and that his daughter is as much a pawn as ever and that he can still be counted on to do the right thing—as far as Samuelson is concerned—about bringing his influence to bear on whatever the government's decision may be. The government whose decision matters, of course, is the British one. He can't influence that. But he can influence the Dutch Government to pressure the British one, which is just about as useful from Samuelson's viewpoint.

"And think what would have happened *had* David Meijer died while his daughter was still in the F.F.F.'s custody. Unlikely, but that's not the point. People range from the soft-headed to the incurably romantic. The 'died-of-a-broken-heart' syndrome has always had a powerful following. Sure, people do die of a broken heart, but it's over months and years and not overnight. No matter. If he had died, the public reaction to Samuelson and the F.F.F. would have been one of revulsion and rejection. Attitudes would harden, resistance stiffen, and the average man in the street would say: 'The hell with these cold, ruthless, murderous madmen. Never give in to them, never. Let them do their worst and see if we care.' That, I should imagine, is the last response that Samuelson and company want.

"Going back to that communiqué. Notice the noble, dignified and selfless fashion in which he refused to give the reasons for his decisions. I didn't know that David Meijer had a heart condition, but for all I know it may be common knowledge. If it's not, I'll take long odds that it soon will be. Helmut Paderewsky, whom Samuelson calls our voice in Amsterdam, will make good and sure of that, and that *his* voice will be heard. Radio and newspapers will be anonymously and discreetly told that David Meijer has a severe heart condition—the truth of that can soon be established—and hints dropped that his gallant hostage daughter had been pleading for his life. For the newspapers, it's a natural, a human-angle story to tug at the heartstrings. Suitably dressed up in the usual sickening journalese, this will be manna to Samuelson, a big plus, an image that puts him in line for tabloid canonization. No matter what he's done or is threatening to do, popular sympathy is going to swing behind him and make it all the easier for his demands to be granted. The whole world loves a reformed rogue, a bandit with a heart of gold. A toast to the Robin Hood of Amsterdam."

"This I do believe," George said. "Among the other accomplishments you don't know I have, is a smattering of Yiddish. Not much, not even a working knowledge, but a smattering. I wondered what senseless instructions he was trying to give in Yiddish to this fellow Paderewsky in Amsterdam. I don't wonder any more. It makes sense."

"Lastly, of course, there's the Dutch reverence for the guilder. What praise, people will say, can be too high for a man who spurns twenty million guilders—the fact that he doesn't have it and probably wouldn't have got it anyway is quite irrelevant—at the sight of a teardrop in the corner of the eye of a lovely maiden. The twenty million, admittedly, is added to the government's bill, but who ever cared about robbing a government? You still think, Vasco, that Samuelson was motivated only by humanitarian considerations?"

"When you put it that way, I have to admit that I don't. He's what you say. Well, it's all very well you having convinced me. It's an unfortunate fact that fourteen million other Dutchmen didn't hear you. I'm convinced that they're going to stay convinced to the contrary."

"Not all of them. Give some of them time and they'll work it out. The great majority won't. And that's what the frightening thing is about Samuelson. It took me quite a time to figure out the angles at the heart of this whole messy business. Samuelson's got a computer mind. He did it all on his feet, within seconds and, it would seem, spontaneously, although of course it wasn't spontaneous at all. Man's brilliant. And dangerous. It would behoove us to have a very long spoon when we're supping with Samuelson."

"Back to the devil again, is that it?" George said. "He's the key. Nothing else fits the lock. He's the one who says that Riordan is prepared to use the devil's tools to fight the devil. I wonder if Riordan uses a long spoon to sup with Samuelson. It must cost thousands of dollars a day to run this operation. Maybe tens of thousands. Agnelli hasn't got that kind of money, and I doubt whether Riordan ever earned a penny in his life."

"Samuelson beyond doubt. The paymaster."

"Pity we're in no position to check with Interpol."

"Wouldn't do us any good even if we were. If he's as diabolical as I think he is, Interpol will never have heard of him. Interpol simply has no idea as to who the world's outstanding criminals are. That's what makes them outstanding. May not even have a criminal past at all—I say criminal past as distinct from criminal record. He'll have no record. And perhaps, as I say, no past. He may even be what Uncle Arthur suggested he was—a bloated plutocrat, a man who has made his immense fortune in oil or shipping or something of the kind."

"Then we would have heard of him."

"We might or might not have heard of him—under another name, of course. May not even be a photograph of him in existence. Some of the world's wealthiest men are never photographed."

George said, "If he's as rich as we think he may be, why is he trying to extract more from other sources?"

"Show. I'm convinced that Samuelson neither wants nor needs money. But for all I know he may have persuaded his partners that his funds are drying up and he's now making a show about money to divert attention from the fact that money is of no value to him and that his interests lie elsewhere. Agnelli makes no secret of the fact that he's very interested in money and this may be Samuelson's way of keeping him happy. He has a large staff to keep happy, and they'll be keenly interested in seeing Samuelson displaying a keen interest in money. He seems to need us—for what purpose we don't yet know, we may well be here on only a contingency basis—but we need money too. And Riordan, above all, has to be kept happy, for Riordan above all needs unholy money to achieve his holy purposes."

"Unholy money for unholy purposes," George said. "Split mind. Dichotomy. There must be something in this Irish-American connection. We know there are men who are willing to trade heroin for bags of gold to help a so-called worthy cause. Purblindness. That the word?"

"Something like that. In medical terms, tunnel as opposed to peripheral vision. We have to accept that it's an illness and try to treat it as best we can."

"How do we go about treating this ailment? The good doctor has something on his mind?" Despite his vast bulk George shivered in the wind. "A prescription? A nostrum?"

"Too late for medicine."

"Surgery? I wouldn't even know which end of a scalpel to hold."

"You don't have to. In the best medical parlance, surgery, at this moment, is contra-indicated."

George cleared his throat delicately, no easy thing to do in a gale-force wind. "You have suddenly developed a newfound regard for his well-being? Of criminals who are prepared to drown God knows how many thousands of our fellow countrymen?"

"No such sea change, George. I know they have their quota of hard men and psychopathic nut cases around here, but do you seriously doubt for a moment that we could kill Riordan, Samuelson and Agnelli and get the girls away unharmed?"

"*I* know we could—I take back my ludicrous suggestion about your tender heart. Tungsten steel, more like."

Vasco's expression didn't exactly register shock, but it did hold a certain amount of apprehension and disbelief.

"You're a policeman, sir. Sworn to uphold the law. I mean, give them a fair trial and hang them in the morning."

"I'm my own court of law and I'd shoot them down like wild dogs if I thought it would solve anything, but it wouldn't. Two reasons—one psychological, one practical.

"The psychological—curiosity, nosiness if you like. I am not convinced that those three are ordinary criminals. I am not convinced that Romero Agnelli is the murderous, ruthless killer we wrongly think he is. He bears no resemblance to his two brothers I put behind bars, who were grade A vicious sadists. The fact that he hasn't laid a finger on either Julie or Annemarie helps bear that out. Or Riordan. He's no psychopath. Loony as a nut or nutty as a loon and a demagogue of some note—but only an occasional demagogue. But being loony, as I keep pointing out, doesn't necessarily mean that you're certifiable. There are quite a number of people tidied up—institutionalized, as they say, who are convinced that they are the only sane people around and that great numbers of people, those responsible for wars, hunger, diseases, genocide, heroin pushers and those who talk glibly of nuclear annihilation, not to mention a few other trivial matters, should be where they are, locked away, and who's to say they're not right?"

"And then there's the factor of demagoguery."

"Dema what?" Vasco said.

"People who are supposed to go in for ranting and raving. A word that has fallen into disuse. A word associated with the likes of Hitler, Mussolini and a few dozen nationalistic leaders in the world today. There are good demagogues and bad ones. Originally it meant people who were opposed to established rules of law, usually bad rules. Christ, if you like, could have been called a demagogue. Riordan, I admit, is no member of the Holy Trinity, but I think he's a sincere and honest demagogue, however misguided. I do not believe him to be evil.

"Samuelson is the question mark. He's the real enigma. You know that he's English?"

Both men shook their heads.

"He is. A wealthy man. Obviously, very wealthy. Sure, rich men are normally under a compulsion to become even richer, but there's a limit even to that and I believe Samuelson has reached that limit. As sane and stable a man as you could ever hope to meet. Beneath that bonhomie and geniality I think he's an obsessed man. A driven man. I want to know what drives him. What do you think of Kathleen?"

Both men stared at him, then George said: "Wait a minute." He disappeared inside the mill and reappeared shortly afterward with three large glasses of brandy in his hands. "If we are to continue this discussion in Verkhoyansk temperatures—what do you mean, Kathleen?"

"What I said. How does she strike you?"

"We hardly know her," George said. "A lovely child, of course."

"There you go again. You and your middle-aged propensities. Vasco?"

"I agree with George. I've never seen—" He broke off. "She seems kind and gentle and—"

"An accomplished actress? A case-hardened spy?" Vasco said nothing. "The smiler with the knife under the cloak?"

"No!" Vasco was vehement.

"No, indeed. When she was watching that TV announcement tonight, you weren't. You were watching her. Not that I blame you, she's as watchable as anyone in the Netherlands.

But that's not why you were watching her. Apropos of nothing, Vasco, I think you'd make an excellent inspector. Under, of course, the watchful eye of George, whom I hope to persuade to leave his ill-chosen role of restaurateur."

"Me?" George stared at him as if either or both of them had taken leave of their senses.

"You. You're wasted. Keep La Caracha, of course; Annelise is the best cook in Amsterdam and you could always hire a couple of thugs to take over your distasteful duties as bouncer. But that's by the by. What did her eyes tell you, Vasco?"

"Her eyes?"

"Kathleen's. Come on now, you were watching her eyes, not her face."

"How did you know—"

"A combination of craftiness, cunning, and experience. Practice is all. Fear, distress?"

"Something like that. Distinctly unhappy. Edgy. Odd thing was, she was looking like that *before* the announcement was made. She knew what was coming or thought or was convinced she knew what was coming and didn't like it one little bit."

"Another driven person," Van Effen said.

"If we're talking about drivers and the driven," George said, "you could also include Maria Agnelli. A great lip-licker is our Maria. We've all met people who lick their lips when they're in a state of sadistic anticipation, but when you're in such a state your lips don't tremble. Hers did. Nervous apprehension. Revulsion, if you like."

"I missed that," Van Effen said.

"Well, we've each of us got only one pair of eyes," George said reasonably. "But you only had to have half an eye to see that Samuelson enjoyed every moment of the broadcast. So what do we have? Three driven people. One of those driven people, Samuelson, is also the driver, going hell-bent, one might say, round a series of hairpin bends down a pretty precipitous mountain slope. The other two are driven, terrified of going over a precipice at the next hairpin."

Vasco said in a complaining voice, "You're going too fast for me. You make those two girls sound relatively harmless, maybe even nice. Joachim, Joop and those two other baby faces in the mill here—Baader-Meinhof, RAF or whatever you call them—they are not nice."

"They wouldn't agree," Van Effen said. "They are the new Messiahs, dedicated to the creation of a nobler and better world. It's merely because of the blind folly of this misguided world that assassination and now the deployment of tactical nuclear weapons have become their stock in trade."

"And those two girls are their associates and allies," Vasco said, biting it out bitterly. "Or do you dip your hand into this witches' brew of murder, mayhem, terrorism and theft and bring them out pure?"

"A little dusting of soot, perhaps. Camouflage. A little coercion here, a little blackmail there, misguided love, misguided loyalty, a warped code of honor, a false sentimentality, a judicious mixture of truth and lies."

"'Conned,' I believe is the word you're after," George said. "But they weren't conning anyone when they kidnapped Julie."

"Of course they were. Sure, they hoped to discourage me, but that was only the ostensible reason. Romero Agnelli would never have thought that up on his own, and as for hurting my sister, I've already given my opinion that he would be reluctant to tread on a beetle. The orders came from his brothers Giuseppe and Orlando, that delightful duo."

"But they're in prison."

Van Effen sighed. "Vasco, Vasco. Some of the most powerful and vicious gangs in the world are controlled by bosses temporarily confined to maximum-security blocks in prisons. Palermo, Cagliari, Ajaccio, Marseilles, half a dozen cities in the United States, even London and Amsterdam and Naples— there's where the criminal overlords—overlords still with powers of life or death—hang out in their prison cells. It's Romero's brothers who gave the orders for the sending of those menacing postcards to me, who ordered Julie's kidnapping. But they're not after Julie. I don't believe they're even after me. Convicted criminals, oddly enough, don't usually harbor grudges against the cops who caught them; their resentment is reserved for the judges who sentenced them. Italy is a classical example of this."

"If they're not after you or Julie," George said slowly, "then my towering intellect tells me they're after something else. And to think that Samuelson had the staggering effrontery to say that it was Riordan who is prepared to use the devil's tools to fight the devil."

"Which is why I said that one would require a very long spoon to sup with the devil."

"Devil?" Vasco said. "With all due respect, of course. What the devil are you two talking about?"

"The devil," George said. "Or devils. Part of the flooding—or non-flooding of the country—and it may even be a precondition—will be that Romero's murderous brothers be released from prison or, heaven help us, be given a pardon."

There was a brief hiatus while George went inside the mill again to get some more anti-pneumonia specific. When he returned Van Effen said: "Well, so much for theory. I think we've got everything right except Samuelson's ultimate motivation. We're not wrong about it—we just don't know. Now, practicalities; that shouldn't take too long. Our options are limited and, besides, it's too damned cold.

"We have agreed that now is not the time to dispose of the three head guys here. There are other and non-theoretical reasons. Samuelson may *not* be the C in C, although I'm convinced he is. There could be others. He has to have someone in the vicinity of the Ijsselmeer to trigger that damned nuclear device of theirs and it's not likely to be a minor figure, some clod with bad breath and a .45. They also told us, unwisely, that this is only a stop-over HQ; the other will be their main one and, almost certainly, the one from which they intend to make their final strike. We have to find it, so, for the moment, we have to go along.

"I'm more than prepared for the fact that they'll breach the dikes north and south of Lelystad and flood the east and south Flevoland areas shortly after midnight because the British will temporize and not throw in the towel before the first bell rings.

With any luck there should be no loss of life—human life, that is; I wouldn't care to guess what is going to happen to the livestock. This nuclear device to be detonated in the Ijsselmeer tomorrow afternoon presents a more serious threat—my guess is that it would be in the Markerwaard—and I wouldn't much care to be in the vicinity of Marken or Volendam when it went off. Nasty things, tidal waves, especially when the height is unpredictable. Things might even be unpleasant in Hoorn or Amsterdam itself, although I doubt it. After all, this is meant primarily as a demonstration for the British Cabinet or whatever. The big bang will come later—considering the steadily worsening conditions that should be at the next high tide afterward. Or the one after that. In daylight, anyway."

Vasco said, "Why daylight?"

"You think they have this helicopter just to make a nonexistent film? They want it to take them someplace a land-based vehicle can't reach. An island, perhaps, though that seems unlikely. The point is that it's very difficult to land a helicopter in gale-force winds, even if air-sea rescue pilots do it regularly. But to try it in a gale in darkness and driving rain—in zero visibility, that is—is foolhardy to the point of suicide, especially if you happen to have as part of your cargo some potentially unstable nuclear devices. So, daylight."

"We might be here for a couple of days yet?" George said.

"My guess is that we'll be off first light in the morning. They'll want to establish themselves in their HQ, near the scene of action. Those ground-to-ground and ground-to-air missiles—they have been deactivated?" George nodded. "How are you when it comes to deactivating tactical nuclear devices?"

"I've never even *seen* tactical nuclear weapons. If I could examine one or see a blueprint, well, yes, perhaps. Otherwise, no. I know I wouldn't feel a thing, but I don't much fancy being vaporized."

"Well, we'll have a look at them later on tonight. They're somewhere on the premises. We don't even have to look. You heard what Agnelli said—'I can show them to you now.'"

"Won't that make them suspicious?" George said. "That we

didn't ask to see them right away? They'll be thinking we have been having a conference and have dreamed up some scheme."

"Let them think what they like and be as suspicious as they like. We're as safe as men in a church. We, my friends, are indispensable." George and Vasco looked at each other, then at Van Effen, but said nothing. "We're also not very bright. Joop, Joachim or some of their psychopathic Red Army Faction pals stole those nuclear devices from the U.S. NATO arms dump near Metnitz on the night of February third. Something else happened on that same night."

"February third," George said. "Of course! We really *are* not very bright. That was the night the De Doorns ammunition dump was blown out of existence. So: Samuelson's explosives experts trying to replenish their supplies. An enormous crater. No replenishments and, of course, no experts. No wonder the F.F.F. were so desperate for our supplies and services. We're probably the only people around who could set off a squib. Lloyd's of London would approve of this."

Vasco said: "A marvelous insurance policy, to be sure. But has the thought occurred that Joop or one of his lunatic associates may know how to trigger those nuclear devices?"

"The thought has occurred," Van Effen said. "So we'll just have to attend to the lunatics or the devices, won't we? Or both. But before we start attending to anything I suggest we go inside, have a wash and brush-up, find out how thoroughly they have examined our luggage, listen to the next riveting communication from the Dutch or British governments or the F.F.F., then join our genial hosts for dinner. One would imagine that Samuelson's resources could run to a cordon bleu chef."

Romero Agnelli greeted them genially on their entrance and at once pressed jonge jenevers on them. "You must be needing this after your long stay outside. I mean, it's pretty cold tonight."

"Not for us," Van Effen said. "We're fresh-air fanatics."

"I thought that applied only to the English. Anyway, I trust you enjoyed your stroll."

"If you call pacing up and down your veranda a stroll, then

yes, we did." Van Effen knew that Agnelli was perfectly well aware that they had not once left the veranda.

"And, of course, the opportunity for a private conversation." Agnelli smiled.

"Well yes. Pondering our probable future, about which we know precious little. After all, you and your friends are hardly very communicative. We don't know what we're here for, what services we are expected to perform, where we're going, even when we're going."

"That last I can tell you—eight o'clock tomorrow morning. As for the rest, well, you and I are great believers in the need-to-know principle."

"True, true. But there's one other thing that we do need to know—where do we sleep tonight? On the floor?"

"Dear me, no. Mind you, this is no Amstel but we do have accommodation of sorts. Come, I'll show you. I've already had your baggage brought up."

He led the way up the curving staircase and along to a door at the end of a passageway. The room beyond was of moderate size with three single beds. Agnelli indicated a door at the far end of the room.

"Bathroom. No marble bath, no gold taps, but serviceable enough." He looked at his watch. "Dinner in twenty minutes."

Van Effen and George sat on their beds, engaged in desultory conversation, while Vasco looked around. In looking around Vasco was a specialist, meticulous and thorough. After a few minutes he said, "Clear. No bugs."

George hoisted his medium-sized suitcase onto his knees. It was one of those fancy cases with combination locks, four figures next to each of the two keyholes, eight in all. George peered at it closely.

"Combinations as set?" Van Effen said.

"As set. But not untouched. Very tiny scratches. This case is brand-new, never been used before. Normally, I wouldn't be seen dead with this junior-executive status symbol, but Annelise gave it to me for my birthday and it would have been worth my life to have left home without it. It's been opened and closed and in very short order, too. I don't know of a safebreaker in the Netherlands who could have done this. Anyone who knows his job can open a conventional safe—a pair of good ears or a doctor's stethoscope can hear the tumblers click. No tumblers in this type of lock."

Van Effen said: "I'll bet O'Brien could open the vaults of the Amsterdam-Rotterdam bank with a bent hairpin."

"I wouldn't doubt it." George adjusted the combination figures and opened the case. "Very neat. Everything exactly where it was, except of course where it's naturally settled in the process of being carried."

"Yours, Vasco?"

Vasco unlocked his case. "Untouched. Spare Smith & Wesson magazines still there."

"Naturally." Van Effen opened his own case—it hadn't even been locked—lifted out a rather battered toilet bag and took from it a burgundy-colored aerosol can with a silvery top, chromed. The side of the can bore the legend: *Yves Saint Laurent—Pour l'Homme—Mousse à Raser.* The aerosol can, in fact, contained no shaving foam.

"Well," George said, "nobody's been touching or sniffing the contents of that."

"Right." Van Effen replaced the aerosol. "If they had, they'd still be here. Horizontal on the carpet. I doubt if they even opened my toilet bag. If there was anything worth finding, they must have reckoned, it would have been in George's thief-proof case." He took a small bar of soap from his toilet bag and handed it to Vasco. "You know what to do with this."

"Hygiene is all." Vasco went into the bathroom while Van Effen and George crossed to the window opposite the beds and opened it. As far as they could judge in the cold dark they were about fifteen feet above the cobbled courtyard below, a courtyard shrouded in black.

"Very satisfactory, George, don't you think?"

"Very. Only snag is that you'll have to make a pretty long detour to keep in the darkness in order to reach the back of the barn. And have you thought of antipersonnel land mines—you know, the nasty kind that jump three feet in the air before exploding?"

"George, this place is run and staffed entirely by local villagers. If, say, a laundry maid were just kind of accidentally blown in half—"

"True. Point taken. But if you were to run into a patrolling member of the F.F.F.—"

"Anybody out on patrol on a night like this has to be a head case. Gale, driving rain, bitter cold, thunder and lightning due any time—"

"But—"

"I'm not going to run into anyone. Someone might run into me. Velvet gloves. Vasco's taking his time, isn't he?" They moved to the bathroom door, tried to open it and found it locked. Van Effen rattled the door handle.

"Put out your light," Vasco said. They did as he asked. Vasco opened the door of the bathroom, which was dark. "Sorry about that, gentlemen, but I didn't want the watcher in the shadows to know that he was being watched by another watcher in the shadows. Not, mind you, that our fellow watcher is very much in the shadows."

The bathroom window was, in fact, directly opposite the door in the loft of the barn that held the army truck on the ground floor. The man standing in the doorway was making no effort to conceal his presence and the courtyard light projecting from the mill's veranda was quite strong.

"Doesn't seem to me to be guarding against anything very much," Van Effen said. "Unenthusiastic. Don't blame him. Must seem like a pretty useless exercise on a night like this."

"And a freezing exercise, too," George said.

"He generates his own heat," Vasco said. "Wait."

They didn't have to wait long. After less than two minutes the guard reached behind him, lifted a bottle to his lips and took what appeared to be a considerable swig from it.

"No mineral water, that's for sure," Van Effen said. "Let's get inside."

They closed the bathroom door behind them and switched on the bedroom light. Vasco handed Van Effen a small metallic object sheathed in polyethylene. Van Effen dropped it in his pocket.

"I've stuck the two pieces of soap together and left them in hot water," Vasco said. "Should be mushed together again pretty soon. I have an idea. Just after I got into the bathroom I saw a man crossing the courtyard toward the barn. That's when I switched off the light. He disappeared round the back of the barn, you know, where the outside stairs are, and then joined the man who was then standing at the loft door. Changing of the guard. That was at seven o'clock. It occurred to me that it might be convenient if the condition of my throat had deteriorated so badly that I would be unable to join you for dinner. It might be very convenient if we found out how regularly they changed guards."

"It would," Van Effen said. "An excellent suggestion, Vasco. Should have thought of it myself. Promotion guaranteed—if, that is, we survive. I'm sure Samuelson will be most distressed. Probably insist on sending you another toddy."

"Make sure it's a large one, if you please. I'm feeling weak."

"Mr. Danilov. George." As Van Effen and George descended the stairs into the living room, Samuelson advanced to greet them, beaming as if they were long-lost friends. "Just in time for the next TV broadcast. Then dinner. But where's our dashing young lieutenant?"

"Our young lieutenant isn't feeling all that dashing. Throat's worse. Flu, I think."

Samuelson clucked his tongue and shook his head. "Damn flu's everywhere these days. This awful weather. Most important that he's reasonably fit tomorrow. Herta!" This to a flaxen-haired young girl who was setting the table for the evening meal. "A toddy. A strong one. Take it up to the lieutenant's room. Dear me, dear me. Ah!"

Agnelli had just turned up the volume of the TV set and a rock band, which had been playing, mercifully, in apparent mime, faded from the screen, to be replaced by the accustomed announcer looking, if possible, even more lugubrious and funereal than he had on the previous occasion.

"With reference to the threats being made against our country by the unidentified group calling themselves the F.F.F., the

Ministry of Defense has just issued a statement. The British Government and ours are in constant contact but no announcement as to the results of those negotiations can yet be made pending the outcome of discussions between Whitehall and the Stormont. The Stormont is the parliament or governing body of Northern Ireland, which is, of course, next to ourselves, the country most closely concerned with the outcome of those negotiations. Whitehall, it must be said, finds itself in a most difficult and peculiar position. Ulster, Northern Ireland, that is, although an integral part of Great Britain, retains a certain degree of autonomy as far as decisions relating to its own future are concerned. When further news comes to hand, the country will be immediately informed.

"The F.F.F. have informed us that they will issue a further communiqué after this broadcast. This will be transmitted to you at eight P.M.

"In the circumstances, the latest report from the meteorological office is relevant. The wind, due north, is force 9 and strengthening. Torrential rain is sweeping over most of Scandinavia and is heaviest of all over the Netherlands. The North Sea is expected to reach its highest level for at least the past quarter century inside the next forty-eight hours."

The announcer's image faded and Agnelli switched off the set.

"Dear me, dear me," Samuelson said. "Things do look very unpromising. Or very promising. All depends upon one's point of view." He gestured toward the bar. "Romero, see to it that our friends are not neglected. Excuse me, ladies and gentlemen." He disappeared up the stairs.

While the Agnelli brothers busied themselves behind the bar, Van Effen wandered aimlessly around the room, apparently admiring the paintings and the bronze and copper artifacts that decorated the walls. He paid particular but brief attention to the telephone; the telephone number had been thoroughly inked out, which neither surprised nor disturbed him. He was reasonably certain that he could, later that night, have given that number to the police HQ in the Marnixstraat in Amsterdam, which would have enabled them to pinpoint the whereabouts of the windmill, but that would not have suited his purpose; the answer to the machinations of the F.F.F. lay elsewhere. Samuelson, presumably and for reasons best known to himself, had gone upstairs to use another telephone to deliver the text of the next F.F.F. communiqué.

Dinner that night was an odd affair. Not that there was anything odd about the food. Obviously, there was no cordon bleu chef within fifty miles. The Dutch, by and large, are not gourmets. Your standard Dutch cook or housewife considers it an insult to her guests if they can see any part of the plate under the mound of food that covers it. The food was palatable enough, but Michelin would not have come there a second time.

What was odd was the contrasting behavior of the diners. Samuelson, Romero Agnelli, Van Effen and George were in an expansive and talkative mood. Daniken made an occasional contribution but was clearly no conversationalist. The Reverend Riordan, apart from delivering a lengthy and, in the circumstances, extremely hypocritical blessing before the meal, remained grave and thoughtful and silent throughout; Riordan, Van Effen reflected, if not quite deranged or demented, was totally detached from reality and possessed of an incredible naiveté. Leonardo was equally silent. He, too, was thinking, but only of his stomach. For a man of his diminutive stature, he was an awesome trencherman. They spoke only when spoken to, smiled but seldom and for the most part were remote and withdrawn.

At one point Van Effen said to Romero Agnelli, "And where's our friend O'Brien tonight? Not down with the flu, I trust?"

"O'Brien's as fit as a fiddle. He's elsewhere."

Van Effen said: "Ah."

Samuelson smiled. "You really are a singularly incurious person, Mr. Danilov."

"Would it help any if I knew where he was or what he was doing?"

"No. Romero has spoken to me several times about your need-to-know philosophy. It is one with which I am in entire agreement." He glanced at his watch. "Romero, it lacks one minute to eight o'clock."

It was the same newscaster. He looked as if he had just heard that his entire family had been wiped out in an air crash.

"We have here the latest communiqué from the F.F.F." He sounded less and less like a news-reader; he intoned the words like a minister delivering a funeral oration. "It is very brief and reads as follows: 'We placed no credence in the Ministry of Defense's statement. We think the Dutch and British governments are either stalling or don't believe in our threats. Or both. We do not intend to stall. We intend to make them believe our promises. A few minutes after midnight the dikes north and south of Lelystad will be breached. The nuclear device in the Ijsselmeer will be detonated at two P.M. tomorrow. We beg you to believe that those two incidents will be regarded as the merest trifles compared to the disaster that will engulf the Netherlands within twenty-four hours of the detonation of the nuclear device.' That is the end of their communiqué.

"We have also had a further statement from the Ministry of Defense. They say that they have no comment to make on this latest communiqué on the basis that there is no way that they can predict the irrational workings of the minds of terrorists." Samuelson clucked his tongue and shook his head sadly. "They say they are prepared to believe that the terrorists are insane enough to carry out their threats"—more cluckings and shakings from Samuelson—"and can do no more than warn all local authorities to effect all possible means of protection.

"Netherlands experts and British nuclear scientists have agreed on the probable results of such a nuclear explosion. It is assumed that this will take place in the Markerwaard. If this device is located in or near the center of the Markerwaard, the tsunami, the tidal wave, reaching the shores should be of minor proportions, averaging between two and three feet. Should it be placed close inshore, the wave could be several times as high and the local results disastrous.

"The nation will be immediately informed of any further developments."

Agnelli switched off the set. Samuelson, half smiling, looked at Van Effen and said, "Do I detect just the trace of a half-frown, Mr. Danilov?" Van Effen made no reply. "Romero has told me that you are prepared to react violently to any threat to the lives of your fellow citizens or, rather, to the citizens of your adopted country. Romero is of the opinion that you and your two friends are highly dangerous men. I concur. You are, I believe, armed."

Van Effen opened his jacket to demonstrate that he wasn't carrying his shoulder-holstered Beretta, then turned to Agnelli, who was sitting next to him, crossed his knees and pulled up his right trouser leg to show that he wasn't carrying his Lilliput either. "I don't consider guns an essential part of dressing for dinner. Do you think I would be so mad as to start a gunfight in the company of four beautiful young ladies? Any ladies, come to that?"

"No. My mistake. The nuclear device is in the Markerwaard but is located precisely in its center. Do you believe me?"

"If I had your unpleasantly suspicious mind I would say that I'd wait until five past two tomorrow afternoon to find out. As it happens, I believe you. Now, Mr. Samuelson, you know that I do not normally probe into anyone's affairs, but I must confess to being just a little concerned about those nuclear devices. My friends and I are experts in conventional explosives, but we know nothing about nuclear ones. We wouldn't recognize one if we saw it, far less know how to arm, activate or deactivate it. But we do know they are nasty, jiggly and unpredictable things. I know you have some on the premises, although I don't know how many. What I do know is that I have a healthy regard for my own skin. I assume you're transporting them elsewhere—they can be of no use to you here. I don't want to be aboard whatever form of transportation is taking those devices from here to wherever elsewhere may be."

Samuelson smiled. "Mr. Daniken here shares your sentiments exactly."

"What has Daniken got to do with it?"

"Mr. Daniken is our helicopter pilot. He doesn't want to carry those things."

"I didn't refuse to, Mr. Samuelson," Daniken said. "I said I was highly reluctant because of the great risk involved. I agree with Danilov. I don't know how unstable or temperamental those damn things are. Flying conditions are atrocious, just on the limit. With an updraft or wind shear, we can go up or down a hundred feet in two seconds. We could make a heavy landing, a crash landing, or just crash."

"You and Mr. Danilov can relax. Should have mentioned it before, but we made our minds up just before dinner. No helicopter. We have decided to use the army truck which Mr. Danilov and his friends have so thoughtfully provided. Those devices are quite small and can easily be concealed in what looks like a couple of extra long-range petrol tanks. We'll have three men dressed in uniforms, Ylvisaker as a full-scale lieutenant colonel, and the rest—"

"Where did you get the uniforms?" Van Effen said.

"I told you," Samuelson said patiently. "We're making a war film. The rest of us go by helicopter."

"Must be some helicopter."

"A war film, I said. A gunship. The end of the Vietnam War caught the U.S. Air Force on the hop and they had over-produced. Going for a song. Elderly but fully serviceable. Stripped of armament, of course, but we ordered dummies. I suggest we move to more comfortable chairs for our brandies, liqueurs or whatever."

Van Effen said, "If I may be excused, I'd like to have a look at the lieutenant."

"Give him my sympathies," Samuelson said. "I suggest he might appreciate another toddy."

"Thank you. I'm sure he would. If he's not asleep, that is."

Vasco was comfortably seated in a small armchair that he had brought into the bathroom. Using the pencil beam of the hooded torch that was an indispensable item of his traveling equipment, Van Effen handed Vasco the glass.

"Compliments of the house. Or, Samuelson."

"Very civil of him. Well, it's eight-twenty now and the same character is still on watch. Judging from his performance with that bottle, he must be half sloshed. Like me, as you can see, he's found an armchair. I'm surprised he hasn't dropped off by this time. Anyway, I'll keep watch until they change guard. The toddy will help sustain me."

Van Effen gave him a quick resume of the Ministry of Defense's statement and the F.F.F.'s reply, promised that he and George would be back by nine o'clock, and left.

He returned to the living room to find that the group had been considerably depleted.

"The lieutenant seems to have benefited from that first toddy. He doesn't sound quite so hoarse. Very drowsy but not too drowsy to attack the second toddy. His thanks. And dear me, the lovely ladies have departed. Shame. But I'm not surprised. They were hardly what you might call vivacious at the table tonight."

"They said they were tired," Samuelson said. Julie, Van Effen knew, had not been tired. She was a notoriously poor air traveler, and the thought of traveling in a helicopter—she'd never been in one in her life—must have been a nightmare.

"What have they done to make them tired?"

"Nothing. They're just nervous and apprehensive."

"Like George and myself."

Samuelson surveyed him dispassionately. "I doubt whether you and your big friend have ever been nervous or apprehensive in your lives."

"There's always a first time. And where's the holy father?"

"You know the Reverend doesn't drink. But it's not that. Every night before he goes to sleep, he spends an hour in meditation and prayer."

Van Effen said somberly: "Let's hope he includes in his prayers the souls of the victims of his nuclear toys."

The silence that followed, of which Van Effen seemed to be unaware, was thick. It was Romero, in an attempt to break the silence, who said hastily, "Speaking of those toys, as you call them, I told you earlier I'd show them to you. You might be interested—"

"Not I." Van Effen waved an indifferent hand. "Same old principles—need-to-know and would it help any if I saw them?" He was aware of George's momentary slight frown but knew that no one else had seen it. Van Effen paused, as if something had just occurred to him, then said, "Someone has to be able to touch off those nuclear devices. Don't tell me it's Joop and his psychopathic pals."

"It is indeed, as you say in your disparaging fashion, Joop and his psychopathic friends." The words held a rebuke but the tone didn't; it required no telepathy to realize that Samuelson shared Van Effen's opinion of the Red Army Faction. "When they got hold of those devices in Metnitz, they also obtained copies of the operating instructions. One would have been useless without the other."

"Remind me not to be within five miles of Joop and company when they arm either of those devices. A palm reader once told me I had a long lifeline, but she could have been wrong. How is this device in the Markerwaard to be detonated?"

"Pre-set timing device."

"And the two other devices?"

"By radio control."

"God help us all. Make that ten miles."

"You don't trust them?"

"I wouldn't trust Joop and his friends with a firecracker. They are fanatics, and fanatics have unstable minds. Unstable hands, too. No, I don't trust them. Neither, I suspect, do you."

"You still wouldn't like to see those devices?"

"I presume you're not lunatic enough to keep those in the mill."

"They're a half mile away in a secure underground cellar."

"I've no intention of going out in that monsoon. And though you might not be lunatic, I think you're guilty of a grave error of judgment. To detonate any device by radio doesn't call for the mind of an Einstein but it can be tricky and is a job for experts. Joop and his band of trusty experts have never detonated a charge in their lives."

"And how would you know that?"

"That's being simple-minded. Why did you have to call me in for the palace job?"

"True, true. Would your scruples, or your objections to monsoons, prevent you from having a look at the operating instructions? We have them in this room." Van Effen looked at Samuelson.

"Scruples? What you have in mind is that we should do your dirty work—instead of Laurel and Hardy. Do you know what would happen if those explosions resulted in the deaths of any citizens?"

"Yes. You would ensure that I joined the departed. I wouldn't like that at all."

"Let's see the plans."

Romero Agnelli handed a couple of papers to Van Effen and George. George was the first to speak and that only after a few seconds.

"This isn't a half-kilo device. It's only for the equivalent of fifty tons of TNT."

Samuelson came close to smirking. "The equivalent of ten tons would have suited me equally well. But it's useful to exaggerate the terror potential, don't you think?"

George didn't say what he thought. After less than a minute he looked up and spoke again. "Only moderately complicated and very precise. Two snags. The first is that Joop speaks fractured English and people who have difficulty in speaking only the simplest form of a language are hopeless when it comes to reading or writing it. The second snag is the jargon."

"Jargon?"

"Technical terms," Van Effen said. "They might as well be in Sanskrit as far as Joop is concerned."

"Well?"

Van Effen handed his paper back to Agnelli. "We'll have to think about it."

Samuelson tried, not altogether successfully, to smother the smile of a man who knows he has won his point. For the next minute or two they sipped their brandies in companionable silence. Then, on the screen, came the familiar figure of the tragedy-stricken newscaster.

"The government have just announced that they have just received two more demands from the F.F.F. The first of those concerned the demand for a hundred and twenty million guilders and how it is to be transferred. The government does not say whether it will accede to the request and refuses to discuss the nature of the transfer. The second demand is for the release of two prisoners who were imprisoned several years ago for crimes of extreme violence. The government refuses to disclose the names of the prisoners.

"We would remind viewers that we shall be on the air again at midnight to find out whether the F.F.F. have, in fact, breached the Flevoland dikes."

Agnelli switched off the set. "Satisfactory," Samuelson said. He was actually rubbing his hands together. "Eminently satisfactory."

"Seems like a pretty silly and stupid broadcast to me," Van Effen said.

"Not at all." Samuelson was positively beaming. "The nation now knows that the government has received details of our demands and, as they have not outright rejected them, it probably means that they are going to accede to them. It also shows how weak the government is and in how strong a position we are."

"That's not what I meant. They've been stupid. They didn't have to make that announcement at all."

"Oh yes, they did. They were told that if they didn't we would radio the communiqué to Warsaw, who would be just too delighted to re-broadcast it to Western Europe."

"You have a transmitter that can reach as far as Warsaw?"

"We haven't got a transmitter, period. Nor do we know anyone in Warsaw. The threat was enough. Your government," Samuelson said with considerable satisfaction, "is now reduced to such a state of fear and trepidation that they believe anything we say. Besides, they'd look pretty silly, wouldn't they, if the announcement came through Poland?"

Van Effen refused the offer of another brandy. He had every reason to keep a clear mind for the next hour or two, and said good night.

Samuelson looked at him in some surprise. "But you'll be coming down to see the midnight broadcast?"

"I don't think so. I don't doubt your ability to carry out your threat."

"I'm going too," George said, "but I'll be back down. Just going to see how the lieutenant is. Incidentally, Mr. Samuelson, if I may—"

"Another toddy for the young lieutenant. Certainly, my friend, certainly."

"He may have a bit of a head in the morning," George said, "but he should be halfway toward recovery."

Vasco was, in fact, in excellent health and showing no signs of an incipient headache.

"Still the same lad. I should imagine the changeover will be at nine. Some guard. Spends most of the time with his chin on his chest, then jerks awake."

"Let's hope his relief is of the same style. Me, I'm going to have a snooze. If he's still there at, say, nine-twenty, give me a shake. If he's relieved at nine, shake me at ten. How do you operate the radio on that army truck? And what's its range?"

"Unlimited. Well, a hundred, two hundred miles I'm not sure. Operation is simple. Just lift the receiver and press the red button. The transmitter is pre-set to the nearest army command base that is always manned."

"I particularly don't want to talk to the army. I want to talk to Marnixstraat."

"Easy. Standard tuning dial, standard wavebands and a switch beside the button for illumination that picks out the wavelengths."

Van Effen nodded, stretched out on a bed and closed his eyes.

10

GEORGE WOKE VAN EFFEN at 10 P.M.

"New sentry took over at nine. Hardly seems an improvement on the other one except, that is, from your point of view. He's middle-aged, fat, wears two overcoats, is sitting in the armchair with a rug over his knees and, you'll be pleased to hear, also has a bottle in his hand."

"Sounds like my kind of man." Van Effen rose and changed his trousers for a pair of denims.

Vasco said: "What's that? Your battle uniform?"

"What's Samuelson going to say if he sees me in sodden trousers or even dry trousers that are so wrinkled that it will look as if I'd fallen into a river?"

"Ah. Well, you're going to get wet enough, that's for sure. Rain's heavier than ever. There are times when we can hardly see the lad in the loft doorway."

"Suits me. That barn wasn't built yesterday and old floorboards in old lofts tend to creak. With rain like this drumming on the roof, he won't be able to hear a thing. Besides, judging from George's general description, the sentry is probably half deaf anyway." He strapped on his Smith & Wesson, shrugged into his jacket and put the aerosol can in one pocket and the hooded flashlight in the other.

"Velvet gloves," George said.

Vasco said, "What's that?"

"Silenced pistol and the canister. That's what he calls velvet gloves."

Van Effen dug into an inside pocket, brought out a small leather wallet, unzipped it, took out the metallic contents, examined them then returned them to the wallet and pocket.

"Skeleton keys and picklocks," George said approvingly. "No self-respecting detective should be without them."

Vasco said: "What happens if you don't come back, sir?"

"I'll be back. It's five past ten now. I should be back by ten-thirty. If I'm not back by eleven, go downstairs. Say nothing. No doom-laden speeches, no warnings that their end is nigh. Kill Samuelson. Cripple the Agnelli brothers and Daniken, and, if Riordan is there, him also. Remove all weapons, of course, and one of you keep an eye on them and make sure that nobody tries to stagger out of the room and summon help while the other gets the girls. As your guns are silenced, there should be no interruptions. Then get the hell out of it. If anyone gets in your way, you know what to do."

"I see," Vasco said. "And how do we get the hell out of it?"

Van Effen touched the pocket where he had replaced his wallet of skeleton keys and picklocks. "What do you think those are for?"

"Ah. The truck."

"Indeed. As soon as you get under way, call the army or the cops. Give them the approximate location of this place— we know it's somewhere between Leerdam and Gorinchen— and leave the rest to them."

Vasco said: "They might try to escape by helicopter."

"You have the alternative of shooting Daniken in both shoulders or taking him with you. I'm virtually certain that none of this will happen. I don't want it to happen and that's not primarily because by the time it happens I'll probably be dead. It would be a confession of failure and I don't like being associated with failure. It would be a most unsatisfactory conclusion; in fact, it would be no conclusion at all. Samuelson has another headquarters and, as we have agreed, other associates. O'Brien has almost certainly departed this evening to associate with those other associates. Even although I doubt it, some of them may—I repeat may—be in a position to carry his plans to a successful conclusion." He opened the window. "Back at ten-thirty."

He slid down the two knotted sheets and vanished into the shadows.

George and Vasco went into the darkened bathroom. Vasco said, "He *is* a cold one, isn't he?"

George said, "Um."

"But he's a killer."

"I know he has killed and would do so again. But he's very selective, is our Peter. Nobody who has ever departed this world at his hands has ever been mourned by society."

Four minutes later Vasco caught George by the arm. "See?"

They saw. The sentry had just taken a long swig from his bottle, laid it on the floor beside him, clasped his hands over his rug, and appeared to relapse into some kind of yogalike contemplation. The shadow that had loomed behind him resolved itself into the form of Van Effen, whose right hand curved around and held the aerosol can an inch or two from the sentry's face for not more than two seconds. He then pocketed the aerosol, hooked his hands under the man's knees and eased him forward several inches to ensure that he wouldn't topple sideways from his armchair, picked up a bottle from the floor, poured some of the contents over the sentry's face, emptied the remainder of the contents over the front of his clothes, wrapped the fingers of the unconscious man's right hand around the bottle, thrust hand and bottle partly under the rug, tightened the rug to ensure that hand and bottle would remain where they were, then vanished into the gloom.

"Well now," Vasco said, "there's one character who isn't going to report himself for dereliction of duty because of dropping off into a drunken slumber."

"Peter doesn't do things by halves. Let's see now. A two-second burst of knockout spray. He should come to in about half an hour. Peter explained those things to me once."

"Won't he know he has been drugged?"

"That's the beauty of it! Leaves no trace. That apart, what would you think if you woke up with your clothes reeking of schnapps or whatever and your hand clasped around an empty bottle?"

The stairs, broad and creaky, just behind where the sentry slept, led to the floor of the barn, now converted into a temporary garage. Flashlight in hand, Van Effen descended quickly, loosed the bolts on the retaining half of the entrance door and turned his attention to the truck. The exterior was as it had been except that the number plates had been changed. He then wriggled under the truck, scraped clear an area on the underside of the chassis just forward of the rear axle and attached to it the magnetic clamp of the metallic device which Vasco had removed from the bar of soap. Thirty seconds later he was in the driver's seat and talking to the Marnixstraat.

"Put me through to Colonel Van de Graaf, please."

"Who is speaking?"

"Never mind who's speaking. The colonel."

"He's at home."

"He is not. He's there. Ten seconds or you're an ex-policeman tomorrow."

In seconds the colonel was on the phone. "You were a bit harsh on that poor lad."

"He's either a fool, an incompetent or was improperly instructed. He was told to keep open an anonymous line." Van Effen spoke in Polish, which the colonel understood as well as he did. Dutch police changed their wavelengths at infrequent intervals and had done so again only that day. As in every major city in the world, criminals occasionally picked up police wavelengths. But the probabilities against one who understood Polish picking up a newly changed wavelength were astronomical. "Please switch on your recorder. I don't know how much time I have and I don't want to repeat myself."

"Proceed."

"I shall spell names backwards. We are south of—this is a name—Utrecht—and between—two other names—Leerdam and Gorinchen. You have that?"

"I have that."

"Do not attempt to locate and do not attempt to attack. The principals are elsewhere"—it was an outright lie, but the colonel was not to know that—"and it would achieve only the deaths of five people who don't deserve to die. You know the people I mean?"

"I know."

"We have here the army truck. You know which one. It has changed identification plates. I will give you the new numbers. Backwards." Van Effen did so. "It will be carrying the nuclear devices you know about."

"What!"

"I have attached a magnetic transmitter to this vehicle. Have an unmarked police car in the vicinity as from, say, seven A.M. It is to track this truck at a safe distance. This police car will also be in radio contact with two or three army commando trucks lying to the west. I am becoming increasingly convinced that this truck will be heading toward the Schelde area. There will be three people in that truck, all dressed in Dutch army uniforms, including a bogus lieutenant colonel called Ylvisaker, who may even call himself by that name. I want that truck seized, along with its occupants, and the seizure to be kept in complete secrecy. If you release that news, then the responsibility for the flooding of the country will lie in your hands."

Van de Graaf's voice took on a complaining note. "You don't have to threaten me, my boy."

"I apologize. I am under pressure and have to make my points in as impressive a way as I can. One other thing. Have TV and radio announce—or just say, if you like—that they are to be of good heart and that you are closing in on the Rotterdam and Schelde areas. The reason to be given is that you want every citizen thereabouts to be on continuous alert and report anything abnormal to the police. This is purely psychological and I don't believe our friends are much good at depth psychology. But please, please, apart from taking this truck in complete secrecy, no other attempts at interference."

"Understood. I have someone with me who would like a

word with you and who speaks Polish even better than you and I do."

"Spell his name backwards."

Van de Graaf did so and Wieringa's voice came on the phone. "Congratulations, my son."

"Those may be a bit premature, Minister. I can't, for instance, stop the breaching of the Flevoland dikes or the detonation of the Markerwaard device. A further thought occurs. You might have the media include in their broadcasts about the Rotterdam area that Whitehall and the Stormont have arrived at an agreement to begin active and immediate negotiations."

"The two parliaments might not like it."

"I'm a Dutchman. Instruct them to like it."

"Very well. Frankly, how do you rate our chances?"

"Better than even, Minister. They trust us. They have to trust us." He explained briefly about the De Doorns ammunition dump and the RAF's inability to handle radio-controlled devices. "Apart from that, I'm not only sure but know that they don't distrust or suspect us. They are basically naive, complacent, overconfident and sure of themselves. They lack the true devious minds of detectives. I have to move, sir. I'll call again as soon as possible."

In the Marnixstraat, the Minister of Defense said, "You agree with Van Effen's assessment, Colonel?"

"If that's what he thinks, then that's what I think."

"Why isn't that young man—well, young compared to us—chief of police somewhere?"

"He'll be the chief here in the not-too-distant future. In the meantime, I need him."

"Don't we all." Wieringa sighed. "Don't we all."

Van Effen climbed up to the loft, patted the sentry lightly on the cheek, got no reaction and left. Three minutes later he was inside the bedroom. Vasco looked pointedly at his watch.

"Ten thirty-three," Vasco said accusingly.

"Sorry. I was detained. Line was busy. Anyway, that's a fine way to welcome back a man who may just have escaped the jaws of death."

"There was trouble?"

"No. Clockwork."

"You didn't unpick the garage lock," George said accusingly.

"Another word of warm welcome. Where are the congratulations for a mission successfully accomplished? Would you have picked that lock if, at the window next to our bathroom, you had seen the Reverend Riordan, who seems to meditate on his feet and pray with his eyes open, gazing out pensively over the courtyard? Instead, I unbolted the garage doors from the inside."

"I hope you remembered to re-bolt them."

"George!"

"Sorry. What detained you?"

"Wieringa, the Defense Minister. He was in the Marnixstraat with Colonel Van de Graaf. If you refrain from asking questions, I'll tell you word for word how our conversations went."

He did so and at the end George said, "Satisfactory. You fixed the bug, of course. So why did you go to all the trouble of getting hold of the operating instructions for the devices?"

"Have you ever known of a cop—or soldier, for that matter—who never made a mistake?"

George pondered briefly, then said, "Present company excepted, no. True, we may yet need that information—Ylvisaker and his friends might just miss the roadblocks. But you didn't tell them that we were going by helicopter?"

"I did not. For the same reason that I didn't take up Samuelson's unspoken offer to tell us where we are going. If I had, his immediate reaction—our Defense Minister's, that is—would be to have called his counterpart in Whitehall to send over a Nimrod, the British bomber that is a virtual airborne radar station and which could have tracked us from here to wherever we're going without our knowing a thing about it." He smiled. "You wear, what shall we say, George, a peculiar expression. The same thought had occurred to you?"

"It had." George looked thoroughly chagrined. "I thought it rather a good idea, myself."

"I don't. I have no doubt that the Royal Air Force would

have been delighted to comply, and I have no doubt that within a short time of our arriving at our destination we would have a visit from our paratroopers and commandos who don't tend to beat about the bush very much. I don't much care for that idea."

"Why not? A few friends . . ."

"Three reasons. I don't want a firefight, a bloodbath. Killing or capturing—killing, more likely—Samuelson and his group would not be the total solution. There may be—in fact I feel certain there will be, don't ask me why, I don't know—enough of his people left to carry out the ultimate threat. Third, I don't much care for the idea of the women being hurt or worse. I wouldn't much like to gun down—wound, I mean, not kill— a countryman who was threatening the life of one of those girls."

Vasco said, "Julie and Annemarie?"

"All four."

George said mildly, "The other two are criminals."

"They associate with criminals. Different matter entirely. Anyway, if the government were to commit this folly, we would be in a position to expose them and dictate our own terms. Wieringa and the colonel would back us up, and they're the only two people who matter. However, this is all academic. It's not going to happen. . . . These denims are rather damp."

When he'd changed, he said, "Our friend O'Brien is missing in more than one way—he's also the key. I'd give a lot to know where he is at this moment. He won't have gone to their other hangout for his skill in debugging and defusing alarm systems that wouldn't be called for there. One could speculate endlessly, but that would be a waste of time."

"I'm neglecting my duties," Vasco said. "If I may be excused. George, would you come and switch the light on again?"

He turned off the light, went into the bathroom and closed the door. No sooner had George turned the light on than Vasco tapped on the door. George switched the light off again and the bathroom door opened.

"This may interest you," Vasco said.

The sentry's head was nodding, intermittently and at irregular intervals. After a few seconds of this he held it in an upright position, then shook it from side to side. After a few more seconds of this—it was too dark to see his expression— he brought up his right hand from under his rug, looked at the bottle still clutched in it, upended it and, having established the fact that it was empty, placed it on the floor and pushed himself back in his seat.

"He's going to drop off again," Vasco said.

"Not him," Van Effen said. "He's making a major decision."

The sentry made his move. He lifted his rug to one side, pushed himself groggily to his feet and took a few staggering steps that brought him perilously close to the loft doorway.

Vasco said, "He's drunk."

"Again, not him. He's seen his bottle is empty and assumes because of that and the fact that he reeks of schnapps that he ought to be drunk and acts accordingly. Autosuggestion, I believe they call it. It could have been awkward if his relief found that he couldn't wake him. Enough."

In the bedroom Van Effen said, "I think we should go downstairs in a few moments. Including you, Vasco, if you feel strong enough."

"I'm a captain in the Dutch army. I'm brave."

George said: "You told Samuelson you wouldn't be down."

"My mind changes along with the circumstances. It was freezing out there. I require brandy. More importantly, I want to see their reaction to the news that the hunt for the F.F.F. is now being concentrated in the Rotterdam-Schelde area. Even more important is that I want those missiles, explosives and other nasties transferred from the truck to the helicopter."

"Why?" George said.

"The roads between here and the Rotterdam-Schelde area will be alive with patrols tomorrow morning; police and Army, but mainly, I suspect, Army. My personal conviction is that Ylvisaker will be intercepted. I want those missiles because the F.F.F. want them mounted for some offensive or defensive purposes and that should give them, from our point of view, owing to the fact that the missiles are useless, a splendid sense of false security."

"You should have been a lawyer, a politician, a Wall Street broker or a criminal specializing in fraud," George said.

"Look who's talking. I also have a hunch that the explosives, grenades and other sundries may prove to be more useful to us than to them. Just a hunch. Vasco, what do you know about the regulations concerning the transport of missiles?"

"Nothing."

"Then let's invent some."

"I'll wager, sir, that I can invent better regulations than you can."

"Gentlemen, gentlemen!" Samuelson's crocodile smile would have shamed an archangel. "Delighted to see you. I thought you weren't coming down, Mr. Danilov."

"Couldn't sleep," Van Effen said with a transparent honesty that would have shamed the same angel. "As a Dutchman, even an adopted one, I just couldn't—well, you understand—well, you know, Flevoland."

"Of course, of course. I understand. *And* the captain—sorry, lieutenant. Delighted to see you, my boy. I take it you are feeling better?"

"My voice is not but I am," Vasco said hoarsely. "Thanks to your kindness, Mr. Samuelson."

"The universal remedy. I suggest another." He looked at Van Effen and George. "Brandies, gentlemen? Large ones?"

"You are kind," Van Effen said. He waited while Samuelson gave instructions to Leonardo. "You know my normally incurious manner, but two things take my attention. The ladies have returned. I was given to understand that they were still in a state of nervous exhaustion."

"As far as I can understand, they still are. Your second question?"

Van Effen smiled. "Your TV is on again. You are expecting a further communiqué?"

"Correct. Both questions answered. You will excuse me a moment, gentlemen. I must tell the Reverend that it is earphones time."

Leonardo brought them their drinks. Van Effen thanked him

and led the other two out onto the terrace. No one raised an eyebrow. Apart from the fact that they had already established a reputation as eccentric fresh-air fiends, if they wished to have a private conversation they had already had a long time to have held it upstairs.

Van Effen closed the door and said, "Well, what do we make of that?"

"The four women and their rapid recovery from nervous exhaustion? They're talking among each other, not animatedly, not cordially, but they're talking. And I don't think they've come down to watch late-evening television." George sipped his brandy. "Somebody wants to talk to us."

Van Effen nodded. "Julie. Could be Annemarie, but my hunch is Julie." He looked across at the loft door where the sentry was now pacing to and fro, perfectly steady on his feet and looking every inch a man devoted to his job. "When we get back inside—which will be in a few seconds, it's like an icebox out here—I want you to wait a few discreet minutes, then wander aimlessly around, playing the role of a genial, middle-aged Lothario—just act your natural self, that is—and see if you can't have a word with Julie. Just a few words, and don't let her talk more than a few words with you. If necessary, just say the word 'helicopter.' She'll know what I mean. I'll try to get next to her and no one can hear a word on a helicopter. I don't want to go near her myself. If Samuelson has got a leery eye for anyone, it's for me."

"Done," George said.

They reentered the living room, both Van Effen and Vasco giving exaggerated shudders; George was too big and well covered for that sort of thing.

Romero Agnelli smiled. "Back so soon, gentlemen?"

"Fresh air is one thing," Van Effen said. "The polar ice cap another." He looked up at the flickering but silent TV set. "Samuelson not down yet?"

"He's hardly had time to get upstairs and back. And he too is called now and then by nature," Agnelli said reasonably. "Your glasses, gentlemen."

At the bar, Van Effen said, "It's a wild night outside and

getting wilder. Do you seriously think it'll be safe to fly tomorrow?"

"Do you fly?"

"As a passenger, a lot. I have—had—a pilot's license. Never been in a helicopter in my life."

"I have a license for a helicopter. Total solo flying time—about three hours. In weather like this, you wouldn't get me within a hundred miles of the pilot's seat. Daniken's had thousands of hours. Superb pilot."

"Well, that's a relief." Van Effen was aware that George and Vasco had drifted away, his eyes made no attempt to follow them. "Nice to think we might get there—wherever there is."

"If Daniken wasn't sure he wouldn't take off."

They continued an amicable discussion along those lines for two or three minutes, until Samuelson reappeared, to all appearances his urbane and good-humored self.

"Any moment now, ladies and gentlemen. I think we should take our seats."

The lugubrious announcer seemed to have aged considerably.

"We have two announcements to make, both concerning the F.F.F. The first is that London and the Stormont, the Northern Ireland parliament, have arrived at an agreement to begin active and immediate negotiations with our government. Such negotiations have, in fact, already begun."

Samuelson beamed.

"The second is that the government advises all citizens of the Netherlands to be of good heart. The Ministry of Defense suspects, although it has no reason to believe, that the F.F.F. will be switching their scene of operations from the Ijsselmeer, where the dike breaches and the explosion of this nuclear device are promised to take place tomorrow. This is because the F.F.F. have established a practice of not striking twice in the same area. The balance of opinion is they will concentrate on the southwest, most likely in the Rotterdam-Schelde. The reason given for this announcement is that the government wants every citizen in that area—repeat *every*—because it affects every citizen, to be on continuous alert and report anything in the slightest way abnormal to the nearest police or army post. It is appreciated that this statement will also be picked up by the F.F.F., but the government regards this as the lesser of two evils compared to whatever use it may be to the F.F.F."

Samuelson was no longer beaming. Van Effen, forehead furrowed and lips pursed, looked at George, then, without altering his expression, at Samuelson, and said, "I don't think I like this very much."

"I don't like it at all." His expression was almost a mirror image of Van Effen's, and the fingers of both hands were drumming on the arms of his chair. After a few seconds he turned to Van Effen and said, "And what do you make of *this* development?" It was significant, Van Effen thought, that Samuelson should have asked him first; it didn't speak highly of his confidence in his associates. Van Effen waited about twenty seconds before he replied; he already had the answers to most possible questions, but Samuelson wouldn't have been suitably impressed by an immediate answer.

"I think they're bluffing. Or, at least, counter- or double-bluffing. They may believe that you intend to strike next in some other spot entirely and that this is intended to put you off your guard and relax while they close in elsewhere where they fondly imagine you are. Or they may not be bluffing and this may be intended to restrict your movements. Either way, they're not very bright, but then, the Minister of Justice, the Minister of Defense, and the chief of police of Amsterdam are hardly renowned for their intelligence." George coughed softly into his hand but retained an impassive expression.

Samuelson looked doubtful. "Don't forget I've met Wieringa. He didn't strike me as a fool."

"He's not a fool. He's honest, straightforward and the most popular man in government. But he lacks the cunning to rise to the top. Plots and counterplots are not for him. Another thing. If the authorities knew where we were, don't you think we'd have had a visit from a battalion of paratroopers some time ago?"

"Ah!" The thought seemed to cheer Samuelson up.

"And still another thing. You have another operations center somewhere. Why don't you call and see if they've suffered any harassment?"

Samuelson nodded to Romero Agnelli, who dialed a number, spoke briefly and hung up.

"Nothing," he said.

"Excellent," Samuelson said. "So we're in the clear."

"No, we're not." Van Effen shook his head in a discouragingly definite fashion. "Lieutenant, is there any chance that it may have been discovered that the truck and weapons are missing from the armory from which we took them?"

"The truck?" Vasco said hoarsely. "Possible but unlikely. The weapons, no. The regular inventory isn't due for another two weeks."

Van Effen said, "Mr. Samuelson, it's not for me to say, but shouldn't we change the identification numbers on that truck?"

Samuelson smirked. "Already done."

"Well done. But there's more to it than that." Vasco spoke huskily and unhappily. "The authorities, as Mr. Danilov says, may be operating in this area. Mention was made of both police and army posts. That means there may be police *and* army roadblocks. Police roadblocks present no danger. The Army's do. They know that missiles in transport—which is in itself an extremely rare occurrence—always travel in convoy. If you want to get them to their destination, they'll have to travel by helicopter."

"Not in *my* helicopter, they won't," Daniken said.

"Mr. Daniken, I believe you to be an expert helicopter pilot." Vasco's voice being in the assumed condition it was, it was difficult for him to speak coldly, but his eyes were cold enough. "The cobbler should stick to his last. I'm an expert on missiles. A missile cannot be armed until it's in flight. It's obvious that you've never been in military helicopters. What do you think the Russian gunships use in Afghanistan? Peashooters?" Daniken remained silent. "I also think the other weapons and explosives should be removed, otherwise you'll be liable to be asked what armory you've taken them from and to what armory or army unit you're taking them. Mobile army controls tend to be very curious, very alert and very persistent—especially when in a national emergency alert."

Daniken looked unhappy. "But the detonators—"

"The detonators," George said comfortably, "will be in their velvet sockets, wrapped in cotton wool, in a lead-sheathed steel box and resting on my lap." He let a note of irritation creep into his voice. "Do you think I want to blow myself up, far less your damned helicopter?"

"I shouldn't imagine so." It was Samuelson who spoke. "What do you think, Romero?"

"I don't have to think, Mr. Samuelson."

"Neither do I. Agreed, gentlemen. Fine precautions. We shall drive the truck down to the helicopter tonight and transfer the missiles and the rest of it after the staff have retired, which may be rather late, especially as they, too, will be watching their TV sets at midnight. Not that it matters much. They are accustomed to the mysterious goings-on of film companies." He paused. "I wonder if one of you three gentlemen would care to supervise the transfer of those materials."

"I will," George said immediately. "No coward like a big coward." He looked at Daniken. "It looks like being a rather bumpy flight tomorrow. As this is an ex-military helicopter, I assume you have clamps, lashings and other devices to secure things that have to be secured?"

"We have," Daniken said. He still looked distinctly unhappy.

"Seems to be all," Van Effen said. "Mr. Samuelson, I'd like another snooze before this midnight broadcast. Not that I'm convinced that we'll see anything. Even if there are ships or helicopters around with searchlights, visibility in this rain will be zero. George? Lieutenant?"

"Me, too," George said. "Any more of this brandy and I'll be dropping detonators all over the place."

Vasco was already on his feet. Without as much as a glance at the four girls, they left and made their way up the stairs. In the corridor above, Van Effen said admiringly, "You really are a couple of terrific liars. Have a word with Julie, George?"

"Certainly not." George spoke in a lofty tone. "We professionals operate on a higher level." He produced a folded bit of paper from his pocket and replaced it.

"Splendid. Vasco, we approach our bedroom door. Has anything occurred to you?"

"Visitors."

Once inside, Van Effen carried on a brief conversation about the weather, the best way of securing the missiles and other weapons aboard the helicopter, and their conviction that the truck should have no trouble in getting through to its destination. Vasco meanwhile carried out his usual meticulous inspection. After a few minutes he returned from the bathroom and put his fingers to his lips.

"Well, me for bed," Van Effen said. "Any gallant volunteers to keep the midnight watch?"

"No need for anyone to keep watch," Vasco said. "I have a traveling alarm."

Seconds later all three were within the bathroom, which had both the mirror and overhead lights on. Van Effen and George had gone in first, from darkened bedroom to darkened bathroom, followed immediately by Vasco, who left the bedroom door slightly ajar and turned on the light as he entered. He then switched on the overhead shower in the bath.

"O'Brien is gone," Vasco said. "He could never have been responsible for the crude device that's attached to the underside of my bed. The one device that can't be deactivated without a listener knowing it is inside a shower head—the listener can hear it being unscrewed—and even if there were other bugs in here, which there aren't, no one can hear a thing over the sound of a shower. Odd, but a fact."

"You're just like our big friend here," Van Effen said. "You should have joined the criminal ranks years ago. You'd have made a fortune. Well, the F.F.F. should now have a tape reassuring them that there's no way they can fail. Let's have a look at that note, George." George did so and Van Effen read it out.

"'Something goes on that neither Annemarie nor I understand but which may be of use to you. We have become quite friendly with our two lady criminal "kidnappers," and if they are criminals, so are Annemarie and I. Hardened criminals don't go around looking as if the Day of Judgment is at hand and trying all the time not to have tears in their eyes. They do.'"

Van Effen broke off and looked thoughtfully at George. "Anyone see Julie slip this note to you?"

"No."

Vasco was perturbed. "What if Julie, I'm sorry, sir, your sister—you must remember I don't know her—has told them about us?"

"Rubbish!" George said. "As you said, you don't know her. Peter's faith in her intelligence, judgment and intuition is total, as is mine. In fact," George added confidentially, "she's a lot cleverer than he is."

"That was uncalled for," Van Effen said.

"'Kathleen is definitely the one who is under the most pressure,'" the note went on. "'She is afraid of Samuelson or something that Samuelson might do. Maria is under less pressure but doesn't seem to like what her brother Romero is up to. But she seems to like *him* and I have to admit that he has been very kind and courteous to us since they took us away.

"'I think that, in their own way, they are as much prisoners as we are. Kathleen and Maria are here under a form of coercion just as Anne and I are here under coercion, but a different kind of coercion.'"

"'Coercion,'" Vasco said. "That's the word you used. On the veranda, remember?"

"I remember. 'We're here—Annemarie and I—simply because we were abducted. They are here, I'm sure, because they have been misled, lied to, because appeals have been made to their love or loyalty or some misguided sense of honor or all three. I think that they, especially Kathleen, have been lured here under false apprehensions.'"

"Jesus Christ!" For once George's massive calm had deserted him. "I've heard of rare cases of telepathy between twins, but she's only your young sister. That's what you said, almost word for word."

"Nothing to do with telepathy. Great minds tend to think

alike. Still question her intelligence, judgment or intuition, Vasco?"

Vasco shook his head slowly, several times, and said nothing.

Van Effen looked at George. "Hah! And you still think she's cleverer than I am?" George stroked his chin and said nothing. Van Effen read on and his face became still. "Maybe you were right at that, George. Listen to this last paragraph."

"'I know why Maria is here. Despite her disapproval of what Romero is up to, there is a genuine bond of affection between them. As for Kathleen, I have mentioned that she is afraid of Samuelson and whatever he has in mind. I have also mentioned misguided love and loyalty. I am convinced that she is Samuelson's daughter.'"

There was a considerable silence. Then George said, "I take back what I said about her being smarter than you. She's smarter than the three of us put together. She has to be right. There's no other explanation."

Van Effen set fire to the note and flushed the ashes away. Then they turned off the shower and left.

Vasco shook Van Effen by the shoulder. "It's time, Mr. Danilov."

Van Effen opened his eyes and, as always, was instantly awake. "I didn't hear the alarm."

"Turned it off—I've been awake for some time. George!"

Only Samuelson, the Agnelli brothers, and Daniken were in the living room when the three men arrived.

"Just in time, gentlemen," Samuelson said. Even though normally cheerful, he seemed to be in uncommonly good humor at midnight, a condition that could have been accounted for by the bottle of brandy by his side, but which was almost certainly due to an anticipatory euphoria. "Ten minutes and we're all back in bed."

"Not me," George said. "I'm staying here. Your loading supervisor, remember. When do we begin the transfer?"

"Of course. Half an hour, say. Leonardo, we are neglecting our guests."

Van Effen looked at Samuelson. He bore no resemblance to Kathleen, but that meant nothing; she probably took after her Irish mother. Van Effen didn't doubt his sister's conviction.

The same announcer, whose depth of depression seemed to be matched only by his stamina, appeared on screen just after midnight.

"It is with regret that we have to announce that we will be unable to show live the threatened breaches of the Flevoland dikes when and if they occur. It is impossible for our TV cameras to operate in conditions of total darkness and torrential rain. We are, however, in constant radio-telephone touch with a number of observers and will inform you at once as soon as any positive news is at hand." His image faded from the screen.

"Pity," Samuelson said. He seemed in no way disappointed. "Would have been a stirring spectacle. Still, we shouldn't have long to wait."

They had very little time to wait. Less than a minute elapsed before the announcer reappeared, replacing a phone on his desk.

"The Oostlijk-Flevoland and Zuidslijk-Flevoland dikes were breached simultaneously ninety seconds ago. Both breaches initially appear to be massive but the appalling weather conditions make it impossible to gauge their extent or the severity of the flooding. The authorities say they must wait until the first light of dawn before the scope of the disaster can be accurately assessed. We shall, however, be on the air every hour on the hour to give you what fresh details are available." He paused to look at a sheet of paper that had just been handed to him.

"A phone call has just been received from the F.F.F. The message reads: 'Markerwaard two P.M. today.'"

11

TWO MEN WERE to play important parts in the morning hours of that day.

One was Sergeant Druckmann, who was accompanied by two other officers. All three were in plain clothes. Their unmarked police car was plainer still, mud-covered and battered. It carried an unusual amount of electronic equipment, two separate sets of radio transceivers and a radar tracking device. The operator sat on the left-hand rear seat with a large-scale road map on his knees. The equipment was, for the moment, covered by a carelessly thrown rug. The car had been in position since six-thirty that morning in a side road just north of Gorinchen.

Two other unmarked cars, similarly equipped, were within a few miles of them. But it was Druckmann's car that was to count that morning.

The other man to matter was one Gropious, dressed in the uniform of a corporal in the Dutch army and sitting beside a private at the wheel of a small Dutch army troop carrier. Two other soldiers sat in the rear. Nobody would have used a photograph of Gropious on a recruitment poster. His uniform was shabby and wrinkled and his long blond locks fell every which way under a hat that was more than slightly askew; the Dutch, for some reason best known to themselves, permit their soldiers to grow their hair to a length that would have had any British soldier confined to barracks for a fortnight. But the blond locks were not his own.

The uniform, too, was a fake. Gropious was a soldier but no corporal: Lieutenant Colonel Gropious, of the Dutch army commandos, was a particularly tough specimen of a tough and elite corps.

The 7 A.M. broadcast that morning—the first breakfast-time broadcast in Dutch TV history—had been at once gloomy and slightly reassuring. Hundreds of square miles of the Flevolands had been inundated but to no great depth. As far as was known, no lives had been lost; the loss in livestock could not be estimated until later in the day. Hundreds of engineers were already pouring even more hundreds of tons of boulders and quick-setting concrete between hastily erected and, it was admitted, inadequately secured vertical steel plates. At best, it was also admitted, this could do no more than slightly reduce the effects of the next high tide and operations would have to cease at least three hours before that.

In the living room of the windmill, where some dozen people were having breakfast, Samuelson was in high spirits.

"Exactly as predicted, ladies and gentlemen." He looked in turn at Van Effen, George and Vasco. "I keep my word, do I not, gentlemen? Maximum psychological impact, yet not a life lost. Things *are* going our way." He paused and listened to the thunderous drumming of the rain on the veranda, gradually lost his expression of good humor, drummed his fingers in echo on the table, looked at Daniken and said, "What do you think?"

"I don't like it much," Daniken said. He rose and walked out to the veranda, closing the door behind him. He was back in seconds.

"The wind's about the same," he said. "That is, gale force. I could fly in that. But the rain is the heaviest I've ever seen, even worse than the onset of the monsoon in India. Visibility is zero. I can't fly in that and keep our flight plan as it is."

"You mean you won't fly?" Samuelson said. "You refuse to fly?" Samuelson didn't seem unduly perturbed.

"Not even if you ordered me. I will not be the person

responsible for the end of all you wish for. *I* am the pilot and refuse to be responsible for the deaths of twenty-two people. Which I will be if we stick to our flight plans. Mass suicide is not my game."

Van Effen cleared his throat delicately. "I don't like this talk of mass suicide, not least because it involves me. Is the need to leave exactly on time a matter of the utmost urgency?"

"Not really." It was Romero Agnelli who answered. "Mr. Samuelson does me the honor of leaving all the organization to me."

"And exceptionally good you are at it, too."

"Thank you." Agnelli smiled almost apologetically. "I'm just a stickler for timetables."

"I don't think you need to worry too much about timetables," Van Effen said. "I know this country, you people don't. George and the lieutenant will confirm that downpours of this extraordinary order rarely last very long. It's been raining hard all night. What's all this about flight paths or flight plans or whatever?"

"No reason why you shouldn't know," Samuelson said. He was relieved by Van Effen's statement. "Daniken has radiofiled a flight plan to Valkenburg, near Maastricht, and this has been accepted. We are today filming a scene in hilly countryside, and the only hilly countryside in the Netherlands is in the province of Limburg, where Valkenburg lies. Romero has had even the foresight to book us hotel accommodations there."

"Where, of course, you have no intention of going." Van Effen nodded his head twice. "Neat, very neat. You take off for Limburg, which lies in a roughly south-south-easterly direction, then Daniken descends and alters course. The Netherlands is a flat country, so one has to fly very low to keep beneath the radar screen. As a pilot myself, I know that altimeters are notoriously inaccurate at very low altitudes. It wouldn't do us a great deal of good if a sudden downdraft were to bring us into contact with a block of high-rise flats or even one of those massive TV antennas. Mr. Daniken has to see where he is going, and I have to say that I am in one hundred-percent agreement with him."

"Mr. Danilov has put it even better than I could," Daniken said.

"And I agree with you both," Samuelson said. "Leonardo, be so kind as to tell Ylvisaker to delay his departure with the truck until further notice. I do not wish him to arrive at our destination before we do."

Ylvisaker, resplendent in his lieutenant colonel's uniform, and his two companions, dressed as a sergeant and private of the Dutch army, departed at 8:45 A.M. The wind had not eased but the rain, as Van Effen had predicted, had lessened to no more than a heavy drizzle.

At 8:46 A.M., Cornelius, the policeman in the rear of Sergeant Druckmann's car, said, "Moving out, Sergeant." Druckmann picked up his microphone.

"Sergeant Druckmann here. Target Zero has just moved out. Will A, B, C, D, E please acknowledge."

The five army patrol vehicles acknowledged in alphabetical order.

Druckmann said, "Two minutes, three at the most, and we should be able to know what route Target Zero is taking. After that, we shall report at minute intervals."

At 8:47 A.M., twenty-two people filed aboard the giant helicopter. All, except the four women, Van Effen and George, were dressed in Dutch army uniforms. Samuelson said goodbye to four umbrella-carrying staff who had come to see them off, assuring them that they would be back the following evening. All the soldiers, with one exception, were armed with machine pistols: the exception, Willi, the feckless guard, was burdened only by a pair of handcuffs.

At 8:49 A.M., Daniken lifted off and headed south-southeast.

Also at 8:49 A.M., Sergeant Druckmann reported: "Tracking Target Zero at just over one mile. Target Zero is now a half mile north of Gorinchen. From there the three main exit routes are east, south and west. Two minutes and we should be able to let you know which direction he is heading."

Van Effen turned to Romero Agnelli, who was sitting beside him, cupped his hand to his ear and said: "Two things intrigue me."

Agnelli lifted his eyebrows.

"I was led to believe that the armament on this gunship had been dismantled and replaced by dummies. Those guns are for real."

"The armament was dismantled and replaced by dummies. Then we replaced the dummies. These things aren't hard to come by if you know where to look. What was the other thing?"

"Why isn't Daniken climbing? We're still under a hundred yards."

"Look to your left."

Van Effen looked. Less than fifty yards away another, much smaller helicopter was flying alongside. Even as Van Effen watched the pilot slid back his window and waved an arm. Van Effen looked forward. Daniken was waving in return. The pilot of the small helicopter closed his window and began to climb. Daniken gently eased the gunship around until it was heading due south.

"Neat," Van Effen said. "Very, very neat. In weather like this there will be precious little private flying in the country today. The odd bored air controller might just amuse himself by tracking this helicopter to Valkenburg. *That* helicopter, of course, *is* heading for Valkenburg." Agnelli nodded. "Your idea, of course."

Agnelli smiled and made a deprecating motion with his hand.

"Target Zero is heading west on the Sliedrecht road," Druckmann reported. "Which patrol is in the vicinity?"

"Patrol A."

"Ah! Colonel Gropious, sir?"

"Yes. I am setting a roadblock one half mile east of Sliedrecht. Close up until you have them visually. But not too close."

"I understand, sir. Target Zero is traveling at a very leisurely pace—perhaps 'circumspect' is the word I'm looking for. Just below thirty miles. I estimate they should be with you in just under twenty minutes."

"Thank you, Sergeant."

Ylvisaker leaned back luxuriously in his seat and lit a cigar. "This," he said with a sigh, "is the life. Thank God we're not aboard that damned helicopter."

That damned helicopter was bumping and lurching its way in a generally west-by-south direction. "Generally," because Daniken was at pains to avoid towns, villages or settlements of any size. It was, Van Effen thought, a superfluous precaution. There was no earthly reason why, say, a lone farmer should report the passage of an unidentified and probably unidentifiable helicopter. Helicopters were ten a penny in the Netherlands.

Van Effen looked around the gunship. Most of the passengers looked distinctly unhappy and their complexions offered interesting shades of color. Annemarie and Julie, who were sitting together, had adopted remarkably similar attitudes— clenched fists and eyes screwed tightly shut. Van Effen himself was untroubled; Daniken was a superb pilot.

He cupped his hand to Agnelli's ear. "How much farther?"

"About fifteen minutes."

"Reasonable accommodations?"

Agnelli smiled. "Nice little place."

Judging by the standards of Samuelson's taste, the nice little place, Van Effen thought, was probably about the size of the royal palace.

The blue-and-yellow sign read: ROAD CHECK AHEAD. PLEASE STOP AT THE RED LIGHT.

Ylvisaker's driver slowed and said, "What do we do now?"

Ylvisaker took a leisurely puff at his cigar. "Drive on, my man."

Gropious' driver lowered his binoculars. "Target Zero for sure, sir." He raised his binoculars again. "And the given number."

Gropious' vehicle was in the left-hand lane; facing oncoming traffic. On the right-hand side, and slightly behind them, was another troop carrier. Two soldiers, both holding umbrellas, were leaning against their vehicle. Both were smoking cigarettes.

"Would you look at that sloppy bunch," Ylvisaker said. "Umbrellas! Cigarettes! I'll bet there's not an officer nearer than Rotterdam. And these, mind you, are the gallant troops sworn to defend NATO to the death."

As they came to a halt at the red light, Gropious and his two men, all three trailing machine pistols in their left hands, approached the stolen army truck, Gropious going to the front of the truck and his two men to the rear. Ylvisaker opened his door.

"What's all this then, Corporal?"

"Colonel!" An embarrassed Gropious, perceptibly stiffening, executed as military a salute as could be expected from a slovenly corporal. "Colonel. If I had known——"

Ylvisaker smiled tolerantly. "What is it, Corporal?"

"Orders, sir. We are under instructions to stop and examine all vehicles, army trucks included, which may be carrying illegally obtained weapons. We were given the registration number of one particular army truck. This is not the one."

Ylvisaker displayed some mild interest. "Are you searching for anything in particular?"

"Missiles, sir. Ground-to-ground and ground-to-air missiles. I must admit, sir, that I don't even know what they look like except that they're copper-colored and over two yards long."

"Duty is duty, Corporal. I see you have two men at the rear. Instruct them to open up and search. Just, you know, for the records."

Gropious gave the instructions, the rear doors were opened.

"My apologies, Colonel," Gropious said. He hesitated, then produced a notebook and pencil. "My instructions are to make a note of the identification of every person passing through this checkpoint."

Ylvisaker reached inside his uniform jacket. Gropious said, "No, no, sir. In your case, no papers are necessary. Just your name, Colonel."

"Ylvisaker."

"Colonel Ylvisaker." Rather laboriously, Gropious wrote down the name in his notebook. How ironic, he thought, that such a confrontation should occur between a lieutenant colonel posing as a fake corporal and a civilian—and criminal—posing as a lieutenant colonel. He put his notebook away and lifted his machine pistol at the same instant as his two soldiers at the rear of the truck.

"Move," Gropious said, "and you're dead."

No sooner had Gropious and his men brought Ylvisaker and his two men out onto the roadside than Sergeant Druckmann's car drew up behind them. Druckmann and his men got out, Druckmann carrying a considerable number of metal objects in his hand. Druckmann looked at the scruffy corporal with the straggling blond locks and said hesitantly, "Colonel Gropious?"

"It is." Gropious removed his hat, took off his wig and threw it beyond the roadside. "Those damn things itch."

Druckmann said, "Congratulations, sir."

Gropious, who without his wig, now looked remarkably like a lieutenant colonel, shook his hand warmly. "And the same to you, Sergeant. Your name, please? All I know is that all the police cars were manned by sergeants."

"Druckmann, Colonel."

"An excellent piece of work, Sergeant Druckmann. Most professional. And what, may I inquire, is all that ironmongery you're carrying?"

"Handcuffs and leg irons, sir. I understand that those are not standard army issue."

"Splendid. Kindly have one of your men attach them at

once." He turned to one of his soldiers. "Instruct all patrols to return to base. I suggest, Sergeant Druckmann, that you instruct one of your men to do the same for your police cars. Emphasizing, of course, the need for secrecy."

"At once, Colonel. But there is no need to emphasize secrecy. All of us, myself included, have been threatened by Colonel Van de Graaf with the equivalent of Devil's Island."

"Ah! Our redoubtable chief of police in Amsterdam."

"Yes, sir. Whose prisoners are those—yours or ours?"

"They are now the property of the nation. We will drive to my base, call up Mr. Wieringa, the Defense Minister, and Colonel Van de Graaf and see what is to be done to them. Meantime, let's have a look at Ylvisaker's truck—well, his stolen truck."

Inside the truck Druckmann said, "I really know very little about what's going on. Those three men are F.F.F."

"They are indeed, and they face three charges. The first is impersonating army officers. The second is being in possession of a stolen army vehicle." Gropious opened the lids of the two fake long-range petrol tanks to reveal the squat, cylindrical shapes of two bronze-colored metal objects. "The third, of course, is to have them explain how come they are transporting a couple of nuclear bombs along the roads of our fair countryside."

The lids were lowered and they stepped outside. Druckmann said, "May I smoke in the colonel's presence?"

"The colonel is about to do the same."

After a few moments, Druckmann said, "Well, all right. I volunteer."

Gropious smiled. "To drive this truck to base?"

"I'm a coward, Colonel. I shall take great care."

"I have a great deal of time for cowards, Sergeant. By the time we get there we shall have two U.S. experts from Germany standing by to deactivate those damned things. I shall lead the way, red lights flashing and all that sort of thing, you will follow close behind and your police car will follow close behind you. You have this consolation, Sergeant Druckmann: If you're vaporized, we're all vaporized."

The time was 9:27 A.M.

* * *

At 9:27 A.M. Daniken touched down outside another isolated windmill-cum-farmhouse, considerably larger than the one they had so recently left. Two men and two women, umbrellas in hand, came hurrying out to meet them.

The living room of the windmill, which had a similar veranda outside, was even more luxurious than the one they had left behind. There were ten people in the room—Samuelson and the Agnelli brothers, Van Effen and his friends and the four girls. Daniken, Van Effen guessed, was presumably parking—and concealing—his helicopter in a nearby barn. Riordan had gone upstairs, no doubt for meditation and prayer.

Samuelson, relaxed in an armchair before a crackling wood fire, sighed like a man content with himself.

"Clockwork, my friends, just clockwork. The penultimate stage successfully complete. I know it's still relatively early in the morning, but then, we shall be having an early lunch. Something in the nature of a soupçon of jonge jenever, I think."

"An early lunch?" Van Effen said. "We're moving on?"

"Just after two o'clock." Samuelson gestured toward a TV set. "After we've seen what happens in the Markerwaard."

"I see." Van Effen made it clear that he didn't see at all. "Well, wherever." He shrugged. "How many of these establishments do you own in the Netherlands?"

"None. The owners of this house, for instance, are presently basking in the sunshine of the Bahamas. The Golden Gate pays well. This, as you are aware, is the dead season for farming. A local farmer, also well rewarded, looks after the cattle and sheep. There are no problems. Do you know where we are, Mr. Danilov?"

"Haven't the faintest idea." Long experience had taught Van Effen to lie with conviction, he knew exactly where he was. "After so short a flight, still somewhere in Holland. Does it matter?"

"You are a singularly incurious person. We are in the vicinity of Middelharnis. You know of it?"

"Middelharnis?" Van Effen frowned, then said, "Over Flakkee."

Samuelson nodded and said nothing.

Van Effen set down the glass that Leonardo had just given him. His face was stonily bleak and his eyes very cold.

"The Haringvliet," he whispered. "You're after the Haringvliet." His horror was all art; he had been well aware of the target for some time.

The Haringvliet dam was variously referred to as the valve or the sluice gate of Holland. It blocked the entry to the Haringvliet estuary and many waterways beyond. In the late spring and early summer, when the snows in the Alps, Germany and France melted, it diverted the waters from the swollen Rhine, Waal and Maas rivers past Rotterdam and into the New Waterway, which joined the North Sea at Europort, simply by keeping its massive hydraulically operated, electrically powered gates closed. It could also, when the level of the river water rose too high, and the level of the North Sea was considerably lower, release water directly into the North Sea simply by opening as many of its gates as was deemed necessary. At this time of the year, however, with the river water shrunk to its lowest level, its main task was to keep out the North Sea except at the very latest of neap tides. The flooding, the damage and the deaths that would inevitably result from the destruction of the sluice gate of Holland were incalculable.

"Yes, Mr. Danilov." Samuelson must have been convinced that his life was in danger, but he remained outwardly calm. "I am, as you say, after the Haringvliet."

Van Effen nodded just once, briefly. "Hence the nuclear weapons. I hope to God they detonate en route and blast Ylvisaker and his friends into outer space."

"A most uncharitable wish." Samuelson sipped his drink. "I see you are wearing your Smith & Wesson, Mr. Danilov. I have no doubt your friends are similarly armed. Romero, Leonardo and I carry no arms—it's a point of principle with us. If you choose to shoot me, there's nothing I can do about it. But wouldn't you consider it rather unfair to shoot a man merely because you're laboring under a vast misapprehension?" Samuelson seemed to be positively enjoying himself.

"Go on."

"The nuclear devices are most definitely not intended for use on the Haringvliet dam. Firstly, I don't relish the prospect of vaporizing myself. Secondly, I want the sluice gates to remain intact and in perfect working order. Thirdly, I intend to take over the dam."

Van Effen sipped his drink in silence for a few moments, as if to take time out for thinking. He'd been convinced earlier that Samuelson had had no intention of destroying it.

"How very ambitious. And how do you intend to set about this takeover?"

"It's already half done. About forty hours ago a skilled electrician carried out a delicate and all but undetectable job of sabotaging three turbo-generators."

"The devil he did. He was an employee?"

"Naturally."

"And Dutch?"

"Yes. Twenty thousand dollars, I've always found, has a most profound influence on even the most patriotic soul. Besides, he had no idea what we had in mind. He, of course, was given the opportunity to trace the source of those faults, and when he failed they called in experts from Rotterdam. Those four are currently lodged in a cellar beneath us. They are being well fed and cared for, as you can see for yourself any time you wish."

"That will not be necessary. And then, of course, you sent in your own four experts."

"Yes. Alas, all four are expert at incarceration. They have criminal records and have served prison sentences but they have a saving virtue: they are probably the four best safecrackers in the country. They also have a considerable knowledge of electrics."

"Such men could not have been easy to come by," Van Effen said. He paused, then said: "Wrong. They could have been easily come by." He looked at Romero Agnelli. "Your brothers, of course. They must have the names and track records of every outstanding—by their standards—criminal in the country."

"They are very able men," Samuelson said, "but better at safecracking than electrics."

"Their purpose being, of course," Van Effen said, "to locate and deactivate all the alarm systems in the dam—pressure pads, rays, panic buttons and whatever. Also to discover the location of both on-duty and off-duty guards."

"Not to deactivate. Not yet. Might not even be necessary," Agnelli said. "The rest, yes. There were one or two points about which they were uncertain, so they asked permission to bring in the best turbo-generator experts in the country."

Van Effen nodded. "And, of course, they got the best expert in a totally different field. O'Brien. Very clever, I must admit."

Samuelson waved a hand. "All Romero's work. He would have made an excellent divisional officer. Has O'Brien returned, by the way?"

Leonardo left the room and returned with an O'Brien who had acquired a beard and a mustache.

"Sorry about this," O'Brien said. Wincing, he tore off both mustache and beard. "As I'm going aboard with you, I thought the sudden transformation of a civilian engineer into a Dutch army sergeant-major might have caused some eyebrow-raising."

Samuelson said, "How is everything?"

"Ready to go," O'Brien said.

"One point," George said. "How are we to recognize those four—ah—colleagues you have on the dam? We don't want to point guns at the wrong people."

"A good question," Agnelli said. "All four are dressed in light-blue overalls."

"And carrying only tools in their tool bags?"

"The odd pistol. A few gas grenades. Useful things like that."

"I'd like some of those," Van Effen said. "Gas grenades, I mean. In a small satchel or suitcase. Like Mr. Samuelson, I'm adverse to unnecessary violence, and the people on the dam are, after all, my adopted countrymen. If it's necessary to restrain any of them, I'd much rather do it with a whiff of gas rather than a bullet."

"My sentiments exactly," Samuelson said. "You shall have them."

"One further point," Van Effen said. "How are you going to account for the presence of two civilians in an army group?"

"Aha!" Samuelson smiled broadly. "Civilians, but not just ordinary civilians. You are two senior members of the Amsterdam police specialist anti-terrorist squad. That should fit the bill rather nicely, don't you think?"

"A perfect idea," Van Effen said. "I always wanted to be a cop. How do you propose to gain entrance to the dam, Mr. Samuelson?"

"Nothing simpler. We land on the roadway on the dam. First, of course, we send a radio message to the dam to the effect that there is a suspicion, nothing more, that the F.F.F. may be thinking of making an attack on the dam either from the sea or from the river side and that patrol boats will be approaching from the river side and a destroyer from the sea side. We, of course, shall be there first—it's only a few minutes' flying time from here. They will be ordered to maintain complete radio silence—no transmissions, no receptions."

"The simplicity of true genius," Van Effen said. "You have your nerve. The young ladies, of course, remain behind?"

"Most certainly not. I wouldn't have Kathleen and Maria miss this splendid denouement for all the world. The rear of the helicopter will be screened off and the four will remain in hiding until we have taken over."

"The other two girls might scream for help or attempt to overpower Kathleen and Maria."

"They'll find it difficult to scream for anything when they're gagged and difficult to attack anyone when their hands are tied behind their backs. As an additional precaution, Joop will be with them. Joop is useful with a gun."

"You think of everything," Van Effen said. He hoped Joop wasn't too useful, for then Joop would have to die.

Samuelson rose, went to a desk and brought out two sheets of paper. "These are the ground and elevation plans of the

Haringvliet dam. Leonardo, go and bring the others here. I want every man to know exactly what to do, to know exactly where every guard will be on duty, where the off-duty guards and workers are, and where each man on duty may reasonably be expected to be. There will be no slip-ups."

Daniken returned as Leonardo left. In seconds Leonardo returned, bringing with him Joop, Joachim and the two name-less RAF youths that had been at the other windmill, four older men in their thirties and forties whom Van Effen had not seen before, and two of the guards he had seen. The last six looked very tough, very competent. They all crowded round the table, followed by Van Effen, Vasco, George, Samuelson, Romero Agnelli, Daniken and O'Brien. Only two men were missing— Willi, who was locked up in a cellar somewhere, and Riordan, who was presumably above such mundane and secular matters.

Although it was Samuelson who had called the meeting, Romero Agnelli conducted it. He pointed out to each man exactly where he was to go and what was expected of him. He insisted that they coordinate their watches so that each man should know exactly what time he should be at any given place. This took about five minutes. He then started it all over again. When he started a third time, Van Effen, accompanied by George and Vasco, headed resolutely toward the bar. Samu-elson, smiling, came after them and moved behind the bar.

"You get easily bored, Mr. Danilov."

"I don't have to be told the same thing twice, far less three times."

"You have a point. Maybe we are overdoing it a bit." He looked at his watch. "I find this a bit worrisome. The truck should have been here by this time."

"Ylvisaker struck me as being an able character," Van Effen said. "Engine trouble, heavy traffic, burst tire, anything. Any-way, you can soon find out. You've said you have a radio transmitter here. The lieutenant is an operator—and, of course, he knows the frequency of the truck."

"Would you, Lieutenant? Thank you." Samuelson pointed across the room. "There."

Vasco seated himself at the transceiver, adjusted his headphones and started transmitting. After two minutes he took off the headphones and returned to the bar.

"Nothing, Mr. Samuelson. Can't raise him."

Samuelson pursed his lips. "You're sure?"

"Sure I'm sure." Vasco spoke with just a faint trace of irritation. "I know what I'm doing. If you don't believe me, let Daniken try. He knows what he's doing too."

"No, no. Sorry, Lieutenant. Worried, you know."

"Two things may have happened," Vasco said. "He may have had an accident. That's the more serious and less likely happening. What's more probable is that the on-off switch is in the off position."

Samuelson's brow cleared slightly. "If he's late, why doesn't he call us?"

"Does he know how to operate the radio?"

Samuelson's brow cleared even more. "Quite honestly, I don't know." He looked up as an aproned maid approached him.

"Sorry, sir," she said. "I thought you might like to know that there is to be a government broadcast in two minutes. Less."

"Thank you, thank you." Samuelson hurried round the bar, gestured to Agnelli to end the lecture, and switched on the TV set. Within half a minute an announcer appeared on the screen, a much younger one than previously, but one trained in the same mortician's school.

"The government have three announcements to make. The first is that the British Government and the Stormont have agreed to withdraw all British troops to barracks. As the troops are scattered all over Northern Ireland, this is expected to take several hours, but the process is already under way. Although no statement to this effect has been made, this is taken to be indicative of London's intentions."

Samuelson beamed in satisfaction. At that moment, Ylvi-saker was the last thing in his mind.

"The second is that the British Foreign Minister, Defense Minister, the chief of the Imperial General Staff and the First Sea Lord are en route to Amsterdam in a VC 10 to witness the detonation of this nuclear device in the Markerwaard at two P.M.

"The third is that the government have offered an amnesty to the two as yet unnamed prisoners whose release has been demanded by the F.F.F.

"We will, of course, be back on screen at two P.M."

"Well," Van Effen said, "it looks like wholesale surrender."

"Matters are certainly proceeding satisfactorily," Samuelson said modestly. "All right, then. We will each take a minimum of luggage with us. This can be concealed in the rear of the helicopter—soldiers on active duty do not carry suitcases. Lunch will be at twelve-thirty, so we have about two and a half hours to wait till then. I do not think it would be a good idea to indulge in any more drink, so I suggest we rest. Although we are not returning tonight, we have quarters prepared for you, to which you will be shown. Tell me, Lieutenant, do you intend to have a snooze?"

"Not I."

"Then perhaps you would be kind enough to come down, say, every twenty minutes, and try to contact Ylvisaker?"

"If you think it's worth trying, certainly. I'll go upstairs, have a wash, pack what little equipment I have to pack, and be down in twenty minutes. After that, I might as well stay down." Vasco smiled. "No furtive trips to the bar, I promise you."

The room to which Van Effen and his companions were shown was almost a duplicate of the one they had left in the other windmill. Vasco carried out the search and pronounced the room clear.

Van Effen said, "Samuelson is rather concerned about the non-arrival of Ylvisaker and his friends who, I think we may take it, are at present being detained at Her Majesty's pleasure. More importantly, Samuelson seems to think that it's all over but the shouting. The possibility of failure doesn't now exist for him. That's a dangerous state of mind to be in—dangerous for him, I mean."

George said, "And what do you think he'll do when he gets to the dam?"

"Take it over. I can't see that giving him any trouble. Then he'll tell the government that he has done just that. Coming so soon after the nuclear explosion in the Markerwaard, it should have a devastating effect on the government, who will all too early appreciate the implications and realize that the F.F.F. have the nation by the throat."

"And then," Vasco said, "they blow a few bits of concrete off the dam just to show they mean business."

"Nothing like that," Van Effen said. "Nothing so crude. The explosives are Agnelli's idea. Apart from being a first-class organizer, Agnelli is a prudent fellow. The explosives are for back-up purposes only, just in case something should go wrong.

"What I do believe is that O'Brien knows as much about the controls of the hydraulic gates as the man who designed them. They just open the sluices."

"And if the authorities cut off the power from the mainland, if you can call it that?" Vasco said. "Then, perhaps, the explosives?"

"There have to be standby generators. O'Brien will have checked. As far as the safety of the country is concerned, the sluice gates of the Haringvliet are the most vital installations in the country. Imagine the sluice gates being open at low tide and a major power failure occurs? They simply cannot afford to rely on a single source of power.

"For the moment, however, and much more importantly, Samuelson and Agnelli have been kind enough to provide us with a detailed outline of their plans."

George rubbed his hands. "And now we make our own plans."

"Now we make our own."

Some forty minutes after Vasco had gone down to the living room he was joined by Samuelson. Vasco, sitting on the radio chair and idly leafing through a magazine, looked up at his entrance.

"Any luck, Lieutenant?"

"None. I've called four times—every ten minutes, not twenty, as you asked. Nothing."

"Good God!" Unmindful of his own admonitions, Samuelson went behind the bar and brought back two jonge jenevers. "Ylvisaker is wildly overdue. What on earth can have happened to him?"

"I've been thinking, Mr. Samuelson. He hasn't blown himself to pieces or the news would be all over the country by now. Let's assume he's had an accident or had a breakdown. Let's further assume he doesn't know how to operate the radio. What would you have done, sir?"

"Gone to the nearest phone and informed us. It's difficult to move far in any direction in this country without coming across a house with a phone or a public call box."

"Exactly. Does Ylvisaker *know* the telephone number of this place?"

Samuelson stared at him, then said, "Ylvisaker has never been here. Wait."

He hurried from the room and returned within a minute, his face grim. "The consensus of opinion is that Ylvisaker does *not* know this number."

"But you know the route he was taking?"

"Of course. Two men, a fast car. Bound to intercept. Thank you, Lieutenant. I'm glad to see that there are some minds still working around those parts."

"Shall I keep on trying, Mr. Samuelson?"

"It's a faint chance, isn't it?"

Vasco shrugged. "Very faint. But nothing else for me to do."

"Thank you." Samuelson handed him the gin. "A trifle like this is not going to hurt a mind as clear as yours."

The car was a tan-colored BMW with Antwerp number plates. Vasco, on the veranda, watched the car and its two occupants disappear round a corner, finished his drink in a thoughtful manner, then returned inside. He went to the radio, switched wave band and wavelength and said softly in Flemish, "Record." He spoke for no more than twelve seconds, then switched back to the previous wave band and -length. He tried again for Ylvisaker and was answered by the same silence. He refreshed his drink at the bar, resumed his chair, glanced through a magazine and again called the missing truck, with the same lack of response. He tried twice more in the next twenty minutes. He was still trying to make contact when Samuelson returned.

"Nothing?"

"Dead. Just how important are those nuclear devices to you?"

"Almost entirely psychological. If necessary, I would have used them to blow off both the northern and southern approaches to the Haringvliet dam."

"What for? No senior military commander in the Netherlands would dream of attacking the Haringvliet dam. Bombers? Never. Fighter planes? Never. Not only is your gunship more than a match for any fighter, not only do you have ground-to-air missiles, you will have a large number of hostages whose lives they would never imperil. Destroyer? Torpedo boats? Ground-to-ground missiles are heat-seeking. They're lethal."

"Not bombers?"

"What would happen if they breached the Haringvliet dam?"

"Of course. Well, no point in trying any longer. Perhaps we should both have a brief rest before lunch."

Vasco gave Van Effen and George a resume.

Van Effen said, "So you've convinced Samuelson of his invulnerability and ensured that we will have two fewer hard men to cope with aboard the dam. Whom did you notify?"

"Rotterdam police."

"I think, George, that we may make a policeman of him yet. Well, another hour or so before lunch."

"Snooze for me," Vasco said. "Jonge jenevers are too much for my delicate constitution."

"What did you say?"

"Dutch hospitality. You know what it's like."

Lunch was more than adequate but less than convivial. Samuelson tried to maintain a cheerful facade but, deeply worried about the fate of his nuclear devices, his worry was almost palpable. The last half hour of the meal was consumed in silence.

Over coffee, Samuelson said to Van Effen, "Do you think it possible that Ylvisaker and his men could have been seized by the authorities, army or police?"

"Unlikely. I don't see how they could have been. Your security is total. Even if they had been, the question is, would Ylvisaker or his men have talked?"

"About the Haringvliet dam? No. Until we got here today, only Riordan, Agnelli, Daniken and O'Brien were privy to the plans." Samuelson smiled faintly. "Your famous need-to-know maxim, Mr. Danilov."

"Without sounding cynical or callous, what the hell are you worrying about, then?"

"As you can see," the TV announcer said, "the weather is as atrocious as ever, with correspondingly poor visibility, such as one would expect as dusk approaches. The rain is extremely heavy and the wind, between force eight and nine, has backed to the northwest. We have four cameras in position—one near Hoorn and one near Volendam, on the west side of the Markerwaard, and one on the opposite shore near Lelystad. This one, I'm afraid, is virtually useless; in spite of its hood the rain is driving straight into the lens. We have a fourth camera in a helicopter and we understand they are having a very rough time indeed. The time is one fifty-eight. Our first shots will be taken from the helicopter."

A white-capped, storm-tossed sea appeared on the screen. Detail was blurred and shifting, because the helicopter was being severely buffeted, making it impossible to maintain a steady camera. Another voice took over from the studio announcer.

"Helicopter camera here. I can assure you that my friend in the studio was not exaggerating. The conditions are abominable and I have to confess that the only person who is not sick is, most fortunately, the pilot. We are flying at twenty-three hundred feet, give or take one hundred feet every time this damn machine is going up or down, which we hope is a safe height if the nuclear explosion and its accompanying waterspout should occur, God forbid, directly beneath us. It is now precisely two P.M. and"—his voice rose almost by an octave—"there it goes! There it goes! Me and my big mouth. It *is* directly beneath us!"

The camera lens had been extended to maximum zoom. The surface of the Markerwaard boiled whitely and then erupted a great column of water climbing vertically skyward toward the helicopter's camera.

"Would you look at that?" the excited voice went on. "Would you just look at that?" It seemed rather a superfluous question, as, unquestionably, almost every eye in the Netherlands was looking at nothing else. "And the air is full of spray. Our pilot is moving as quickly as possible to the northwest—we want to get out of this area as quickly as possible. We are making poor time against this northwest gale, but he is clearly hoping that that same gale will blow the spout and spray away from us. So do I."

Van Effen looked at Samuelson. He appeared to have gone into some kind of trance. The only sign of movement came from his hands. His fingers were interlocked but his thumbs were revolving slowly around each other.

The studio announcer appeared. "I am afraid the helicopter's lenses are clouded by that spray. We regret that none of the other three cameras are in visual contact. The detonation appears to have occurred almost exactly in the center of the Markerwaard."

The helicopter's commentator's voice came again. "Sorry about that. What with the spray and rain, we are at the moment quite blind. We are still moving steadily northwest. Wait a minute, wait a minute. We have eyes again."

The spout was collapsing on itself. The camera, zoom half retracted, was only momentarily on the spout, then began panning the surrounding area. A circle of water could be seen moving steadily outward from the center.

"That," the commentator said, "must be the expected tidal wave. Doesn't look much like a wave to me, but then, from this altitude it is impossible to gauge the height of the water."

The picture faded, to be replaced by the studio announcer. "We are trying to—wait, wait, we have Volendam."

A camera, at full zoom, showed a swell of water, little more than a ripple, it seemed, rapidly approaching the shoreline. A commentator said, "I agree with my colleague in the helicopter. This is hardly my idea of a tidal wave. However, I understand those tsunami tend to increase in height as the water shallows. We shall see."

There wasn't, in fact, much to see. With the wave less than a hundred yards from land, the commentator estimated its height as just under a yard, which was pretty much in accordance with the scientists' predictions. Samuelson gestured for the set to be switched off.

"A few wet feet, no more," he said. "And not a life lost. An impressive performance, wouldn't you say, Mr. Danilov?"

"Most impressive." True, probably not a life had been lost. Not that day. But the years to come might well record a different story; the radioactive fall-out would be falling over the already flood-beleaguered Flevolands. But it hardly seemed an appropriate moment to point this out.

Samuelson said, "Romero, radio the message to the Haringvliet dam. Emphasize the need for absolute radio silence. Where the devil are those two who went in search of Ylvisaker and his friends?" Nobody knew where the devil they were. "Five good men lost to me. Five!"

"It's annoying, Mr. Samuelson," Vasco said. "And worrisome. But it can have no effect on the outcome. We have seventeen men. With the element of surprise in our favor, I could take the Haringvliet with only four men."

Samuelson smiled. "That's a comfort. We leave in twenty minutes."

They left in exactly twenty minutes. All the soldiers were armed, all carried rucksacks or satchels. Neither Van Effen nor George was armed, at least not visibly, but they, too, carried satchels, both crammed with gas grenades. In addition, Van

Effen had taken the precaution of taking his Yves Saint Laurent aerosol.

As they climbed aboard the gunship, Van Effen said to Samuelson, "Gas, not guns?"

"Gas, not guns."

12

THE GUNSHIP TOUCHED down on the Haringvliet dam roadway at 2:38 P.M.

Romero Agnelli, dressed as a major and in nominal command of the party, was the first down the steps. A fair-haired, youngish man with horn-rims detached himself from a small group of observers, hurried forward to greet Agnelli and shook him warmly by the hand.

"Damned glad to see you, Major, damned glad. Have you seen what those devils have just done in the Markerwaard?"

"That we have," Agnelli said somberly. "That we have."

"How seriously do you take this threat to the Haringvliet?"

"Well," Agnelli said reasonably, "there's no threat now. Quite frankly, I don't take it seriously at all, but as soldiers, ours is not to reason why. Again, frankly, the country is in a state of near panic, and ninety-nine percent of all intelligence reports and agitated phone calls we receive turn out to be groundless. This, I say, may be the hundredth, although, as I say, I don't believe it." He took the man's arm and led him a few steps from the helicopter as soldiers followed down the steps and others opened the loading doors. "May I have your name, sir?"

"Borodin. Max Borodin. Manager. What on earth are those things they are unloading?"

"Missiles and their launching platforms. We'll have one

303

facing the North Sea, the other the river. Ground-to-ground missiles and ground-to-air missiles. Heat-seeking. Lethal." Agnelli did not add that they could be swiveled on their platforms to cover both road approaches to the Haringvliet dam. "Totally superfluous precaution. The F.F.F. are a mad lot but not mad enough to launch a frontal attack on the Haringvliet dam. We expect a destroyer and patrol boats to be standing by shortly. Again, quite unnecessary."

"Unnecessary or not, you've taken a load off my mind. Who are those two civilians?"

"Senior police officers from Amsterdam. Specialists —antiterrorist squad. They'll be wanting to look for any weak spots in your defenses. Pure formality, but they insist. We shall leave two soldiers by the missiles to keep watch. Inspector Danilov—that's the less portly one—also insists that my men accompany us. He wants, understandably, that they should familiarize themselves with the general layout of the interior of the dam."

Twenty minutes it was, and a very surprising twenty minutes it turned out to be for Borodin, not least when four blue-overalled mechanics produced Kalashnikov machine guns that had been assembled from their tool bags. It was a completely painless and bloodless operation. Borodin, his staff and his guards had simply no chance. They all finished up in one of the many giant cellars in which the dam abounded. Agnelli was about to turn the key in the lock when Van Effen stopped him.

"No. Rope. Tie them. Come, come, Mr. Agnelli, you're the man who never overlooks anything."

"I've overlooked something?"

"You've overlooked the fact that O'Brien may not be the only man in the world who can pick locks."

Agnelli nodded. "Of course. Rope." Rope was fetched, enough to secure a hundred men. When Borodin and his men had been bound hand and foot, Samuelson, looking every inch the successful Roman general back from Gaul and making his ritual entry of triumph into the city of Rome, led them all up to the control room. Van Effen and his two friends lingered behind while Van Effen opened a small tin and brought out six sodden balls of cotton wool. Those they stuffed into their nostrils. Vasco winced.

"What the hell is this? Sulfuric acid?"

"You'll get used to it," Van Effen said.

"And what was this rigmarole about people being able to pick locks? It's a million to one against there being another O'Brien down there."

"We're going to need rope. Lots of it. There's a couple of hundred yards of it down there, wound around those guys."

Vasco looked at George. "The man thinks of everything." He shook his head. "Agnelli is not the only one who overlooks things."

They entered the control room. It was wide and spacious with serried ranks of control panels lining the right-hand wall and paralleling tables. O'Brien was in the vicinity but not examining them; Van Effen knew he didn't have to.

"Ah!" Samuelson said. "The very man, Lieutenant. I want to talk to Wieringa, the Minister of Defense."

Vasco showed no surprise, merely thought for a few seconds.

"The Defense Minister will be out at Volendam, I imagine. Doesn't matter where he is. No problem. Wherever he is, office, car or plane, he's never more than an arm's length from a telephone. I'll call the War Office and they'll patch him in."

"How long will it take?"

"A minute. Less."

"A minute!"

"In the Netherlands," Vasco said with a trace of loftiness, "the Army has overriding priority." In less than the specified time he handed the phone to Samuelson, who took it, his eyes the eyes of a man whose dreams have come true. Or a madman whose dreams have come true.

"Mr. Wieringa? This is the leader of the F.F.F., the Fighters for Freedom. I trust you appreciated our little demonstration in the Markerwaard this afternoon. I have more rather unwelcome news for you. We have taken over the Haringvliet dam. I repeat, we are in complete control of the Haringvliet." There ensued quite a lengthy pause, at least on Samuelson's part, before he continued, "I am glad, Mr. Wieringa, that you appreciate the significance of this. Any attempt to retake the Haringvliet, by force or by stealth, will have disastrous effects on Holland. I might also add that we have mined the dikes at Hollandsch Diep and the Volkeral. We have observers there. Any attempts to send divers to investigate will compel us to radio-detonate those mines.

"At four P.M. we will be giving a slight demonstration of what awaits your country if our demands are not met immediately by opening a few sluice gates for a few minutes. You might find it instructive to have a helicopter around to take a few pictures so that the people of the Netherlands may understand what lies in store for them.

"I do hope you speed up negotiations with the British Government. End."

"That was quite a performance, Mr. Samuelson," Van Effen said. "You really do have those two dikes mined?"

Samuelson laughed. "Of course not. Why should I? That pusillanimous lot now take our every word for gospel."

Van Effen and friends drifted unobtrusively into the space between the table and wall controls and opened their satchels while Samuelson and his men talked excitedly and congratulated themselves. In just over two seconds ten gas grenades, fairly evenly spaced around the room, exploded. The effects were spectacular. Within a few seconds everyone was staggering about and most were unconscious before they crumpled to the floor. Van Effen snatched a key from Agnelli's pocket and the three men hastily left the room, closing the door behind them. Their noses were protected but they could hold their breaths for only so long.

"Five minutes and we'll be able to go back in there," Van Effen said. "They'll be asleep for half an hour at least." He handed Vasco the key. "The ropes. Cut Borodin free and tell him to do the same for the others. Explain."

Vasco entered the cellar and cut an astonished Max Borodin free, then handed him the knife.

"Cut the others loose. We're police officers—genuine ones. The one with the scarred face is Lieutenant Van Effen of the Amsterdam police."

"Van Effen?" Borodin was understandably dazed. "I've seen his picture. That's not him. I know his face."

"Use your head. So does nearly every criminal in Holland."

"But the F.F.F.—"

"Are having a short nap." Vasco gathered up the spare ropes and left at a run.

Van Effen approached the man on the seaside missile site. "Samuelson wants you. Quickly. Control room. I'll keep watch." The man was just disappearing from sight when Van Effen crossed to the other man on the river missile site, his hand around the burgundy Yves Saint Laurent aerosol with the special fragrance. He lowered the man to the roadway and headed for the helicopter.

The man from the first missile site that Van Effen had visited stopped when he saw George, who waved him on encouragingly. As the man passed, George chopped him on the back of the neck. For George, it was just a little chop, but the man, had he retained consciousness, would probably have regarded it differently. George lowered him gently to the floor.

Van Effen pulled back the curtain and said, "Ah, there you are, Joop. Keeping a good watch, I see." Joop's watch lasted seconds before he slumped to the floor. Van Effen produced his Beretta, waved it in the general direction of Kathleen and Maria, and sliced Annemarie's and Julie's bonds free. He raised both women to their feet, helped them free their gags, and, gun still in hand, put his arms around their shoulders. "My beloved sister. And my dear, dear Annemarie." The eyes of Kathleen and Maria were as round as the proverbial saucers.

"You took your time about it, didn't you," Julie said. There were tears in her eyes.

"Gratitude was ever thus." Van Effen sighed. "There were problems."

"It's over?" Annemarie whispered. "It's all over?"

"All over."

"I love you."

"I'll have you repeat that when you are in a more normal state of mind."

The other two seated women were still staring at them. Kathleen said, "Your *brother*?" Her voice was husky, disbelieving.

"My brother," Julie said. "Peter van Effen. Senior detective lieutenant of the Amsterdam police force."

"A nasty shock, I will admit," Van Effen said. "There may be an even nastier one awaiting you. There are those you might like to see or who might like to see you. When they wake up, that is."

All of the F.F.F. were still sound asleep, bound hand and foot, or in the process of being bound.

"Not bad, not bad," Van Effen said. "And what else have you been doing with your time?"

"Would you listen to him," Vasco said. He tightened, with unmistakable enthusiasm, the last knot on the rope binding Samuelson's legs. "To start with, half the police cars and vans in Rotterdam and Dordrecht should be on the dam inside fifteen minutes. I thought that up all by myself."

"A promising officer, as I said." Van Effen turned to Kathleen, who was staring at her father, her face ashen with shock and fear. "Why, Kathleen?"

Instead of replying, she reached inside her handbag and brought out a small pearl-handled gun. "You're not going to take him. You didn't know he was my father."

"Yes, Kathleen, I did."

"You did?" Her voice faltered. "How did you know?"

"Julie told me."

Julie stepped between the gun and Van Effen. "You'll have to shoot me first, Kathleen. I'm not being brave, because I know you could never do it."

Vasco moved quietly forward, removed the gun from the suddenly nerveless hand and replaced it in her handbag.

Van Effen said again, "Why, Kathleen?"

"I suppose it will all come out, won't it?" She was crying openly now. Vasco put an arm around her trembling shoulders, and instead of resisting she seemed to lean against him. "My father is English. He was a lieutenant colonel in the Guards, not under that name. His father was an earl, who left him a fortune. His sons, my brothers, went to Sandhurst. Both were killed in Northern Ireland. One was a lieutenant, the other a second lieutenant. My mother was killed by a renegade off-shoot of the IRA. He's never been the same man since."

"I figured as much." Van Effen sounded as tired as he undoubtedly felt. "He may be tried in this country or be extradited by the British. In either case, diminished responsibility will apply."

"You mean he's mad?" she whispered.

"I'm no doctor. Some kind of temporary derangement, I imagine. Tell me, Maria. Had either Romero or Leonardo anything to do with the murder of my wife and children?"

"No, no, no! I swear it. They wouldn't hurt a fly. My two other brothers in prison. I *know* they arranged it. They are hateful, evil men. I will testify to that in court. I promise."

"That could mean another five or ten years to their sentence."

"I hope they remain there till they die."

"Okay. No charges will be brought against you and Kathleen. Accessories are one thing, accessories under duress another. Vasco, be so kind as to release her and put a call through to Uncle Arthur. Tell him all. George, take those four beauties out for a restorative. There's bound to be a supply in their mess or canteen or whatever. If not, the helicopter is not exactly bereft. Beware of suicide attempts."

Julie said, "I don't think that anyone is going to commit suicide."

"Your feminine intuition, I suppose. Well, I agree. And, George, you could bring something back here. I feel weak."

George smiled and ushered the four from the control room.

Vasco was two minutes on the telephone, then turned to Van Effen, his hand over the mouthpiece. "I believe Uncle Arthur would like a word with you. May I—ah—join the ladies?"

"By all means." Van Effen picked up the phone as he heard the first sound of screaming police sirens. Colonel Van de Graaf's congratulations were fulsome in the extreme. So were those of Wieringa, who eventually handed him back to Van de Graaf.

Van Effen said, "Not to be ungrateful for your gratitude. But I am, Colonel Van de Graaf, getting tired of being the handmaiden who does all the dirty washing for you. I want a new job, increased salary or both."

"You shall have both. An increased salary is what goes with my job." He coughed. "Six months, say? A year?"

ABOUT THE AUTHOR

Alistair MacLean, once a schoolteacher, saw little future in writing. Twenty-five years as a bestselling author have proven him to be emphatically, happily wrong. Today, H.M.S. ULYSSES, THE GUNS OF NAVARONE, and WHERE EAGLES DARE are classics, while his recent blockbusters, PARTISANS and RIVER OF DEATH, continue to earn Alistair MacLean an enthusiastic international following.